THE SHADOW
CATCHERS

THE SHADOW CATCHERS

Thomas Lakeman

 ST. MARTIN'S MINOTAUR ✳ NEW YORK

THE SHADOW CATCHERS. Copyright © 2006 by Thomas Lakeman. All rights reserved. Printed in the United States of America. No part of this book may be used or reproduced in any manner whatsoever without written permission except in the case of brief quotations embodied in critical articles or reviews. For information, address St. Martin's Press, 175 Fifth Avenue, New York, N.Y. 10010.

www.minotaurbooks.com

Book design by Irene Vallye

Library of Congress Cataloging-in-Publication Data

Lakeman, Thomas.
    The shadow catchers / Thomas Lakeman.—1st ed.
    ISBN-13: 978-0-312-34799-4
    ISBN-10: 0-312-34799-5
    1. United States. Federal Bureau of Investigation—Officials and employees—Fiction. 2. Kidnapping—Fiction. 3. Nevada—Fiction. I. Title.

    PS3612.A53 S48 2006
    813'.6—dc22

                                                                    2006042391

First Edition: September 2006

10 9 8 7 6 5 4 3 2 1

For Mouse

Acknowledgments

I am greatly indebted to Detective Steve Greene of the Jefferson County Sheriff's Department, Dr. Lois Wims of the Criminal Justice program at the University of South Alabama, and retired FBI Special Agent Volney Hayes. Special thanks to Dr. Eliana Gil, who served as my guide to the fascinating world of child psychology and play therapy. Needless to say, any factual errors in the narrative are mine alone and do not reflect on the wisdom of these smart folk.

I am deeply grateful to everyone who stayed with the manuscript through many revisions: Victoria Lakeman, who recognized a spark within the story (even though the story has since changed beyond recognition); Carolyn Haines and the Deep South Writers Salon—Aleta Boudreaux, Susan Tanner, Stephanie Chisholm, and Renee Paul; and my friends and readers Nancy Boykin, John Gale, Bill Bly, Mark Kines, Leah Lowe, Randy Davis, Marta Anderson, and—for excellent chats over many fine cups of English tea—Keira Mallinger.

You would not now be reading this book were it not for a wonderful agent, Marian Young, and a brilliant editor, Kelley Ragland. Nor would I be here to write these words without my parents, the Reverend Ed Lakeman and Dr. Patricia Burchfield, who always believed in me and my work. To all, my heartfelt thanks.

I saw under the altar the souls of them
that were slain for the word of God,
and for the testimony which they held:
And they cried with a loud voice, saying, How long, O Lord,
holy and true, dost thou not judge and avenge our blood on
them that dwell on the earth?
—Revelations 6:9–10

Look, children, it's just something to put you to rest.

—Jim Jones

THE SHADOW CATCHERS

ONE

"Okay, now do me," said the waitress at the Silver Star Café. "Tell me whatcha see."

Three hours out of Vegas and six miles from nowhere, the Silver Star was supposed to be southern Nevada's oldest eating establishment. Its walls were covered with antique tintypes: cowboys lining up for shots of Nockum Stiff, sporting girls in striped tights, a dead rustler with a sign around his neck that read, THIS IS WHAT HAPPENS TO CATTLE THEIFS IN DYER COUNTY. I don't know what I found more disturbing—the satisfied grins of the lynch mob, or the fact that they had misspelled *thieves*.

"Quit stallin', handsome." The waitress playfully flicked a dishrag at me. "You already told Luther and Bill their whole life stories just by lookin' at 'em."

I shrugged. "Those guys were easy. They have tattoos."

"I got tattoos." She pouted. "I'm easy."

There were five of us in the diner. Two old-timers with fourteen teeth between them, someone playing video games in the room next door, the waitress—her name was Meghan—and me. It was four o'clock on a Friday: Halloween.

"What'd you say your name was?" She leaned toward me, baldly hinting where one of those tattoos might be.

"Mike."

"Give you some homemade cherry pie, Mike. Now come on, make a girl happy."

I looked her over. Late thirties, sexy in a last-call-at-the-roadhouse way, with a C-section scar smiling over her jeans. There was also a recently chipped front tooth and a badly concealed bruise on her neck. She smiled pretty. But every time she looked away, the life went right out of her eyes.

With the old men it was mostly a game. With Meghan I'd have to be careful. If I gave it to her straight, I could forget about seeing the inside of that Wonderbra. Or I could make a girl happy. A night on the trailer-park mattress, then silence over cornflakes while her kids stared sullenly away. Meghan's fleeting look of desolation as she tried to smile me out the front door. Who knows. I could even wind up trading punches with the slime-ball who gave her that bruise.

But what the hell.

"You're a model." I winked. "Twenty-seven, right?"

Meghan smiled. "One slice, comin' right up."

So it's finally come to this, I thought. Ten years of hard-core training at taxpayers' expense, just so I could play mind reader in Where-the-hell, Nevada. Will Profile for Food.

She picked up my empty plates and bumped the kitchen door open with her ass. "Say, how'd you get so good at readin' people, anyh—" Then the color drained from her face.

Everyone was looking through the front window.

Motorcycles flanked the gray hearse as it rumbled down Highway 313, followed by an old green Jeep Cherokee and a long procession of mourn-ers: Dodges and K-cars with bad mufflers and busted headlamps. The faces of the drivers—when I could see them—were solemn and confused.

"Sweet Jesus," someone whispered.

"Who are they burying?" I asked.

Meghan gave me a pinched expression, letting me know I'd crossed some invisible line.

"Mexican boy," she murmured. "Six years old."

"Jesus, that's tragic."

One of the old men snorted. "Damn criminal is what it is. People who let their kids run out in the road—"

Meghan winced. "Shame on you, Luther."

"It's folks like them need shamin'." He slammed his fist down. "Oughtta be the parents who died instead of the kid. If there was any justice."

I glanced over at him. "I'm sure there's a couple of people in that pro-cession who'd agree with you."

He gave a dry chuckle. "Yeah? Like who?"

"The parents."

Luther looked away before I did.

"What exactly happened to him?" I heard myself say.

Nobody answered. These were local matters, private matters, and my car had Pennsylvania tags. The last of the mourners passed, and now the only sound was tinny music from the game room next door.

"Didja see that coffin?" Bill shook his head. "Best piece o' furniture them wetbacks own, and it's goin' right in the ground."

"You hush now." Meghan reddened. "They ain't wetbacks anyhow." Her voice faltered as a red Ford pickup tore down the highway, its right front tire screaming. For a second I took it for a late mourner. Then the truck braked hard into the parking lot, dragging gray dust behind.

Luther scratched his jaw. "Hell, that's Dale." The floorboards creaked as Dale came into the diner.

He was six and a half feet tall, three hundred pounds on the hoof. His mouth was surprisingly childlike, lost in a brick-red beard. Dale wore shit-kicker boots and a yellow Windbreaker labeled DYER COUNTY FIRE AND EMERGENCY RESCUE. He didn't look like he was there to check the extinguishers. His right hand was pale and blotched, all gooseflesh. Probably just out of a cast. Every few seconds it flexed and extended, as though he were trying to bring it back to life.

" 'Lo, Dale." The waitress tried to smile.

"Rob here?" His voice was thick and slow. As Dale touched his cap I noticed a deep crease in his left temple. An old scar, badly healed. The words SEMPER FI were stamped on the gold ring on his little finger.

Meghan was wringing her hands. "Robbie's over in the game room. Been here maybe—whatya think, Luther? An hour?"

"Near about." Luther nodded. "Every day at three, he's here."

Dale barely saw me as he lumbered past: I was just some guy eating lunch. As he entered the game room, the diner began to breathe again.

"Oh boy." Meghan passed a hand over her forehead. "You don't think—"

"Reckon I don't." Luther's eyes dropped to his fried apple pie. "Ain't no trouble of mine."

If Robbie had been a deadbeat gambler or some redneck Romeo with a hard-on for Dale's sweetheart, I might have agreed. But something that old man said bothered me. *Every day at three, he's here.* Three o'clock is when school lets out.

I shifted for a better view of the game room.

Robbie was small for his age—seven or eight, maybe forty pounds. He had to stand on a box to reach the video game controls. His slender legs were clad in metal braces. A brand-new walker stood beside the machine. As Dale's shadow fell over him, the boy said something too soft to hear. Dale put his hand under the boy's armpit and lifted him like a puppet.

Robbie yelped, "I need my walker."

Dale grabbed the walker, tucked it under his right arm, and started for the door. I kept my eyes on Dale. Again he brushed past me without looking. Then Robbie came within reach of my arms, and for one awful second his brown eyes gazed deep into my own.

My hand tightened on the brass rail.

"Excuse me." But Dale didn't stop. I turned to the waitress.

"Call the police," I said. "Now."

"Don't be crazy." She grabbed at my wrist.

"Just do it."

By the time I got to the parking lot, Dale was fumbling for his keys with Robbie pinned beneath his left arm. Whatever he planned to do to the boy, he was damned well going to do in private. I was thirty feet away, walking steady. My palms were sweating.

Dale flung the walker into the bed of the truck, where it landed with a dull clatter. Robbie screamed.

"Let go!" Robbie swung his thin legs, clawed at Dale's shirt. "Leave me alone! I hate you!"

His fingernails swiped Dale's left eye. The keys flew from Dale's hand and disappeared under the front tire.

"God *damn* it!" Dale took the boy's face in one enormous hand. "Cut this shit out! Tell me what the fuck she said!"

Robbie bit his lip.

"Look at me when I talk to you, Robbie!"

"Let *go* of me! You're not my daddy!"

"Dale." I was ten feet away.

He turned. "Who the hell are you?"

"My name is Mike." I spoke softly enough to make him lean forward. "Is everything okay?"

"Fuck you care?" His breathing slowed a little.

"I'm a little worried about Robbie." I could feel the blood in my temples. Why was I doing this? I didn't have any authority here, not anymore. And

I sure as hell didn't look forward to getting pounded. But Robbie was watching.

Dale's hand slipped from Robbie's face, leaving a bright red mark on the boy's cheek. "Never mind about Robbie. He's fine."

"Come on, Dale. He's scared out of his mind."

Dale drew back slightly, balancing on the razor's edge.

"Just take it easy," I said. "And let's do the right thing."

For a second he seemed about to let go. I reminded myself not to move until he was at least two strides away from the kid. Then we both heard it, a keening sound on the wind. Police sirens. Dale's face went white.

"You son of a bitch." He pushed the boy hard, trying to get him into the cab. Robbie slipped and collapsed on the pavement. I reached to stop his fall and that pushed the trigger. A moment later Dale hurtled toward me.

He drove the first punch—a haymaker—straight at my solar plexus. I darted to one side and his fist rammed against my ribcage, sending a dagger of pain through my lungs. Then he landed a left to my jaw. My head snapped back and the ground swung around me. I was going down. I feinted with my left, hooked the back of his leg with my instep, and slammed his chin backward. We both fell hard, but I was ready for it. He wasn't. He instinctively threw out his hand to break his fall: the wrong hand.

"Mother*fucker!*" Dale bellowed, taking three hundred pounds hard on the pavement.

By instinct, I reached for my pancake holster . . . but of course it wasn't there. Dale had a killer look in his eye, and the squad car was still half a mile away. I had to take my shot before he got his feet under him. Throwing all my weight into my stride, I ran up and planted my toe as hard as I could into the cleft of that dent in his skull.

The shock traveled all the way to my hip. I'd struck something harder than bone. Dale's head swung away and his eyes rolled like he'd touched lightning. Then his cheek hit the pavement. Blood trickled from his ear.

"Okay, that's enough." I leaned over, out of breath. "Robbie, stay where you are. It's gonna . . . be all right."

Dale slumped against the side of his truck—making a soft sound, like a dove cooing.

"I didn't want to do that," I said. "You were losing control. I had to stop you."

He only looked at me in confusion, as if wondering who the hell I was and what he was doing on the ground. Then, in a clear soft voice, he spoke.

"Did you hear that?"

"Hear what?"

"Just then." His eyes rolled upward. "Did you hear a baby cry?"

At that moment all I could hear were the sirens of a sand-colored Crown Victoria as it pulled to a stop. The crest on the side read, DYER COUNTY SHERIFF'S DEPARTMENT.

"Day early for Sattidy wrasslin', ain't it boys?"

The lead officer, small and compact, wore desert-drab plainclothes. A gold detective's shield dangled from his worn leather belt. He stood from the vehicle, his narrow yellow eyes checking for danger. His deputy was an aimless-looking goof with fresh acne scars. Both of them wore black armbands and carried twelve-gauge shotguns.

The detective's lips curled in amusement. "Now what's this looks like to you, Clyde?"

" 'Pears to be dis-orderly conduct, Tippet." Clyde whistled. "Damn, Dale. You let that little wart of a guy break your hand all over again?"

Dale looked up. "I have to go home now."

"Lieutenant." I looked Tippet straight in the eye. "My name's Mike Yeager. I—"

"I'll getcher name when I want it," Tippet sneered. "And keep those hands clear of your body. I just got called from a funeral, and I'm in no mood for shit."

I held my palms out. "Look, I'm the one who told the waitress to call in. I saw this man grab that young boy over there, and—"

"Boy?" He glanced around. "Ain't no boy."

I looked back at the tailgate. Robbie was gone. So was the metal walker.

"Clyde, you see any boy 'round here?"

"Guess he musta run off." Clyde nodded back to me. "All right, sir. Need you to turn 'round slow and face the vehicle. Keep your legs apart and put your palms together behind your back."

"You, too, Dale." Tippet kept a tactical distance, a park ranger eyeing a wounded grizzly.

"Cassie's gone," Dale said with dull certainty.

Tippet threw a weary glance at his partner. "We go through this twice a week, Dale. Your daughter ain't gone nowhere."

"She wasn't at school when I went to get her." Dale furrowed his brow. "Somebody said they saw her talking to Robbie. So I thought . . ." His voice trailed off.

"Mean to tell me that was Robbie McIntosh you grabbed hold of?" Tippet rolled his eyes. "Dale, for chrissake."

Clyde cleared his throat. "Tip, maybe we oughta call this one in."

Tippet barely nodded. "Dale, if I go check on your daughter, you ain't gonna give us no trouble—right?"

Dale stumbled to his feet. "I gotta look for my Cassie. Maybe she's home by now."

"Shoulda thought about your little girl before you got in a fight."

"We'll call the Maidstones for ya." Clyde circled behind Dale. "They'll keep a look out for Cassie."

The cuffs trembled in the deputy's hands as he fumbled to get them around Dale's huge wrists. I stood still and waited my turn, certain that Clyde didn't know what the hell he was doing. With his back to me, it wouldn't be too much of a job to get the jump on him. I could even try and take that twelve-gauge away if I felt crazy enough. And that bothered me. A dumb local cop can get a man killed.

But then there was Tippet, covering his partner with a shotgun on tight choke. He looked like he might enjoy having me resist arrest.

"All right, sir. What was that name again?" The cuffs bit my wrists as Clyde forced them home.

"Yeager. Michael Francis Yeager."

"On your way down to Las Vegas, Mr. Yeager?"

"Just came to take pictures of the mountains."

Tippet cocked an eyebrow. "What do you do for a living exactly?"

"Right now exactly nothing." I glanced over to my car. "My cameras are in the old Nash over there."

A rattlesnake gleam shone in Tippet's eyes. "Get his wallet."

Clyde started to reach into my hip pocket. "In my jacket," I said. The deputy warily plucked out my billfold.

"Whatta we got there, Clyde?"

"Outastate license." He held it up for his partner. "Filla-delf-yuh, P-A. Subject is five foot seven, one hunnert and sixty pounds. Age, forty-two. Black hair, blue eyes. Organ donor. I guess he about donated some organs today."

Tippet frowned. "Keep lookin'."

Clyde continued to flip through the wallet. "Holy Christ. Tip, check this shit out."

"Whatya got?"

"Holy Christ on a mother-lovin' pony." Clyde held up up the laminated ID card. "This fella's FBI."

"FBI my ass." Tippet leaned over Clyde's shoulder. Then he gave a low whistle. "Well, shit on a brick. That right, Mr. Yeager? Are you FBI?"

I sighed. "Once upon a time."

TWO

I'd driven all day hoping to photograph the mountains at sunset, and there they were: a jagged range of desert sandstone, fading to red in the dying light. Even through the police cruiser's dirty windows, it was easy to see how the mountains earned their name: Sangre de los Niños. Blood of the children.

"Gonna be dark soon." Dale said. "Gotta find Cassie."

He'd been repeating that ever since they cuffed us, and he didn't seem to notice that nobody was answering. His swollen wrist was pinned behind him and he was sweating like a bull hippo. Dale smelled of engine oil and wood smoke, and something even worse—dark blood, caked on his face and ears.

"My Cassandra needs me." His breath came in short hitches. "Why won't they let me go look for her?"

Tippet had been inside the diner a lot longer than it should have taken to confirm my story. A few times he stood close to the window. I could see him on a walkie-talkie, his mouth working in clipped phrases. Finally he came outside. He checked around, then deliberately holstered his police radio and took a cell phone from his vest pocket. Now I could see Tippet's game. The radio chatter was to let everyone see him in charge—tracking down Dale's daughter, running my car tags, whatever. The second conversation was private. And this time he was mostly listening.

"They said you was in the FBI." Dale was talking to me.

"So it seems."

"Why'd you let them piss ants cuff you? Why didn't you call somebody and make 'em let you go?"

I glanced sideways at him. "I'm not above the law."

He snorted. "Or maybe it's that you got nobody left to call."

I didn't answer. Tippet had pocketed his cell phone and was beckoning Clyde over for a head-to-head.

"I wasn't bothering you none," Dale said. "Why'd you kick me?"

"Why'd you hurt a helpless child?"

Dale lowered his head. "He ain't so helpless."

"That's not an answer."

His lips were working hard to form words. "You wouldn't care if I told you. Why should I?"

"It's okay, Dale. I already know."

"You do?"

"Sure. You want me to understand that you'd never really hurt your nephew. But the boy is just so damn willful. All you wanted was to make him respect you, the way a boy ought to respect his uncle." I looked at him. "That is what you were going to say, right?"

He was uncomfortably close, and I guessed he could still break me in two even with the cuffs on. But then he smiled. It was the first time I'd seen Dale smile and I didn't like it. His eyes didn't smile with him.

"So in other words"—he paused—"the reason you kicked me was to make *me* respect *you*."

I had to admit his answer caught me off guard.

"I did it to stop you, Dale. That's all."

He tilted his head to look at me. "You proud of yourself, bein' in the FBI?"

"Sometimes."

"Proud." He nodded. "That's how I felt bein' in the Marine Corps. Protecting people. Knowin' if I hadda die in an evil place, it'd be for a reason. And now it's all gone." His smile fell. "I was tryin' to do somethin' before. And now I can't remember what it was."

"You were trying to push your nephew into your truck."

"Oh." He nodded. "Tell me somethin'. If you met somebody bigger and meaner than me . . . if you saw him hurting a kid. Would you try and stop him, even if you could die?"

I nodded.

"You're not so big." He eyed me keenly. "But you knew what I was gonna do to Robbie even before I did. Only one other guy I ever met was that smart. He's dead now."

"Sorry to hear that."

"I'm not," Dale said. "Not one little bit."

Now Tippet had the walkie-talkie to his ear, holding it so Clyde could listen in. Tippet didn't seem to like what he was hearing.

"Dale," I said. "When you fell—you asked me if I heard a baby cry. Why'd you say that?"

"I don't remember. Sometimes I hear it, though." Dale took a ragged breath. "Things don't work right inside me. Can't sleep. Can't feel nothing. You know what happens to people when they're too fucked up to feel anything? They don't last long, I'll tell you that." He looked back at me. "What'd you say your name was?"

"Mike."

"You did right to kick me, Mike."

Tippet had been barking into the walkie-talkie loud enough for me to catch a few random phrases. *Under control* came up a lot. So did *federal bullshit.* There was a long silence—Tippet rolled his eyes—and finally he said, "No sir, she's fine. Got it covered." There were a couple more *No Sirs.* Then he slapped the walkie-talkie into Clyde's hands.

I turned to Dale. "Looks like you may see your daughter tonight after all."

"I hope so." Dale shifted. "This is a real bad place you came to, Mike. Worse than I hope you'll ever know."

"How's that?"

"You won't believe me," he said. "But you know that guy? The one I told you about that I said was dead?"

"Yeah?"

"He might not be."

Then Tippet returned to the cruiser.

"Boys, seein' as it's almost trick or treat, we decided to let you off with a warnin'." Tippet had unlocked Dale's cuffs and was taking his time removing mine. "Think you can stay outa each other's hair?"

"I gotta go find Cassie." Dale cradled his injured wrist. The handcuff had cut an angry red groove into his flesh. My own hands were numb and useless, as if they'd been soaking in ice water.

"Your little girl's fine," Tippet was saying. "I just talked to Mary Frances. She said it was her day to pick up Cassie from the after-school program, and you musta got confused."

Dale blinked. "Mary and I got divorced. She don't live with us anymore."

"I know that, Dale. But she's still got part custody of your daughter. Now go home and sit tight, and Cassie'll be home soon enough. You hear me? Sheriff said to brand your butt if I caught you out again tonight."

Dale nodded, chastened if not entirely soothed—then turned and stared right at me. He seemed to be gathering his courage to say something. Finally he looked from me to Tippet and simply exhaled.

"You did right, Mike." Then he stumbled to his truck.

"What the hell was that all about?" Tippet asked as Dale's taillights faded down the highway. "You did right how?"

"Tickets to the Fire Department barbecue." I massaged my wrists, feeling the blood tingle. "I told him to put me down for a dozen."

"That ain't till April," Clyde said. Tippet shot him a dark look and began writing in his pad.

"Well?" I said. "Do I get my car keys now?"

Tippet nodded to Clyde.

"Sorry to inform you, Agent Yeager," said Clyde, "but we're gonna have to impound this here vehicle of yours."

"On what account?"

"Standard procedure, sir." Clyde darted an anxious look to his partner. "This bein' disorderly conduct and you bein' outa state, we gotta run a check—"

"That's horseshit."

Tippet raised an eyebrow. "You'll want to watch that lip, sir." He tore off a pink slip and threw it at me. "You can pick your car up Monday—assuming there's no wants or warrants."

I snatched the receipt from the air. "Maybe I should take this up with your sheriff."

Tippet's eyes were smiling. "His orders, Mr. Yeager. You can make an appointment to see Sheriff Archer on Monday."

Clyde cleared his throat. "Sheriff says to drive you to a motel, Agent Yeager. Seein' as it's special circumstances. And you bein' FBI and all."

"Why'd you lie before?" Tippet asked from the driver's seat, spoiling the silence of Highway 313. "I mean, if you're FBI, why not just say so—'stead of all that 'nothin' exactly' crap?"

"Maybe it's nobody's business," I said.

He shrugged. "Man has a right to take pictures of rocks and sagebrush if he's a mind to. Just seemed like you were a mite ashamed of your federal connections. Or vice versa."

"You'd have to ask the Bureau about that."

Tippet tossed me a look. "Don't think I won't."

"I sure gotta hand it to ya, Agent Yeager." Clyde leaned forward from behind the wire screen. "Never seen anybody lay ole Dale out that way before."

"Dale's a fighter, is he?"

"Yessir. War hero. Served in Operation Desert Storm back in 'ninety-one. Fella sure has had a hard life, though. When he—"

"How'd you know he was gonna shake Robbie like that?" Tippet lit a Chesterfield. "Four people in that diner didn't have the first clue."

"They all had a clue," I said. "They just didn't do anything about it."

"Folks here keep to themselves." He blew smoke my way. "Somebody like you starts interferin'—askin' questions about how some local boy died, for instance—people get mighty spooked."

I casually rolled the window down. "Incidentally, how did he die?"

"Hit and run." The end of his cigarette glowed.

"So what's the story on Dale's daughter?"

"No story. Every time Cassie has a sleepover or comes home late from school, Dale starts thinkin' she's run off. He just forgets things. Like Clyde said, he's had a hard life."

Clyde whistled. "It sure was somethin' the way you took him down. Maybe you could come give us some tactical training. We'd love to have ya."

"Didn't you hear the man?" Tippet asked. "He ain't on duty. He came out west to take pictures of the Sangre de los Niños." He snorted smoke. "Though I bet that ain't the end of the story by a mile."

"Thought you said folks here keep to themselves."

"They do, I don't. Way I figure, there's only two reasons for a G-man such as yourself to get off the beaten path. Either the federals sent you here to snoop around . . ."

"Or?"

"Or they don't know you're here. And maybe don't particularly care."

I smiled. "Let's just say I had a bad day at the office, Lieutenant."

"Sir," said Clyde. "You ain't had a bad day in your life. Not till you get where we're takin' you."

THREE

Where they took me was the Lucky Strike Motel on Highway 313, a courtyard rattrap with a marquee sign reading

G D BLES AMER CA
ADU T MOVIES
KIDS SL EP FREE

"If this don't suit you," Tippet said, "we can make room for you down to the lockup. Special FBI discount."

I stood from the vehicle. "I'd like my ID back now."

"Your ID. Right." His mouth curled. "Where is that damn thing? You ain't got it, Clyde?"

"Not where I could put a hand to it."

Tippet patted his shirt pocket. "Say, now. Here it was all along." He strummed the laminated card with his thumbnail. "Matters to ya, does it?"

"Get out of the car and I'll show you."

Tippet offered a jackal grin. Then he let the card fall to the pavement.

"See you Monday." He put the engine in gear. "Sleep tight, now. Don't open the door to strangers."

I waited until they were well out of sight before I bent down to pick it up.

My room smelled like cattle drainage, but at least it gave me a view of the giant neon cowboy at Wild Pete's Hotel and Casino. The lights of Langhorne, the county seat, glowed fitfully in the distance. No trick-or-treaters out tonight. It was weirdly quiet for Halloween.

I emptied my leather jacket, setting the laminated card next to the Gideon Bible. FEDERAL BUREAU OF INVESTIGATION gleamed at me in dark gold letters. SPECIAL AGENT MICHAEL F. YEAGER. My name was the only thing I didn't surrender on the way out.

I showered under tepid brown water, starting to feel the ache in my joints. My jaw was swollen where Dale had clocked me with his Marine Corps ring, and I had a bruise under my ribs. Plus a jammed toe from kicking that metal plate in his head.

The phone was ringing as I turned off the taps.

"So who won, you or the windmill?" asked a woman's familiar voice.

"Special Agent Weaver." I smiled. "I figured you'd be the one they called."

"Only because I'm your former squad leader. They don't know I'm also the former future Mrs. Yeager. Sweetie, what happened? They said you got in a fight with some ex-marine in—where are you? Nevada?"

"Dyer County. It's a long story, Peggy. I needed to get out of town. I wish they hadn't bothered you."

"You wish—? Mike, it's been weeks since anyone's heard from you. I seriously thought I was going to wind up matching your dental records. You don't disappear when you're on administrative leave."

"Funny. I thought making me disappear was the whole point."

"The inquiry's still in progress, Yeager. It's a brain-dead move and you know it."

I took a pained breath. "Look, it was totally shitty of me not to call. I surrender, okay?"

Silence. "How'd you wind up fighting this guy, anyhow?"

"They didn't mention the boy?"

"No. What boy?"

"I made a mistake. I saw him shaking this handicapped kid, and—"

"—you intervened and controlled the situation."

"I got lucky. Maybe I taught him a lesson."

"Sure. You taught him not to do it in public." Her voice softened. "You just can't help yourself, can you? You hear a scream and you storm the castle."

"That was the mistake. This marine, he looked scared. Maybe I should have tried harder to calm him down."

"Maybe. But that's twenty-twenty hindsight."

"My speciality." I laughed. "So who called you? The sheriff?"

"Yeah. I'd watch out for that one. He's spinning something. Not that you listen to me lately, but I think you need to get out of Dodge."

"They've got my car," I said. "What did you tell him about me?"

"The truth. Mike Yeager is an outstanding agent and we all miss working with him. Particularly me."

"He didn't ask about the administrative leave?"

"He asked, that's all."

"Well, thanks for covering for me. I better go see if I can get my heater working. You wouldn't believe how cold the desert gets at night."

"I've still got a nice warm bed in Hunting Park."

"Yeah?" I laughed. "Last I heard, some strapping fellow named Tyrone was warming that bed."

"Tyler," she said. "Your intel's way off. Tyler's a friend. Somebody I work out with, that's all."

"So he's what, a personal trainer?"

"He's a—you know what? None of your damn business. He's not you." She laughed weakly. "That's my trouble. Nobody's you."

"I'm not myself," I said.

"Have you been sleeping?"

"About as much as ever."

"Take one of your pills after we get off the phone."

"Yes, Mom."

"Don't 'yes, Mom' me. This happened because you weren't looking out for yourself. What are you doing out there, anyhow?"

"Maybe I just want to see if I can live without you."

She took a careful pause. "You shouldn't say things like that. I'm liable to believe you."

"Let me put it this way," I said. "The ex-marine asked me why I didn't drop any names from the Bureau. I realized your name was the only one that still mattered."

"Then why didn't you call me?"

"Because then you'd come find me," I said.

She was quiet a moment. "How long are you gonna keep doing this?"

"Well, first I've gotta get my car back. After that I'm on God's time."

"No, Mike. How long until you forgive yourself for Tonio Madrigal?"

I took a long breath. "Peggy, I did what I had to."

"Yeager, please stop selling tickets to your own execution. You had no right to walk away. Not while other people were putting themselves on the line. The Office of Professional Responsibility tried to exonerate you. They wanted to. If you hadn't vanished two days before the final hearing."

"That's why I vanished," I said. "Because they *wanted* to exonerate me."

FOUR

I sat on the bed and shook two pills from my toilet kit. FOR RELIEF OF ANXIETY. DO NOT TAKE WITH OTHER MEDICATIONS. My psychiatrist's phone number was on the label. I briefly thought about calling him to ask if Thunderbird counted as medication. Then I dry-swallowed and awaited the inevitable fuzziness. It was going on nine-thirty. I dressed as warmly as I could, then went out to see if there was a steak buffet at Wild Pete's Casino. One step out the door and my balls shriveled up. Fifteen degrees and falling.

If Peggy didn't understand why I had to leave Philadelphia, it was a sure bet nobody would. And there was no way I could make her see. Peggy's mind worked in straight lines and well-lit passages. That was the first thing I noticed about her, as soon as I was done noticing her auburn hair and hazel eyes and the pleasant way she filled out her regulation black suit. For Agent Weaver there was only right and wrong. You did right and feared not, and in the end only your actions mattered. I liked that about her. There was a time when I liked that about myself.

Wild Pete's, despite having a very bright neon cowboy, was dark and deserted. CLOSED BY ORDER OF DYER COUNTY HEALTH DEPT. So much for steak. I double-timed back to the motel. The manager, an elderly Mexican in coke-bottle glasses, was staring at me from the lobby counter.

"Why'd you go there?" he asked in a rusted-out voice. "Ain't nothin' in that casino."

I put a dollar down. "I need some change for the machine."

His coffee-colored eyes widened. "Hungry, eh?"

"That's the general idea."

He shuffled back into his office. A moment later he was back with a brown paper sack.

"Burrito," he said. "*Mi esposa* make. Two dollar."

A smell of ancient flesh rose from the bag. I waved it off. "Just the quarters, for chrissake."

He sourly punched the register open. I bought a stale candy bar and a soft drink, then went back to lie down. The telephone jarred me awake.

"Mike?" said a heavy voice. "Oh, thank God."

"Mm?"

"I'm sorry to bother ya this late, man. It's just I figured you'd be at the Lucky Strike, and—"

"Who is this?"

"It's Dale." He was suddenly timid. "From, you know. Today. You remember, right?"

"Yeah, Dale. My jaw remembers you real well." I could hear music on his end—some kind of gospel program with the volume cranked way up.

"Oh," he said. "You're probably still pissed off. But it's just right now I'm in a bad way, and—"

"Dale?" I said. "I don't wanna be rude, but—"

"She's gone, Mike."

"What?"

"Cassie." He strung the word like piano wire. "They said she'd be home when I got here. Didn't you hear 'em say that?"

"I thought your ex-wife had her."

"They was here earlier. My neighbor said they came inside, but that ain't right. Nobody's here. Not even the damn dog."

There was a loud rapping on his end.

"Things are goin' nuts around here." He was starting to hyperventilate.

"Just calm down," I said. "Did you check the neighbors? Or call the sheriff?"

"No. No. They'd say I'm crazy and I can't deal with that shit anymore." The rapping again. "Maybe she's all right. Probably just went trick-or-treatin', huh? You think?"

It was two minutes after ten. Unthinkably late for trick or treat. "All right, Dale. So you came home and nobody was there. Was the door open or shut?"

"Shut." He hesitated. "I usually lock it, but sometimes I forget."

"And does your ex-wife still have a key?"

"No," he said with conviction. "It wasn't Mary Frances's day to pick Cassie up. Tip was full of crap. Cassie wasn't even supposed to go trick-or-treat anyway, on account it's Harvest Night."

"Harvest Night?"

"At the church," he said. "Mike?"

"I'm here, Dale."

"If I have to go away," he said. "Will you come look after my Cassie?"

"Go away where?"

"Promise me, okay?"

"Dale, just tell me—"

The rapping came again, insistent. "I gotta find out who that is. Call me back."

"Dale."

But he'd already put the receiver down.

I was about to hang up when I realized Dale's phone was still off the hook. I heard music and praising from the TV. Dale's heavy boots on the linoleum, a door swinging open on heavy springs.

"What the hell is that?" Dale asked. "Looks like you're carryin' a damn bazooka in there."

A male voice answered, his voice drowned out.

"Jesus, am I glad to see you," Dale said. "I'm in a world of hurt."

Then the receiver clicked off.

I lay still with the phone on my chest, listening to my rapid heartbeat and thinking: *This is why you don't get involved.* I thought that all the way down to the lobby. I asked the manager for a phone book, but he suddenly seemed to have lost all his English. Finally he pointed to the pay phone outside.

Searching for a guy named Dale in Nevada turned out to be a lot like looking for somebody named Paulie on Staten Island. There were seventeen Dales in the Dyer County phone book, plus any number of first-initial *D*s. Then I remembered what Deputy Clyde said about "calling the Maidstones." That had to be a neighbor. Sure enough, there was a listing for Delbert and Evelyn Maidstone on 714 Angel Hair Road, Caritas, Nevada. And six pages back, at 712 Angel Hair Road, was Dale A. Dupree.

This time there was no answer at the Dupree residence. I used the last of my change calling the only other number I had for Angel Hair Road. By then I was royally freezing my German ass off.

"Hello?" croaked a whiskey sour voice.

"Mr. Maidstone?"

There was an indignant pause. "Mrs. Maidstone," she replied. "I done talked to my lawyer. He said I got ninety days to make that payment."

"I'm not a bill collector, ma'am. I'm a . . . friend of Dale Dupree's. I was wondering—"

"Friends!" she cackled. "Dale ain't got no friends. I bet you're the law. This ain't about that little runt he beat up at the Silver Star, is it?"

"I'm not sure that's—Ma'am, we were talking and got disconnected. Could you maybe ask Dale to come to the phone?"

"Hell, I'd freeze like a nun's underpants, walkin' all that way. Besides, it's past ten o'clock and I got drinkin' to do."

"I understand, Mrs. Maidstone. But he seems worried that his daughter's gone missing."

"Swear to God," she huffed. "Cassie's been home since before supper. That whore wife of his took her right in the front door."

"He's pretty sure that she's not in the house."

"The boy's crazy as catshit. I just heard him yellin' at Cassie not ten seconds ago."

I stopped. "You're positive about that."

"You can probably hear him if I hold the phone up." She paused. "Sounds like they've got a wrasslin' show on TV. Lights flashin' inside."

"What exactly was Dale saying to his daughter?"

My only response was a dead line.

By then I wasn't sure whether to feel concerned or stupid. All I'd wanted when I came to Dyer County was to eat some local food and take pictures of the damn mountains. And there I was standing in the cold, courting hypothermia. Peggy was right. I needed to start looking out for myself. As I went back to my room, I silently prayed for one good night's sleep, one forgettable weekend in the shitty motel. Then goodbye to Dyer County.

Come morning I'd hitch out to Caritas and see what was what. And in all likelihood it would be nothing.

As it turned out I wouldn't be spending the weekend at the shitty motel, because early next morning Tippet and Clyde were pounding on the door. For one dizzy moment I thought they'd brought me my car keys. But they had come to take me into custody for the murder of Dale Alexander Dupree.

FIVE

The first thing I noticed was dried blood on their boots: they'd come straight from the crime scene. There was more blood on Clyde's knees and elbows, probably from collecting evidence. Even though I was the guy standing in his boxers, they were the ones who looked exposed.

"Don't I get a Miranda warning?" I asked.

"You ain't bein' questioned," Tippet said dully.

"You're supposed to instruct me not to touch anything." I reached for my trousers. "Integrity of evidence, remember?"

"Get your goddamn clothes on."

As we emerged from my room, the motel's other guests—mostly hookers and drifters—were lined up to watch the FBI guy get pinched. The manager regarded me with a twisted grin, as if to say: You should have bought my burrito.

We passed nothing of beauty on the long drive north to Langhorne, only miles of fences with potato-chip bags hung on the barbed wire. Skinny, pink-eyed cows nosed through cheatgrass near the skeletons of their lost calves. Trailers stood on lousy foundations beside rusted swing sets that had no children to play on them. Dead lizards lay flattened on the shoulder of the road. The sky was corpse-white, the Sangre de los Niños a barren gray. This was Dyer County without makeup.

Then we hit the end of the road.

The Dyer County Sheriff's Department was three stories of white cinderblock and arrow-slit windows, surrounded by yellow sodium-vapor lamps. U.S. and Nevada flags waved in a courtyard of stadium-quality grass. Even the county courthouse was a shack beside that sheriff's station.

We drove over the Severe Tire Damage teeth and past two checkpoints to the lockup. All the way, deputies sniffed me out like junkyard dogs.

As soon as we were inside the steel doors, Deputy Clyde removed the cuffs and they took everything I had left: my wristwatch and wallet, my jacket and belt, my shoes and loose change, and last of all the St. Christopher's medal Peggy had given me for my fortieth birthday.

"We'll take good care of it for you." A pretty young deputy, Ada Rosario, accepted the pendant with the solemn compassion of a burn-ward nurse. Her eyes were heavy with dark circles and her hair was freshly cropped. "Come stand on the yellow line, so we can take your picture."

I stared up into the camera and the strobe flared blue.

"It was a gospel program," I muttered.

"Pardon?" she said.

Mrs. Maidstone had mentioned flashing lights in Dale's house. She said it sounded like he was "watchin' some kinda wrasslin' show on TV." But I was almost positive it was a religious program I'd heard. That wrestling show had to be the sound of Dale being murdered.

"Just talking to myself." I smiled apologetically.

"We don't have TV," she said. "I can get you religious tracts if you want them."

The Friday night drunks were still asleep in their cells, wrapped up in their blankets like cadavers. Dale had probably spent many a night in there. By now he had to be in the local morgue. That swollen wrist hanging down from beneath a plastic sheet, never to heal.

I got a cell to myself; I was valuable property. The metal door shut and, for the first time in my life, I was standing on the side without a doorknob as the lockbolts slid home.

Hours later, Detective Tippet finally brought me to the interview room.

"Mike, we know you talked to Dale last night."

Suddenly, it seemed, we were on a first-name basis.

"Yeah, we pulled the motel records. You were on the phone close to—" he checked his notes "—three minutes. Then the Lucky Strike manager says you went right out the front door, and that's the last he saw you till mornin'."

I shrugged. "If you know I talked to Dale from the Lucky Strike, then you also know I wasn't anywhere near him at ten o'clock when he died."

He didn't bat an eyelash. "And what makes you so sure about the time of death?"

"Because that's my job, Detective. What are you really asking?"

"I ain't askin' a thing, Mike." He leaned back. "All the same, I think you're gonna tell me what you and Dale talked about. Short of that—well, what would you do in my place?"

"Read me my rights," I said. "Charge me with homicide, if you think you can make the case. I don't think you've got too many options."

Tippet seemed about to offer a sour reply when a knock came at the door. He nodded to the window, and seconds later a man in his late thirties entered.

He was tall and lean, with serene brown eyes and sandy hair. Judging from his outfit—Reeboks and khakis—I guessed him for a university type. He seemed not quite sure where to sit; Tippet motioned him to the far end of the room. In his hands was a cardboard box with my name on the lid.

"Try and see this from my point of view, Mike." Tippet tapped his pencil. "I've got real problems since you blew into town. I've got a dead man in a county with a zero homicide rate. And worse besides."

"By 'worse' you're referring to the fact that Cassandra Dupree really is missing this time?"

Tippet and his comrade exchanged a look.

"Evelyn Maidstone told me she saw someone bringing Cassie up the walk," I said. "Less than a minute later, Dale was murdered. I'd say there's a connection, wouldn't you?"

He squinted. "Keep your shorts on, Mr. Yeager. Cassie's no concern of yours."

"Is she a concern of yours?" I said. "Because yesterday you called your sheriff and told him Cassandra Dupree was safe and you had the situation under control."

He looked back at me with a thousand-yard stare.

"For the love of God," I said. "Tell me you're not wasting time grilling me when you've got a missing child out there."

Tippet burned cold white. Then he gave himself away. An involuntary upward glance, straight to the hidden camera in the ceiling. From the corner of my eye I saw the stranger watching me.

Tippet cleared his throat. "If you had this information—"

"What time is it?" I said.

"What?"

"Time. Watch. When?" I grabbed Tippet's wrist, turned it over. He yanked it away.

"You try that again," he said, "you're gonna be spittin' teeth."

"The time is one-twenty-four A.M.," I said. "Sunday, November second. Since my arrest at eight o'clock yesterday morning I have not been charged with any crime. You're allowed to hold me like this for exactly twenty-four hours. Then either you file charges or I turn into a pumpkin."

He finally saw where I was going with this. "You little shit."

"As long as we're on the subject of shit," I said. "Tell your sheriff I'm not impressed with his procedures. Because so far he's handled this case like a gorilla with a spare tire. And if I'm not out on the street by eight A.M. with my car keys and all my belongings in the trunk, then so help me I'll eat every last one of you cornpone Barney Fifes for breakfast and crap tin stars all over this toxic waste dump you call a sheriff's station. You got all that? Or do I repeat it slow?"

"I heard you fine." He seemed ready to bite—then shot a look at his comrade. Some kind of silent agreement seemed to pass between them.

"He's all yours." Tippet pushed himself away from the table. The stranger waited until the door had shut before looking my way again. He smiled, friendly and a little cautious, as if I was some kind of captive animal. Here comes good cop, I thought.

"So what's going on?" His accent was mid-Atlantic, no trace of Nevada twang.

I shrugged. "Looks like I'm in jail."

He looked around, as if noticing for the first time. "Does seem that way."

"So we agree. Mind telling me who you are?"

"My name is Connor Blackwell." He didn't offer his hand: no physical contact on the cell block. This guy knew the rules. "I'm a clinical psychologist. I have a private practice in the area, and sometimes I do work for the county."

"You're here to find out if I match the profile for argument-related homicide," I said. "Violent tendencies, impulsive behavior . . . possible amphetamine use?"

"Don't forget conflict with authority figures." He grinned. "The sheriff told me about your law enforcement background. Maybe it'll make both our jobs a little easier."

"My job is getting out of here in one piece," I said. "I'm assuming yours is to give me tests out of that magic box of yours. Are you working with the new Minnesota Multiphasic? Or just phrenology skulls and chicken entrails?"

"A little of each," he said. "I'm assuming you've taken the MMPI before?"

"I used to administer it to arrest subjects," I said. "For the record, I don't hear voices, I don't think the government is recording my dreams, and I'm not unusually attracted to fires. Does that make your job any easier, Dr. Blackwell?"

"Connor." He leaned forward, intensely calm. "How are you feeling, Mike? Honestly."

"Honestly?" I gave a sharp laugh. "I'm hungry, I'm tired, I'm pissed off. And I'm increasingly convinced that very little is being done to find a missing child. What do you think?"

He furrowed his brow. "I'm sure they're doing everything they can."

"Really?" I said. "Has anyone put out a skip trace on the mother?"

"I don't know. I'd guess so."

"Is Cassie's description in the hands of interstate authorities? Has she been placed on NCIC as a missing person? Amber Alert?"

"To be perfectly candid, Mike, I know next to nothing about your case. I got a call asking me to come see you, and that's about it."

"My case?" I said. "Don't you mean the Dupree case?"

"Dale's case," he said. "My apologies."

"Did you know Dale?"

"Yes, I did."

"Personally or professionally?"

"That's not really relevant to why we're here, is it?"

"It could be very relevant," I said. "Dale might have told you something in therapy that would explain his behavior on Friday afternoon. Why he was trying to force his nephew into a truck, saying 'Tell me what the fuck she said.'"

"You heard him say that?"

I nodded. "You know, it's very possible you have two missing children. Robbie vanished right after that incident. A handicapped child on a walker."

Connor smiled. "I can set your mind at ease on that, anyway. Robbie is home safe with his family."

"And you know that for a fact."

"Yes." He lifted an eyebrow. "What do you think Dale meant by his comment to Robbie?"

"If 'she' is Cassie . . . it's possible she gave her cousin some kind of warning just prior to her disappearance."

He nodded. "Which could imply that she knew she was about to be abducted."

"And that she knew her abductor. Just as Dale knew the identity of his killer when he opened the door to him on Friday night."

"Ah." Connor nodded. "And this is why you wanted Tippet out of the room? So you could tell me this?"

"So I could tell the sheriff." I pointed up to the hidden camera.

"Right," he said. "You don't think there's anything I can do to help you."

"Is that really why you're here?" I smiled wearily. "Look, you seem all right. But don't think you're going to worm a confession out of me just because you're a nice guy and Tippet's a bastard."

Connor shook his head, as if I were a wild child trying to fool the babysitter. "I guess it's back to the skulls and chickens, then." He took a notepad from his shirt pocket. "Mind if I check a few facts?"

"It's your party."

"Michael Francis Yeager," he read. "Born June first, nineteen sixty-four, in Lancaster, Pennsylvania. Raised . . . Lutheran."

"Missouri Synod," I said.

He made a note. "Says here you wanted to be a minister, once upon a time. NCAA semifinalist in wrestling . . . Eagle Scout . . . speech and debate champion. Both parents deceased. Can you tell me anything about your folks?"

I tried hard not to show my amazement. He'd gotten a hell of a lot in seventeen and a half hours. "My father owned an apple farm," I said. "Between that and his other job, he worked eighty hours a week. He dropped dead when I was twenty-one."

"And your mother?"

I said nothing. He raised his hand, letting the question fall out of bounds. "Let's see—Bachelor of Science from Lancaster Community College, M.A. with honors in Forensic Psychology from U Penn. You hung in three years, waiting for a slot at the FBI Academy. Did I miss anything important?"

"I have a lovely singing voice."

He closed the notebook. "It's a pain, I know. But I have to make a complete report."

"Sounds like you've got enough for several complete reports."

He smiled, taking the compliment. "Let's rewind a bit. A while ago I asked how you were feeling and you somehow managed to change the subject."

"I answered the question."

"I need a little more," he said. "Tell me why you feel personally responsible for Cassie's welfare."

"Well, for one thing, it's my job."

"Yes, but—aren't you currently on leave from the FBI?"

"I didn't say anything about the FBI. I said it was my job."

"So let me understand. Dale called you Friday night. He was upset, he told you his daughter was missing. What did you do?"

"Called the neighbor to check on him."

"And then?"

I stopped, seeing the trap too late. "I went back to my motel room and fell asleep. I did crap, all right? The neighbor told me the daughter was home safe. I feel rotten about it, if that's your point."

"I'm not asking you to feel rotten," he said. "The neighbor said everything was fine. You assumed the situation had resolved itself. That's reasonable, isn't it?"

"The first rule of my profession is to assume nothing."

"And what's the second rule?"

"Situations don't resolve themselves."

"Like with Dale and Robbie at the Silver Star," he said. "You trusted your instincts then. Why not later on?"

"Trust is the ability to predict," I said. "Lately it seems my ability to predict . . . isn't what it used to be. As you'd say, it's not relevant." I averted my eyes. "I now believe I misread the situation in the parking lot. I don't think Dale was trying to hurt Robbie. I think he was just misguided and scared. And maybe putting Robbie into a truck was his mixed-up way of— protecting him."

My answer seemed to throw Connor off balance. "From whom? Protect him how?"

"I don't know," I said. "I never gave him a chance to tell me. Just like when I busted Dale's hand, I may have taken away his only chance to defend himself."

"Then you feel responsible for Dale's death."

I didn't answer. Who was this person, this therapist?

"If I tell you," I said, "are you going to use the information to help save a child's life?"

"My job is to report what I see, Mike, and let other people decide. If you have something important to say, I'll make sure you get your audience."

"With the sheriff."

Connor nodded.

"Dale asked me to look after Cassie if he went away," I said. "I'd say that creates some responsibility."

"Did you tell him you would?"

"If I did, then I've most definitely failed."

"Not necessarily," he said. "If you know something that could help this investigation—wouldn't that keep your promise? By helping to catch Dale's killer, you'd be helping Dale's daughter. True?"

Here was a fine question. If Connor had a line to the sheriff, then he might be presenting me a bona fide opportunity. On the other hand, his spur-of-the-moment proposal could easily be a well-laid trap. In my time I'd interrogated countless suspects who offered to "assist" a child abuse investigation by turning me on to the "real culprits," satanic cults and international child-sex rings. The leads were invariably bogus, but sometimes they were useful in getting a subject to implicate himself. He was very good, this Connor Blackwell.

"I suppose so," I said at last.

"Would you expect to be set free in exchange?"

"I expect to be set free because I haven't done anything wrong. I'm not asking for any deals."

"And if you were set free? Would you stay and assist, or—where would you go?"

"I haven't thought that far ahead. I sure as hell don't plan on settling down."

"Considering the welcome you got, I don't blame you." Connor looked at his watch. "I'd better check in with the sheriff. This case is high priority for him."

"Why is that?"

"Ask him yourself." He stood and rapped on the door.

"Connor," I said. "You can tell Sheriff Archer something else for me."

He waited. Keys jangled in the lock.

"Someone was taking pictures at the crime scene last night," I said.

He raised an eyebrow. "How could you know that?"

"I just do." I pointed. "You forgot your magic box."

He smiled. "No I didn't."

I waited until the door closed before reaching for the box. The bottom was warm, slightly damp. A familiar smell of bacon and eggs.

Breakfast.

SIX

The paneled hallway leading to Sheriff Archer was lined with newspaper photos, mostly of the sheriff himself. ARCHER BUSTS MOB RACKETS, read a headline from the early 1960s. The picture showed a perp walk of fat men shielding their faces with cuffed hands. The sheriff was at their heels—a square-shouldered lawman with heavy eyebrows, looking for all the world like Randolph Scott.

"So your boss ran the Mafia out of Dyer County," I said.

"Nawsir," said Clyde, my escort to the top floor. "Fact is he never let 'em in."

"Maybe they didn't want in that bad."

As the years flew down the hallway, Archer got older and the headlines got louder: ARCHER RE-ELECTED IN LANDSLIDE and RECORD PLEDGES FOR SUMMER CAMP and even ARCHER WELCOMES THE GIPPER. He did shake hands with President Reagan. Also Barry Goldwater, "Duke" Wayne, and somebody who was either Elvis Presley or a damned good Elvis impersonator. And in every blessed picture, Archer was wearing a revolver. It was a Colt .45 Buntline Special with a twelve-inch barrel and a walnut grip. No matter if he was kissing orphans or wearing a tux, he always kept that gun right on his hip.

"You like working for the sheriff?" I asked.

"I get moved around a lot," Clyde exhaled.

I noticed how the closer we got to Archer's office, the more Clyde seemed to drag his feet. By the time he knocked on the heavy oak door, Clyde was practically crawling.

"Come," said a gunmetal voice on the other side of that door. I was standing in the private office of Sheriff Rafe W. Archer.

The room was a study in mahogany and oxblood leather. Brass Remington cowboys topped the mission-style tables. A Russell painting titled "The Last Buffalo Hunt" dominated the back wall. Next to it the grandfather clock showed ten minutes till eight. Coffee and Bull Durham hung in the air. If it hadn't been for the modern push-button phone, you could have strung a velvet rope and called it a museum.

And yes, there was the Buntline Special, hung in an ebony frame over the sheriff's desk. The man himself was nowhere in sight, but I could hear his voice through the half-open washroom door.

". . . twenty deputies and twice as many volunteers," he was saying—to someone on the phone, I guessed. "All wanderin' around like dumb ants while I sit here jawin' with you."

The toilet flushed noisily. Clyde bit his lip and stared straight ahead.

"Christ, I've been hearin' calls to retire since Pike's Peak was a pimple. Buford Warburton's got his hooker money, and I've got his nuts in a sack. Who'd you rather lay odds on?"

A large U.S. Geological Survey map lay across Archer's desk. It looked like he'd staked out a lot of canyons and back roads for the search. A sheet of Sheriff's Department letterhead was covered with notes: *white Silverado* was about all I could read upside down.

"Sorry if I offend your virgin ears, Reverend," the sheriff continued. "But right now I got more troubles than Judas on Judgment Day, and the damn election just ain't a priority. Now go do your job and we'll talk after church . . . Because it's part of a crime scene, that's why. Give the kids their apple juice somewhere else. And for chrissakes tell Martha to stop bawlin' till my men arrive. I got enough misery without her wakin' me up at all hours."

He hung up the phone. There was a trickle of tap water. "You still here, Clyde?"

"Sir." Clyde gulped. "I brought Muh, Mister Yeag—"

"I know who it is," Archer said from behind the door. "You got that watch detail at the preacher's house like I told you?"

Shit, Clyde mouthed. "Um, yessir. Safe as Fort Knox."

"Clyde, I just got done talkin' to the man. Now get on it before I skin you."

Clyde hastily backed out of the room. The washroom door swung wide.

The sheriff's gray eyes shone beneath his heavy brows like silver in an abandoned mine. That was all that remained of the brash young gunfighter in those newspaper photos. He seemed not to have aged so much as eroded, until only the hardest and least forgiving part of him remained. Beneath a snow-white mustache his teeth were the color of old ivory. He held a file in two gnarled and knotted hands. Despite his years he inhabited the room like a ruined king—but a king all the same.

"Boy ain't worth a cup of warm piss." Archer didn't look my way as he sat behind his massive desk. "What's on your mind, son?"

I pointed to the Buntline. "I was just wondering what a weapon like that is doing behind a pane of glass."

"It's an antique," he said. "Some folks'd put me in a frame like that, if they had their druthers."

"I bet it could still punch a hole in a man."

"That it could," he said. "Sit down. You're making me nervous."

He didn't look nervous, but I sat down anyway. He sized me up in two rapid glances. One at my palms—probably to see if they were sweating—the other straight into my eyes.

"You're a piece of work, ain'tcha?" He offered a perfunctory smile, as if he'd already seen my hole card and didn't think much of my wager.

"I imagine I don't smell much better than the cell I slept in."

"You're not bad off for a fella who went two rounds with Dale Dupree."

"One round, Sheriff," I said. "I went one round with Dale. Somebody else had the last one."

He reached for the old percolator behind him. "Coffee Mike?"

"Sure, Rafe."

He poured out two mugs and added a slug of bourbon to his. "That Colt revolver was a gift of my predecessor, old Sheriff Fox. Which he inherited after the war—and so on, back to the year that model was first made."

"Eighteen seventy-seven," I said. "That was quite a gift."

"It was," he said. "I'll never forget what he told me. 'You will never win a fast draw with the Buntline, Rafe. The barrel's too long and the action's like draggin' barbed wire through the mud. But it never misfires, and it's steady. So don't aim that weapon unless you intend to kill. Because it will do terrible things to a man.'"

"And have you ever aimed it?"

"I hear you're none too impressed by our procedures." His eyes gleamed cold. "You know, when I heard what you did to Dale, I was almost impressed with you. I thought, 'Now there is a man who understands the philosophy of the Buntline.' Figured I'd have to make your acquaintance one way or another."

"I'd have accepted a dinner invitation. You didn't have to impound my car."

"That Tip." He shook his head. "He's an ambitious fella, and he can shoot a bird flyin'. But between us, I don't think he'll ever inherit that Colt. I guess he's just one more gorilla playin' with tires."

"Spare tires," I said. "You said 'almost impressed.' "

"You wanted a shot and now I'm givin' it to you." He drummed his fingers on the table. "But from where I sit—*Agent* Yeager—you appear somewhat low on ammunition."

"I won't waste your time," I said. "I'm not the one you want."

He raised an eyebrow. "Said the deer to the hunter."

"I'm guessing you've talked to Connor Blackwell, and that's why I'm here."

"Connor's a smart young man," he said. "I leave him in charge of the five-dollar-word department. And from what I understand, he thinks highly of you. On the other hand . . . my detective lieutenant, Jackson Tippet, believes you are sandbaggin' evidence on my investigation. And I don't think you know just how much that pisses me off."

"Sheriff, I'm well aware of how important this case is to you."

"Really." He settled back. "Are you now."

"I told Connor everything I know. If you don't believe me, have Mrs. Maidstone confirm it."

"Ev Maidstone don't always know what planet she's on."

"But you're aware I talked to her."

"I'm aware somebody called her from the Lucky Strike. Wouldn't give his name. Said he was a friend of Dale's. Is that what you are now? His friend?"

"I guess he thought so."

"Even though you were tryin' to kill each other that afternoon."

"I did what I felt was necessary to defuse the situation."

He snorted. "I'll say you defused him, all right. Gave little Robbie somethin' for a future nightmare."

"I regret that," I said. "Has anyone talked to Robbie about what happened?"

He look a long pull of his coffee. "What's a boy like Robbie to you?"

"He may know something about his cousin's disappearance," I said.

"And, as you say, he's bound to be traumatized. Somebody needs to tell Robbie that what happened wasn't his fault. And that grown-ups are going to stay with him and keep him safe."

"Don't you think he knows that already?"

"Children believe what they see every day," I said. "I haven't seen much in the way of justice in Dyer County."

He didn't blink once in half a minute.

"You're the man from the Justice Department," he said finally. "My job is keepin' the peace. When someone like you shows up, I know there's gonna be trouble. In my long experience, y'see, only two kinds of strangers come to Dyer County. The ones who think they're gonna find the lost Dutchman's gold mine . . . and the ones lookin' for the only thing this desert has in abundance."

I shrugged. "Empty beer cans?"

"Death," said the sheriff. "You don't look like you expect to find a gold mine."

"You already know I didn't kill Dale," I said. "Precisely because I am a stranger. If you've looked at the evidence, you've seen that Dale was killed by someone close to him—maybe even a person he's known all his life."

For the first time I saw a flicker of surprise. "Is that so."

"Dale opened the door to the killer. And he died relatively quickly, which means the attacker was able to get close without raising suspicion. I'm betting on a blitz-style attack from behind, at extremely close range."

He hesitated thoughtfully. "How do you know he died quick?"

"Less than two minutes after I hung up with Dale, the killer was taking pictures of the victim."

Archer gave an indifferent shrug. "Yeah, Connor mentioned somethin' about photographs. You mind explainin' that?"

He had a better poker face than his deputies. "Evelyn said she saw camera flashes," I said. "It's the key to your entire case. In a personal-cause homicide, where the subject is close to the victim, the attacker is generally afraid to look into the victim's eyes. So they'll go from behind. Usually they'll aim for the face, to erase the victim's identity. Was Dale's face injured in any way?"

Archer was stone-faced. "You were tellin' me about photographs."

"Some killers take a memento of the victim—a personal belonging. Sometimes it's a body part. Taking photographs is unusual. It suggests both a desire to preserve an image of the victim in death, and the need to achieve psychological distance. Dale thought of the killer as a friend. But the killer only saw Dale as an object. Like a scientist studying a lab rat."

"False friendship," he said. "You are one smart monkey, Agent Yeager. I'll give you that."

"That's why you brought me here, isn't it? You knew I could help you catch the man who took those pictures. It's what the FBI trained me to do. I've spent the last ten years of my life looking at photographs."

"In that case"—he raised his eyebrows—"what do you make of these?"

He spread the file open and turned it around.

"Jesus wept," I said.

SEVEN

It was true; I had spent the last ten years looking at photographs for the FBI. My job was to know when the victim had last eaten, whether she had been raped or injured, whether anything in the camera frame would reveal the abductor's state of mind. As a matter of preference I relied on faces. Faces of the dead and those about to die. Faces of children who were in terrible pain and yet ordered to smile, and sometimes all too willing to try.

But Dale had no face to study. His head had been severed at the base of the neck.

There were twenty-one black-and-white glossy photographs in the set Archer laid out for me. Pictures of Dale, lying nude on the floor. His bare skin had been hacked until it shredded away like wet toilet paper. Strips of limp flesh hung to either side—exposing the naked ribs, the collapsed lung. There were angled cuts along both forearms, straight to the bone.

"Nothing to say?" the sheriff asked. "All that FBI training up and run away?"

The photographs were good enough for an Academy textbook—maybe too good. Every shot was surgically precise. Each mangled tendon, every lipless wound caught the light and modeled itself in garish relief. I started to speak, then realized I'd forgotten to breathe.

"These aren't crime scene photos." I barely masked the tremor in my voice.

"We don't know who took 'em," he said. "Thought maybe you could tell me."

"He's a perfectionist," I said. "You see the microwave clock in three different shots—ten-fifteen, one-thirty-four, three-seventeen. Always in focus.

He's telling us how long he was at the crime scene. Sheriff, how did you acquire these pictures?"

"Why?"

"The subject could be a professional photographer," I said. "That or a talented amateur. It takes practice to get that deep focus—and these prints weren't developed at Wal-Mart. You're going to need your own darkroom, and it's got to be top-drawer. Chemicals and equipment would have to be specially ordered . . . all that's going to leave a paper trail."

"We don't have any photographers in town." He paused. "Not professional, anyhow."

"Even an expert would need half a day just to produce the prints—never mind travel time." I took a whiff. "You can still smell the developer. I'll walk out on a limb and say they were left for you between two to four hours ago."

He nodded. "Found 'em on my doorstep at six this mornin'."

"So he's local. The subject's got to have three things working for him—money, privacy, and time. That'll narrow your range of suspects. The job will get easier once you type the film stock and camera."

"And you think whoever took these pictures did the killin'."

"At the very least he watched it happen. But I'm willing to bet it's the same guy. Look at the quality of these prints. He wants us to admire his work." I leafed through them. "Hardly any close-ups. He keeps the camera ten to twelve feet away . . . probably to get the deep focus. But then you also have to look at what the subject's choices tell us about his personality."

"What do they tell you?"

"He wants to get as far from the victim as possible," I said. "Probably to detach himself emotionally. And even though he sends photographs to the authorities, he clearly doesn't expect to be caught. Looks like he used a tripod to disguise his height. No shadows, no reflections. Not even footprints in the blood. It's like he's making himself invisible. Did you find any prints at the scene?"

"Nothin' good enough to match," he said. "How'd they take Dale's head off?"

"Bladed weapon." I took a closer look. "I'm not a knife expert, but I'd say it was one made for slicing, not stabbing. There's two different wound patterns. The first set are deep, precise—the subject has good upper-body strength, so it's probably a male, thirty to fifty. The rest are hackwork—this one can barely draw the blade out. So that's two assailants. Where's Mary?"

"Mary?"

"The victim's wife," I said. "She was—"

"We don't know where Mary is," he said.

I returned to the photographs. Dale lay on his side, bloody and naked as the day he was born. Most likely he'd been stripped postmortem. In almost every picture he was curled in a fetal position, his arms gathered to his chest like a sleeping child. A dark cloth was wrapped around his neck stump, replacing his head.

"What's that cloth?" I said. "Flag? Looks like forty-eight stars."

"That's from his daddy's funeral," he said. "He was a marine like Dale—died at Khe Sahn. See that triangular frame on the wall? They broke it open to get that flag."

"Undoing," I said.

"Undoing?"

"The killer's posthomicidal remorse. Posing the victim, washing or dressing him. The killers attempted to 'undo' the murder by covering the victim's wounds with an object they knew had significance for him. Like giving a child his teddy bear. It generally happens only when the killer is unusually close to the victim."

"Like family?"

"Someone who's known him since childhood," I said. "Got any candidates?"

He was suddenly cautious. "Keep talkin'."

The last photo, Number 21, was a stark contrast to the others: an eye-level closeup of Dale's neck stump. The flag had been removed to display the severed windpipe. Both hands were gathered to the neck, as if clutching for the missing head. They were in perfect focus. The rest of the picture was slightly blurred. I noticed a tiny dog-ear in the upper right-hand corner.

"Semper Fi," I said.

"Hm?"

"Dale's Marine Corps ring," I said. "It's the focal point of the entire image."

"Is it important?"

"I don't know yet," I said. "Okay. Those are defensive cuts on his arms, so Dale must have had at least a second to turn around. But then there's that downward slice between the sternum and right clavicle. Which is . . . odd."

"Why so?"

"The blade would have severed at least two major arteries. He wouldn't have had time enough to stand up, let alone fight back."

"Dale wasn't much on brains," Archer said. "But he was a fighter."

"It doesn't add up. You'd have to be standing over the victim to make that deep cut. And he'd have to be holding still, or you'd likely glance off the bone. So that couldn't have been the first blow. I'd have to see the body to know for sure. But the victim was obviously moved postmortem, so there's no telling where—"

"How do you know that?" he said.

"Blade marks on the floor don't match the wounds." I held the photograph closer. "They time everything perfectly—but then the first blow doesn't kill. The victim had time to stand up. Dale was fighting back."

For a moment there I could almost see it happening, like a movie in three dimensions. The victim on his knees, face bent downward as if he were saying his prayers. The killer standing behind him. An arc of steel, a fountain of blood. But then the victim looked up with those anguished blue eyes and became Dale again. *I'm in a world of hurt.*

It took me a moment to realize that Sheriff Archer was studying me. Not with contempt this time, but with a curious and shadowed expression.

"What did I say?" I asked.

"For a second there," he said, "you looked like you were in a lot of pain."

I carefully stacked the photographs.

"You should have told me what these were before you let me touch them," I said. "There might have been usable prints or DNA traces."

"I just figured you'd know that without my saying so," he said. "Until you looked at those pictures I'd have sworn you were a tough hombre. Then it was like your face broke wide open."

"Just the bruise on my jaw."

"I recognize that look," he said. "Used to see it every day in the mirror till I got old and mean. You got wounded eyes, Mr. Yeager."

I looked past him to the grandfather clock. "It's two minutes to eight, Sheriff. Are you going to book me for murder or let me go?"

"That depends how truthful you are," he said. "I'd rather hang a liar than a killer any day."

"I haven't told a lie since I walked in your door."

"You ain't exactly drawn a map for me either. But I think I got a bead on you now. You can't stand to see people in pain. That's what you do in the FBI, ain't it? Protectin' kids. I hear you were good at it."

"I protected children," I said. "So what?"

"Well, look at you," he said. "Scratchin' around this desert . . . gettin' in fights and wakin' up in jail, so old farts like me can push you around. Time was you did the pushin' around. Must've been like biting your arm from a steel trap to leave all that. Hadda damn near killed you."

"It damn near killed me."

"I was just thinkin' you might like a chance to get that arm back."

He spoke as easily as he had when he poured my coffee.

"Not if the trap's still attached," I said.

"But you promised Dale you'd look after Cassie. Or did Connor misquote you?"

"He got it right."

"And you could help me find her. It's what you want, isn't it?"

I was beginning to see why Clyde lived in fear of the man. Archer didn't need the Buntline. He had those gray eyes.

"I'm sorry," I said at last. "I'm just not the man for that kind of work. Not anymore."

"You won't even look at her picture?"

Without waiting for an answer, he handed me a framed color matte from his desk. School portrait. Cassandra Dupree looked nothing like her father. She was pallid and underfed, with a large round face and long red-gold hair that needed a mother's combing. An absent half smile. Her eyes were pure green, large and intensely watchful.

"How old is she?" I asked.

"Seven," he said. "Same as her cousin Robbie. You got kids of your own, Agent Yeager?"

I shook my head.

"I got two, myself," he said. "Sometimes I don't think they'd miss me much. But it terrifies me thinking what Cassie must be goin' through right now. Wherever she is, she's got to be scared right out of her mind."

"I'd start looking for the mother," I said.

He frowned. "You keep bringin' up Mary Frances. You just shakin' my apples, or do you know something?"

"Mary Dupree could easily be the second assassin," I said. "Recently divorced, possible custody battle. A good candidate for domestic-revenge homicide. And she was at the scene. If you're looking for the photographer, a place to start would be her list of lovers. Evelyn Maidstone called her a whore. Was that just a slur, or had Mary actually worked as a prostitute?"

Archer folded his hands. "Still does, so I'm told."

"So look for her pimp," I said. "Find the pimp and you'll have Mary. Find Mary and you'll get Cassandra. That's how you do it, Sheriff. Follow the chain of abuse."

For a moment his eyes blazed like he'd stepped on a nail. Then the clock began to toll. With each chime the pale fire dimmed, and then he was only the dusty old lawman again.

"I guess there's wisdom in that," he said.

There was a knock behind me.

"Sheriff?" A familiar voice over my left shoulder.

"Detective Tippet," the sheriff grunted. "Agent Yeager thinks instead of wastin' time on him, we should be trackin' down Mary Dupree's ex-boyfriends. I believe he mentioned her pimp. You mind gettin' on top of that?"

Tippet's mouth fell open. "Nosir."

"No sir," Archer repeated. "Please discharge Agent Yeager and give him a ride to the impound—and, of course, sincere apologies for our piss-poor arrest procedures. You're a free man, son. For what it's worth to you."

"Sheriff." I rose from my chair. "If you need help, I can put you in contact with—"

"Purely for my peace of mind," he said. "Your reluctance wouldn't have anything to do with a boy named Antonio Madrigal . . . would it?"

The old bastard. All this time and he'd known.

"So it would seem." Archer nodded. "Good-bye, Agent Yeager."

E I GHT

Tippet kept his cool right down to the ground floor. Then he threw a fat manila envelope at me.

"You've got your shit," he said. "Now get your smelly ass out of my sight."

I made a big deal of counting the bills in my wallet.

"Goddamn FBI gloryhound," he said. "You think because you did an end run with the sheriff, that makes you Jesus? You just better not try and foul my investigation. There won't be enough angels in heaven to pray for you."

"The investigation's all yours, Tippet. You may not credit this, but I hope like hell you succeed." I slipped my belt on. "Since you're so keen on the chain of command, I may as well ask. Who was it you called on your cell phone Friday—before you reported back to your sheriff?"

His face dissolved in cold rage. "Find your own way to the fucking impound."

Tippet stalked away. The pretty clerk, Deputy Rosario, came out shyly from behind her counter.

"Don't you mind him," she said. "I'll give you a ride."

We walked out into the clear light of morning. The distant mountains were pale silver. Ada's perfume, cedar and cinnamon, was sweet and refreshing after a day in jail.

"They're beautiful," I said.

"Hm?"

"The Sangre de los Niños. You know, if it wasn't for those mountains, I wouldn't even be here. I saw pictures of them in *National Geographic* when I was a kid, and they've never let me go. I always thought one day I'd become a photographer and live out west, like Ansel Adams."

"Oh," she said. "So this is like a vacation for you?"

"It's a long story," I said. "I was facing the end of something . . . trying to get my life together. Then two weeks ago, I woke up on the floor of my apartment and realized—'I've never taken pictures of the Sangre de los Niños.' I know it's silly, but it gave me a reason to keep going."

"I understand. We live close to the mountains. So . . ." Her voice dropped. "I'm sorry this happened to you. There's good people here, too."

"I'm sorry I won't be around long enough to find out. You might have changed my mind about Dyer County."

She looked at me intently, as if my comment raised issues too complex for a stranger to understand.

"Lots of us are glad what you did for Robbie," she said. "I got a little boy his age. At least . . . he would be."

"What happened to him?"

"He's dead." Her face suddenly froze, twisted. "Someone killed him with their truck."

We had arrived at her car—the same green Jeep Cherokee from the funeral procession. A child's car seat was strapped into the rear, M&Ms crushed into the upholstery.

"My God," I said. "Your boy . . . I had no idea."

"My mama and brothers don't understand why I came back to work," she said. "They told me I was dis—dishonoring my baby boy. But I have to do something. If I stayed at home, I think I would die."

"What's your son's name?"

"Espero."

We drove to the impound in silence. My old Nash Rambler waited among the junked pickups.

"I'd better get back," she said. "I'm not supposed to leave my desk."

"I'm glad you did."

I stood from the car. Her hands were tight on the steering wheel.

"He shouldn't have died," she said. "It was my fault."

"How could it be your fault?"

"Mama says he ran off because I work all the time. If I'd been there, instead of—"

"You weren't the one driving the truck, Ada." I looked down at her. "How did it happen?"

She closed her eyes. "He . . . was out playing in the yard in the evening. And he wandered away into the road."

"How far do you live from the road?"

"About a mile."

"Seems a long way for a child to wander," I said. "Had he ever done it before?"

She looked at me, startled—stitches ripped from a fresh wound.

"No," she said. "Nothing like this has ever happened before."

Then she left me alone in the impound yard.

NINE

The Unocal station at Highway 313 and Sparks Valley Road was the last stop before leaving Dyer County. From there it was a straight shot to the interstate—south to Vegas, west to Los Angeles—or wherever I wanted to go, now that I was a free man again.

"... reached the mobile phone of Special Agent Weaver of the Federal Bureau of Investigation," said Peggy's recorded voice. "To leave a voice message, press one. To send a numeric page ..."

I pressed 2 and tapped in the number of the Unocal pay phone, then added the three-digit code Peg and I used for personal messages. It was 8:45 A.M., just shy of noon in Philadelphia. By now Peggy would have finished her morning jog and bagel run. If I was with her, we might be hashing out reports or trying to smarten up for a Monday court appearance. Maybe we'd play hooky if the weather was good. But no matter what, we would be together. Sunday afternoons we could occasionally take off the badges and pretend to be an ordinary couple.

Two minutes later the pay phone rang.

"You weren't kidding about the sheriff," I said. "He was spinning something, all right. I just escaped being indicted for first-degree murder."

"Mike?" Peggy said. "Where are you?"

"On the other hand, maybe I didn't escape." I looked around. "Peg, do I have the right to feel sorry for myself?"

"Probably not. Why are you suddenly asking?"

"I was moaning about my aches and pains to somebody, and it turns out her son just died. Somehow she found a way to keep going. It makes me wonder how I could fall apart after one bad case."

"That one bad case hit you a lot harder than you want to believe," she said. "We need to talk."

"Seems that way." I took a breath. "What did you tell Sheriff Archer about me?"

"What I said Friday," she said. "Good things."

"About Tonio Madrigal?"

"About—okay, back up. I see from the area code that you're still in Nevada. Do you have your car?"

"Yes."

"Get in your car, drive across the nearest state line, and call me back. Then we'll talk about Tonio, or . . . whatever else you've gotten into."

"Who else could have spoken to him? Are you sure you didn't tip him off somehow?"

"Yeager, did it never occur to you that the Madrigal case might be public knowledge?" Her voice tightened. "Jesus, even in the boondocks they must get the *Inquirer*. And since when have I ever shafted you about—anything?"

"I didn't mean it like that," I said. "I'm a little keyed up. I just spent the weekend in jail."

"Of course. For murder. Your ex-marine." She took a slow breath. "Why do you think they let you go?"

"Oh, I don't know. Maybe because I didn't kill anybody?" I tried to laugh and it came out sounding pissed off. "Sounds like you're not too surprised by any of this."

"Nothing you do surprises me lately." She sighed. "I got the call half an hour ago."

"The sheriff again?"

"Yes, the sheriff. And before that, the Special Agent in Charge of the Las Vegas field office. Asking why one of my agents was assisting a homicide investigation in his jurisdiction."

"Homicide and kidnapping," I said. "You don't have to worry about a pissing match with the Vegas field office. I already turned the sheriff down."

"It's already gone beyond that. Archer's not accepting any other offers of assistance. Whatever you told him seems to have him convinced you're the only man for the job. Do you even know what the job is?"

"Just a quick-and-dirty read on some photos," I said. "Plus there's a missing girl. You know, the kind the media go for—strawberry blonde, green eyes."

"He showed you her case file?"

"School picture. It sounds like this sheriff's under pressure to retire. My guess is he's just scared of bad publicity."

"Think about it. Where did he keep this school picture? An evidence bag?"

"On his desk."

"In a frame, right?"

"Yeah, how did—oh, shit."

You got kids, Yeager? I got two, myself.

"A school picture on his desk," I said. "How the hell did that get past me?"

"You're tired. I can hear it in your voice."

"His granddaughter," I said. "Has to be. Which means—Jesus, I actually called his daughter a prostitute."

"And he still let you go. He must have known you wouldn't go far."

I exhaled. "What do you think I should do?"

"Probably nothing. The Office of Professional Responsibility would have to agree to return you to active duty—which almost never happens in a pending inquiry. If you want an excuse to stay clear, I'd blame the bureaucracy."

"Why would I want an excuse?"

"Because the sheriff is personally running the search for his own granddaughter. If the case goes south, he's going to be out for blood. And you're vulnerable, Mike. Which means the Bureau is vulnerable. I hate saying this, but if it starts looking like a replay of Madrigal . . ."

"I hear you." I closed my eyes for a moment. "But now wait."

"It always scares me when you start sentences with 'But now wait.'"

"Suppose it works, Peg. What if I actually manage to save this one?"

She took a careful breath. "If there's a successful recovery, it could put you back on the side of the angels. The Bureau loves good press. And maybe the inquiry will vanish in a puff of smoke, and you'll start sleeping again." She hesitated. "But honestly, it's a hell of a long shot."

"Well, like you said, the Bureau probably wouldn't let me within a mile of this case anyway."

"Who knows? This sheriff seems to have a lot of pull. And he wants you. He's made that very clear. Plus there's one more factor on your side."

"What's that?"

"You really are the right man for the job."

I smiled. "Would you be willing to swear to that in open court?"

"Look, if you're serious, I'll back your play. But I need to know something first—no jokes, no bulletproof-Mike routine."

"You want to know what I'm trying to prove."

"In a word, yes. Because if it's just to get your job back—or for somebody else you couldn't save . . ."

"It's not just that. It's Dale, and—it's that picture of Cassie, too. Something in her eyes."

"You think you're the only one who can save the kid."

I took a breath. "I just want to know that I still can."

"Keep driving, Mike. It's too soon. And you're still hurting. Which could damage your judgment at a critical moment."

"I hear you," I said. "Peg, you got that little electronic notepad on you?"

"Yeager, for God's sake."

"I can't make this decision without background. Nothing fancy. Priors and known accomplices, that's all."

She sighed. "Go ahead. Start with the mother."

"Mary Dupree—that's D-U-P-R-E-E, adult Caucasian. She'd have left the area between ten P.M. Friday and eight A.M. Saturday, in the company of her daughter and an adult male—a boyfriend or pimp. No description on him, but—"

"She's literally a prostitute?"

"Yeah. Any ideas about that?"

"State of Nevada requires sex workers to register with an employer," she said. "That'll lead us to the boyfriend. What about the daughter?"

"Seven years old," I said. "From the picture I'd guess . . . three and a half feet, forty to forty-five pounds."

"Where was she at the time of the murder?"

"Most likely on the scene."

"If they made her watch . . ."

She didn't finish the sentence. She didn't have to.

"I better get on this," Peggy said. "What's her name?"

"Cassandra," I said. "Don't wait for the full packet. Just fax me whatever you've got in an hour."

"Fax you where?"

"Hang on. I'll get you the number for the motel."

"Yeager, are you sure you want to take this on?"

There was a long silence.

"All right," she said. "You're wandering in your desert. But promise me something. If not as . . . well, as somebody who cares about you. As a friend."

"Name it."

"Don't go so far in you can't hear me anymore."

TEN

Forty-five minutes later I was waiting for Peggy's fax in the lobby of the Lucky Strike Motel. I killed time reading a recent issue of the local newspaper, the Dyer County *Ledger*. There was a flash flood warning, a list of Halloween activities—and a very interesting front-page headline:

RECALL SURVIVES FINAL COURT CHALLENGE
Sheriff Archer to Face Critics in Nov. 4 Referendum

Apparently the County Commission, having failed for the umpteenth time to force Archer's retirement, had finally succeeded in getting a recall initiative onto Tuesday's ballot. The sheriff had, in so many words, dared his enemies to come get him if they had the sand. As of Friday he was still expected to squeak past a field of seventy-six candidates, most of whom had no party affiliation or reported income. Archer's only serious opposition, a used-car dealer named Buford Warburton, was rumored to be in the pay of local gaming interests. "Hooker money," Archer had called it.

It was now going on ten A.M. I crossed around the desk, knocked again, then pushed the door open. The manager sat reading sheets of paper topped with the FBI seal.

"Thought they locked you up."

"That's official business," I said. "Confidential, understand?"

He held the pages to his thick glasses like a jeweler sizing up a diamond. "Fax for guest only."

"Swell. I'm a guest."

He weighed the documents. "Forty dollars."

I put down two twenties and snatched the pages away. "Ask for anything else," I said, "and you're gonna eat that fax machine."

According to her license to practice prostitution, Mary Dupree was thirty-two years old, five foot six, one hundred and seventeen pounds—with bottle-blonde hair, her father's gray eyes, and no sexually transmitted diseases. Even in a faxed copy you could see Mary's face was her fortune. The rest of her wasn't exactly bankrupt. But there was nothing beautiful about that list of priors: Narcotics possession, DUI, a juvenile hall stint for "loitering" near California's Ft. Sherman—in police vernacular that meant underage prostitution.

In 1990 she married Dale and things seemed to settle down for a while. Then, a week before their fourteenth anniversary, she was picked up in a vice raid on the Las Vegas strip. Her husband and sister appeared on her behalf and no action was taken. But apparently it was the last straw for Dale, and that summer he sued for divorce on grounds of adultery. The inevitable custody battle ended with an October 15 ruling in Dale's favor.

As of September 15, Mary Dupree was under a six-week contract at the Sweet Charity Ranch in nearby Caritas, Nevada. There were two likely reasons for her wanting to stay that close to home. One was her daughter. The other had to be the guy on the following page.

Peter Stimson Frizelle, aka Paul Stimson, aka Farrell Stone, aka Wild Pete. Thirty-seven, five foot nine, a hundred and forty-five pounds. His photo showed him in Armani, mustache trimmed, trying to look respectable; the pothead grin and gambler's eyes gave him away. Prior arrests and convictions included grand theft auto, statutory rape, narcotics possession, narcotics trafficking, pandering, and solicitation. The guy didn't learn from his mistakes—but somehow he always managed to beat the serious charges. Then in 1985 he graduated to interstate felony with a Mann Act violation, transporting minors across state lines for immoral purposes. Frizelle spent the rest of the eighties in the California prison system, then moved to San Francisco, where—against all probability—he actually stayed clean. In 1997 he wrangled a license from the state gaming commission—officially it was in his mother's name—and opened Wild Pete's Hotel and Casino.

I looked up at the giant neon cowboy across the highway. Wild Pete's.

The date of Frizelle's Mann Act violation was the same as Mary Dupree's loitering charge: June 16, 1985. Which meant he had been trading her flesh since she was at least fifteen years old. Sheriff Archer, it seemed, could kick the Mob out of Dyer County . . . but he couldn't keep his daughter away from Pete Frizelle.

In 1995, while he was still building his bankroll in California, Peter Frizelle had entered a family court petition for paternity of Cassandra Dupree. Apparently he'd gone so far as to request a DNA test. The motion was swiftly denied—it was Archer's family court, after all—but that wasn't what interested me. On the application, Frizelle listed his profession as "importer-exporter." And in the space for "Place of Employment," he'd given the address for Shogun Swords & Military Collectibles, San Francisco, California.

On the phone I'd heard Dale say that the killer was carrying something that "looked like a damn bazooka." That would be just about the right size. Because the weapon that ended Dale's life was a blade for slicing—and for that kind of killing there was nothing cleaner than a Japanese sword.

I grabbed a map of Dyer County from the lobby desk. Then I was back on the road to Langhorne.

ELEVEN

Tree of Life Interdenominational Church—the Reverend Gavin McIntosh, Pastor—was a big white corrugated metal building. If it wasn't for the fake bell tower, I'd have guessed it for a feed storage. FALL HARVEST FESTIVAL, FRI–SUN, read the sign out front. BRING THE KIDS! The parking lot was packed. Parked across two handicapped spots was an off-road vehicle marked SHERIFF.

The inside was as plush as the outside was plain. Thick blue carpet, gold ceiling fixtures—like the last days of Louis XVI, I thought. The altar wall was floor-to-ceiling glass, offering a brilliant view of the Sangre de los Niños.

" 'Suffer the little children to come unto me,' " recited a clear tenor voice. " 'And forbid them not, for of such is the kingdom of heaven.' "

I had walked in on the tail end of the pastoral prayer. Reverend McIntosh was on his knees, a broad-faced man in a Panama shirt. Sunlight filtered down, making a kind of halo in his coiffed, white-blond hair.

"Lord, Thy will be done, but sometimes it's hard to understand," he said. "Rain won't come. . . . Enemies surround this great land . . . and our children, Lord. You take our children from us. Just this last week, little Espero came home to You. And now our Cassie's in trouble. Where's it all gonna end?"

The faces of the congregation were bent in prayer. Fat-bellied bikers and mothers-to-be, bent old ladies and teenage girls sharing their Bibles. Trembling with grief. Holding each other in fear.

"We know You're not a cruel God. You won't look coldly on our suffering. We pray . . . make this desert live again. And as you sent Your child to die for us, protect our young ones from the darkness. Amen."

"AMEN!" the congregation echoed.

Music started again, and now the collection plates were coming around. Three hundred handbags, wallets, and change purses opened wide. Finally I saw the sheriff, standing against the far wall. As he saw me he began to smile.

"How'd you know to look for me here?" The sheriff met me in front of the altar as the service ended.

"You were on the phone with the preacher when I came into your office. Dale mentioned something about a 'Harvest Festival' on Friday, so I figured this might be a hot zone for the investigation."

"Whole damn county's a hot zone today." Now that I was closer I could see a streak of red in his eyes. From tears, maybe, or exhaustion. His voice was softer in the empty church.

"I wanted to apologize for some of the comments I made about your daughter," I said. "I would have been more careful if I'd known."

"I didn't want you to be careful," he said. "I wanted you to tell me the truth."

"Good. Then we're square."

He half-smiled: Cassie's smile. "Are we?"

"I think I'm owed a few answers," I said. "You already knew about Mary's history with Pete Frizelle. And I'm betting you also knew he'd worked for a company that imports Japanese swords."

Archer calmly lit a hand-rolled cigarette from an altar candle. "Actually, he owned it. Might be the only honest work Pete ever did. Where you takin' this, Mr. Yeager?"

"You knew your daughter was a prime suspect before you ever met me. I don't like that, Sheriff. I spent the night cooling my heels over nothing. Don't say it was Tippet's doing, because those boys don't twitch a nostril without your say-so."

"Maybe you should follow their example." Smoke passed across his narrowing features. "You might have been free a lot sooner if you hadn't pitched a fit."

"Those were twenty-four hours we could have been looking for Cassandra," I said. "Think about it."

We were interrupted by coughing.

"The Lord Sayeth No Smoking." Reverend McIntosh smiled as he approached.

"Son-in-law." Archer snuffed his cigarette between two fingers. "This here's that FBI fella I was tellin' you about."

"Agent Yeager." Gavin's blue eyes lit up as he shook my hand with both of his. "You're an answer to a prayer."

"I am?"

"Absolutely. We called on the Lord to send help, and here you are."

"Here I am."

"Let's go see that kiddie school of yours, Gavin." Archer grunted. "I want to know exactly how Pete Frizelle managed to get his hands on my granddaughter."

Gavin led us to the Sunday school. I noticed he had an odd habit of tilting his head upward as he walked, as if reading God's instructions off the ceiling. It took me a minute to realize he was simply trying to straighten out his double chin.

"The sheriff called you 'son-in-law,'" I said.

He nodded. "Robbie's our little boy. Martha and I are very grateful to you for looking after him."

"I'm just glad he's all right."

"Robbie's fine," Gavin said, a shade too quickly. "Scared, of course. As you can imagine, he's terribly worried about his cousin. As are we all."

"I'd like to ask your son a few questions." From the corner of my eye I saw Archer bristle—reminding me I was on his turf, not mine. "With the sheriff's permission, of course."

Archer nodded. "We'll come by later on, Gavin. Go ahead and tell Mike about Friday."

"I wasn't here," the preacher said. "I'd just gotten the call that Robbie had missed the church shuttle, and went out looking for him. Normally I'd have been here to troubleshoot."

"How often has he missed the after-school program?"

"Robbie? Once or twice."

"An old man at the Silver Star says Robbie's there every afternoon playing video games."

"Oh. Well, that's . . . not good." The minister flushed. "Anyhow, the girl we had on duty is very young. So when Mary Frances showed up on the wrong day, she got confused."

The sheriff watched as I knelt down to the floor. "Yeager, you hearin' this?"

I nodded. "Why is there dog food on the carpet?"

Gavin raised his eyebrows. "Cassie brought her puppy with her. Its name is . . . Bonnie? Bella?"

"Belle," Archer said.

"She'd had it at school. We don't usually allow that. I don't know why the school did."

"Sounds like a lot of procedures weren't being followed on Friday," I said. "This girl of yours . . ."

"Leta," he said. "Leta Brauning."

"Does she have any teacher training? Child care certification?"

"Our youth program director holds the certificate. He was out buying candy for the festival."

"So you weren't here . . . the supervisor wasn't here . . . and you have how many kids being watched by an untrained assistant?"

"Twelve—excuse me, eleven."

"Well, which is it, eleven or, twelve?"

He threw an imploring eye to the sheriff.

Archer sliced the air with his hand. "Gavin, where is this girl of yours?"

"I'd rather she didn't get yelled at again, Rafe. Your detective questioned her yesterday, and the poor child just broke down. She's only sixteen. She didn't know what to do."

"We'll still need to talk to her, Reverend." I stood up. "What was the interaction between mother and daughter? Were they arguing?"

He took a deep breath. "All I know is that Mary Frances started—well, screaming. Kicking things over, like that tree. There was no one here to make a judgment call, so Leta finally had to let Cassie go."

I looked to where Gavin was pointing. A cardboard tree, covered with instant photographs, had been knocked on its side. "And then what?"

"Then they left in Pete's truck." He gestured to the window. "Apparently he was outside waiting for them."

"Waiting?" Archer's eyes blazed. "You mean she saw Pete Frizelle out there and still let Cassie go?"

"Rafe, please."

"Jesus on the turnpike, Gavin. You put my granddaughter's life in the hands of a teenager not old enough to drive, and—Christ, take me to the little bitch right now, or I swear to God—"

"Rafe, she's already said she was sorry."

"Yeah, well, you can teach a mynah bird to sing 'Rock of Ages,' it don't mean he's goin' to Heaven." Archer stormed out of the room.

"Why is all this happening today?" Gavin murmured as he took off after the sheriff.

I was about to follow, then stopped to examine the fallen cardboard tree. The photos were Polaroids of the Sunday school children. One had been knocked loose: it showed a plump-cheeked Hispanic boy with dark hair and a curiously familiar smile. His name was printed on the bottom.

Espero Rosario. He had Ada's eyes; the Cupid's-bow mouth had to be his father's. Espero sat as if propped up, listing slightly to the left. He held a brand-new stuffed tiger in his right hand—but it was his left eye, not his right, that led toward the camera.

The classroom was neat as a pin. Four low tables surrounded by tiny chairs, boxes of crayons, and stacks of butcher paper. Twelve cubbyholes, all empty. All but one. Espero's tiny red jacket still hung from its hook.

"Mike."

The sheriff was standing in the doorway. His eyes were pinched, nervous.

"Did you find the girl?" I asked.

"She ain't here." Archer clenched his jaw. "We're burnin' daylight. You gonna help me do this?"

"Let's go." I pinned Espero's photograph back to its cardboard branch.

TWELVE

We headed south under a merciless glare. While the sheriff drove, I examined the Dupree case file.

"Here's the statement Tippet took from Leta on Saturday," I said. "It pretty much confirms what the reverend told us."

"Pretty much?"

"She says Mary arrived alone." I thumbed ahead. "They argued, then Mary went outside to make a phone call. Pete showed up a few minutes later in a white Chevrolet Silverado. Just like the one Mrs. Maidstone reported seeing in front of the Dupree trailer late Friday night."

"No surprise there. Everybody in Dyer County knows Pete's Chevy."

"Something doesn't add up," I said. "Maidstone saw Mary leading Cassie into the trailer around four o'clock. Then, at ten o'clock, she heard Dale yelling at his daughter. But Dale swears he was alone the whole time."

"You're wonderin' where they were those six hours?"

"That—and why Mary would bring Cassie home in the first place if she was planning an abduction. Or why she told Tippet she had Cassie. Or, for that matter, how Tippet was able to track her down so fast."

"Mary ain't always that smart," he said. "And Tip's smarter'n he looks. Not like you are. Good enough for Dyer County, I guess."

"But not good enough to make captain?"

He eyed me from behind his shades. "How do you figure that?"

"In most of the departments I've assisted, Detective Bureau is headed by a captain. Or even the chief himself. Do you not have a second in command, or have I just not met this person?"

"You're askin' me if I think Tippet is seasoned enough for this investigation?"

"In so many words."

"He does what I tell him to." Archer paused. "Mind, you get a nip of bourbon in the man, he'll tell you I'm holdin' back his natural genius. Reckon if he wants it bad enough, he's welcome to run for sheriff with the rest of the fools."

A yard sign went spinning across the road, caught in the wind: RECALL ARCHER. The sheriff drove right over it.

"I swear, you could hide an elephant in this damn desert," he said. "And walk right by it without ever knowing."

"Where would you go, if you were on the lam?"

"Canyons," he said. "But you'd have to be shit-stupid to hole up in the de los Niños. That, or a mountain lion. And my daughter ain't no mountain lion. Wherever she is, it's inside four walls."

"I've always wondered—why do they call the mountains 'the Blood of the Children'?"

"Band of Spanish settlers got lost," he said. "Legend has it they lived the whole winter off the blood of their own children. Supposedly you can hear their dyin' screams echo in the canyons, late at night."

"Jesus."

"It's only a story, Mike. Somethin' kids tell to scare each other."

By daylight the Sangre de los Niños seemed anything but frightening—remote, proud, but beautiful. Still, I reminded myself, winter was just getting started.

"I tell you, this is a cruel and dyin' time," he said. "Take an old man's advice and stay on the roads."

"You have to respect the desert," I said.

He tilted his chin at me. "That's exactly right, Mike. You'll never love the desert, and she'll never love you. But you live here long enough, you do learn to respect her. That or she'll put some hurtin' on a man."

We pulled off the highway at an auto wrecking yard, where a small evidence team was taking plaster impressions from the ground.

"Tow truck driver said he saw a white truck pulled over here late Friday night." The lead deputy led us through a maze of wrecked automobiles. "It was gone when he came back Saturday morning."

Archer raised an eyebrow. "Pete's Silverado."

The deputy nodded. "Seems that way, sir. We're about walkin' distance to the Duprees, so this wouldn't be a bad place to stow a getaway vehicle. Take a look at that second pair of treads."

I bent down to where the deputy was pointing. The Chevy's tracks ran parallel to another set of marks, newer and cleaner than the first.

"Toe-in on the right front tire," I said. "I remember that wheel was shaking on Dale's pickup when he pulled into the Silver Star."

Archer nodded. "Dale's truck was gone when Tippet showed up Saturday morning. I'll say Pete stashed the Chevy here and walked to the scene. Then him and Mary came back in the Ford and split up. Probably plannin' to meet up north somewhere—Reno, maybe."

"The Ford kicked up a lot of dirt on the way out." I walked slowly beside the tire treads. Midday sun shone off scattered bits of chrome and plastic. "Deputy, did your team recover any small objects that might have fallen?"

"Not that I know," he said. "Seems like you're right about Pete headin' north, Sheriff. We did some checkin' on highway motels. Found the name 'Farrell Stone' on a register just outside Lake Tahoe."

"That name sound familiar to you, Yeager?"

"One of Pete's aliases. I remember." Then I stopped.

"Find something?" Archer came up behind me.

"There." I pointed to a glint of brass in the yellow-gray dirt.

Archer suddenly went pale. "Pick it up."

"Let's get a couple of photos first—"

"Get it out of the goddamn dirt."

I reached down and brushed the dirt away. BELLE was engraved on the heart-shaped tag. REWARD OFFERED.

"There's blood on the collar," I said.

"What's it mean?" Archer said as we drove on south.

"It's not good," I said. "Sometimes a kidnapper will threaten harm to a pet as a way of controlling the kid. Once the threat's actually been carried out . . ."

"Just tell me one thing." Archer cleared his throat. "What's Frizelle want with my granddaughter anyhow?"

"She could be a hostage," I said. "A way for Pete to keep Mary under his thumb."

"Think he's going to whore her out?"

It seemed strange to me—almost surreal—that this would be the sheriff's first concern. "Why do you think he'd do that?"

"It's just what he did to Mary Frances," he said. "When they were little, my girls wouldn't even give Pete the time of day. He was just a hooker's kid from the wrong side of the tracks. Then they hit puberty, and all of a sudden Pete had 'em shopliftin' . . . stealin' drugs . . . Lord knows what else. Martha, thank God, she got sense early. But Mary Frances . . . somethin' went wild in that girl. Got so's we couldn't do a thing with her."

"So finally you did something with Pete," I said, recalling Pete's 1985 Mann Act violation.

Archer nodded. "It was Dale who called me. He was stationed at the Marine base over to Ft. Sherman. Told me the MPs had picked Mary and Pete up for prostitution. But I guess you knew that already."

"Only what I saw on her arrest record."

"Well, Pete was now officially a pimp. Which made my daughter a fifteen-year-old whore. Base commander told me, 'We don't want her in jail. We just want her off the grounds.' And I asked him what they were gonna do with Frizelle. He said if they let Mary off the hook, they wouldn't have much on Pete either. But he reckoned it was up to me."

"So what did you do?"

"What else could a man do? I told him to send Pete away for the pimp that he was. He got six years in federal penitentiary, and Mary spent ninety days in juvenile hall for whoring."

I looked in his eyes for regret and found none. Maybe some weariness.

We pulled off to the shoulder, under the shade of a large billboard. It showed a beckoning blonde, wearing little more than a cowgirl hat and a smile. TURN HERE! it read. OPEN EVERY DAY BUT CHRISTMAS!

"Pop that glove box open, wouldja?"

Inside was the .45 Buntline Special, fully loaded.

"I thought we were going to your daughter's house."

"We are." Then he slid the long gun into his holster and we turned up the dirt road to the Sweet Charity Ranch.

THIRTEEN

From the front, the brothel looked like a Disneyland version of an Old West saloon. From the back it was all double-wide trailers. There were other cruisers out front, and deputies herding sleepy hookers into a paddy wagon.

Inside was sheer pandemonium.

"You dickless fucks!" the madam yelled, a broad-hipped woman in lavender pajamas. "Come back with that cash register, damn your behind!"

The sheriff's deputies were tearing the place apart. Meanwhile the girls were yowling and scratching as they tumbled into the parlor, protesting that they'd just got to sleep and what the *fuck* was this ungodly shit on a Sunday morning?

"Rafe Archer." The madam's eyes were an uncommon green. "Damn your hide, this is restraint of trade! I got a fifteen-thousand-dollar permit from the goddamn state of Nevada. You think this horse manure is gonna scare me into takin' my money out of the race?"

"Ain't nothin' to do with that, Nell. Shut up and leave me to my work."

"Your work." She laughed. "You ain't got power or money enough to shut me up no more. Come Tuesday sundown it's the Lord's own reckoning for all the harm you done."

The sheriff only sneered. "You, Tippet."

Tippet's eyes bulged as he came into the room. Evidently he hadn't been expecting his boss. "Sir, it's no need to trouble yourself. We got it all under control—"

"Yeah, seems like. Kindly put this lady where I don't see her. And for God's sake take charge of your crew. This ain't a damn panty raid."

"Yessir." Tippet stalked away.

"Sheriff," I said. "I was under the impression we were looking for Cassandra. What's with the harassment?"

"I believe I've found your darkroom," he said.

The Sweet Charity's VIP room was decorated in the height of brothel luxury—crown molding, mirrors, black velvet sheets adorned with the Harley-Davidson logo. Cologne and disinfectant hung in the air. Close to the walk-in closet, a floor-length mirror had been pried open to reveal a 35mm Nikon mounted on a tripod. Beyond that was a pocket-sized darkroom.

"Give those pictures to Agent Yeager."

Someone handed me a stack of black-and-white 8 × 10s. I leafed through them, careful to handle them by the edges. They looked like classed-up Internet porn—some kind of Fourth of July romp starring the Sweet Charity girls, along with a few customers who probably weren't aware they were part of the show. Not the kind of thing to bring a tear to a patriot's eye. But you wouldn't get arrested for selling them on the streets of Vegas.

"They all seem to be consenting adults," I said finally.

"Keep looking," Archer said. Then I saw what was making his blood boil. A candid shot of Mary Frances Dupree, in an American-flag bikini, hugging her daughter from behind. Cassandra seemed more interested in her paper and crayons than anything going on around her. But she was still a seven-year-old child in a brothel.

Archer pointed to the Nikon. "Those pictures look like they mighta been taken by the same camera as the others?"

I paused before answering. "The same camera, maybe. It's a decent setup. Developing's not bad for a kitchen darkroom. But I'm not sure it's the same person who took those shots of Dale. These people are having fun. And our man is a sadist."

"Give those to me," Archer said. I handed him the pictures and he separated the photo of Cassie and Mary from the stack. We all watched as he struck his butane lighter and set fire to the picture. He dropped it to the carpet, where it slowly curled and blackened to ashes.

"Jesus God," I muttered.

"All right, boys," said the sheriff. "You know what to do. And, Tip, you tell Mrs. Frizelle that, taxpayer or no, her line of business is no longer necessary to our local economic base."

"Sir." Tippet drew a sharp breath and left.

"Mrs. Frizelle?" Now I realized what was so familiar about those green eyes. "Pete's mother owns this place?"

"What place?" Archer tossed the remaining pictures into the flames. "I don't see a thing here worth takin' a crap on."

He set off for the door. The deputies followed him with their eyes, stock-still. Like a pack of wolves.

"Yeager," Archer said from the doorway. My eye caught sight of something on the floor. I picked it up without stopping.

"What'd you find?" he asked.

"Nothing." I pretended to toss away the strip of 35mm negative as I slipped it into my pocket.

FOURTEEN

"What's bitin' your butt?" Archer said, as we drove back to the highway.

"I was just thinking what a shame you didn't bring your newspaper photographer along. That would have been one to hang on your wall."

He looked at me with cemetery eyes. Then his face broke into a wide grin. "Are you offended, Mike? You think these are nice folks, turnin' young girls out for money? You saw that picture of Cassie. What did that look like to you?"

"Sheriff, I'm not dainty. I've seen a lot of bad shit go down. But today was the first time I ever watched a fellow officer deliberately destroy evidence in full view of witnesses."

"My boys see what I want 'em to," he said. "Anyhow, I wasn't destroyin' a thing. I was protectin' a minor from shame and embarrassment."

"You were whitewashing," I said. "And not helping your granddaughter one bit. There might have been information in that picture we could have used."

"Your lady friend in Philadelphia said you've got a photographic memory."

"Let's get something straight. I'm not one of your 'boys.' I'm here to help find Cassandra. Not to protect your political interests . . . or participate in abuses of authority."

"Is that a threat?"

"It's a reminder," I said. "Exactly how the hell are you going to defend what you did today in any courtroom?"

"You're serious? Christ Almighty, son. You're ridin' in the damn courtroom." He shook his head. "If I didn't know more about you, Michael Francis Yeager, I'd swear you were the last virgin in the state of Nevada."

"What do you mean, 'if you didn't know more about me'?"

He only smiled.

We came to the town of San Cristobal, a walled community just south of the county seat at Langhorne. SECURITY AND SERENITY, read the sign at the front gate.

"Nevada Highway Patrol's lookin' for Dale's Ford." Archer spoke evenly, as if our altercation had never happened. "Any ideas?"

"With that bad alignment on the front tire, they won't get too far off the paved roads." I did some mental arithmetic. "The earliest the subjects could have left the scene was four A.M. And they'd have to ditch the truck before dawn. I'd say you're working inside a radius of a hundred and fifty miles."

"That's spittin' distance from Tahoe," Archer said. "So let's find that pickup. What next?"

"Follow the money," I said. "Sooner or later, Frizelle will have to draw funds. In the meantime we notify U.S. Customs, put out a wants-and-warrants flag to Nevada Highway Patrol. Contact the U.S. Postal Service about change-of-address filings . . ."

"You're talkin' a lot of paperwork."

"I could use some help," I said. "Somebody motivated, good with details. Deputy Rosario, maybe."

"You got her." He stole a look my way. "What else?"

"Publicity," I said. "The National Center for Missing and Exploited Children will post Cassie's description on their Web site. Plus we should start talking to the media, issue an Amber alert—"

"No," he said.

"No to what? Everything?"

"I ain't about to make a three-ring circus of my family."

"It's going to make our job a lot harder if we can't build public awareness," I said. "Is it just invasion of privacy you're worried about, or—"

"I believe I've said my piece."

We pulled up to the gatehouse, where a security camera kept watch over the automated barrier. Archer punched a number into the intercom box.

"Hello?" It was a young boy's voice—one I'd heard recently.

"Robbie, it's Grampa," Archer said. "Be a good boy and open up."

"Did you find Cassie?" Robbie asked.

"Not yet, honey."

We waited. The barrier didn't move. "Rob, push the button. No games, hear?"

"Okay," the boy said sullenly. A moment later the gate lifted. The video camera's red light flickered on as we drove through.

"You think he did that on purpose?" he asked.

"Maybe it just takes him a while to reach the buttons."

"He's a mite slow in the head. Seems like if the Lord's gonna take a boy's legs, he oughtta give him somethin' else upstairs."

I didn't know what to say without losing my temper, so finally I said nothing. To drive around that neighborhood you'd never know you were in a desert. All the lawns were planted with flower beds and new grass. Archer braked for a golf cart and exchanged waves with the driver, a pleasant, gray-haired man in a pink shirt. It took me a few seconds to recognize him from the pictures I saw at the brothel. He looked different without his diapers on.

"That's the judge Mrs. Frizelle would have to see about the damage to her property," Archer said. "With all the golfin' he does, I don't imagine he'll have much time for her grievance."

"Sounds like Mrs. Frizelle's laid out some serious money," I said. "Isn't the judge worried about Tuesday's election?"

"Not as much as he's worried about Mrs. Judge." We started rolling again. "Take a look around. Here's where the serious money is nowadays. Don't need gamblin' or whores to make a fortune—or even cattle or silver, like in my grandpappy's day. There's only one word a fella needs to know and he can coin his own money: *retirement.*"

"So this is where you plan to retire?"

He grunted. "I'll retire the day I die."

We parked in front of a white colonial house. The door opened and a four-year-old girl—vanilla curls and yellow organdy—came bounding down the steps.

"Grampy!" she squealed, casting herself into his arms. "Hey, you smell like perfume! Perfume, and . . . smoke!"

"Hadda help an old lady out of a burnin' building," he said with a wink in my direction. "I reckon that deserves about a million kisses, don't it?"

She giggled as he peppered her cheek with kisses. Reverend McIntosh ambled down the driveway. Perspiration had matted Gavin's fine yellow hair. His face, so perfectly bronzed under the altar lights, was a mass of freckles. For some reason it embarrassed me to realize Gavin had been wearing makeup during the service.

"Where's that no-account deputy of mine?" Archer asked.

"Out back with Robbie." Gavin took the little girl from the sheriff. "Hannah, go ask Mommy to please set two more places."

"I ain't stayin'," Archer said. "I got to join the search. I brought Mike so he could talk to Robbie."

"That's fine," Gavin said in a way that seemed to imply the opposite. "At least come inside, Rafe. Martha will have my hide."

"Watch me, Grampy." Hannah twirled back up the walk.

"Don't know how I feel about my grandchildren playin' in the yard, Gavin."

The minister seemed about to protest, then simply nodded. "You're right, of course."

"Why exactly do they need guarding?" I said. "You expect Frizelle to come after them?"

Archer exchanged a dark look with Gavin. "I wouldn't put it past Pete. Or that bitch who whelped him."

Gavin dropped his voice. "How did it go?"

"It's still goin'." The sheriff glanced at me. "Mike, I wonder if you'd be kind enough to tell my deputy to play games on his own time. Right now I want him out front protectin' my family."

I could feel the hairs on my federally funded neck rise as he said this. I was being shooed away like little Hannah. But it would give me a chance to talk to Robbie alone.

"Not at all," I said.

I turned to see the sheriff pass a plain brown envelope to Reverend McIntosh. Gavin took one look at the contents and went as white as his shirt. Apparently Archer hadn't burned all the photographs he'd found at the Sweet Charity Ranch that morning.

"Hurry!" Robbie yelled, surrounded by an army of dolls. *"We must reach the secret shelter before dark!"*

He held a Spider-Man action figure in his hands. Then he answered for a Barbie doll with flame-red hair. *"All the others are dead,"* the boy said in a high-pitched voice. *"It's just two of us now. I'm afraid."*

Other dolls were broken to pieces or lay half-buried in the sand. A giant Japanese robot lurked behind an upended bucket.

" 'Lo, Yeager." Clyde stretched out in a lawn chair, reading a comic book. "Let you out on good behavior, huh?"

"Agent Yeager," I said. "Sheriff wants you on the door."

"Christ on a fuckin' pony."

"Relax. I'll tell him you were inspecting the fence." I took the comic book away. "Don't swear in front of the kid."

He nodded gratefully and left.

"I've heard people say cuss words before," Robbie said.

"I'm sorry to hear that." I knelt down to him. "Quite a game you've got going on there."

"The slaves are re-bel-ling." Robbie turned his pale face to me. "That's my word for the day. Do you know that word?"

"Sure. Who are they rebelling against?"

"They just are. They run away to places to hide."

"I see. Like the secret shelter." I pointed at the broken toys. "It doesn't look like those slaves got away."

"No," he said sadly. "They always die at the end."

"Maybe I could help you, and this time the good guys could win."

He raised his eyebrow, as though wondering if such a thing could be possible. "You talk like Miss Corvis."

"You remember me, don't you, Rob?"

He nodded. "You hurt Uncle Dale."

"Yeah. That must have scared you, huh?"

He shrugged.

"Rob, I'm looking for Cassie. Want to help me find her?"

He seemed to consider the offer. "Grampy says you look at pictures."

"That's right. I try to figure out what they mean. Are you interested in that?"

"I can take pictures," he said. "But they don't turn out so good. You can help me play this game, if you want."

"All right." I held up the Barbie doll. "How do you think she's feeling today?"

He pursed his lip. "She's scared."

"Do you know what's scaring her?"

Robbie glanced at the toy robot. It was painted black, with multiple arms and clawed hands. The robot's face was a blur of melted plastic.

"Did you do this? Melt the face off?"

"He did it to himself," Robbie said. "He's the Shadow Catcher."

"Why do you call him that?"

There were those deep brown eyes again. "Do you really want to know? Or are you just a pretending guy?"

"I'm pretty sure I'm not a pretending guy."

"He takes things from inside you," Robbie explained. "All the bad parts nobody wants."

"What does he do with them?"

"Takes them to his invisible place. Then he makes all the shadows into . . . something. Then that something comes and—eats you up." He said it as plainly as if he were describing the taste of oatmeal.

"So how do we help Barbie get away from the Shadow Catcher?"

He looked right at me. "If somebody tried to hurt a kid, would you shoot him?"

I remembered that Dale had asked me a similar question on Friday.

"If I had no other way to stop him—yes, I would."

"Would you shoot him until he died?"

I said nothing. The frankness in his voice as he spoke that last word— died—had left me a little stunned.

"That's what I thought," he said. "You won't find Cassie."

"Why not?"

"The Shadow Catcher is after her."

He placed the robot on top of the bucket.

"I tried to tell Uncle Dale," he said. "That made him mad."

"Robbie!" said a sharp feminine voice behind me. "How many times have I said not to play with Hannah's—well now, look who's here!"

I turned—and found myself looking at the spitting image of Mary Frances Dupree.

FIFTEEN

She wore a white kitchen dress and her hair was auburn, not blonde. She had maybe fifteen pounds on her sister, not to mention a telltale bulge in her belly. But her eyes were the same piercing gray as Mary Frances's. The sheriff's eyes.

"I'm Martha McIntosh." She smiled and extended her hand.

I stood up, wiping dirt off my trousers. "Sorry, I don't mean to stare."

"Mary and I are identical twins. Don't worry, everybody makes the same mistake." She led me into a living room decked out in high-class Western chic. "I apologize for Robbie bothering you. He's very moody nowadays."

"In what way?"

"Oh—you know how little boys are." She stooped to pick up a child's plastic pony—bracing her back with her hand, the way pregnant women do. "Would you like some coffee, Mike? Or maybe just a glass of iced tea— or Diet Coke—I need to open another bottle . . ."

"Coffee's fine," I said over my shoulder. "Only if it's already made."

There were family portraits on the mantel, mostly of Gavin and Martha and their two children. A few were from her own childhood. Little Martha and Mary Frances were always dressed alike, posed like two dolls from the same shelf. One look at Mrs. Archer and you could see where they got their curves.

Martha handed me a mug of instant. "I didn't hear you say how you took it."

I took a sip—amaretto cream—and tried not to wince. "I've always wondered what it would be like having a twin."

"Sometimes it was hard knowing where my sister ended and I began.

When we were little girls . . . if Mary Frances got a spanking, I was the one who cried. And she did get a lot of spankings, let me tell you."

"And what are you feeling from her now?"

"I can't feel her any more." Her smile faded. "When she had to go away it was like I was . . . being amputated." She tossed her head. "You must think I'm crazy, sayin' such things."

I smiled.

She furrowed her brow, just like Robbie. "Have you had any luck . . . finding her?"

"We're just getting started," I said. "Your father can probably tell you more than I can."

"My father." Martha rolled her eyes. "I should have been a detective myself, the way I've had to read him all these years."

"Think he'd have allowed you to join the force?"

"Never in a million years." She laughed. "I must see to dinner. Is there anything else I can . . . ?"

"Pictures of Dale and Mary," I said. "With Cassandra, if you have them."

"Oh. Well, now, we took one at Cassie's birthday party." She cast about the room. Her eyes lit briefly on an end table, then darted to the bookcase. "I've had to move so many things around lately—oh, that's right, I put it behind my Precious Moments . . ."

I could see why she'd hidden her sister's photograph behind a row of sad-eyed porcelain children. The Duprees looked like living hell. Dale was trying to coax his daughter with a slice of cake while Mary gripped her tightly around the shoulder. Meanwhile Cassie seemed to shrink from both of them, holding a tiny beagle puppy in her lap. No, not holding: clinging. As if the dog might fly away or disappear.

"This was taken right before Dale filed for divorce, wasn't it?"

"Yes—how did you know?"

"Dale and Mary are holding Cassandra, but not each other," I said. "Plus Dale is hiding his broken hand from the camera."

"Yes, he—put it through a wall," she said. "How do you notice those things?"

"Part of the job. Interesting how nobody's looking at the camera. As a matter of fact—" I went back to the mantel. "I don't see a single photograph of you or Mary looking straight at the camera."

"We were shy kids." She glanced to the end table again.

"Of course." I set the portrait on the mantel. "I hate to put you to any trouble, Mrs. McIntosh. I should have mentioned I don't take cream in my coffee."

"Oh. Here, I'll take that." She grabbed the cup. "I'm so inconsiderate not to ask. You must think I'm an awful person."

She never stopped smiling, but there was real fear in her voice. And she wouldn't look me in the eye.

"I don't think you're an awful person," I said. "It's just coffee."

"I'll get you exactly what you want this time. Don't move."

She went back to the kitchen. If Martha was the daughter who "got sense," then Mary Frances had to be a real basket case. I walked over to the end table. There was a thin rectangle on the tabletop that was darker than the surrounding finish. Inside the drawer was a framed picture.

It was an outdoor shot, faded Kodacolor from the late seventies. Mary and Martha looked maybe eleven or twelve, posed on the deck of a sailboat stranded in a dry lake bed. It didn't take long to identify the two boys clowning around with them. One was a tall, big-boned redhead: Dale Dupree. The small, wiry teenager at the prow had to be Peter Frizelle. Archer, it seemed, was off the mark when he said the girls wouldn't give Pete time of day. Because there they were as children, wearing camp T-shirts and shorts, a quartet of kids trying to seem grown-up and cool. And all four smiling right into the camera, as if they'd never known a dark day in their lives.

I opened the frame. *Cathedral Lake Camp, 1977* was written on the back in girlish letters. Then someone had added in a mangled scrawl: *FOUR CAME HOME.* The photographer's angled shadow was clearly visible. Shaggy hair, chubby arms. The shadow of a child—or a very small adult.

From the kitchen I heard a microwave beep.

"Dinner's on." Martha returned with my coffee. "Bring this to the table if you want to, Mike."

I stood between her and the end table, the picture safely stowed.

"It's good this time, isn't it?" she said expectantly.

I took a sip of hazelnut mocha. "It's like you read my mind."

SIXTEEN

"I just can't make myself believe it," Martha said. "I know Mary Frances was never much of a mother. But even so, Gavin. It's not possible."

We ate sloppy joes at the kitchen table—or at least I did. Nobody else seemed to have much of an appetite. Hannah might have gotten in a few bites, but her mother kept dabbing at her mouth with a wet paper towel.

"Honey, you know I don't want to believe it either." Sauce dribbled from Gavin's sandwich. "But Mary's always surrounded herself with darkness. It doesn't necessarily make her evil, or beyond redemption. Just . . . lost."

She frowned. "Mary Frances hasn't 'always' surrounded herself with anything, Gavin. You don't know my sister well enough to judge her that way."

"My bear got broken," Hannah said to me plainly.

Martha patted her daughter's hand. "Hannah, shh."

"It's all right," I said. "What happened to him?"

"He-err," Hannah said. "She used to could talk. Then Robbie broke her."

"Did not."

"Liar."

"Children, please." Martha fixed her gray eyes on me. "Mike, do you think—is it possible Mary Frances could have been—forced?"

The children didn't seem to care much for the grown-up conversation. But that didn't mean they weren't listening. "It's still early in the investigation," I said. "Anything's possible."

Martha rolled her eyes. "God, I hate police talk. It's all evasion and—Hannah, sweetie, you're gonna get Manwich on that Sunday dress I made for you."

"I don't wanna wear this dress no more."

"*Any*more," Martha said. "Don't you want to look nice for Mr. Yeager?"

"No! I'm tired of dressup an'—everybody bein' here alla time!"

Martha gave me an embarrassed, kids-say-the-darnedest-things look. "Sweetheart, don't make our guest think you're a white-trash girl."

"What's—white trash?"

"A rude little girl who raises her voice at the table and smears food all over her brand-new dress," Martha said.

"Mike, do you and your wife have a church?" Gavin smiled.

"Well—no to both, actually. No wife, no church."

"No kids?"

"No time."

Martha looked up. "Be careful, Mike. You're being recruited."

Gavin chuckled. "My apologies. We're just so proud of our little church, sometimes I don't know when to quit. Ten years in the area, and already we're the largest congregation in Dyer County. Next year we're opening a new hospital, a new K-twelve school—we're going to make this desert bloom again."

"So you didn't grow up around here?"

He shook his head. "I had a ministry in Phoenix, but—well, it was a rewarding experience. It's all in my book."

"Book?"

"*Arise and Go.* It got some very nice reviews in the evangelical press. I'll give you a copy if you like. Martha's always after me to write a sequel."

She gave me a thin smile. "And where is home for you, Mike?"

"I grew up in Pennsylvania. Home is . . . kind of up for grabs right now."

"Well, maybe you'll decide to stay with us awhile."

"Were there Ay-mish people where you grew up?" It was Robbie saying this. As I'd guessed, he was a lot more attentive than he let on.

"That's right," I said. "But it's pronounced Ah-mish. I'm impressed."

"Thanks," he said. "Did you find Cassie's puppy yet?"

"Not yet, Rob."

"Her name's Belle," he said. "She's already been spayed."

Gavin cleared his throat. "That's not table talk, Rob."

"I bet it wasn't Pete who hurt her," Robbie said. "Not like Grampy thinks."

Gavin and Martha exchanged a tense look.

"Really?" I said. "Why's that, Rob?"

He shrugged. "I bet he spent the night with his whores."

Martha blanched. "Robbie!"

Gavin was ashen. "Pal, you better tell me where you got a word like that."

"Who gives a care?"

"I'll care your behind, Robin Archer McIntosh. You see how you just upset your mama? Now you apologize to her. And to our guest."

"Reverend—," I started to say.

"All right, kiddo. Go to your room till you learn to be sorry." Gavin put his hands on the table. "Now."

"I'm just saying." Robbie stared at his plate. "If Pete or his wh—"

Martha slammed her fist down. Silverware clattered. "Robbie, shut *up!*"

Robbie looked straight at me—then bit his lip, pulled himself behind his walker, and limped away.

"Where would he have heard that?" Gavin said.

"Reverend," I kept my voice even. "I don't mean to interfere—"

"Mr. Yeager, no offense, but you *are* interferin'." He turned to his wife. "Angel face, are you okay? You wanna lie down?"

"Stop treating me like a little girl," she said.

"Sweetie—"

She stood up. "You know damn well where he learned that word."

"What the hell's that supposed to mean?"

She ran out of the room. Gavin was on her heels.

"Martha, I asked you a question. What—"

A door slammed. Hannah wiped her hands on her dress.

"What's *whores*?" she asked.

SEVENTEEN

The McIntoshes went upstairs to settle their dispute, and my ride back to the station was still at least twenty minutes away. I found the quietest room with a phone—Gavin's office, littered with invoices from building contractors—and started making calls. Fifteen minutes later I was still bouncing between desks at the Nevada Highway Patrol. Apparently my FBI creds didn't mean much to the local bureaucracy. Finally I dropped Sheriff Archer's name: that got some action.

"Sorry to keep you waitin'," the trooper said. "Turns out we had that vehicle all along. Red Ford half-ton, right? Picked it up last night, twenty-six miles outa Reno."

"Fantastic." I grabbed a pencil. "Where was it?"

"Up a dry wash. They'd hid it pretty good, only the sumbitches forgot to turn the headlamps off. Typical dumb criminals, huh?"

"I'll need it returned stat," I said. "In the meantime fax me some photos of the vehicle—interior, dashboard—"

He whistled. "Sir, you could drive up here faster'n I could get you photos. It's just me here till Monday mornin', and I'm all backed up."

"Trooper, you understand this is a homicide."

"Yessir, welcome to Nevada. We get ten of those outa Vegas every Satur—"

"And it's a missing kid," I said. "The sheriff's granddaughter. Now I don't know what you'd consider a higher priority, but I'm starting to feel a little neglected here. First you say you don't have the vehicle, then you tell me I have to wait till Monday."

"Agent Yagger, I don't know who you need to yell at, but it ain't me. We go by whatever case numbers we get from you people. I got two stop-and-detain requests outa Dyer County, and when they sent you over I got handed the wrong reference code."

"What was the other vehicle?"

"Black Nissan four-by-four, tinted windows."

"Not easy to mistake for a red pickup, is it?"

"No sir, I see your point. But it's got almost the same file number, see? SV-ADR-ten-thirteen. Yours is ten-thirty-one, Agent Yagger."

"Yeager," I said. "I didn't file a case number."

"Well, I got one right here. It's not our system, which is how I got so mixed up." He took a breath. "Honest, sir, I'da told you sooner. We think the world of Sheriff Archer."

"In that case, I'm sure you'll find a way to get me those photos tonight." I paused deliberately. "Just so I don't have to drive up there in person."

"Yessir," he said sourly. "We'll get right on it."

I hung up, by now aware that someone was standing behind me.

"I am awful sorry to bother you," Martha said.

"I won't keep you out of a room in your own house."

"Please let me apologize for my family." She shut the door behind her. "Daddy'd strap me naked if he saw how I let my kids behave."

"No apology necessary," I said. "To be honest, Mrs. McIntosh, I'm a little concerned about your son."

"Oh?"

"I honestly think he's trying to help. What he said at the dinner table— about 'Pete and his whores' . . ." I let the word hang in the air. "That's not something a seven-year-old just drops out of the blue. You can shut him up, but I think it's more important to find out what he was trying to say."

"I understand," she said. "I promise you won't see that happen again."

"That's not really my point." I leaned in. "Mrs. McIntosh, do you think your son knows something about Cassie's kidnapping?"

"Why would he?"

"The game he was playing in the yard . . . wasn't exactly a game. He mentioned someone called the Shadow Catcher. There were definite overtones of violence and fear. He'd melted the face off this robot—"

"The face . . . ?" Martha paled.

"Children frequently use games to act out real-life trauma. Possibly it represents someone Robbie's afraid of. Does your son have a lot of contact with Frizelle?"

"I don't let Pete anywhere near my children. Never." Martha began rubbing the base of her neck. "Robbie gets weird lately. I don't know why he burned the face off that doll."

"Actually, I said 'melted,' not 'burned.' Weird how?"

"He . . . wets the bed. He didn't use to do that."

"Have you noticed any changes to his physical environment?"

"Like what?" she said, suddenly alert.

"Well, is there any sign he may have been—"

"Abused?" She pulled back. "We don't beat our children, thank you."

"Mrs. McIntosh, please."

"You child abuse people think everyone was abused. That's your answer to everything."

"It's not my answer to everything."

"I don't want you planting scary ideas in my son's head, that's all." She aimed her sharp chin at me. "Do you enjoy frightening people?"

"I don't enjoy seeing children in fear, if that's what you mean."

"Stop pretending to be the white knight. You were snooping around. When you put that old picture back, you forgot to close the drawer."

"When people don't hide something very well," I said, "it's often because they want it to be found."

"I wasn't hiding anything. I was in a hurry to clean up."

"All the same, that summer at the lake must have been a special memory for you."

She blushed.

"Tell me," I said. "What does 'Four Came Home' mean?"

"It's just a picture. They don't always have to mean things."

"In that case, I apologize." I stood up.

"Where are you going?"

"Obviously I've offended you, Mrs. McIntosh."

"Martha," she said. "Don't go."

She perched on the edge of the yellow love seat.

"Why do you—" She put a hand to her chest. "Why don't you have any children, Mr. Yeager?"

"It's like I told your husband," I said. "Law enforcement's just not a family-friendly profession. But I guess you know that."

"Yes," she said. "Still, don't you ever feel that part of yourself has been—denied?"

"I can live with the decision." I shrugged. "Actually, I always thought of the children on my cases as my kids."

"That's—very beautiful," she said. "Those are lucky children."

"I wouldn't put it that way," I said. "Why are you asking?"

"Family can be such an awful burden." She glanced away. "My sister, for example. She's my dark half. I live to thank God I never got mixed up in any of the terrible stuff Mary Frances did." She furrowed her brow in sympathy, but her eyes registered fear. "When Mary Frances went to reform school, it all fell to me to protect the family reputation. If she had just stayed away from that Pete Frizelle—"

"Martha, I know you and Frizelle have a past together," I said. "Say what you have to. But let's not play the convent schoolgirl, okay?"

She crumpled into the love seat, as if I'd struck her down.

"Gavin mustn't know," she said. "Last week I went to visit my sister. At that—place she works."

"The brothel?"

"Yes. The brothel." She looked up with her father's steely eyes. "Mary Frances was talking up and down the county . . . and Daddy's so worried about the election. I knew it'd just break his heart if bad things got back to him."

"What kinds of bad things?"

"She was mad because Daddy took Dale's side in the custody hearing. I begged her to stay quiet, at least till after Tuesday. Mary said she didn't care if Daddy did get tossed out on his rump. And one way or another, she'd get Cassie away from Dale. I feel like a traitor telling you this."

"Did she explain what she meant by 'one way or another'?"

Martha shook her head. "She kept saying, 'Something bad has happened. I have to get Cassie away before it happens again.' "

"Something bad," I said. "Was she implying that Dale had harmed their daughter?"

"I can't imagine Dale ever hurting Cassie." Martha was shaking. "This only started after that custody business. I'm convinced it was Pete who put her up to the whole thing."

"Is that why you wanted to know if I thought Frizelle was controlling Mary?"

"I guess I'm just grasping at straws. Daddy seems to think she did things . . . because she wanted to." She put a hand over her face. "You won't hurt him, will you?"

"Who? Your father?"

"Pete," she said. "He's not strong."

"Why are you suddenly worried about Frizelle?"

"It's like you said." She looked away. "We have a past together."

"Did your sister say anything else? When you—"

"I'm sorry, I just can't do this anymore." She broke into sobs. "I can't be what everyone wants. My whole family's falling apart, and I feel like it's my fault. What am I doing wrong, Mike? To feel so . . . *bad* all the time?"

All at once she was on my shoulder. Her thin arms twined around my back. Tears ran into my shirt collar. I mentally commanded myself not to notice how warm and full Martha's breasts felt against my chest.

"Okay, okay," I said. "Mrs. McIn . . . Martha—"

"I just w-wish I could hold her again," she whimpered. "Be together with my suh, sister, like it was—when everything still felt real . . ."

I reached up to her neck, trying to find a gentle way to disengage. Then my hand touched a jagged ridge near the base of her skull. A scar.

"Martha?"

She pulled away quickly. Her husband, Gavin, was standing over us.

"Martha," he said. "For God's sake."

EIGHTEEN

Reverend McIntosh walked me to the door.

"I kept looking around for you." He took a paperback from a table in the front hall. "Never occurred to me that you might be right under my nose."

"Reverend—"

"I promised you a copy of my book, didn't I? This is the only one I have at home, but—well, I can always order more from the publisher."

He put the book into my hand. *Arise and Go: A Prodigal's Journey.* On the cover was a photograph of the reverend—big smile, pompadoured hair. It made an odd contrast to the plump, disheveled man before me.

"Thanks," I said. "Gavin, about what you just saw . . ."

"Don't." He raised both hands. "Even in the best of times, Martha . . . Well, she gets out of balance." He lowered his voice. "You must have seen by now that the Archer family is . . . troubled."

I nodded, waiting for him to say more.

"Certain patterns repeat," he said. "I believe a great evil happened to the twins. No one's ever said a word, but you'd have to be blind not to see it. And I'm starting to fear that evil will pass on to the next generation." His eyes darted to the driveway, where my driver was waiting. "The sheriff's not going to be pleased with me for detaining you."

"Reverend, I have been nothing lately if not detained. What exactly do you mean, 'certain patterns repeat'?"

"Have you met Connor Blackwell?"

"The psychologist?"

Gavin nodded. "Connor came with me from Phoenix. He's very good with these things."

"I'll call him," I said. "Reverend, I think it would be a good idea if I talked to your son some more."

Naked terror washed across the minister's face.

"No," he said. "I'm afraid I don't agree, Agent Yeager. I think it would be a very bad idea for you to talk to my son."

Then he disappeared into his beautiful home.

NINETEEN

According to my driver, three teams were working the search for Cassandra Dupree: one collecting evidence at the crime scene, another watching the highways, and the third—the largest by far—combing the desert outback. Sheriff Archer was leading this team personally. I decided to join him.

It was near dusk by the time we reached them, a line of dust-covered men with their heads bent down. Big Rhodesian Ridgebacks roamed and sniffed the ground.

"Cadaver dogs," the lead deputy explained. "Got 'em on loan from the Nevada state police. Still no luck getting helicopters."

"Helicopters?" I raised an eyebrow. "How much desert are you fellows trying to cover?"

"Ten thousand acres, not including the mountains." He pointed to the Sangre de los Niños. "That's where the sheriff is right now."

"By himself?"

"Yessir. Three times since yesterday. I can try raisin' him for ya, but the mountains play hell with reception."

"I'll be damned," said a voice behind me. "Mike!"

Connor Blackwell had broken from the line and was coming toward me. "Sheriff said you'd decided to stay. It's like an answer to a prayer."

"So I keep hearing." I looked around. "How's it going here?"

Connor waited till the deputy was out of earshot. "It's not easy keeping everyone's spirits up," he said. "We're only two days in. Still . . ."

". . . Two days is forever when you're looking for a child." I nodded. "What's this about the sheriff searching the mountains alone?"

Connor shook his head. "Is it a problem?"

"Just a little strange," I said. "You don't happen to have a cell phone on you? I had to let my driver go."

"Sure, but—do you need a ride? Things are kind of winding up here anyway."

I looked back at the broken line of men: the end of a long and fruitless day.

"Let's wait a little while longer," I said. "They need to know somebody's watching."

Connor's Honda was littered with protein-bar wrappers and empty Powerade bottles. As he cranked the engine, a confident male voice boomed from the speakers:

"—punishments that are rarely effective and often harmful." The voice was familiar—that coal-walking guy, maybe. "But the greatest punishment of all is neglect."

"Sorry." Connor punched the eject button and a white audiocassette popped out. "This guy's awesome, though. Absolutely changed my life. Do you ever listen to audiobooks on the road?"

"I drive a 'fifty-seven Nash Rambler." I massaged my ear. "I can sometimes get AM radio, if the wind's right."

"Well, maybe you'll want to borrow the tape sometime. The desert's damned lonely if you only have yourself to listen to." He looked over his shoulder as we backed onto the road. "So how was your first day?"

"Eye-opening," I said.

We drove north on the highway, toward town. "Anything I can do to help?"

"Maybe. You don't know anything about Cassandra's custody hearing, do you?"

He nodded. "They had me interview her. So she wouldn't have to testify."

"How did it go?"

He frowned. "I was a little out of my element. Most of my work is with adults."

"What I meant was, how was Cassie?"

"Nervous," he said. "Why?"

"I saw some photographs of her today. One was taken this summer and the other one just a few weeks ago. Big difference."

"How so?"

"In the first picture she was still a kid," I said. "In the second one she looked . . . very old for her age. Like someone who's resigned herself to her fate."

"Divorce is always hard on children," he said. "This one in particular."

"Did you keep a copy of the interview?"

"Maybe a transcript somewhere." He furrowed his brow. "But you know, it's all under seal of the court."

"Seeing as it's the sheriff's granddaughter, shouldn't we consider it unsealed?"

"You'd have to ask the sheriff about that."

"Right now I'm asking you. Did anything come up during that hearing that might indicate child abuse?"

He took a breath. "Cassie was pretty withdrawn. I finally got her to talk about a nightmare she'd had."

"What about?"

"Her puppy," he said. "She dreamed that somebody wanted to hurt it."

"Did she say who?"

"Not right away. But when I convinced her to do a picture . . . she drew a man with dark brown hair and green eyes. I asked her who it was, and she said 'my daddy.' Obviously that wasn't Dale."

"Isn't Pete her biological father?"

He shifted uncomfortably. "Yes. And Mary always told Cassie to refer to Pete as 'my daddy.' But look, that by itself proves nothing. She could have been coached."

"Well, at least I know why Archer's been so hot on Frizelle as a suspect."

His eyes caught mine. "You don't think Pete's guilty, do you?"

"I'm still deciding."

He nodded soberly, taking my measure. "Let's see if we can't find that transcript."

The Arbor Vitae Community Center was one of the bigger and newer buildings in town. The locals seemed to be making good use of it: Swim Team, Scrapbooking Class, Al-Anon, and something called Jump Bump Giggle Wiggle. Connor's counseling office was a hideaway next to the administrative suite.

"This is just temporary." He fumbled through a dozen or so keys. "Next year they're moving me to the new psychiatric wing at the hospital."

"Who's 'they'?"

"Well—Gavin, mainly. He's the rainmaker."

"He seems to place a lot of faith in you."

Connor smiled modestly. "He likes to call me his prodigy—or is it protégé? I could never keep those two words straight. Anyhow, 'charity case' is probably closer to the mark."

Connor's shelves were jammed with self-help books, including a thoroughly dog-eared copy of *Arise and Go*. IT'S NEVER TOO LATE TO HAVE A HAPPY CHILDHOOD read his computer's screen saver. All of his degrees and certificates were from Arizona.

"Is this you?" I looked closely at a framed picture from the late '70s—a family of three in fishing gear, standing hip-deep in a mountain stream. Dad had Connor's brown eyes; Mom was a sandy blonde. The boy between them, skinny and tan, proudly held a fish on the line. He looked secure and simply happy.

He smiled at the picture. "That's near Vallecito, Colorado, where I grew up. Probably the last happy memory I had for a long time."

"Nice catch," I said. "What is that, speckled trout?"

"Cutthroat trout. Four pounds. Dad made me throw it back. He said nothing has to die to prove a man's worth." He shuffled through papers on his desk. "I lost my folks a year after that picture was taken. Messed me up pretty bad. If it hadn't been for divine intervention, I don't know where I'd be." He looked up. "Was it like that for you?"

"Minus the divine intervention," I said. "I'll confess you scared the crap out of me with that dossier. I don't think even the FBI knows I wanted to be a preacher."

"I get my information from a higher source." He winked and pointed upward. "Plus a few random Internet searches. What changed your mind about the ministry?"

"A little problem of not believing in salvation," I said. "I guess my father had something to do with that."

"He was an atheist?"

"No," I said. "He was a minister."

The phone rang. Connor answered, then gestured for privacy. I nodded and stepped around the corner. A moment later I heard children singing from the auditorium.

> *Three blind mice . . .*
> *Three—blind mice . . .*
> *See—how they run . . .*

I pushed open the door. The big space was hung with enough TV lights and cameras for a small-scale awards show. Twelve kids sang tunelessly on stage, shuffling in half-finished mouse costumes. For a bare instant I forgot about murder and kidnapping. I could almost imagine myself a lovestruck father, watching his own kids stumble through Mother Goose.

> *They all ran after—a—farmer's wife . . .*
> *She cut off their tails with a—carving knife . . .*

Then a triplet of handclaps broke the spell.

"Okay, that was beautiful!" a woman's clear voice called from the pit. "You guys are doing great! Only Chelsea, Clemenza—no tickling, okay? Judah? You gotta remember, sweetie, the audience is *this* way. Your folks are gonna want to see your pretty—now what is getting into you little mice?"

The children giggled and muttered and shrank into each other. Who was this strange grinning grown-up coming toward them? Then a dark-haired young woman rose from the orchestra and turned her astonishing blue eyes to me.

TWENTY

"Well, it's no good trying to make 'em pay attention now." She smiled as she made her way over to me. "Are you looking for one of the other rooms? I get lost in here all the time."

She was in her late twenties, a latter-day flower child. Hints of amazing curves beneath her sweater and Navajo skirt. Her brilliant blue eyes were ever so slightly crossed, giving her an air of perpetual curiosity. That scent around her wasn't perfume. More like incense from some new-age emporium of beingness.

"Just waiting for someone," I said. "I take it this is Jump Bump Giggle Wiggle?"

"That name was not my idea." She blushed a little. "Mine's Dorothy Corvis, by the way."

"Mike Yeager." Then I remembered. "Robbie mentioned you today."

"Yes, I'm his teacher. When did—I'm sorry, should I know you?"

"Probably not. I'm still a stranger here." I nodded to her. "Maybe you can help me with that."

She tilted her chin, smelling a line—but then smiled anyway. "Maybe later. Tonight I've got my hands full with this pageant." She glanced back at the children. "It's nice to see them laughing again. They've been so worried about Robbie—especially after what happened to poor Cassie. I keep telling them he's all right." She looked back to me. "He is, isn't he?"

"To be honest, I'm really not sure."

"There you are." Connor stepped up to us. "Is this guy bothering you?"

She looked at me approvingly. "Not yet."

"Well, be careful what you say about the government. He's FBI."

"Cut it out," she said. "Really?"

"I'm afraid so," I said.

"You mean—oh." Her mouth fell open. "I don't mean to be rude. You're that guy from the parking lot, aren't you? The one who got in the fight with Cassie's dad?"

"I wish that wasn't the first thing people knew about me. But, yeah."

"He's assisting the search for Cassie. Speaking of which—" Connor gestured to the door. "Whenever you're ready, Mike."

She watched him leave, biting her lip. "You're 'afraid' you're in the FBI?"

"It's a long story."

"Come by tomorrow and tell me," she said. "Maybe I can answer some questions about Cassie."

"I'd appreciate that."

"But right now I gotta get back to the munchkins." She raised an eyebrow. "You don't seem like a typical cop. How did you wind up here, anyway?"

"It was involuntary. They arrested me."

"No way! Will you be my friend?" She laughed. "That's how my kids say hello to each other. They haven't discovered rejection yet."

"Let's hope they never do."

She smiled as she took my hand, then turned it over. "Wow."

"What is it?"

"You have got to let me read this palm some time. All these amazing lines."

"Battle scars," I said. "Trigger calluses."

"No," she said. "It's not a hand for holding weapons."

By now the children were calling her name.

"What's the story on her?" I asked as Connor drove us back to the sheriff's department.

"Dorothy? Business or personal?"

"Either way."

"She just started teaching first grade at Dyer Consolidated. Supposed to be very good—Stanford, Peace Corps, Phi Beta Kappa. We keep trying to hire her away, but no luck so far. Nobody's really sure why she came to Dyer County with that resumé."

"Probably just looking for a fresh start."

"We all deserve a second chance." He grinned. "Not hard to look at, is she? Every schoolboy's first crush."

I made a noncommittal smile. "What happened to those transcripts, by the way?"

He shook his head. "They collected everything after the hearing. I thought I still had a copy, but—"

"You didn't keep any notes?"

"Yes—but I had to surrender those as well." He steered into the county square.

"Twenty minutes ago you said you could get me the file." I looked closely at him. "This wouldn't have anything to do with that phone call you got, would it?"

Suddenly he wouldn't meet my eyes.

"Just drop me off," I said. "I'll handle it myself."

He pulled up to the curb in front of the station.

"Please understand, Mike. It's not just the court seal. It's patient confidentiality." He cut the engine. "Don't you have a code of ethics in the FBI?"

"Connor, I don't mind you having a code of ethics. But please don't pretend to be incompetent. I think we both know better." I opened the car door. "Anyhow, thanks for the ride. And for breakfast, too."

"You looked like you could use it." He waited as I stood from the car. "Mike?"

I looked back at him.

"I know what happened to you," he said. "About your mother's death, I mean. It was in your file."

"Swell."

"I wasn't looking for the information, but when I found out . . . I just wanted you to know I understand."

"Is this supposed to help me find a lost child?"

He stopped, flustered. "It could. I mean, I see the pressure you put yourself under. And what you said before . . . about losing your faith in redemption . . . it got me thinking. Maybe it's okay to let go of the past."

I shrugged. "Suppose somebody told you he felt responsible for another person's death. Would you tell him to let go of the past?"

"Not in so many words. But yes."

"What if he really was responsible?"

He hesitated. "There's nothing that can't be forgiven," he said. "Except the refusal to be forgiven."

"Here's where we part company," I said. "Some people don't deserve a second chance."

TWENTY-ONE

"So I'm calling you from my spacious nine-by-twelve office at the Dyer County Sheriff's Station," I said to Peggy. "Woke up this morning in jail, and twelve hours later I'm ass-deep in paperwork. Not bad for a day's work."

"At this rate you'll have your prime suspect before the transfer comes through," Peggy said. "How's it feel?"

"It'd feel a lot better if everybody wasn't so determined to nail this guy. Don't get me wrong. At face value, Frizelle's perfect. Criminal record, demonstrated grudge against the victim. Meantime the physical evidence keeps popping up like Easter eggs."

"Sometimes that's how it plays out. They don't all have to be brain-breakers."

"There's two problems," I said. "One, Frizelle doesn't match the killer's profile. Our unsub is precise, methodical . . . controlled. Frizelle can barely keep himself out of jail. More significantly, there's not one arrest for violent crime on his record. Not so much as a fistfight."

"What do you call the rape charge?"

"Statutory. He was eighteen, the girl was a year younger. All I'm saying is, he's probably a low-down bastard. But if he's not the guy who killed Dale, then he doesn't have the kid. Which leads me to my other problem. Archer's got a real grudge against Frizelle. Seems to go way back."

"So what's your third problem?"

"I only said two."

"There's always at least one you don't tell me about," she said.

"I get the oddest feeling that I'm under a microscope here. Did I ever tell you about my family?"

"Only that you don't like talking about them. Why?"

I started to tell her about my conversation with Connor—then held my breath at the sound of approaching footsteps. "I guess every family has its secrets," I said finally. "But there's something very strange about the Archers."

There was a knock at the door.

"Gotta go?"

"Sounds like it," I said. "Maybe I'm just overthinking this, Peg. I mean, if Pete and Mary are innocent—why would they run?"

"How do you know they did?"

"Good point." I hung up with Peggy, then opened the door. Deputy Ada Rosario stood outside, cradling a stack of files.

"You wanted to see me, Agent Yeager?"

I waved her to a chair. "Sheriff tell you what I'm looking for?"

She nodded. "It means a lot, your asking for me." She glanced at a cardboard box by the door. J. TIPPET, LT. OF DETECTIVES, read the discarded plate on top. "I don't guess Detective Tippet is very happy you're staying."

"No, I guess not." We shared a smile. "How're you holding up, Ada?"

"I'm fine," she said. "I want to get to work."

"You're on." I handed her the documents from my desk. "Here's what's going out tonight—first, a request to open a file on Cassandra with the Nevada Attorney General's office. Also an application for a UFAP warrant. You're familiar with that?"

"Unlawful Flight to Avoid Prosecution," she said.

"Correct. If we can prove Frizelle crossed state lines knowing he was a suspect, we'll have at least that much on him. Now here I've made a list of chemicals and equipment that could have been used in the Dupree photos. Tomorrow we start canvassing suppliers in the region . . . see if they have any Dyer County customers."

She read the list carefully. "Ilford . . . Perceptol?"

"That's a brand name," I said. "I'm almost certain it's the developer they used. It gives you flawless, grain-free prints. You trade off film speed for clarity—but since they were shooting a dead body, it doesn't really matter. It comes in powder form." I caught her eye. "Have you seen it around here?"

She shook her head.

"Okay, let's deal with victimology. We need a list of behavioral features—anything that might indicate Cassandra's general condition just before the kidnapping. Any sudden or unexplained injuries, new friends, changes in her living situation . . ."

By then I'd noticed Ada's pen had stopped moving.

"I can see you've done this before," I said.

"When my Espero got lo—when he died. We did this for him, too."

I noted how quickly she'd stopped herself from saying *lost*. "Ada, would you mind closing the door?"

She glanced over her shoulder. "Sheriff doesn't like closed doors around here."

"Well, he's going to have to deal with one for the next few minutes."

She looked both ways before shutting the door.

"When exactly did your son die?"

"The doctor pronounced him dead on October twenty-seven," she said.

"I realize that. What I'm asking is when he died."

She began straightening her files. "I don't understand."

"I think you do, Ada." I checked my notes. "I see where the Dupree case has the local designation . . . SV-ADR-ten-thirty-one. I'm assuming you're the one who opened the file?"

She nodded. "Yesterday morning."

"And SV stands for . . . ?"

"Special victims."

"Right. Now Dale was murdered October thirty-first—I guess that's why the code is ten-thirty-one . . ."

The blood drained from her face.

"But then there's this other SV file opened on October thirteenth," I said. "Asking for a trace on a late-model black four-wheel SUV with tinted windows. Was this the vehicle that hit your son?"

"We didn't see who hit him." Her voice was paper-thin. "Why are you asking me?"

"Your initials are on both files," I said. "Ada Delfina Rosario. ADR."

I had to hand it to her. She didn't even blink.

"That was a mistake," she said finally. "That case number doesn't exist."

"Not around here, anyway. But whoever purged the files apparently forgot to call Nevada Highway Patrol to cancel the request."

She took a careful breath. "You're making me think about things I don't want to."

"Ada, you told me your son was a hit-and-run. And now I find out he was missing ten days before you recovered the body."

"I didn't lie to you, Mr. Yeager. I told you how he died."

"Look, I'm sorry."

"No, you're not. Don't even say you are. Somebody dragged him—dragged my baby up and down the canyons. And left him for the coyotes. It was so bad we couldn't even open his coffin for the funeral. Now do you see? Or do you want me to show you the pictures they took?"

Her cheeks were burning. But she looked me straight in the eye, and suddenly I found it hard to look back.

"If nobody saw the vehicle that hit him, how did you know to look for this SUV?"

"I told you it was a mistake," she said. "My brother saw it, but it turned out to be wrong. And I thought . . ."

"What did you think?"

She put a hand to her face. "I think you'll have to find another person to help you, Mr. Yeager."

"Ada, was Cassandra the first child to be abducted?"

"Does it make a difference?"

"If she wasn't the first," I said, "she might not be the last."

Ada gazed at her hands for a long time—bare of any jewelry, fine and strong. Finally she looked back at me. "Then I guess she might not be the last."

A knock came at the door.

"What is it?" I asked.

Deputy Clyde put his head in. "Sheriff wants you down in the garage."

"Tell him I'll be right there." Clyde didn't move. "Thank you."

Clyde glowered at me, then down at Ada.

"So tell me, Deputy Rosario," I said, as Clyde's footsteps echoed down the hall, "what are you and I going to do about this?"

"Ask me things I can do." She brushed at her eyes. "Don't make me do things I can't."

"Such as what?"

"I won't go against the sheriff."

"Did he tell you to withdraw that vehicle warrant?"

She said nothing.

"All right. I'm guessing you have access to county records."

Ada nodded.

"Go to the courthouse and pull everything they've got on the Dupree custody hearing. I'm particularly interested in an interview they did with Cassie. Think you can manage that on a Sunday night?"

"The clerk likes me," she said. "Is that all, or . . . ?"

I shook my head. "I also want you to get the names of every registered sex offender in Dyer County."

"We don't have any," she said. "Sheriff Archer wouldn't allow it."

"Maybe so, maybe not. Will you help me?"

"You'll tell the sheriff you asked me for this." It wasn't a question.

"If it'll make you feel better, sure."

"I think that would be good." She stood up. "You shouldn't keep the sheriff waiting, Agent Yeager. He'll say it was my fault."

"Ada?"

She stopped at the door.

"You're doing right by your little boy."

But her eyes were dark and empty as she turned away.

TWENTY-TWO

Archer met me outside the elevator. I noticed reddish dirt on his boot heels.

"Thought I was gonna have to come get you," he said.

"Just wrapping up some paperwork," I said. "How did it go in the mountains today?"

"I didn't find my granddaughter." He shot me a fast look. "How'd you make out with Robbie?"

"Not so good," I said. "His parents could be a roadblock."

"Martha's a pistol," he said. "But you'll manage her fine. Way I hear, you gave the come-to-Jesus to some state trooper in Reno."

"I asked him to send pictures of Dale's truck," I said. "Did they arrive?"

"Better'n that." He pushed open the door to the garage. "We got the truck."

There it was at the bottom of the ramp, the same red Ford half-ton I saw tear-assing into the parking lot of the Silver Star Café. Now two drivers from the Nevada Highway Patrol were rolling it down a flatbed ramp. A team of deputies—Clyde among them—stood ready to take possession.

"Has anybody touched the interior?" I asked one of the troopers.

He shook his head. "Only to ID the vehicle and get her in neutral. You said treat it like crime scene evidence."

"Get me a photographer," I said. "And somebody to take samples."

There were two different shades of dirt on the truck: Old dirt, bluish gray, was crusted in the wheel wells and headlamps. A spray of copper-brown coated the hood and windshield. Same color as the dirt on Archer's boots.

"That gray dirt's local," Archer said. "They'd have picked up the rest of it up north. See all them rocks in the tire treads? Wild Pete musta been hell-bent over the fire trails."

The crime scene crew arrived, and we spent the next thirty minutes working around the outside of the vehicle. Finally I was ready for the cab.

"Sure is clean inside," the photographer said. "What's that smell, Armor All?"

One of the other deputies chuckled. "Looks like Pete was aimin' to get his security deposit back."

It was clean, all right. As shiny and neat as any car off the lot.

"There's another smell underneath," I said. "Lye. Sheriff, come take a look at the dashboard."

He bent in. "Needle's on empty. Reckon they didn't want to stop for gas."

"Maybe." I turned to the trooper. "You fellas found the truck after dark, right? Was the ignition like this?"

"Nawsir, it was turned over. Like I said."

"So the headlamps were on." I carefully turned the dashboard switch. The lights came right on. "There's no way the lamps could have burned continuously from eight in the morning till after sundown. Not without draining the battery. Unless . . ."

". . . Unless the engine was runnin'." A light dawned in Archer's eyes. "They wanted us to find it."

"Hey, look here." Clyde was on the passenger side.

"Clyde, get the hell away from there," I said. "We haven't lifted prints from it."

"Yeah, but there's somethin' stuck under the seat . . ."

Now all the deputies were crowding around him.

"Mash that button right there."

"I did," Clyde grunted. "Feels like somebody's jacket got crammed under. Got oil on it . . ."

I circled the truck. "Clyde, goddammit."

"Jesus fuck." Clyde pulled his hands free, sticky with dark liquid.

"Oh boy," somebody said behind me. "That ain't oil."

TWENTY-THREE

It took the mechanic twenty minutes to get the seat off its rails. By then the smell of blood had filled the garage. Archer stood stock-still while a deputy gently placed Cassie's beagle on a clean plastic sheet. As it passed by, I saw him wince.

"Hell and damnation—" Then he turned on his boot heels and left.

The sheriff was sitting with his back to me as I came into his office.

"Sheriff—"

"Gave her that puppy for her birthday," he said. "She made me a card—I got it around here somewhere—picture of my granddaughter. And her puppy." He turned around, his face darkened with rage. "Earlier today, you were tellin' me what it means when they kill the dog."

"It means there's no going back," I said. "If the subject's already crossed that boundary, it's only a matter of time before he—"

"Does it to her." Archer clenched his jaw. "By *subject* I take it you're still referrin' to Pete?"

I took a breath. "At this point I'm not sure."

His eyes widened. The phone rang before I could say another word. "Right," he said into the receiver. "Tell him to get his ass up here. It's supposed to be his goddamn investigation." He slammed the phone down.

"Sheriff, I think it's time we talked about my visit to your daughter's house."

"Yeager, I already got chapter and verse from Martha and Gavin. Frankly I got more important things to think about than my grandson's cussin'. I need you for one thing only, and that's to help me find my granddaughter."

"That is exactly what I'm trying to do."

"Really? You sure there ain't just a little FBI cover-thine-ass goin' on here? This very mornin' you put the hat on Pete Frizelle. Now you're sayin' he ain't guilty?"

"Will you hear me out?"

He gestured to a chair. I sat down.

"If we move on the wrong man, we lose our shot at Cassandra," I said. "First we have to understand the motive. From what I've seen, this is looking less and less like a simple parental abduction."

"In other words, that whole song-and-dance you gave me was flat wrong."

"Wrong—maybe. Definitely incomplete. The revenge motive is obvious. But it's not against Dale. Dale's dead. The question is, who does the killer want to suffer? He takes photographs—and he sends them to you. He kidnaps your granddaughter. He leaves the truck right where it can be found, so you'll be sure to see what happened to the dog. This is all aimed at you, Sheriff. Tell me the same thoughts haven't crossed your mind."

He raised an eyebrow. "And you don't think that sounds like Frizelle."

"I don't know the guy. Based on what I've seen, no. Right now I've got Deputy Rosario over at the courthouse pulling files. Maybe it'll ring the cherries on Frizelle. But just in case it doesn't . . . I've also asked her to get the names of Dyer County's registered sex offenders."

"We don't have sex offenders in Dyer County," he said plainly. "Not unless you count Pete."

"Sheriff, what do you really know about Frizelle?"

"Enough to know he's a sorry excuse for flesh."

"Is he clean? Physically?"

The sheriff snorted. "Not since the day he was born."

"Really? Because that's what our subject is. Compulsively. You saw the interior of that cab. He doesn't just wash it down. He polishes it with Armor-All to kill the smell of the lye. That's beyond careful. It's obsession."

"I suppose if you were drivin' around in a truck full o'blood, you wouldn't take five minutes to wash 'up?"

"Where's he gonna wash up? The local gas station? Nobody drives for hours soaked in blood—and they're not about to clean up in a canyon. My guess is you're going to find a lot of blood and soap down the septic drains at the Dupree trailer."

He paused thoughtfully. "We already did."

"It's too easy, Sheriff. That Ford was planted right where we expected to fluid It. Meanwhile, did you see how the mirrors were angled? The seat and steering wheel adjustments? How tall was the last person to drive that truck?"

"Five foot nine," he said. "Give or take."

"Pete Frizelle's exact height. Now why would someone careful enough to hide himself in the photographs . . . smart enough to avoid leaving blood or fingerprints anywhere . . . be so stupid as to leave the mirrors adjusted to his own height?"

Archer drummed his fingers. "What were you gonna say about your visit to Martha's?"

"I think Robbie knows something. How much I can't tell. Seems like Martha and Gavin are worried about where the questions might lead if he starts talking. Gavin had alluded to past events—"

"Gavin needs to stick to preachin' and leave police work to professionals."

"He seems to enjoy your confidence on some level. What exactly was in that envelope you showed him this morning?"

"His future." Archer's lip curled slightly. "He's still got one, as long as he remembers who set him up here."

"I'm sure he won't forget you on Tuesday," I said. "Here's another one for your collection."

I handed him a sheet of photographic paper from my jacket.

"I just had these printed up," I said. "They're from negatives I found at the Sweet Charity. You'll recognize them as belonging to the same set as the ones you burned."

He frowned. "What's that last one, cut off in the middle? All I see is a girl's . . ."

If I thought Archer was capable of embarrassment, I'd have said he was blushing.

"The last exposure on the roll," I said. "You'll recognize Mary's American-flag bikini hanging over the bed."

He turned the sheet over. "Coulda sworn I saw you toss that film away, Yeager. Where's the negative?"

"Safe," I said. "I didn't make this print just to shock you. I wanted you to understand how the killer operates differently than Pete Frizelle. Do you still have the Dupree photos?"

He looked at me with jaundiced eyes. Then he reached into his desk and handed me the folder.

"See what happens to the film in Pete's camera when it's blown up to eight-by-ten? Grain marks . . . slight blurring. Now compare it to the killer's pictures." I held them side by side. "Practically grain-free. Needle-sharp focus. We're talking about a large-format negative—five-by-four stock, maybe bigger. The camera had to be a portrait model. The kind professionals use."

"Like that camera of yours, maybe."

"Maybe. But there's no way Pete's Nikon took these pictures. The killer's camera weighed . . . let's say fifteen pounds, once you factor in the peripherals. Not to mention a tripod, lights, reflectors . . ."

"The murder weapon?"

"All together—forty pounds, easy. That's a hell of a lot to hump in on foot. So the killer's got to be strong enough to swing a blade but agile enough to maneuver in a small kitchen. And familiar with law enforcement technique. That's key. The truck was hidden with the lights on so it wouldn't be found until after its importance as evidence had been established."

"You're tellin' me a cop took these pictures," he said. "Or a deputy."

"Maybe a wannabe cop—security guard. Somebody who washed out of police academy, or missed a promotion—"

"—or got himself sent down by the FBI?"

He reached back for his Bull Durham, easy as you please.

"Sheriff," I said. "If you think you can make the case on me, go ahead."

"Yeager, I made the case on you before you ever walked in my door." He set to rolling a cigarette. "You're like them Indians who nail themselves up on crosses every Good Friday. They think the more they bleed, the holier they get. Least they only do it once a year."

"I'm just doing my job."

"Men like you don't have jobs. What they have is crusades." He lit up. "Lotta people get killed in crusades. Like that Mexican boy in Philadelphia—what was his name?"

"I think you remember his name."

"Tonio Madrigal," he said. "Sure did make you a popular fella with the newspapers back east. Seems like in every story I read, you were sayin' somethin' real intelligent—just like you're tellin' me now. Too bad none of it saved a little boy's life." He exhaled a stream of gray smoke. "Or am I wrong? What do you think?"

"Does it matter what I think?"

"It matters if my Cassie could live or die by your judgment."

"Fair enough," I said. "What do you want to know?"

"This Madrigal boy. What did he mean to you?"

"I never met him," I said. "I knew his father. Everyone in Philly knew Sandalio Madrigal. Everybody liked him. He was a big-time real estate dealer. Seven kids by two wives . . . oldest boy, Baldomero, went to Harvard. Overachievers."

"Must have had high hopes for Antonio."

"Tonio was deaf. I think that disappointed the Madrigals." I took a breath. "Anyhow, you know the facts. At two o'clock on the afternoon of June fourteenth, Antonio disappears. No sign of struggle, no witnesses . . . and no suspects. Sandalio Madrigal didn't seem to have enemies. Two weeks later, his office receives a proof-of-life photo. The boy's in terrible condition. And right across him is the shadow of a naked man."

"Jesus."

"When I saw that picture I knew—no way was this a kidnapping for ransom. As I said, once certain physical boundaries have been crossed . . . the worst part was the waiting. For the first time I started to feel real hatred for a subject. Not just a desire to stop him. I wanted—"

"You wanted to rip his balls off and cram 'em down his throat," said Archer.

"Yes," I said. "I wanted him to suffer. All the more as I really began to study that proof-of-life shot. Tonio was holding up his right hand—defensively, I thought. And there was this awful look of recognition in his eyes. He knew his abductor very well. A week later we arrested the boy's father."

"And all because of a picture?"

I shook my head. "Sandalio fit the profile. He was inexplicably absent when his boy was reported missing. He'd arranged for a secretary to open the ransom note. That's something subjects do when they're afraid they won't be able to feign genuine surprise. When I talked to him, he seemed fearful . . . but mainly for his own reputation. It turned out he had plenty to hide. His ex-wife showed me pictures of the bruises he'd given her and the kids. Then . . . we found the camera that took the proof-of-life shot. By the third day of questioning, I'd truly come to despise the bastard. He seemed to have absolutely no remorse for his son. To listen, you'd think he was the victim."

"But finally you broke him," Archer said.

"I broke him," I said. "But not the way I wanted to. Sandalio Madrigal hanged himself in his cell. He never confessed. Then we received another picture of Tonio . . . dead. This time the photographer got careless and left some of his DNA behind. Blood and semen. Belonging to the oldest son."

"The Harvard boy?"

"Tonio's half-brother," I said. "It started as revenge against his father . . . later, he said, he learned to enjoy it. When I put the cuffs on, the kid smiled at me and said—'I couldn't have done it without you.' And I knew he was right."

"Because you were wrong about the father."

"Because I'd completely misread the picture. Tonio wasn't holding his hand up as a defense. He was making sign language—a letter *B,* for *Baldamero.* He'd been trying to communicate through the photograph. I was so focused on my suspect—the wrong one—that I never understood."

Archer frowned.

"That's why I left, Sheriff. I couldn't risk that happening again."

"And yet here you are."

"Here I am."

There was a knock at the door. "Come."

It was Tippet. Holding his forsaken nameplate.

"Sheriff, you called?"

"Just tryin' to keep track of you, Tip. Thought you might be happy to know Mike managed to find that truck. Already got the prints lifted."

"Yeah." He threw me a dark look. "I just got back from dealin' with the business from this mornin'. All due respect, sir, it wouldn't have been my move."

"Noted," Archer said. "Anything else?"

"My . . . office is locked."

"Agent Yeager's office," he replied. "Good night, Lieutenant."

An odor of gasoline and burning plastic followed Tippet out.

"What wouldn't have been his move?" I asked.

" 'Pears Tip has a soft spot for the hard-workin' gals." Archer frowned. "We done here?"

"I'd like to study those photographs some more."

He tensed for a moment, then nudged the file toward me.

"By the way," I said. "Your grandson has an interesting theory about all of this. He doesn't think Pete's guilty, either."

Archer gave a thin smile. "Yeah? Who's his prime suspect?"

"Somebody called the Shadow Catcher," I said. "Good night, Sheriff."

" 'Night." Archer's voice was pale as smoke.

TWENTY-FOUR

The Sweet Charity photographs had almost certainly been taken from a concealed position. Their edges were slightly blurred, as if from a pinhole. In the incomplete photo Mary Dupree crouched over her unseen client. All you could see of him were a pair of Durango boots.

I set Frizelle's pictures aside and returned to the Dupree photo set. Once more I found myself mesmerized by the quality of the camera work—so much so that I had to remind myself they weren't taken for my benefit. The standout was Number 21, the close-up of Dale's neck wound. It was the only picture taken at floor level, the only one using a narrow depth of field. Of all the pictures, Number 21 seemed to reveal a little of the victim's humanity. You could count the hairs on Dale's wrist. You could see the pale line where his wedding ring had been. And the Marine Corps ring on his little finger.

"Hang on," I muttered.

I grabbed a loupe and bent closer. On the back of Dale's neck, a hairs breadth from the spinal column, was a circular puncture wound. Three-eighths of an inch wide, smooth-edged—like an icepick or a sharpened screwdriver. It had been almost completely obscured by the decapitation wound.

"There's our sneak attack," I said. "Bastard stood right behind Dale and put a shiv in." It made sense. Take him down quick with a slice through the brain stem. Dale would have been dead before he hit the ground. It had missed its target by less than a centimeter.

It was getting late now, and Ada Rosario still hadn't returned from the courthouse. The paperwork I'd given her was already finished, neatly stacked on her desk; she'd even started making a list of photography suppliers. But Ada herself was unaccounted for. Three calls to the county clerk's office got only a recording, so finally I decided to head over and see for myself. I was halfway out the door when I realized I'd left the Dupree photos spread across my desk. I thought about taking them down to the evidence locker—then remembered that, in this case at least, the evidence locker was Sheriff Archer's desk. Finally I slipped them into my jacket lining along with the Sweet Charity negatives. As a final measure I emptied Tippet's ashtray across the threshold. There was no telling who else had a key to my office—but at least I'd know if anyone had been there.

Dyer County Courthouse was an old Victorian building that looked like it might have started life as an opera house. I walked directly across the square, my boots crunching the frozen grass. By the time I reached the flagpole, I was fairly certain somebody was watching.

"Hello . . . ?" There was nowhere I could turn without getting blinded. The whole square was lit up like Philadelphia Stadium. I heard another pair of boots in the dry grass, hidden beyond the floodlights. Twenty yards to my right.

"Who's there?" The footsteps were moving faster. Long strides. I kept my voice light. "Hell of a night, huh?"

There was no answer. And no sound. I started walking again. Then I heard a car door slam. An eight-cylinder engine roared into life, its fan belt whining. Broken headlamps shone weakly as the old white Silverado shifted into second. It was too dark to see inside, and there was no license plate. But as the truck skidded around the corner, I noticed a bumper sticker for Wild Pete's Casino.

"I told Ada she couldn't take anything." The county clerk, a portly gnome of a woman, led me through a forest of bookshelves. "Most I could do was show her the inventory. I'd of left by now, except she promised she was comin' right back. Oh well. So did Jesus, I reckon."

The basement room was low-ceilinged, windowless. Pipes ran along the concrete walls, sweating steam onto the wooden filing cabinets. The whole place smelled of old newspapers and rust.

"Did Deputy Rosario say where she was going?"

The clerk shook her head. "She was real upset, though. Poor girl locks it all inside. And, you know, her whole family ganged up on her over that rotten business with Espero."

"Why so?"

The clerk eyed me suspiciously. "Thought you was a detective. You ever see a wedding ring on Ada's left hand?"

"I didn't think that was any big deal nowadays."

"It is for some," she said. "Them Rosarios are proud people. Been here longer'n anybody . . . since this was all Mexico, even." She took a mighty breath. "I am way too old and fat for this job. Okay, here's where Ada was lookin'. Like I told her, nothing leaves. Clear?"

"As crystal."

"I mean it, now. You don't want me to search ya."

That was one warning I was determined to heed. I thumbed back through the family court records until I reached *Dupree v. Dupree*. The transcripts were mostly banter between Pete Frizelle and the judge:

> JUDGE: Mr. Frizelle, if you and Mary Frances get married, do you intend to keep her employed in her current profession?
> FRIZELLE: No sir, I plan to keep that 24-hour-a-day good lovin' all to myself. Wouldn't you?
> [LAUGHTER]
> JUDGE: "24-hour-a-day good lovin'" is no way to maintain a family, Mr. Frizelle.
> FRIZELLE: Maybe not, Your Honor. But it is the best way I know to get one started.

The files were suspiciously thin. REMOVED PER ORDER OF FAMILY COURT was stamped on just about every entry in the document log.

"Excuse me," I said. "You wouldn't happen to know where the evaluations for the Dupree hearings are, would you?"

"Sonny boy, I don't live in these damn files. I just try and keep the dry rot out of 'em." She wheezed her way over.

"Here's the last folder Ada had out." DEPREE, CASSANDRA S. was printed in neat red letters on the tab.

"But it's empty," I said. "There's not even a log."

"Sometimes the judge seals the records in these custody cases." She wiggled her thick eyebrows. "Especially when it involves a certain elected official facin' recall."

I held the folder to the light. Along the spine was a line of ridges—the kind of marks a spiral-bound notebook might leave.

"I see your point," I said. "What do you think the sheriff's enemies might have found to use against him?"

"All I know is, Rafe's lived a sight too long to let a piece of paper bring him down."

She ambled away. I flipped back through the transcripts, looking for any reference to the missing documents. Finally I found one:

> JUDGE: Now we have Dr. Lund's physical examination, and I've taken a pretty careful look at Mr. Blackwell's interview. So I find no grounds for putting Cassie through the ordeal of appearing in open court. Motion denied.

"Sir?" The clerk cleared her throat. "You fall asleep in there?"

"This room's too small for all the records you'd have to keep," I said. "Don't you have a warehouse annex, or . . . ?"

She shook her head. "Budget cuts. Tell you true, half the stuff they send here gets shredded after two years. Only records anybody's interested in is water rights. People kill for water."

"The paper said it's supposed to rain," I said. "Flash flood warning."

"People read the *Ledger* so's to know what not to believe." She shrugged. "We've had twenty-five years of drought in Dyer County. Time was you could legally draw water from Cathedral Lake so long as you could trace your land grant to before 1920. Now it's back to 1874 . . . and all in the hands of fat cats. Like we're in a goddamn time machine goin' the wrong way."

"Where exactly is Cathedral Lake? I couldn't find it on the map."

"Up in the high hills," she said. "Been a dry sink since—oh, twenty years. Folks call it Lost Lake now. Used to be a summer camp, but they hadda shut it down."

"Because the lake dried up?"

"Forest fire in 'seventy-eight."

"So who still has water rights around here?"

"None but a couple families to speak of," she said. "The Archers got the best part of it. Only they don't raise cattle no more, so Sheriff gets to sell his water to that fancy-britches neighborhood—San Cristobal. You know the place?"

" 'Security and Serenity,' " I said, quoting the motto over the gate.

She laughed. "Somebody oughta add 'Senility' to that. They get to play golf while our livestock die on the hoof."

"Who else has a claim?"

"The Rosarios." She switched off the overhead lights. "Come on, sir. Don't you have a nice home to go to?"

I was halfway back across the square when I heard the distant howl of fire trucks. The southern horizon glowed a faint orange. It got me thinking about that smell of gasoline on Tippet.

My car was still back at Tree of Life Church, half a mile down the road. I strode off down the highway, keeping to the loose gravel shoulder. The night air was cold and still and clear. Orion the Hunter wheeled overhead, the Pleiades close beside him. There really was no beating desert stars.

A moment later there were headlights behind me, throwing my shadow down the road. I moved over to give it room. The scream of the fan belt was the last sound I heard before darkness took me.

TWENTY-FIVE

There was an awful moment of spinning, followed by a snap of pure black. A moment later I was staring at steam rising from the front grille of an old white Chevy truck. Dust on the cracked headlamps. I touched the back of my neck and my palm came up dripping with blood.

Somebody was laughing.

Truck hit me? My legs felt rubbery—but they were moving, scrabbling against the gravel shoulder.

"Lookitim," a dry voice cackled. "He's fucked up."

"Not enough—"

Something thick and solid connected with my jaw. Fire exploded in my eye sockets and the headlamps spun around. I was rolling into a ditch, dirt and pebbles sliding down my shirt. Heavy boots crunched my way.

"Is he out?"

"Shh! No, he's getting up—"

A shotgun racked behind me.

I took hold of the rough bark of a Joshua tree and pulled myself up. My feet were under me now, but I couldn't get my balance. It felt like I'd been standing still a long time when a cold iron ring touched the flesh under my right ear. Shotgun muzzle. A sound like a metal spring tightening: finger on the trigger.

"Let's see what you got." An iron voice, muffled by the hood.

I threw my right hand against the barrel, swatting it away. There was a loud report in my ear and a shudder of buckshot hurled past. I swung round and saw a tall figure through the smoke, his face hidden behind a dark hood. Moonlight shone off a silver belt buckle engraved with a cowboy and rider. I aimed my boot three inches under that buckle. He howled.

I grabbed for the shotgun but he pulled it right back. Bruised balls or no, this was one strong mother.

A moment later something bit hard under my chin. Steel chain, choking me. I didn't grab at it—that was a way to die. Instead I threw my head back against my attacker's face. There was a satisfying crunch from beneath the canvas hood.

"*Ahjesusfuckbrokemyfuckinnose—*"

He fell backward and now the chain was in my hands. His partner was raising the shotgun. He racked it again, balancing it against his hip.

"Put it down!" he commanded.

I swung the chain at the shooter's neck. He tried to catch it and the end snaked around his right forearm, tearing a gash right through the cloth. We both pulled hard and fell into each other—but he was on the downhill side. I got a tight choke hold from behind, close enough to smell him. Gasoline. Sweat. And smoke.

"Weak move, Tip," I whispered. "Real weak."

White headlights pinned us, followed by the deep thunder of an eighteen-wheeler's horn. I got a sharp elbow in my bad rib. My attackers fell away like wildcats up the shoulder. As the tractor-trailer hissed to a stop, the Silverado peeled away into darkness.

"What the Christ." The driver climbed down. "I coulda killed—what the *Christ.*" He shone a flashlight down at me. "Buddy, you okay? You need some help up?"

I couldn't feel air in my lungs. "Did you . . . see . . ."

He turned his flashlight down the highway. "They're gone. Boy, they was haulin' ass." He stepped down. "Guess they gave you a workin' over, huh? Man oh man."

I started to sway. The trucker caught me. *Come on buddy looks like you've had enough fun,* I heard his voice echo as my blood spattered his boots.

TWENTY-SIX

I was dreaming about getting the crap kicked out of me when the pounding started. It grew louder until I realized I had leapt to the door. I was back in my motel room.

"Who is it?" I slurred.

"Archer," the sheriff said from the other side. "Late for the autopsy."

I squinted against midday light as he pushed into the room.

"Usually when one o' my men don't show up Monday mornin', I give him his walkin' papers," he said. "But I figure . . . shit on a brick, Yeager. You look like somebody ran you through a meat grinder."

I sat on the bed, still fully dressed. My clothes were caked with dust and dried blood. There was more on the sheets.

"Two guys jumped me about half a mile out of town."

"You see their faces?"

I shook my head. "But don't be surprised if Clyde has a broken nose the next time you see him."

"Clyde?"

"And Tippet—he near about blew my head off with a ten-gauge."

"Why the hell would they wanna jump you?"

"Seems like that's how Tip likes to collect evidence."

His eyes widened. "Mike, there's somethin' wrong with the back of your neck."

I touched the base of my skull. My hair felt like it had been greased with motor oil. Dark blood. I looked in the mirror and saw my ears had been bleeding, too. There was a mean red streak across my neck from the chain. That explained the raw throat.

"I'm fine," I said. "Just got the wind knocked out of me."

" You don't look too goddamn fine."

"We can either waste time putting me in a hospital bed or we can stay with the search." I turned on the bathroom sink taps. "Which do you think is more important?"

He was silent a moment.

"I'll be waitin' outside," he said.

"How'd you get back to the motel?" Archer asked from behind the wheel. "Your car's still at the church."

"Trucker brought me back," I said. "I'm guessing he didn't file an incident report."

"Not that I know. What's that part about Tip wantin' to shake you down?"

"I'm still trying to figure that out," I said. "Did Deputy Rosario show up for work this morning?"

He shook his head. "But now, you let me worry about Ada. Right now I need your mind on where we're goin'."

We drove in silence.

"Don't make a bit o'sense," he said. "Tippet's a crack shot. He coulda killed you from a runaway train."

"Then obviously he wasn't trying to kill me."

He shook his head in disbelief. "It just don't sound like the boy I know."

"Does he have a silver belt buckle with the Winchester logo on it?"

"I recollect so."

"Maybe you don't know him as well as you thought."

We pulled up to a low-roofed building the color of baby aspirin. A weathered sign out front depicted a pair of vintage 1950s children.

SIEGFRIED LUND, M.D.
Pediatric Medicine

"I thought we were going to an autopsy," I said.

"We are," he said. "This is it."

The waiting room, packed with children and anxious mothers, smelled faintly of rubbing alcohol and apple juice.

"Morning, Sheriff!" the nurse called, as we pushed through the swinging doors. "Doc Lund asked if you'd mind waitin'—" By then we were already down the hall. Archer nudged open the door to an examination room. A boy of five sat on the table, crying his eyes out. Holding a needle to his arm was Dr. Siegfried Lund.

He was a tall, thin birch of a man, all knots and gnarls from his sneakers to the plume of wild, gray hair from his high forehead. He was maybe six foot two but stood much shorter. All those years of leaning over toddlers must have permanently warped his spine. Dr. Lund's heavy black glasses looked like he'd bought them on the cheap from some Truman-era five-and-dime. The eyes behind those lenses were a soft and dreamy blue. Lund's ratty tweed and frayed button-down shirt gave him the air of an ad-dled English professor, the kind who knew the name of Shakespeare's English Setter but couldn't find his own socks. I wouldn't have pegged him for a pediatrician—or a coroner. Evidently he was both.

"Now—Jasper," said Dr. Lund. "Didn't you just tell your mom you could take all your shots without crying?"

"Um, yeah." The boy sniffled. "But I think I musta been lyin' when I said that."

"No shame, son," he said. "Tell you true, I'd howl like a banshee if some-body stuck a needle in my hindmost."

Jasper giggled. Lund exchanged a friendly wink with the boy's mother. Then he looked up at us and his smile faded. He quickly excused himself and closed the door behind him.

" 'Lo, Sig," Archer said.

"Damnit, Rafe. You don't belong in this part of the office. These children deserve their privacy same as anybody." He threw a sharp glance at me. "So this is your wonder boy."

Archer nodded. "Mike wanted to get a firsthand look at the body."

Lund's head twitched like an old hunting dog's. "Oh, is that what Mike wants? Well, that's a horse of a different color. Maybe Mike should just handle the autopsy and let me get on with my business."

"Now, Sig, don't take on so."

But Lund was already halfway down to the steel doors. "I could cer-tainly use a topflight FBI agent to instruct me in the fine points of my foren-sics work, I surely could."

He pushed through the swinging doors and disappeared.

"Don't pay him no mind," Archer said, as we followed. "It don't take much to tread on his corns. He's good people."

"I've yet to meet the coroner or M.E. who was glad to see me," I said. "He's got an interesting day job. Must have a lot of energy."

"Hell, he's slowin' down. Used to bring babies on top of it all. Time was the first thing every kid in Dyer County saw was Sig Lund's face. It's a wonder he didn't scare 'em back into the womb."

We were both laughing as we came through the double doors. Cold air and formalin hung in the air. Lying on the steel table was Dale Dupree.

He had been dead seventy-two hours. Most of the blood had drained off, but several wounds had closed themselves when the veins collapsed. There was postmortem lividity on the left side of his body that matched the fetal position in the killer's photographs. Now he lay on his back. Lund had broken out the rigor mortis to give himself room for the Y-shaped autopsy incision. A hanging metal pan, like a butcher's scale, held Dale Dupree's heart: it weighed 325 grams. The dead man's wounds puckered around the edges, bruised from the pressure of the blade. The exposed tissue was the color of calf's liver. Dale's skin was otherwise a mottled yellow—drawn so tight that the hairs of his arms and legs stood on end, as if he too were feeling the cold in that refrigerated autopsy room.

"Look at him." Archer's breath showed white. "Too big for the table, even."

"He weighed ten pounds the day he was born." Lund put on his oilcloth apron. "Breech birth, you know. Very nearly died. I remember his mama saying, 'He's all I got in the world, Doc. All I got left now that my husband's dead.' And he was, Rafe. He was a little miracle baby." Lund's face twisted in grief. "Christ, look what they did to our boy."

"That ain't him, Sig. That ain't the baby you brought. That ain't Dale."

"Yes it is." His water-blue eyes filled with tears. "Year after year, we get older and our babies keep dying. It's wrong, Rafe. It's not the natural way of things."

"Maybe not," Archer said. "We still gotta till the soil."

"Dig graves, you mean." Lund wiped his eyes. Then he looked at me. "What in God's name are you doing?"

"I need to take some pictures." I held up my camera bag. "For reference."

He shook his head in wonder. "Stand back from the body and don't get in my way."

Lund put on a pair of gloves—black rubber, made for rough work. I set my 35mm and we both went about our business.

"Now what might I have failed to discover, Agent Yeager? Please enlighten me."

"I'm sure your preliminary report is fine, Doctor. I'm just trying to get a sense of how the victim was decapitated."

"Two cuts," he said. "One in the shoulder from above. The other with Dale lying facedown."

"What kind of blade are we talking?"

"Narrow kerf," he said. "Minimal pressure bruising. Cut through that bone like suet. It'd about have to be a surgical or military-grade weapon."

"A samurai sword?" Archer asked.

"Consistent with a Japanese sword, yes. If you can find one for me, I'll know better."

"Doctor," I said. "Can you tell me anything about that puncture wound—?"

"—In the neck, yes. Almost missed that one myself." Lund probed the edges of the wound with his little finger. "Clean incision, minimal tearing. It entered here, right below the axis vertebrae—close to the base of the skull."

"Downward thrust?"

"Upward. From the angle, I'd say they were aiming for the medulla oblongata—a very tricky shot. But severing it would have cut off Dale's breathing like turning a switch."

"In other words, a painless death."

"Relatively speaking."

"Assuming that's true, about how tall would that make the assailant?"

He glanced at me. "Six, six and a half feet, judging from the angle."

"Thought you told me it was somebody Pete's height," Archer said.

"That's what you said, Rafe. I said maybe." Lund shook his head. "Wish you'd listen to me like you used to."

"Even if it was somebody five foot nine," I said. "The killer would have to be standing less than a foot away."

Archer glowered. "Yeah? And?"

"Considering all the bad blood between those guys," I said, "would Dale ever let Pete Frizelle get that close?"

Neither one of them spoke—but to my eyes, Dr. Lund seemed oddly relieved.

I bent down to the wound. "The diameter seems large for an icepick. What do you think, Doc? Screwdriver?"

"Nothing so crude. The point would have to be high-grade steel. Approximately nine and a half millimeters wide—and hollow, like a hypoder-mic needle. There would have been a jet of fluid from the point of contact—wouldn't you say, Rafe? Seem like anything you've found in your travels?" He threw a telling glance at the sheriff.

Archer returned a beady stare. "Seems like."

I got the feeling a coded message had just passed between the two old men. "I take it you have some ideas about the weapon."

Lund nodded silently as he pulled open a metal drawer, rummaging through a rack of tools till he found the right one. Cold surgical steel gleamed in his hands—a thin tube, finely machined, with a hollow trian-gular point at the business end.

"It's called a trocar," he said. "Normally they're used to create a path-way for exploratory instruments—obstetric procedures, laparoscopic sur-gery. The one they used on Dale would have a thicker shaft."

"Where would the subject have got hold of one?"

"Oh—medical supply warehouse, I suppose. Not so easy for the man on the street. But it's a trocar, or I've never seen one."

Archer looked at his watch. "We about done here, Yeager?"

"Just about," I said. "Dr. Lund, would you mind bringing his hands up around the windpipe?"

"Would I what?"

"I need to see the hands in relation to the decapitation wound."

He silently brought Dale's hands together near the neck stump. I was now seeing the victim from the killer's point of view, through a camera lens. I zoomed in on the hands. The swollen right wrist with its handcuff mark. The left hand that had clocked my jaw.

Something about the shot felt wrong. Then I saw the indentation on his little finger. "Doctor, who else besides yourself has had access to the body?"

"Nobody. Least not since Tippet brought him here."

"And you haven't removed anything."

He was watching me intently. "No."

"Thank you," I said. "I think that'll do."

Archer shivered. "Sig, we 'preciate your time. We'll let you get back to work now."

Lund came close to me. "Here now, what's this?" He took off his rubber glove and pressed an ice-cold palm against the nape of my neck. "I don't have to ask if that hurt."

"It's nothing," I said. "I got in a . . . minor altercation last night. I'm sure there's no lingering effects—"

"Mm," he said. "And where exactly did you study medicine?" He looked into my right ear. "Let's get you someplace warm."

Archer coughed. "We got a live investigation, Sig. Right now we're supposed to be at the school."

"Your wonder boy has suffered a mild concussion," Lund said. "Possibly even a hairline skull fracture. You wanna let him walk around with his ears bleeding, it's your affair. But I can't imagine he's much good to you this way."

"Now just a goddamn minute—"

Lund stared him down. "Go sit in the waiting room, Rafe. Read some parenting magazines."

Archer threw me a tense look, as if suspecting me of having injured myself on purpose. "Swear to God, Sig. You fret just like an old woman."

The sheriff stalked away. As soon as the door shut, Dr. Lund's features seemed to soften. He motioned me into an empty examination room.

"You really think I've got a skull fracture?" I asked.

"By rights you ought to." He closed the door. "Looks like somebody heaved a rock at your head. Brick, maybe. We'll take X-rays to be sure."

"Wouldn't you rather get back to your patients?"

"As of this moment, Mr. Yeager, *you* are my patient. And a damned lucky one, I'll say. Take off your shirt, please. I'd like to see what else happened during your 'minor altercation.' "

I felt silly disrobing in a room papered with Richard Scarry lions. But it seemed like Doc Lund wasn't going to take no for an answer.

TWENTY-SEVEN

An hour later I found Lund in the radiology room, staring at a row of X-rays.

"You don't have a skull fracture," he said. "I'd put some tape on that sprained rib if I thought there was the least chance you'd wear it. How are those stitches treating you?"

I touched the bandage. "I'll be glad when my hair grows back. I haven't had a crew cut since my Academy days."

"That's where they taught you to fight, eh?"

"The FBI gave me a career. My father was the one who taught me to fight."

He seemed to understand. "I was going to ask you about those old breaks. Whoever set them did a good job."

"The doctor put a cast on me and sent me back home. If you want to call that a good job, go ahead."

His chin dropped as he pretended to sort the X-rays. "You seemed . . . very interested in Dale's hands. What did you see when you looked at them?"

"It's what I didn't see. Dale's Marine Corps ring is missing from his little finger. You didn't happen to find it among the victim's personal effects?"

"No." He raised an eyebrow. "He's always worn that ring—I gather it belonged to his father. But how did you know to look for something that isn't there?"

"Well, for one thing, he nearly broke my jaw open with it. But it was also in the photographs." I waited. "The ones the killers sent. Archer must have shown them to you . . ."

"Photographs." Lund paled. "From the killers."

"Take a look." I reached into my jacket.

The photographs were gone.

"I don't understand," I said. "I could have sworn . . ."

"Short-term memory loss is normal after a concussion. Think of it as a preview of old age." Lund cast about his desk. "Which is why I can't seem to put a hand to my prescription pad . . ."

There was no way those pictures could have fallen from my jacket. I had zipped it up for the walk, even buttoned the collar. Then I remembered I'd put the Sweet Charity negative in there as well.

Lund brightened as he found the pad. "There you are, little dickens."

"So you did treat Dale Dupree as a child," I said.

"Mr. Yeager, there has not been a child born in Dyer County over the past forty years that I didn't treat at one time or another."

"Then can you tell me how he got that scar on his head?"

Lund stared at me for several seconds.

"You're referring to the fracture in his left temporal area," he said. "As I recall there was a forest fire, up in the mountains."

"Near the camp, you mean."

"Somewhere in that vicinity. He got lost hiking, I believe."

"You remember the location of the wound but not how it happened?" I shook my head. "Was anyone else with him during this nature hike? Say, Pete Frizelle or the Archer girls?"

"It was a long time ago." He tensed. "Is there some relevance to these questions?"

"I think so. Yesterday I noticed that Martha also has a head scar—similar to Dale's but located near the base of the skull. I also saw a recent photograph of Mary Frances Dupree, showing healed burn marks on her legs. Some of them look very old. So you tell me, Doctor—do you think there's any relevance?"

He looked straight at me. "No."

"You're giving your word as a physician that none of these four people were traumatized as children."

"As I said, it all happened long ago." He went back to scribbling in his pad. "I treated Dale and the others as children. But children, I'm sorry to say, always grow up."

"Not the ones who die."

He stopped writing. "What is it you want from me, Mr. Yeager?"

"A little straight talk would be nice. If there's a pattern of abuse here, I need to know. When you examined Cassie for her custody hearing, did you find any evidence of maltreatment?"

"Absolutely none whatever."

"May I see the notes of your examination?"

"Bring me a court order and I'll be happy to oblige."

"Done," I said. "To save time I'll also bring one for Espero Rosario."

"Espero?"

"It's your signature on his death certificate," I said. "I was wondering what conclusions you drew."

"Wrongful death," he said. "Trauma resulting from multiple injuries. Most likely he died at least a week before the body was found."

"Where was the body discovered?"

"In the dirt road leading to the Rosario home. So I'm told."

"In other words, deliberately planted," I said. "How does that make you feel?"

Lund took off his glasses. "I think I would rather have died than see that little boy lying on my table."

"And yet you say nothing," I said. "I saw the look you gave Archer during the autopsy. There's something foul going on here. And I think you want to tell me."

He was silent for a long time.

"Perhaps," he said. "But you're not asking the right question."

"All right. In your opinion, what was the exact cause of Espero's death?"

Lund closed his office door. "It wasn't from being dragged," he whispered. "Those wounds were postmortem. Espero was exsanguinated."

"How did they bleed him?"

"Not with a truck," he said. "A trocar. Very possibly the same one used on Dale Dupree."

"Did you include this in your report?"

He cast a weathered eye at me. "I told Rafe. I can only assume he spoke to the Rosarios, because the very next day they withdrew permission for an autopsy."

"And that's where it ended."

"Apparently so."

"Hold on. You're telling me that Sheriff Archer personally shut down the investigation of a child's death? For God's sake, why?"

"You can ask him. I don't think he'll answer. You're going to find that Sheriff Archer keeps the law in his vest pocket."

"Sounds like he's got the coroner there, too."

"So it would seem." He tore the prescription from his pad. "I can't help you, Mr. Yeager. I don't expect you to understand why. I will offer a suggestion, though. Stop looking for answers among the dead."

"Odd thing for a coroner to say."

"It's only a part-time job. I was a pediatrician long before Rafe Archer made me a coroner." He handed me the slip. "Take good care of your head. It's not an easy thing to replace."

There was a knock on the door. The nurse peered in.

"Dr. Lund, Miz Cantrelle don't wanna let me give her daughter a shot. She says only you—"

"—Only me." Lund rose to his feet. "So many of them, only one of me."

"Doctor, please," I said. "If you know something—"

"Make sure Spence checks the prescription carefully," he said. "He's getting on in years. And old men's eyes are rarely to be trusted."

A moment later a timid, brown-haired girl was taking him by the hand.

"Well, hello, little miss." He bent down. "If you haven't grown three inches since I saw you last."

TWENTY-EIGHT

Archer was out front by his cruiser, a savage light in his eyes.

"Damn kids were like to drive me crazy," he said, as I climbed in. "Doc Lund fix you up all right?"

"Tolerably." I caught his eye. "Something's happened. What is it?"

"Somethin's happened, all right." He started the engine. "We got Pete Frizelle. Arizona troopers pulled him over west of Virgin River Canyon."

"Long way from Reno," I said. "He was alone?"

Archer nodded. "Mary's suitcase in the passenger seat." He studied me from the corner of his eye. "Never saw an agent so unhappy to get his man."

"I was just wondering what might have lured him back."

"He's gonna be here tomorrow, ask him yourself." He took a breath. "Look here, Mike. I reckon you're just doin' your job, thinkin' through all the angles and makin' sure the *I*s are dotted. So I guess I'm square with you wantin' to keep an open mind—up to a point. But now that point's behind us, and it's time to act. You see?"

"Sheriff—"

"Yeah?"

"You're right. It's time to act." I pointed off to the right. "You mind dropping me off at the church? I need to pick up my car."

"Hell, we're already an hour late to the school. Meantime I got deputies turnin' the county upside down."

"So I'll visit the school by myself. If the kids drive you crazy . . ."

"Yeah, okay," he said. "Just don't waste any more time, hear? We're due to walk the crime scene at four."

"I'll be there."

We turned into the church parking lot. There was my Nash, all by its lonesome.

"I talked to Tip while you were gettin' your head worked on." The sheriff cleared his throat. "Seems he was on search detail last night."

"Did you really expect him to tell you different?"

He glowered. "In ten years that boy's not once told me a bald-faced lie. And I've yet to meet the man who could pull the wool over my eyes."

And with that he drove away.

TWENTY-NINE

Just south of Courthouse Square I found the broken chunk of cinder block they'd hurled at my neck, lying on the shoulder of the highway. Two sets of skid marks led up to it—first the white Chevy truck, then the big tractor-trailer. I followed the spray of gravel down to the Joshua tree I'd grabbed during the fight. The blast had knocked one of its branches to splinters. That could have been my head.

The ground cover was a mess of sand and gravel. Absolutely no sign of the Dupree photographs anywhere. Finally I found a readable bootprint in the lee of a large boulder: sharp toe, high instep. Brand-new Durangos—just like the ones Mary's unseen customer had been wearing.

Whoever broke into my office was careful, I thought, as I unlocked the door. They had stepped right over the spray of ash I scattered, leaving only a thin crescent of a left boot heel in the threshold. Durangos again.

"Administration," drawled the voice on my office phone.

"Sorry, I was—isn't this Deputy Rosario's extension.?"

"She called in sick this mornin', Agent Yeager. Figure she's got a right. What can I do ya for?"

"I've been trying to track down Detective Tippet," I said. "Can you tell me the location of his vehicle?"

He chuckled. "The lieutenant's made it pretty clear he don't need us playin' mother hen on him."

"I'll just call his cell phone. You got that number?"

He didn't have the number. Neither did Directory Assistance. I rifled through the desk, praying Ada hadn't done too thorough a job of cleaning out Tippet's belongings. As I reached into the back of the file drawer, I felt something caught in the slider. Finally I managed to get it loose.

It was a plain evidence packet. Inside was about a yard of old Super 8mm film, badly scratched and musty-smelling. It was too dark to make out, even when I held it to the light. NEG. FOR PRINTS was scrawled on an attached sticker from the lab. Tippet couldn't have thought it much of a priority: the note was dated October 29, more than two weeks after he'd sent it down for analysis. I took it for later and kept digging. Finally I discovered a recent phone bill in the wastebasket. Ten minutes with a customer care representative—a rookie who fell over himself when I said "FBI"—and I had Jackson Tippet's outgoing calls for the past seventy-two hours.

All but one of his conversations were with a private number in town. The first one went out at 4:46 P.M. on October 31—that had to be the call he'd made outside the Silver Star. He rang that same number again on Saturday at 7:05 A.M., probably right after arriving at the Dupree trailer. The longest conversation took place at 10:50 P.M. Sunday, approximately fifteen minutes after I was attacked on Highway 313.

I punched up the number. BLOCKED flashed on the caller ID as a molasses-heavy voice answered. "Yeah?"

I held my breath. In the background I heard an amplified voice: "Customer waiting in finance dep—"

"Tip?" he said. "What the hell are you doin', callin' from your office? You wanna let the whole world—hello?" I could hear his nostrils venting.

"Asswipe," he said, as the phone clicked off.

I tried the other number.

"Freebairn and Son," came the reedy voice on the far end.

"Yes, this is Special Agent Yeager with the FBI. Could I have a word with Mr. Freebairn?"

"Speaking."

"Sir, I've been following up on some paperwork. I understand you gave a statement on Saturday afternoon in relation to the Dupree investigation?"

"No, I'm afraid you're mistaken."

"I have confirmation you spoke to Detective Tippet at"—I glanced at the phone sheet—"three-twenty P.M. on November first."

"I spoke to one of Rafe's boys. Can't vouch for the time. But it didn't have a thing to do with Dale."

"In reference to what, then?"

"You just said you were following up. Don't you know?"

"Naturally, sir. I'm just doing my job and—"

"I swear, it's either drought or flood with you fellows." His voice rose, impatient. "Three weeks I've been bringin' my complaint, and nary a word till now. Guess ole Rafe's forgotten how to treat his friends and neighbors."

"You could say that's why I'm calling. What were the details of the break-in?"

"I already told everything to that detective. He was here two solid hours on Saturday, turning the place upside down. Couldn't get any work done."

I had been jotting down notes as he spoke, but now I stopped. On the critical first day of a major homicide investigation—with Cassie's wherabouts unknown, with only me for a suspect—Tippet had seemingly dropped everything to deal with a routine B&E.

"Mr. Freebairn, I know this is frustrating. But if you could please tell me what went missing."

He sighed. "Oh, nothing that can't be replaced, I guess. It's just such a nuisance dealing with insurance. A couple of stainless steel buckets, some tubing . . . electric needle gun plus thread, incision staplers. Also two gallons of cavity fluid, some assorted trocars, a Porti-Boy—"

"Excuse me. Did you just say 'trocars'?"

"T-R-O-C-A-R-S. Am I not speaking clearly?"

"Is this a medical supply company?"

"This is a funeral home," he said. "Don't you even know who you're talking to?"

THIRTY

I had been rapping on the locked door marked MEDIA ROOM for close to a minute before a chipper young deputy finally ambled past.

"Help you?"

I nodded. "They told me I could examine some film here."

"They'd be right." He unlocked the door. "Sorry to keep you waitin'. We got a lotta sensitive stuff in here."

The room was wall-to-wall steel racks filled with cassettes. A row of monitors displayed views of the entire department—lockup, interview rooms, impound yard. Twelve factory-fresh recorders quietly cranked away.

"Your sheriff seems to like to know what's happening under his roof," I said.

"And then some." He sat down. "Okay, whatcha got?"

I handed him the film from Tippet's desk. He grimaced.

"Not much I can do about this," he said. "I ain't seen a Super 8 projector since my granddad's estate sale."

"Have you got a high-res scanner? And some kind of photo editing software?"

He didn't like where this was going. "Think so."

"All right, scan it in. Make sure the light and color's properly balanced. I want to see the whole thing frame by frame."

"Frame by frame?"

"That's what I said."

THE FUTURE OF DYER COUNTY IS SAFE HERE, read the sign over the gate at Dyer County Consolidated School. It had seemed picturesque at first, a fenced-in courtyard of Spanish Revival buildings. It was only after I made it through the gates and the metal detector that I realized how much the place seemed like a prison. There were no banners or trophy cases lining the walls. Instead there were photographs.

They were framed pictures of the student body for each year, going all the way back to 1920. That first class was only a few solemn children, shown standing around an old Ponderosa pine. From then on the arrangement was always the same—grammar school kids in front, high school in back, junior high in the middle. Always in front of that tree. I was fairly sure I knew those two dashing young men at the rear of the class of 1948. Even as a boy, Siegfried Lund had that wild hair. And young Rafe Archer had that Cupid's-bow mouth.

There was a break in the lineup after 1968, where two hallways met. On the other side of the hall was the student body photo for 1979.

There was no mistake: an eleven-year gap. In the second row of the '79 photo, between the teenagers and little kids, were the quartet—Pete, Dale, Mary, and Martha. They had already lost the innocence of that summer camp photo. They were sullen, remote, a group apart. Dale had a deep, barely healed scar in his temple. Pete's arm was still in a sling. And the twins were not looking at the camera. Somewhere between the summer of 1977 and the Spring of 1979 childhood had been stolen from them.

The bell rang, flooding the hallway with twelve grades of children:

"Go play with your Barbies!"

". . . gotta hook me up . . ."

"Dude, she's psycho!"

"Hey, fag!"

"Skank!"

"X-Box."

"Duh!"

"Whatever . . ."

Then the children vanished in a clatter of echoes.

"Kind of like a flash flood, isn't it?"

Dorothy Corvis was standing close beside me and smiling.

Dorothy's classroom—empty during the lunch wave—was a riot of interesting clutter. Easels and puppets and musical instruments hung on the wall. Her degrees were from Stanford—with honors, I noted. Dorothy threw herself down behind her desk, waving me into a chair that was about three sizes too small for my butt.

"Fair warning." She tossed back a wayward strand of hair. "We've got maybe five minutes till my kids come blasting back, full of sugar and . . . you want tea? Anything?"

"A larger chair, maybe."

She laughed. "You must feel like Gulliver in here. I'm sorry, I usually only have little visitors. Here. Take my chair."

"It's all right," I said. "I'm afraid I can't stay long."

"There you go, being afraid again." She looked at me with gentle irony. "Okay, I can tell you're stressed. What do you need from me?"

"Last night you were asking about Robbie. In your experience, is he the kind of kid to make things up?"

"I'd say he's imaginative. What do you mean by making things up?"

"Well—what do you mean by imaginative?"

"He's a born actor," she said. "Rob was gonna be the star of the pageant till his parents put the kibosh on."

"What part was he going to play?"

"The Pied Piper of Hamelin. He's the one who asked if we could do it. Helped find the script and everything. Now we're left with a dozen mice and nobody to lead them out of the village."

"I thought it was rats."

"You can't ask these beautiful children to play rats." She shook her head in reproach. "So why did you ask if he makes things up?"

"A few things he said seemed out of the ordinary. Has he ever mentioned a toy or game called 'Shadow Catcher'?"

She shook her head. "That's a new one on me. What exactly was he doing?"

"There was this robot called the Shadow Catcher who stole children. And the children were trying to run away. The robot's face had been melted off."

"Did the children get away?"

"He told me, 'They always die in the end.' "

Her face darkened. "That . . . does not sound like any toy or game I know."

"I'd have to agree. Can you shed any light?"

"You probably know this," she said. "For some kids, these play activities are like recurring nightmares. They'll keep playing through until they find a way out. Did it seem like he saw himself in danger, in this game? That this monster was threatening him personally?"

"More like he cast himself in the role of the protector. The one being chased was a Barbie doll."

"Blonde Barbie?"

"Redhead."

"That's not Barbie, that's her best friend Midge. Not that you'd be expected to know these things. Unless you had sisters."

"My sisters had to make their dolls out of corn husks," I said. "So obviously Midge represents Cassandra."

She nodded. "He's very watchful of her. It could be he's trying to deal with feelings of helplessness over her kidnapping. Turning those fears into a monster."

"What if the monster is real?"

"The monster is always real." She raised an eyebrow. "Your sisters' corn husk dolls . . . That was a joke, right?"

"Not to them it wasn't," I said. "Miss Corvis, do you think Robbie had reason to be afraid for Cassandra?"

"Dorothy," she said. "Sorry. Do I call you Detective, or Agent, or . . . what?"

"Mike is fine," I said. "Let me explain. I'm trying to see if Cassie might have known what was about to happen to her. If there'd been any dramatic change in her behavior over the last few days."

"God, yeah." She nodded. "During that whole awful courtroom thing, she'd start crying an hour before her mom or dad showed up. Most days she'd be too upset to keep her food down."

"Did she seem to be avoiding contact with her parents?"

She shook her head. "It wasn't either of them individually. Not even her mom's boyfriend. I think it was just the situation—knowing they were fighting over her. She's a really sensitive girl. And you know how kids think everything's their fault."

"You don't think Dale was mistreating her."

She seemed to consider her answer carefully. "Not consciously. But he was really going downhill. There's no way he could have avoided affecting her."

"You know, the other day—after our fight—he said something very strange. He asked me—"

" 'Did you hear a baby cry?' "

"How did you know that?" I said. "What does it mean?"

"Cassie told me he said it whenever he hurt himself. As to what it means . . . Sometimes, when children are harmed, they create a little wall inside themselves. All their pain and rage goes over that wall . . . until it becomes almost like a second self."

"You're talking about disassociation. They'll tell you about some other child getting hurt, and then you find out it's them."

She nodded. "When Cassie's dad felt pain, he heard a baby cry. Most likely he didn't realize the baby was himself."

"Then you believe Dale was a victim of childhood abuse?"

"Based on what little I've seen, yes. But he was trying not to give it to Cassandra. That's important."

I nodded. "Did she seem better after the hearing ended?"

"She was a lot quieter. But better?" Dorothy held her hands out. "She wouldn't eat in front of anybody else. Also she was doing a lot of this—" Dorothy placed a hand over her lips. "When she had to talk."

"What does that say to you?"

"Kids often take instructions literally. My guess is somebody told her to keep her mouth shut." She reached into her desk drawer and pulled out a drawing. "I wanted you to see this. It's a self-portrait Cassie did for me."

The drawing was, I thought, pretty good for a seven-year-old. Cassie had shown herself standing on a grass lawn, holding a brown puppy in her arms. She'd accurately depicted her own features—green for her eyes, red for her strawberry-blonde hair. But something was missing.

"There's no mouth," I said. "When did she do this?"

"Thursday. That's why I thought it was strange when you said the Shadow Catcher didn't have a face. When I asked Cassie what happened to her mouth, she said, 'I traded it for a puppy.' "

"She traded her silence for her puppy's life," I said. "Who else did you tell about this?"

"My principal. He didn't get it. 'Kids draw weird pictures all the time, yadda yadda.' Anyhow, I was supposed to meet with Child Protective Services . . . wow." Dorothy put a hand to her face. "It would have been today."

"So that's why she brought the puppy to school?"

"We couldn't make her let go. She just clung to poor Belle all day." She shook her head sadly. "Right before she got on the shuttle, Cassie said something that just about broke my heart. 'I don't guess I'll get to see my daddy today.' "

"She said that?"

"Yeah. At the time I told her something stupid like, 'I'm sure you will. He'll come and get you.' I keep thinking . . . I hope she doesn't know what happened to her dad."

She looked at me for a long time, intensely reading my silence.

"Anyhow, it's good you came by," she said at last.

A moment later there was a violent pounding of feet on the ceiling. "Okay. In exactly thirty seconds this room's gonna be full of children, ready for story time. So unless you want to stay and help me read *Make Way for Ducklings* . . . "

"Maybe tomorrow." I stood up, glad to be free of the tiny chair. "The script Robbie found for your Pied Piper play. You don't happen to have a copy, do you?"

"Right here." She handed me a stapled chapbook. "Do you mind if I ask you a question?"

"Fire away."

"What happened to the back of your neck?"

I touched the bandage. "Cut myself shaving."

She didn't laugh. "Let me see."

"It's fine." I pulled away. "I can barely feel it."

As she leaned back there was a look of quiet compassion in her eyes. "You're not used to this, are you?"

"I've been knocked around before."

"That I can tell." She smiled, a little sadly. "What I mean is, you're not used to someone caring about it."

The children came bounding downstairs, yelling and whooping as they swarmed past us.

"I guess not," I said.

THIRTY-ONE

... And the piper said to the rich men, You are GREEDY. I saved you from the rats who bit your babies and licked up all your milk. And this is how you pay me back! Oh how I will fix you. I will take from you a treasure worth all your gold. Your children will serve me forever in my kingdom under the bloody mountain, while you just keep getting older and fatter and feel sorry. Yes. You should have paid attention.

I was so deeply focused on Robbie's big speech that I nearly ran into the county clerk as we both crossed the square.

"Slow down there, bucko!" She laughed and patted her abundant chest. "Give an old woman a heart attack. Whatcha got your nose in?"

"The greedy men of Hamelin," I said. "I'm glad I ran into you. That forest fire in nineteen seventy-eight. You don't have any records of an inquest . . . ?"

"I can send you old newspapers—copies, anyhow." She raised an eyebrow. "Or maybe I shouldn't give you the time of day. Seems like you're runnin' with the wrong pack."

"What do you mean?"

"Hmm. You po-lice all smile like angels on Sunday morning." She shook her head. "Your friend Mr. Archer's gonna be readin' want ads if he keeps up these shenanigans."

"Shenanigans?"

She pointed to the newspaper vending machine.

SWEET CHARITY BURNS
Dyer County's Only Legal Brothel Lost in Electrical Fire

"It gets less than a hundred words," I said to Peggy from my office phone. "Not even a photograph. Meanwhile, there's no mention of the sheriff's raid that morning."

"What does that tell you?" Peggy said. "Besides the fact that your sheriff's got the newspaper on a leash."

"Archer did it to lure Pete back to Dyer County. His mother owns—I should say, *owned* the brothel. And it worked like a charm. Pete was pulled over by Arizona state cops—driving five miles under the speed limit, no less—in a Jaguar XK, British Racing Green."

"So he's a scumbag with a little taste. So what?"

"His warrant advised to look out for a white Chevrolet Silverado," I said. "Everybody saw him driving a white Chevy on Friday. Just like the one that attacked me last night."

"Incidentally, why aren't you dead?"

"Obviously they didn't want a dead FBI agent—even a disgraced one. Just the pictures." I heard Peggy sigh. "Why is everyone so damn concerned about my head? You'd think I'd never gotten a bump on the noggin before."

"Yeah. Well. It's your noggin. So . . ." She paused. "How do you think this Rosario boy ties in?"

"I have a few theories. This is not the behavior of a sexual predator in a panic. The planning, the weapons involved—everything indicates that the victims were chosen with an overarching goal in mind. Not a crime of passion. More like—Peg, my other line's going. Can I call you back tonight?"

She hesitated slightly. "Sure. Talk to Yoshi if I'm not around, okay?"

"What, I don't rate the boss's ear any more?"

"It's not that. Finish what you were going to say, Mike. It's not a crime of passion."

"More like paying the piper," I said. "Never mind. It'll keep."

I punched to the second line. The display ID'd a public pay phone in east Dyer.

"Agent Yeager?" said the woman on the other end.

"Ada," I said. "Where are you? I've been trying to call."

"Yeah. Don't do that again. Can you come see me? I'll be at home."

"Did you find something, Ada?"

She didn't answer.

"I don't know my way around," I said. "Why don't you meet me at the station—"

"No. Please. It's better you come here. There were these people drove by last night. My brothers chased 'em off, but I think they're gonna be back. Will you?"

"Of course," I said.

"Soon?"

I looked at the clock. "I'm supposed to be somewhere at four. If it's urgent, I'll cancel. But then some people might think something's up. Do you see what I mean?"

"Yeah," she said. "God, do I ever."

I took a short breath. "I'll come now. You have people with you?"

"My family." There were the voices again, and Ada was saying *Sí, sí, es él*. "Mr. Yeager, there's a big black dog in our yard, but he won't bite. I'll see you soon."

She hung up. According to the wall map in my office, the Rosarios lived in the east end of Dyer County—high in the foothills of the Sangre de los Niños.

" 'Your children will serve me forever,' " I muttered, " 'in my kingdom under the bloody mountain.' " It was right there in Robbie's speech from the play.

THIRTY-TWO

". . . name is Buford Warburton and I approved this ad," drawled the heavy voice from my car radio. Static washed over the signal as I navigated the canyon roads. *". . . riff Archer wants to keep our law enforcement stuck in the last century. Join with me on . . . as your sheriff I'll lead . . . future for our children. Or my name isn't—"*

"—Asswipe," I mimicked. Hearing that voice again on the radio was simple confirmation. The moment I heard the loudspeaker calling the finance department, I remembered that Archer's chief opponent in the recall was a used-car salesman.

The sheriff had warned me to stay on the highway, and driving through east Dyer made a believer of me. The way to the Rosario ranch had seemed simple enough—from a map. But maps don't tell you what roads have been washed out since last winter. Or what creatures might be hidden among the limber pine, waiting to pick your flesh clean. Once you left Highway 313, driving Dyer County was like navigating an anthill. Ada had told me to watch out for a big black dog. All the yards around there had big black dogs. One fallen-down shack appeared to belong solely to a family of Dobermans. Some places you don't stop for directions if you want to live.

From a distance, the Sangre de los Niños were spectacular. Now they were close enough to seem menacing. Redstone cliffs reached over the road, ready to bury me under a hundred million years of rock. Indian petroglyphs were scratched deep into the cliff face, depicting serpents and hunters and what looked like herds of antelope. I was in a part of Dyer County that seemed to belong to another age.

THIS WAY TO CATHEDRAL LAKE SUMMER CAMP! read a worn-out sign on my left. A SERVICE OF THE DYER COUNTY SHERIFF'S ASSOCIATION. I pulled over for a closer look. The old dirt road was narrow and thick with under-brush, but there were fresh tire tracks leading up. After a moment's hesita-tion, I drove on up to the summit.

Twenty-five years had done little to erase the scars of the 1978 fire. Black-ened aspens and ponderosas rose above the low scrub like iron spikes. Most of the log cabins had long since burned or rotted away, but the granite shell of the main lodge was still standing. As I walked through the open space I saw odd survivors—an orange life vest, an overturned coffee urn. SIGN UP HERE FOR ACTIVITIES, read a fallen sign half-buried in ash and rubble. But activity there was none: Cathedral Lake Camp was as dead as yesterday.

Then I came to the lake itself.

Just as the clerk said, the lake was lost: a dry salt bed about half a mile across. The old sailboat from Martha's picture was still there, now com-pletely buried except for the mast and prow. I got out of the Nash and started down the steep banks. Ten feet from the bottom I tripped on an ex-posed drainage pipe and nearly went ass over teakettle. At the last second I recovered my balance and half-slid, half-fell down the loose gravel fall.

Brilliant, I thought. Now how do I get back up?

It was only as I heard the sound of my feet crunching the sand that I re-alized just how quiet the lake really was—like walking the surface of the moon. A pair of heavy bootprints led me to the sailboat. Twenty-five years of sun, dust, and wind had stripped it clean, like driftwood. All except for a flesh-colored smear on the mast cleat. It was palm-shaped, with two smaller spots like fingerprints on the underside. Radial loops—enough to match partials if not full latents. I scraped the edge with my thumbnail. It peeled up like oily latex paint.

I carefully pocketed a sample for later analysis. Then, as I looked closer, I noticed initials carved into the mast:

D. D.

M. A.

M. F. A.

P. F.

Dale Dupree. Martha Archer. Mary Frances Archer. Pete Frizelle. On an impulse I brushed some of the sand away from the mast. There were faint lines that might have been a fifth set of initials—or not. Someone had hacked through them with a knife.

"Four came home," I said.

Hearing my own voice made me shudder a little, as if I might have woken something that was better left asleep. A moment later I was startled by the sound of a rifle bolt.

"Don't move." He was eighteen, stocky, with fierce dark eyes and a rope of black hair. The rifle, a war-vintage thirty-aught-six, was aimed about an inch above my nose.

"Mind if I come up for air?" I was a sitting duck in that trap door. Fortunately he nodded and I climbed, very slowly, to ground level. The wind chill was already below forty, and yet here this guy was without a jacket. His feet were bare. "Aren't you cold?"

"A little," he said. "Ada said you were comin' to the house. No offense, but we've had strange people 'round here lately."

"Where is Ada?"

"Where we're goin'." He threw a backward glance. "Anybody follow you?"

I shook my head. "What's your name?"

"Raymundo," he said. "Okay, move."

"I don't go anywhere at gunpoint, Raymundo."

He lowered the barrel but his eyes stayed on me.

"You drive," he said.

We returned to my car and drove back down to the main road. Raymundo gave directions—a nod here, a gesture there. I never would have found my way alone.

"You're Ada's brother, huh?"

"Half brother," he said. "My mama's southern Paiute. Long time ago this was all our land. Used to be lotta my red brothers and sisters here. And more food than a man could eat. Now we got barely enough to water our horses."

"You proud of your sister, working for the sheriff and all?"

"Useta be."

"What changed your mind?"

"Turn right here." His broad face blazed in the afternoon light. "First time I looked into my nephew's face. And saw Sheriff Archer starin' back at me."

I nodded. "You can really see the resemblance around the mouth. I noticed that when I saw Espero's picture."

He registered mild interest. "What picture?"

"The one at church," I said. "Funny thing about it—Espero's eyes weren't tracking the camera. You know what might have been wrong with him?"

"Last spring he started havin' nightmares. Ada was the only one who could keep him quiet—but she always worked nights. Couple weeks ago he started wanderin' off."

"So you saw the black SUV the day he went missing?"

"Yeah, that was me. I was watchin' him on the front lawn. My eyes are off him five minutes, dude."

"What were you doing when he wandered off?"

"Fuck's that supposed to mean?"

"Did you actually see him leave?"

"I was smokin' a joint behind the barn, all right? Go ahead and arrest me if it makes you feel good."

"Take it easy, Raymundo. Your eyes are off him five minutes . . ."

He snapped his fingers. "Like that—bam. I run down to the road. No Espero. So we get in the truck and drive around. And there's that SUV, parked near the entrance to the kiddie camp. We chase it down the canyon for a while, then it gets away. Ada put out a, y'know, APB—then took it back after she found out it belonged to that rich-ass mama."

"What rich-ass mama?"

"Preacher's wife," he said. "Sheriff's daughter. She's all"—his voice reached a falsetto—"'I was scared. I thought they was gonna run me down.' How's I supposed to know who she was? That bitch probably did take Espero. Only Ada's so fuckin' meek, she just rolls over like a dog."

"And you were there when they found Espero's body."

Raymundo nodded. "And not a drop of blood in him. Obscene." He sniffed the air. "Somethin's wrong. Pull over."

I braked. "So what kind of nightmares was Espero having?"

"A man," Raymundo said. "A man with no face."

"You're telling me—"

"Holy shit." Raymundo's eyes went wide. There was a deep rumble under the tires. The steering wheel trembled.

"Holy fuckin' shit," he said. "The horses."

Then they were all around us, at full gallop down the canyon road. A moving wall of flesh and hooves, eyes rolled back white. Trailing thick plumes of dust. Or—

"Smoke!" cried Raymundo. "Oh, Jesus, fire—!"

He leapt from the car and ran against the herd, in the direction of the black column rising over the screen of junipers. I beat my horn but there was no getting round the panicked horses. By then I could hear screams.

THIRTY-THREE

The whole family had turned out to fight the flames. An entire wall of the ranch house had ripped away, and shards of aluminum siding lay scattered across the dry bunchgrass. Children were crying. As I passed the barn I saw an old man rolling on the ground, covered in a blanket. Ada's black dog lay whimpering on his side.

I grabbed a middle-aged man by the arm. "Did you call the fire department?"

He merely wept and pointed.

Raymundo was running toward the burning house. I tackled him just short of the porch. Even ten feet away the heat was enough to knock you out.

"Lemme go!" he yelled. "Ada's in there! She's—!"

"We'll go together," I said.

I pulled off my jacket and we ripped off our shirts, winding them around our faces for masks. I took my last breath of clean air and we ran inside.

My eyes swelled shut as soon as the smoke hit, and it was all I could do to keep breathing. The fire hadn't reached the living room—but there was an acrid stench from the kitchen, where the flames were hottest. Raymundo took hold of me, jabbing his finger down the hallway. A slender form lay on her stomach: Ada. I threw my jacket over her and we each took an end. She couldn't have weighed a hundred pounds, but with all the smoke it was like carrying a sack of grain up a mountain. We half-ran, half-stumbled to the porch. Two men were waiting to take her from us.

"Keep moving—," I gasped. "Propane line—"

We scrambled another twenty yards and hit the dirt. A brilliant fireball swept up from the house, bringing fresh shrieks from everyone around us. A wild clanging of metal. The shredded end of a water heater crashed less than fifteen feet from my head. Pieces of the burning house were still falling as I crawled over to Deputy Rosario. Now I saw what the fire had done to her. Flesh fell from her arm like cooked meat.

"Ada," I said. "It's Mike."

"Mister—Yeager." She was barely breathing. *"Usted aquí."*

"I'm here."

"No quiero morir," she said. "But I'm gonna . . . see my baby." She tried to smile. "Drawings . . . in the back. Under his . . . *asiento.*"

"Ada, nobody's going back into that house," I said. "Whatever was in your boy's room is gone now."

"No, no . . . ," she coughed. *"No para nada.* Please . . . not for . . . nothing . . ."

Her voice trailed off. The breath escaped her body. Raymundo was weeping. And now that it was too late for Deputy Rosario, suddenly there were all the flashing lights of the emergency vehicles.

They put an oxygen mask to Ada's face, but she wasn't breathing. One of the medics asked if I needed assistance and I waved him off. As I leaned against Ada's battered Jeep, my eyes fell on the child's car seat.

Asiento. In back. The door was locked. I walked to the rear of the ambulance as they lifted Ada's stretcher.

"Whoa, whoa." The EMT waved me off.

"Give me her car keys," I said.

"No. Absolutely no goddamn way."

"What's goin' on here?" The fire chief approached—a rough-hewn man in a yellow turnout coat.

"FBI," I said. "I'm assisting the Dupree homicide investigation. Deputy Rosario was holding evidence."

"You're tryin' to find whoever killt Dale?"

Several firefighters turned my way.

"Yes." I pointed to Ada. "So was she."

He turned to the paramedic. "Give him the keys."

A moment later the keys were in my hand, still warm from Ada's body.

"You find the bastard what killt our Dale," he said. "And you hang him from the first tree you find. Hear?"

Then he returned to the flames. The ambulance doors were closing.

"You better go with them," I said to Raymundo. "You need to be with Ada now."

"I shoulda been here sooner," he said. "I shouldna been gone so long."

"It wasn't your fault," I said.

The paramedics took Raymundo into the vehicle. A moment later the ambulance drove away.

I opened the rear door of the Cherokee, catching the slightest trace of her perfume over the smoke. Cedar and cinnamon. Under Espero's car seat was a purple spiral-bound notebook, covered with Powerpuff Girls stickers. Written on the front in big, badly formed letters: *C.S.D.*

Cassandra Sarah Dupree.

THIRTY-FOUR

It was getting dark by the time I reached Angel Hair Road. The odor of wet kitty litter greeted me as I entered the tumbledown home of Evelyn Maidstone, neighbor of the late Dale Dupree. A round-bellied man sat in the living room, watching a porn channel on TV.

"Mr. Maidstone," I said. "Sorry, but the door was open."

He didn't move. A fly lit on his spaghetti and took off again.

Somebody laughed in the darkness behind me. "Delbert don't say much since the spaceship brought him back."

Detective Tippet was leaning against the kitchen door, grinning like a demon. Wearing Durangos and a long-sleeved shirt.

"Sheriff here?" I asked.

He cocked a thumb at the kitchen. As I passed he casually reached across the doorway. For a moment I thought he was going to block my way. Then he turned the knob, leaning in close as he pushed the door open.

"Whatya lookin' at my arm for, Yeager?"

"I was just wondering if you'd rather move it or get it broken in half."

He stepped aside. I kept one eye on him as I went into the yellow kitchen.

"I heard him ask her how she was gonna get in when she didn't have a key . . ."

Evelyn Maidstone had lavender poodle hair and wore a dirty pink night-gown. A pair of long-haired cats twisted around her feet as she poured vodka into a jelly glass. Sheriff Archer was leaning against the kitchen table. He saw me but said nothing.

". . . So finally he drives away, and she's standin' there with Cassie, and—omigod! You scared the crap outa me!" Her last yelp was directed my way.

"Sorry I'm late." I turned to Archer. "I've just come back from east Dyer."

He strode past me into the living room. "I know where you were."

"Then you know Deputy Rosario is dead."

His face was hard to read in the darkened living room. "Yeah. I heard."

"But now, Sheriff!" Evelyn wobbled after us. "I forgot to tell you somethin'! When Pete was arguin' with Mary that evenin', I saw him pull her sunglasses off. And she had a big ole cut—right here." She touched beneath her left eye. "Bet you know who gave her that."

"Is that so." Archer barely seemed to listen.

Tippet shook his head. "Miz Maidstone, didn't you tell me yesterday it was her right eye?"

"I did not either."

"I think you did, ma'am. That's what I put in the description I gave to the Nevada state police."

"Oh."

"And I don't see how Mary Frances was wearin' sunglasses if you saw 'em arguing at night."

"Then it wasn't nighttime," she said. "But I know Mary Frances had an argument with Pete. He was tryin' to put his top up, and she kept wantin' him to come inside. He pulled her sunglasses off, and then he drove away. And she went in."

"You just now told me she didn't have a key." Archer waited for an answer.

"I guess . . . I musta been confused about that."

He shook his head and walked out the door. Tippet cautiously followed on his heels.

I stopped at the door. "What time would this have been, Mrs. Maidstone?"

"I'm all mixed up." Evenly frowned. "I don't know why it matters which eye. What I know is that Pete drove away. And that woulda been . . . ah hell, what time *was* that . . . ?"

"Foah thuddy," said a gravel voice behind me. It was Delbert Maidstone, not once looking up from his dirty movie.

"Something about that doesn't wash," I said, as I followed the sheriff down the driveway. "Why would Pete leave Mary and Cassie at the house in broad daylight?"

"Ask her tomorrow, she'll tell you somethin' else," Archer said. "What's the story on this fire? Chief Espy said a propane tank blew."

"That's how it was supposed to look," I said. "According to the family, the tank was nearly empty the day before. Someone must have tampered with it during the night." I turned my collar up against the cold. "Sort of like that freak accident at the Sweet Charity yesterday."

Archer stopped. "I can't see for shit out here. Tip, go fetch the car so I don't step in a gopher hole."

Tip stood his ground. "Sheriff, we got deputies on hand. Why don't I—"

"Get the goddamn car before I pound your empty head open," the sheriff barked.

Tip squinted hard, then turned away.

Archer was a silhouette against the red sky. "What'd Ada give you?"

"Not now," I said. "After what happened on the highway last night, I'm not sure I want to put anything where Tippet can see it."

"Still chasin' phantoms, are ya?" He snorted. "I don't guess you were plannin' to tell me you somehow managed to lose the Dupree photos during your mysterious scuffle."

The car engine roared to life behind us.

"You can quit lookin' for 'em," he added. "Patrolman found the envelope on the side of the highway—right where you dropped 'em, I'd venture."

"What about that negative of your daughter?"

"Guess that one musta blown away south." He was impassive. "Now I ain't gonna insult a man by askin' how critical homicide evidence got left flyin' in the breeze. But I would like to know if your bosses at the FBI put up with the kind of shit you're sellin'. First you scare hell outa Sig Lund, askin' about Dale's medical records—"

"Now why would you consider that request out of line?"

"Because it is, damn your hide. It don't make no difference how Dale got a scar on his temple. The man is dead. And tomorrow the Arizona troopers are gonna bring us Pete Frizelle, and you're gonna get a confession. And no more runnin' around cuttin' the fool in east Dyer. End of goddamn story."

"Who are you covering for, Sheriff?"

"Say that again," he said. "Go ahead."

"Or is it only yourself you're trying to protect?" I nodded. "Because you don't want anyone to know . . . just how helpless you've become?"

Now that Archer was caught in the approaching headlights, I could see the terror in his eyes. "I thought we had a deal, Mike."

"So did I, Sheriff."

His face went cold. "God damn it, no wonder that Madrigal boy died."

He stomped away, then turned. "You comin' or what?"

"I'll walk," I said.

"Suit yourself." The door slammed and the cruiser screamed past me to Dale's house.

It was easy to see why the killer had taken the trouble to approach on foot. Headlights you could spot from a mile away. But one man walking alone at night wouldn't be noticed until he was ready to show himself. I was glad for the long walk, because it gave me a chance to see Dale's home as the killer had, approaching in darkness. It also gave me a chance to cool down.

The trailer had been empty only three days, but it seemed to have been abandoned long before. Aluminum skirting was falling off the foundations. There was an empty bike rack beside a rusted set of free weights. Nobody will ever live here again, I thought, as I passed the walkway where Dale had pressed his enormous hand into the cement. Beside it was Mary's smaller, long-nailed hand. Then Cassie's delicate print. Belle's front paw. And the tiny pawprint of a cat.

The cat was watching me from the porch—a rake-thin black tom with yellow eyes. He leapt down and vanished under the foundations, then peered out and meowed.

"Here, kitty," I said. "Come on, nothing to be scared of." He shrank back—as if to say, Think again, buddy.

"That's Inky!" Evelyn Maidstone was staggering toward me. The cat disappeared. "That's their boy cat! I keep trying to feed him but he won't come. I think he must smell my kitties on me."

Maybe he just doesn't like your brand, I thought, smelling alcohol from twenty paces.

The sheriff came out on the landing. "Evelyn, go on home and don't pester the man. Yeager, this is for your benefit, not ours." I waved to let him know I'd be right there, and finally he went back inside.

"Mrs. Maidstone, wait," I said. "What were Pete and Mary arguing about?"

She sniffed. "I don't snoop on my neighbors."

"No, of course not. But if they were arguing loudly . . ."

She resettled her gown, mollified. "Mary Frances wanted to pack some clothes for Cassie, and Pete said, 'For chrissakes, we don't got room. We'll buy her new clothes.' And he said he couldn't see why all this had to happen today, and was she back on drugs. That's when she—I didn't wanna say this in front of the sheriff, but that daughter of his has a foul mouth. Mary said she wasn't gonna let no blankety-blank like Pete tell her what to do. This was all right in front of Cassie."

"What was Cassie doing while all this was happening?"

"Tryin' to keep her dog from runnin' under the house."

"They weren't restraining her in any way?"

Evelyn shook her head. "They acted like Cassie wasn't even there."

The cat appeared again, putting one paw out from under the house. This time there was no mistake. He was making eye contact with me.

Evelyn laughed. "He thinks he's people."

Inky skittered away again.

"Now I remember!" she said. "The dog was chasin' the cat, and Cassie started sayin', 'Belle, don't be mean to Inky!' Anyhow, the dog wouldn't shut up and Pete finally said, 'This is ten kinds of bullflop'—and drove away."

"Those were his exact words?"

She nodded. "Only he didn't say *bullflop*."

"Yeager," Archer said from the landing.

"One last question," I said. "I want the sheriff to hear this. What color vehicle was Pete driving that afternoon?"

She blinked. "Well, I saw a white truck about ten o'clock."

"You said they were arguing while he put his top up."

"Yes he was—wasn't he?" She stopped. "Well now, it wasn't a truck at all. Not when he came by that afternoon. It was . . . a little green convertible, all nice and new. That must've been why he said there wasn't room for Cassie's clothes. It didn't have a backseat."

"Thank you," I said.

She gave an unsteady nod and wandered away.

"What was that all about?" Archer said.

I joined him on the landing. "It's time to reopen the investigation."

THIRTY-FIVE

The crime scene crew had mopped up most of the blood, but a few dark patches still clung to the edges of the linoleum tile. Black blood soaked the wallpaper, a downward streak across the greasy range hood. The pattern was fine and narrow, like water through a straw.

"That was from the initial blow to his neck." I traced the path with my finger. "Dale was on his knees in front of the kitchen table. His head would have been right about here—" I held my hand a few inches above the bare Formica table "and his back was to the room. Tippet, come here a second."

Tippet was down the short hallway, between the bathroom and master bedroom. "What for?"

"I need you to kill me."

He looked to Archer. The sheriff nodded. Tippet straightened his shoulders and approached cautiously.

"All right, I'm Dale." I got to my knees. "In order to get the right angle on the neck, the killer wants me in this precise position. Nobody's going to just do that on command. Something has to be on this table that I want to see at eye level. If it was just an ordinary object—food, or a magazine, or whatever—Dale's natural impulse would be to lean over it. After all, he's just been in a fight, and he's got a busted hand. And the guy is almost three hundred pounds. But he gets down on his knees without thinking. Giving the killer just enough room to swing the blade down."

I looked back over my shoulder. Tippet was standing directly behind me. "You won't get a better chance than right now, Tippet."

His hand was balled in a tight fist. As his eyes met mine, a fleeting look of surprise crossed his face, quickly washed away in a sneer. "Fuck you, Yeager." He stepped two feet back.

"Okay, Mike, I get your point." Slow awareness crept across Archer's face. "What do you think they put on the table?"

"I wasn't sure before," I said. "But now I'm fairly certain it was Cassandra."

The sheriff went ghost-white. "You better make damn sure you know what you're talkin' about."

"Seconds before the murder, Dale was heard shouting Cassie's name," I said. "The killer came in—and suddenly Cassie is there. Now look at the table. Dale wasn't much of a housekeeper, but the table is clean. It was clean in the photos. When the killer came in, all he'd have to do was lay Cassie down—unconscious, maybe drugged—right there in the space prepared for her. Dale saw his daughter and instinctively got down to table level."

Archer furrowed his brow. "Tip, what do you think?"

Tippet shrugged. "Awful lotta trouble to go to, just to kill a man."

"But you will agree he was on his knees when they attacked him."

Tippet looked down, not liking this conversation one bit. "Seems that way."

"So lemme ask you," the sheriff said. "They've already got Cassie. Why do they need to kill Dale at all?"

"Good question. Obviously the murder was about more than just taking your granddaughter. Think of the moment of Dale's death. The child is on the table, like a lamb on the altar. The victim is on his knees in front of that altar. Like a ritual of sacrifice."

"All that is assuming," the sheriff mused, "that it happened the way you said."

" 'Sides which," Tippet said. "How'd they get in and out without leavin' footprints? There's only the kitchen door. The front door's blocked by the TV."

I looked down the hall. "The windows?"

"Let's take a look," the sheriff said.

There was something uncomfortably familiar about Dale's home. Without opening the cabinets I knew the drinking glasses were mostly from Taco Bell. That the big-screen TV was just barely wide enough to cover grape juice stains on the rug. I knew the television was two payments behind, that the furniture was rent-to-own. I knew that in happier times, Dale had made plans to build an addition to the trailer so they could have a nursery for their second child—a project that never got off the ground. I knew he'd never had the heart to throw away his wife's issues of *Cosmopolitan*. I knew Dale kept pictures of his Marine Corps buddies in a shoebox, and there were a few he couldn't look at without crying. Most nights he'd slept with a Coors in his hand.

I knew these things because that was how it was in the home I grew up in.

"This is the way the killers went," I said. "The blood trail tapers off past the bathroom. They probably washed up in the shower." I threw open the sink cabinet. Inside was a bottle of Bon Ami and a half-empty jug of Red Devil Lye. "You probably won't find prints, but check anyway. Christ, this guy's a fanatic."

We walked past Cassie's room. Most of the trailer was painted the same milky beige, but Cassandra's little room was a study in purple. Purple sheets, purple walls, purple everything.

"Fella could go crazy in here," Tippet said.

I opened the top drawer of her bureau. "Sheriff."

Archer looked over my shoulder. "Don't look like anything's missing."

"Unfortunately, you're right," I said. "Supposedly Mary Frances came by to pack a suitcase. But all of Cassie's clothes are here."

The sheriff's face darkened. "Guess they didn't think she . . . needed any." Archer tested the window. "Locked. And the bathroom window's too small."

"That just leaves the master bedroom," I said.

"When I was here before," Tippet said, "I saw marks in the dirt out back. Could be from a ladder."

"Go check," Archer said. Tippet left. The sheriff took a heavy breath. "I guess we better see what's in there."

The queen-size bed was still unmade, and Dale's side of the bed was slightly caved in. The mirrored closets were shut.

"Why were you sayin' it's time to reopen the investigation?"

"If Evelyn Maidstone's even close to right," I said, "Pete could not have been the guy who planned this. I'm not even sure he knew what the hell was going down."

"How—"

I took him by the arm. "Shh."

We waited. A moment later something shifted inside the closet.

Cover me, I mouthed. Archer drew the Colt from its holster as I stepped to one side of the closet.

"What was that Tippet was saying about ladder marks?" I kept my voice casual.

Whatever was in the closet moved again—a creaking board, like something scrabbling to get out.

"Dunno." Archer's hand was shaking on the revolver.

I threw the door open. Inky the cat leapt out at me.

"What the hell—?"

Now it was clear why the cat kept running under the trailer. And how the killers had left the scene. And what they had left behind. I pushed the square of carpet aside and lifted the loose subfloor. A formaldehyde smell rose from the cold earth. That was how we found Mary Frances Dupree.

THIRTY-SIX

Sheriff Archer lived in a stone-and-timber ranch house in the west end of Dyer County, and it seemed like it might have been a handsome place in its day. Years of neglect had left it a near-ruin. You could tell at a glance that no one had played or laughed or made love in that old house for years. Parked out front was a brand-new black Nissan 4 × 4. FORGIVEN FRUIT . . . TREE OF LIFE! read the bumper sticker on back.

Connor Blackwell opened the door to me, looking like a whipped greyhound. I could hear Archer shouting in the next room.

". . . God oughta mind his own rutting business." I well knew the sound in the sheriff's voice: the hoarse ranting of someone drunk beyond rage.

"It's been that kind of night," Connor said. "I guess none of us is doing well. Did you . . . see her?"

I nodded.

"Quote me one more proverb and I'll make you eat that goddamn Bible," Archer said. "You helped this happen."

"I'm not used to seeing him like this." Connor shivered. "I feel sick, Mike. I should have been more cooperative yesterday."

"It wouldn't have saved Mary's life," I said. "But I do think it's time I saw that interview with Cassie."

"I'll bring it tomorrow," he said, resigned.

"Tell me something," I said. "That picture Cassandra drew—where the man tried to hurt her puppy. Did she do anything to the face?"

He looked surprised. "Yes. She tried to erase it. How did you know?"

"I can't explain right now. Just get me that transcript. And the drawing. But be careful. Evidence has a funny way of disappearing around here."

He nodded slowly. "It must be awful, looking for somebody who's so careful about covering his tracks."

"He's careful, all right. But he's arrogant, too. The arrogance is what's going to bring him down."

"All I meant to say is—I know this hasn't been easy on you."

I shrugged. "Compared to what Cassie's going through? It's a cakewalk."

I went into the living room.

The sheriff sat upright in a morris chair, a glass of watery bourbon in his hands. There were two other highballs on the oak table. One was half-empty. The other sat untouched in front of Gavin McIntosh.

". . . good idea to send Martha and the children away," he was saying in a low voice. "At least until after Tues—"

Archer waved him off. "Mike?"

"We're done," I said. "This time I did the evidence collection myself."

"Where's my daughter?" His voice was oddly calm.

"She's with Dr. Lund," I said. "I'm just on my way back there. I thought you and I should have a few minutes alone."

"Think about what I said, Sheriff. They won't need an answer till tomorrow." Gavin stood up. "Hold on to the good memories, Rafe. Those are the ones that matter."

Archer seemed ready to lash out again, then looked at me. "Those are the ones that hurt," he said simply.

"How is Martha?" I asked the preacher.

"Terrible," he said. "Just . . . terrible. The twins took different paths over the years, but . . . the bond between them was very close."

"I heard you say Martha and the children might be going away."

"We're discussing it."

"I know this is a rough time," I said. "But I'd advise against anyone leaving. We'll need to talk to Robbie some more."

Gavin looked to the sheriff, then back to me. "I'm afraid that's out of the question. Martha is . . . well, quite frankly, she became suspicious after your last visit. She thinks you're planting ideas in Robbie's head. I know it sounds crazy, but . . . he is a very sensitive child."

"All the same—and I hope the sheriff will agree—right now is not a good time for your family to be on the move."

"Mr. Yeager, my wife is with child. I won't put her under additional strain."

"Go on home, Gavin," the sheriff said. "Chrissakes, I got men watchin' her. Ain't nothin' gonna happen tonight." He cleared his throat. "You too, Connor. I've had my fill of holy people tonight."

Connor exchanged a look of alarm with Gavin. Finally the two men left. "What are you drinkin'?"

"Nothing," I said. "What does Gavin want you to think over? Sending Martha away, or . . . ?"

"He suggested I read the writing on the wall." Archer pushed the newspaper my way.

"Yeah, I saw that. An 'electrical fire' at the Sweet Charity—"

"I ain't talkin' about the *Ledger*, for chrissakes. That there is tomorrow's Las Vegas *Sun*."

The article was dominated by a photo of the Dupree trailer: SLAUGHTER IN DYER COUNTY. Cassie's school picture topped a two-column story—in which several "highly placed sources" reported that Sheriff Archer, having botched the investigation, was crumbling under the strain.

"Finally hadda unplug the damn phone," he said. "Looks like you're gonna get your publicity, Mike."

"You didn't really expect to keep a lid on this, did you?"

He took the paper back. "Gavin's senior warden sits on the county commission. Says even if the recall vote does go my way, they're fixin' to put me on compassionate leave."

"I take it Gavin thinks you should resign and spare yourself the ordeal."

"Only person I'd be sparin' is Buford Warburton. Man can't even keep his odometers honest, and he's gonna be law and order in Dyer County." He swirled the bourbon in his glass. "I dunno, Mike. What do you think I oughtta do?"

"Sheriff, I think we have a crime to solve."

He nodded. "Damn straight. What have you got?"

"It's time for you to see what Deputy Rosario found at the courthouse." I held out the spiral-bound notebook. He hesitated only slightly before taking it.

"Most of the drawings up front are typical kid stuff," I said. "But if you turn to the back . . ."

"Good Christ."

Between the purple covers of that child's notebook, Cassandra Dupree had created a vision of hell. Drawings of children lying down in a burning building. Naked children hanging from hooks. Children cut to pieces like broken dolls. And, dominating an entire page, a portrait of a tall red-haired figure with a sharp gray line rammed into his neck. Blood sprayed backward in a narrow jet, just as it had in the Dupree kitchen. And always—in every drawing—the man with the missing face.

"Where did Ada . . . find this?" Archer said.

"As far as I can tell, in the back files for Cassie's custody hearing."

"That was two weeks ago. You're tellin' me she drew a picture of Dale's murder before it happened?"

"I'm not a big believer in ESP. But it's pretty clear she based that drawing on something she'd seen or heard about."

"Or maybe it's a forgery," he said. "Pete worked it up, sneaked it into the files—"

"Rafe," I said. "Turn to the last page."

The killers wanted Dale to be found right away. His body was left by the kitchen door. Photographs were taken and sent to the sheriff within twenty-four hours of his death. They had been no less diligent with Mary Frances. She was prepared in precisely such a way as to delay discovery.

Mary Dupree had been embalmed.

Nearly all of her blood had been drained through the left femoral artery, replaced by heavy-grade arterial and cavity fluid. The organs most susceptible to decay had been removed and were not on the scene. All of this served a practical, if morbid, purpose. But the killers hadn't stopped there. They had taken her apart. They had turned Mary Frances into a monster.

The child's drawing showed every detail.

"What was," Archer said, "what was the cause of death? Was it quick?"

I could have lied. Probably should have. "Dr. Lund isn't sure," I said. "But he thinks . . . she might have been alive for some of it."

His hand tightened, and for a moment I thought he would rip the drawing from the notebook. But he let it fall. I took it back just as he burst into tears—a powerful flood, like a dam bursting. I had never seen any man so unstrung.

"I knew I was never gonna see her again," he said. "The minute they told me about Dale I knew my baby girl was dead. I just . . . kept hoping. I'd almost rather she was guilty of murder than be dead, Mike. Ain't that crazy?"

"I'm sorry, Rafe. It's ugly." I took a breath. "But now it's time to focus on what's most important."

"Cassie."

"Yes. As long as we believed Cassandra was with her mother, we could assume Mary Frances was keeping her—if not safe, then alive. We now know that's impossible. Whoever did this to Dale—and Mary—is not going to hesitate to harm your granddaughter. Especially if she's a material witness to homicide."

"I'm gonna do it to him," he said. "What he did to Mary. So help me God, I'm gonna gut Pete Frizelle like a frog. And if he so much as touched my granddaughter—"

"Rafe, we both know Pete Frizelle was not the man who did this."

He said nothing.

"What happened to Mary takes time," I said. "Pete didn't have the time—and I honestly don't think he had the motive. If his plan was to kill Mary . . . slowly and carefully . . . he would never have left her and Cassie unattended all afternoon."

"You're basin' that on the word of an old drunk woman."

"Partly, yes. But I'm also basing it on what's right in front of your eyes." I turned the notebook around. "See what Cassie drew in both of these pictures? Standing next to her mother and father at the moment of death?" I flipped back and forth between the two drawings. "A man whose face has been deliberately rubbed out. Just like the doll Robbie called the Shadow Catcher."

"So they both play the same games. That's gotta mean somethin'?"

"Kids play the same games. They have bad dreams. They see bogeymen in the closet and nobody believes them. But three children don't independently come up with something as specific as this."

"Three?"

"Just before he disappeared, Espero dreamed about a man with no face."

"You and Sig." He looked away. "Talkin' about Ada's boy—"

"I'm talking about a boy who was murdered with the same trocars that killed your son-in-law—and drained the blood from your daughter's body." I picked up the notebook. "Your son. Espero."

Archer froze.

"Sheriff, why did you hinder the investigation of Espero's murder?" I waited. "Your daughter Martha was close by on the day he went missing. Were you protecting her?"

"Son, you are treadin' a yard too close to the fence line." His voice was like barbed wire. "Best you keep my family out of this."

Archer's face paled as his hands tightened on the chair. I took a breath, casting about for a more diplomatic approach—then decided, screw it; the old bastard needs to hear this.

"You'd best look to your family's safety." I raised my voice to match his. "Remember last night when I told you these crimes were an act of revenge? That's just what they are: a vendetta against the Archers. Unless I'm very badly mistaken, it won't stop until every member of your family pays the price."

He sneered. "Now that does sound biblical of you, Mike. And here I thought you were a man of facts."

"So let's deal with facts. Even to an outsider like me it's obvious you've got no shortage of enemies in Dyer County. Not the least of whom is a detective selling your secrets to Buford Warburton."

"Selling secrets . . ." He blinked, dazed.

"Tippet's got a hotline to Buford," I said. "The Frizelles are backing Warburton . . . and Tippet's got a dirty little secret at the Sweet Charity Ranch. Don't bother denying it. We both know he was in the other half of that picture with your daughter."

Archer was surprisingly cool. "If Tip's workin' for the Frizelles, why would he want Pete charged with murder?"

"He doesn't," I said. "Remember, *I* was his first suspect, not Pete. My guess is Tippet's letting you chase your tail on Frizelle while he pursues his own investigation. You saw him give himself away at the Dupree trailer. I asked him to 'swing the blade down'—before he caught himself, Tippet automatically stood close behind me with his fist closed. Exactly how you'd hold an icepick—or a trocar."

"So what?"

"So he's been following up on that trocar for two days—evidence that connects Dale's death to Espero's."

"You're callin' this a frame-up?"

"There's no doubt in my mind that Pete's being framed by somebody. The only question is whether you're being played—or you're the one who planted the evidence."

Archer's gray eyes were rimmed with fire.

"Take this Silverado of Frizelle's," I said. "The vehicle that ran me down was a white Chevy—with a Wild Pete's bumper sticker, no less. Every statement mentions a white Chevrolet . . . until Evelyn Maidstone corrected herself. Before I came here, I asked the Arizona state police how they knew to look for a green Jaguar, when Pete wasn't even breaking the speed limit. They told me you filed the warrant for a Chevrolet—then Detective Tippet called to amend it."

"How the hell did he know to do that?"

"Better you should ask *why*. My guess is he wanted to make sure Pete was in his custody, not yours. As far as how he knew—well, it seems Frizelle bought the Jag from Buford Warburton after his Chevy was impounded."

The sheriff brooded for a long time. "I noticed how Tip was standin' in the kitchen. And Ev's statement was a little mixed up from what he wrote. On the other hand, we are talkin' about a woman who thinks her husband was abducted by aliens."

"She's probably crazy as a loon," I said. "But she doesn't have a motivation to lie."

"And Tip does."

"He certainly stands to profit from your downfall." I pointed at the newspaper. "There's your 'highly placed source.' Think how it plays out. Tippet lets you hang yourself trying to make the case on Frizelle—then, just in time to tip the scales of the election, he and Warburton triumphantly reveal the evidence they've been sandbagging. Probably before the polls close tomorrow."

"You go to hell," he said. "You're tellin' me he'd put Cassie's life in danger for an *election?*"

"He wouldn't be the first," I said. "Sheriff, I need to hear it straight from your lips. Have you concealed or falsified evidence on this case?"

"No."

"Then why was Espero buried without an autopsy?"

"That tears it," he said. "I'm havin' another drink. And you're gonna drink with me." He stood up. "S'pose everything you're sayin' is true, Mike. How're you gonna make this case?"

"First we cut through the bullshit politics and find out what Tippet's holding. Then we reopen the Rosario investigation. We take Robbie's statement in a neutral environment. We get the deep background and put all the evidence to work on a new profile."

He poured out two glasses. "What exactly do you mean by 'deep background'?"

"I'm talking about what happened to four children at Cathedral Lake a quarter century ago. You were up there three times this weekend. You must have thought you'd find something."

"Now how would you know that, Mike?"

He thrust the tumbler into my hand. I set it down.

"Sometimes you just know things," I said. "How did you know I didn't kill Dale?"

"I showed you the photos," he said. "And I looked into your eyes."

"And what did you see?"

He half-smiled. "Somebody who needed a second chance."

"Speaking of those photos," I said, "I'm going to need them back."

He slid the envelope across his coffee table.

"Try not to lose 'em this time," he said. "Wanna know what I see now?"

Archer drained his glass.

"I see myself," he continued. "The boy-scout deputy I was thirty years ago. Pure of heart. Arrogant. An almighty angel of justice. You know what justice is? I'll save you thirty years, Michael Francis Yeager. Pain. World gives you pain, you give pain back. Blood for blood. The goddamn election don't matter. God himself don't matter. All that matters is *they hit me*—and when somebody does that, you hit back so hard they don't have time to pray for death."

"That's vengeance, Sheriff. Not justice."

His mouth drew back in a cheerless smile. "Know what else I see? You, in some air-conditioned office at the FBI. Wearin' a tie so tight it's liable to choke while you tell your bosses it's time to arrest Tonio Madrigal's dad. You're so ready to fry him you can taste it. Only you don't have the smokin' gun. But you sure as shitfire had it the next time you sat down in that office—didn't you just?"

"The camera," I said. "The one that took the picture of Tonio."

His eyes glittered like steel pennies. "Was it really? Or just kinda sorta like that camera? Did it somehow magically appear—say, in a safety deposit box that only Papa Bear had the key to? And when somebody else had the bad manners to be guilty . . . did anyone ask if Agent Yeager of the FBI might've actually planted evidence?"

"Are you trying to frighten me off this case?"

"Not at all, Mike. I'm tellin' you why I wanted you in the first place. You and me, we're cut from the same hide. Both of us shoot to kill. And neither one above makin' his own justice."

"I don't know where you get your information," I said. "But no action's been taken by the FBI Office of Professional Responsibility. And I promise you I told them the truth."

" 'No action taken,' " he chuckled. "The truth is you didn't care about the truth. All you wanted was to hurt somebody. No shame, son. Every law-man does it once or twice. You could say it's how you bust your cherry."

"And how many times have you done it, Sheriff?"

"Only as often as the world's fucked me. A wolf takes a calf, a wolf dies. The herd stays happy."

"What if you get the wrong wolf?"

"Drink your drink," he said.

I took the pictures and stood up. "I don't think so, Sheriff. Either you fire me now, or I'm driving back to assist in your daughter's autopsy."

He picked up my glass and poured it into his. "You're not fired."

"What are you going to do about Tippet?"

"I'll take care of Tip."

"Like you promised to take care of Ada Rosario?"

"Like I been takin' care of my herd for thirty years."

"Purely for my peace of mind, Sheriff: Who protects the herd from you?"

Rafe Archer merely lifted his glass and drank. I left him that way—alone in his empty, dying house.

THIRTY-SEVEN

The wagon from Freebairn & Son Funeral Home was pulling away from Lund's office just as I arrived. Dr. Lund waited on the loading dock.

"North wind's always the cruelest." He shivered as he pulled the rolling door shut. "How did Rafe take the news?"

"Badly," I said. "What was that van doing here?"

"They're burying Dale tomorrow," he said. "I didn't want to give him up, but it seems Rafe approved it this afternoon."

"Did you get everything you needed?"

"As much as I'm going to." He sighed. "I suppose it's all for the best. I've only got the one table . . . and Dale always knew to give up his place for a lady."

Coming from him it didn't sound like gallows humor. Lund looked awful. Mary Frances lay across the autopsy table where her ex-husband had been only hours before. I had a hard time looking her way. My eyes drifted instead to the slight, sheeted form on a wheeled gurney. Ada Rosario. A charred odor mingled with the scent of preservative.

"I was hoping Davis Freebairn would come himself. This embalming business is over my head. So many of my usual cues—histology, blood, decomposition—all shot to hell. But he won't set foot in here." He threw me a look. "What's on your mind?"

"I spoke to Freebairn this afternoon," I said. "The trocars were stolen from his funeral home three weeks ago."

"Yes." He nodded slowly. "That would follow, wouldn't it?"

"Why won't he help you?"

"Davis used to be coroner, until Rafe had him fired. Guess he's still bitter. Lord knows why. It's no great joy to me."

We stood on opposite sides of the table, looking down at the body of Mary Frances Dupree. Her right eye stared sightlessly, its gray iris reflecting the autopsy light. The entire left half of her face was gone.

"I've seen people die," I said. "I've never seen anything like this."

"People are . . . so very easily broken." He ran his hand softly through Mary's bleached hair. "It's the only part of her they didn't mutilate. Only part that . . . feels like her."

"Probably they didn't want to slow down identification."

"Even as they raped her humanity from her," he said. "Just like Dale."

"Not exactly. Dale's death was all about surprise. Quick, violent, bloody. If everything had gone perfectly, he wouldn't have felt a thing. With Mary they took their time. They wanted her in mortal agony. And yet . . ."

"And yet there are no ligature marks," he said. "Or any defensive cuts."

I nodded. "Almost as if she submitted willingly."

He shuddered, as if that was too horrible to contemplate. "That hole in her belly was the very first thing they did." His face twisted in rage. "I'm sorry, Mr. Yeager. I can't keep doing this."

He pulled a heavy plastic sheet over Mary Frances.

"When you look at this poor woman," he said, "what do you see?"

"Pain," I said. "Cruelty."

"Mary Frances was pregnant, Mr. Yeager. That's why they cut her abdomen first. They made her watch. Do you understand? They. Made. Her. Watch."

He removed his gloves and slumped into a couch.

"How did you know?" I asked.

"She came to me two months ago," he said. "I tried to warn her that Dale wouldn't be overjoyed."

"Because it wasn't his," I said. "Frizelle's?"

He nodded. "Mary Frances was a silly child. She actually did it on purpose. Of course she had to tell Dale. And he put his fist through a wall. Whenever he was afraid of losing control . . . he would take it out on some inanimate object. Or himself."

"And you treated that hand."

"They didn't know how to do anything but hurt each other," he said. "They'd always come back to me . . . broken and bewildered . . . and I'd try to put them back together. I suppose I owed it to them."

"Owed them for what?"

He looked up as if he'd been caught speaking his thoughts aloud.

"Dr. Lund, I get the feeling you want to tell me something, but you're afraid. I can be sympathetic to a point, but eventually I'm going to lose patience."

Lund was silent for a moment. "Do you know what a tontine is, Mr. Yeager?"

"Some kind of insurance scheme," I said. "The last survivor collects everything."

"That is precisely what I'm bound to. Except in my case, I collect nothing but secrets. My reward is to carry those secrets to the grave."

"Doesn't sound like much of a payoff."

"It isn't. But if it's broken, innocent people will suffer."

"Innocent people already have."

Lund rubbed his eyes. "Tell me what you've learned so far."

"This is all about revenge on the sheriff. The closer the victims are to him, the worse they die. Which means Archer himself is almost certainly on the killer's list."

Lund nodded. "But surely not until he's been forced to watch the others die before him."

"Exactly. Our subject may have cherished revenge fantasies for years—then something triggered him to act. Probably this recall election, which suddenly made Archer vulnerable. The killer loves weakness. He's got a lone-wolf mentality . . . waits until his victim's most in need of help, then strikes without mercy."

Lund raised an eyebrow. "Or perhaps in his own way, he thinks he is being merciful. Have you considered the choice of weapons?"

"I did find it interesting that in all three murders, he employed a surgical instrument that's normally used for pregnant women and embalming."

"Birth and death," he said. "What does that suggest?"

"He wants to be God."

"And God is both just and compassionate. Not so?" He pulled himself to his feet. "It's a very ancient and storied thing, the trocar. Roman surgeons used something like it to drain toxic humors from the body . . . making holes to let the poison out. Since then, fiber-optic cameras and harmonic scalpels have replaced bloodletting. Even so, beneath its scientific veneer, the trocar is essentially a magical device—releasing disease, evil spirits . . ."

"Ghosts?"

"If you like. The point is not to overlook the possibility that your killer may see himself as benevolent. At the very least, in the service of a higher power. And his victims are, to his own mind, willing sacrifices."

I nodded. "That's why he wanted Dale to invite him in. The subject needed to believe he had permission to kill. And afterward, rituals of undoing to absolve himself—wrapping the flag around Dale's head, laying Espero's body on his mother's doorstep . . ."

"And putting Mary under the house," Lund said. "Always bringing the victims home."

I watched him look at me, then away.

"You know who he is, don't you, Doctor?"

"Yes—and no." He turned back to me. "The only person I could reasonably suspect . . . is someone who couldn't possibly be responsible."

"Why not?"

"Because this person is no longer alive."

"You know, when Dale mentioned somebody coming back from the grave, I'll admit I thought he was crazy. But when a guy like you starts talking about the undead . . ."

"I'm not asking you to believe me," he said. "Frankly, I've said more than I should. If Rafe even suspected we were having this conversation—"

"Doctor, you are district coroner. These people were once patients under your care. Are you honestly telling me your loyalty to Archer comes first?"

"For the love of God," he said in a cornered voice. "Don't you think my heart bleeds? I made my bargain long ago. I'm not proud of myself. But this—it's between you and Rafe. He holds the contract on this particular tontine."

"Some insurance scheme." I pointed at Mary and Ada. "His own daughter, his mistress—"

Lund's eyes registered surprise. "You knew about Ada?"

I nodded. "These women are dead. And yet Archer sits there like the great stone face. This is more than grief. If I didn't know better, I'd say he was—terrified by this case. Or haunted."

"Rafe's old, but he's not superstitious. He doesn't believe in ghosts any more than I do. I will tell you this, but then you must leave."

"Go ahead."

"You said you'd never seen anything like Mary Frances's murder. Or Dale's, I'm sure. But I have. And so has Rafe."

"What?" I said. "When?"

"A long time ago. And what happened then is happening now."

I waited. "And that's all you have to say."

"It's more than I should have told you." He drew a resolute breath and opened the door to the wind. "I'm going to begin my autopsy now, Mr. Yeager. I should take it as a kindness if you'd leave."

I moved for the door.

"Suit yourself," I said. "I'll find out on my own."

"You won't find anything more tonight," he said. "Tired people make mistakes. Especially the walking wounded. Did you get your prescription filled?"

I shook my head.

"Take your medicine." His voice was oddly gentle. "Hardy's drugstore should still be open. You'll see better when your mind is clear."

I went to the door. "Whose lives are you—protecting—with this bargain of yours, Doctor?"

"Yours, for one." He inspected my bandage. "Safe journey, Mr. Yeager."

THIRTY-EIGHT

Hardy's drugstore was a carefully reconstructed relic of old Americana, complete with a brass-rail soda fountain. Vintage ads for old patent medicines and snake-oil remedies cluttered the walls. Hardy himself, a porkpie of a man, cheerfully took my prescription.

"Bitch of a night, huh? I'm thinkin' early winter this year." He leaned in close. "You know the difference between the desert and a woman?"

"I guess I'm about to find out."

"The desert only turns green when it gets wet," he said. "A woman only turns wet when she gets some green." He laughed hard enough to bulge his veins. "Say, lemme get this for ya." He looked at it and shook his head. "Doc finally got some religion?"

"Hm?"

He handed it back. Under his hieroglyphic scrawl, Lund had clearly written:

LUKE 15:18

I paid and started to leave. Hardy whistled at me. "Don't you want the rest?"

"The rest of what?"

He gave me a printed coupon.

℞ ONE (1) SCOOP ICE CREAM
ANY FLAVOR

ADMINISTER AS NEEDED
NO REFILLS

"No charge to Sig Lund's little patients," he said.

Three boxes from the county clerk were waiting for me at the motel: DYER
COUNTY LEDGER, 1977–78. I spent an hour sorting through the microfiche
copies, then opened my Gideon Bible to the Gospel According to St.
Luke—chapter fifteen, verse eighteen:

> I will arise and go to my father, and will say unto him,
> Father, I have sinned against heaven, and before thee, and
> am no more worthy to be called thy son: make me as one of
> thy hired servants.

I skimmed through my copy of *Arise and Go,* then reached for the phone.

"The dead speak!" exclaimed Special Agent Hiraka. "How've you been
keeping yourself, chief?"

"In trouble, as usual. Where's your boss, Yoshi?"

"Peg's probably in bed, Mike. It's going on two A.M. here in Philly."

"I couldn't raise her at home. Can you patch me through? It's important."

"Sure." He seemed to hesitate. "Anything I can help you with?"

"Maybe. Do Shintos have Bible study?"

"For the record, Mike, I'm Presbyterian. Whatya got?"

"Bible stories," I said. "The parable of the prodigal son."

"Isn't that where the bad son blows his father's inheritance and gets a
fatted calf?"

"He gets forgiveness, yeah. The Bible doesn't say what happened next.
Probably locked his dad away in some third-rate nursing home. Anyhow,
there's a preacher out here named Gavin McIntosh. Started a church
called"—I checked the back cover—"Tree of Life Interdenominational Min-
istries. He wrote a whole book about prodigal sons. See if there's anything
funny on their nonprofit status."

"I'll talk to my guy at Treasury. Anything else?"

"I need to know if there were any child abductions or mutilations in this
area between the summer of nineteen seventy-seven and the fall of nineteen seventy-eight."

He whistled. "It's gonna be tough pulling records that far back. Any matching features?"

"The primary weapon would have been a medical instrument called a trocar. That's spelled—"

"It's okay, I know what you're talking about."

"You do?"

"My wife just had an amniocentesis. We're gonna have a little girl. Wicked cool, eh?"

I flinched. Even by the FBI's starched-collar standards, Yoshi's ability to compartmentalize was mind-boggling. "Yeah, Yoshi. Very wicked cool."

"Seems like they'd have this information locally, wouldn't they? Police morgue? Serial killer trading cards?"

"You'd think so. I've got a whole stack of printouts here. . . ." I rifled through the newspapers. "No mention of child abductions during the fall of 'seventy-eight. Or any major crimes, period. On the other hand, the paper did have this regular feature called 'Cute Baby of the Week.' . . ."

"Maybe we should check the names of those babies," he said. "Sometimes those contests are fronts."

"I think it's just filler. Looks like they're recycling the same five or six babies week after week."

"Whatever happened in nineteen seventy-eight, it's not half what Peggy's gonna do if she finds out I'm working for you on her clock."

"Put me through to her."

"Uh-oh, Mom and Dad are gonna fight."

The phone rang several times. I was all set to leave a message when a man answered.

"Hello?" yawned a sleepy baritone.

"I'm sorry, I was looking for . . . Agent Weaver . . ."

"Hang on." He put his hand over the phone. "Punkin? It's one of your boys."

"What's happening?" Peggy was alert as usual.

"Please tell me you're not sleeping with somebody who calls you 'Punkin.' "

"Mike?" she said. "Oh no."

"I was just thinking about your big warm bed in Hunting Park. I guess my intel on Tyler wasn't so far off after all."

"I have to go to another phone," she said. "On second thought, now is not the right time for this conversation."

For a moment there was only strained silence.

"I shouldn't have bothered you," I said finally. "I've got trouble here. My trailer-park homicide is a serial murderer. Four victims so far, all relatives of the sheriff. One of them is his illegitimate son."

She was alert now. "How old?"

"Six. At first I thought Archer was just blind to the evidence connecting these murders. But he's blocking the investigation, Peg. He's trying to shut me down."

"Even with his own granddaughter on the line?"

"He wants her back," I said. "But he's got secrets. I think he's afraid of being exposed. Tonight he even tried to blackmail me."

"Blackmail you how?"

"The camera. That whole evidence-planting thing on the Madrigal case."

"Shit, that guy hits below the belt."

"Yeah. Anyway, if you've got time for a conference call tomorrow . . ."

I heard fingers tapping on a keyboard. "How's eight A.M. your time?"

Good old Peggy: an old boyfriend on the phone and a new one in the sack, and still keeping her calendar organized. "Eight A.M.'s just fine. I should let you know, I've already got Yoshi working on background."

"Forgiveness is easier than permission," she said. "What kind of background?"

"Better I read it to you." I opened Gavin's book. " 'Sometimes the best way to get a second chance—' that's our local minister talking '—is to offer a second chance to somebody else. Case in point: By the end of the 1970s, our Arizona ministry had fallen on hard times. But a small donation we'd made to a Nevada summer camp had meanwhile reaped a windfall. The local sheriff, Rafe Archer, said the camp was closing and wanted to repay me with interest. Thus began a warm friendship that ultimately brought Tree of Life to Dyer County . . . and introduced me to my beautiful wife.' "

"I take it that's not the end of the story."

"Cathedral Lake is where the water used to come from. It also seems to be related to something terrible that happened to Dupree and the Archer girls back in nineteen seventy-eight. The camp was burned—crime reports and medical files are nonexistent—and now somebody's killing the survivors."

"What kind of somebody?"

"By the book? I'd say—white male, mid-to-late thirties, athletic build. He's organized, aware of consequences, minimizes risk . . ."

"Not impulsive."

"Absolutely not. The subject knows his victims, knows the area—so he's got to be local. Probably a native."

"How's the search for photography suppliers going?"

"I had a deputy working on it, but—" I halted, grimly recalling Ada's charred form on the autopsy table. "She died before she could turn anything up. So far as I can tell from her notes, there haven't been any recent shipments to Dyer County. Which doesn't prove much. The developer has a long shelf life as long as you keep it in powder form—the subject could have bought it years ago. Film is a different matter. From the quality of the prints I think we're looking at four-by-five sheet film—it's fragile and it doesn't keep. Also you can leave thumbprints while handling it . . . which of course our subject didn't. The bastard's too careful for that."

"He's got to have some kind of day job to afford all of this," she said.

"And he's highly socialized. He can approach his victims without arousing suspicion. He's got a mammoth ego—loves to dangle clues in front of us—so he's going to stay close to the investigation. We'll see who shows up at Dale's funeral tomorrow." I rubbed the back of my neck. "Anything else I've forgotten?"

"You said something earlier today about paying the piper."

"It's a long shot. Robbie wrote this strange play for his school pageant— all about children being tortured and forced to serve the piper under his bloody mountain."

"As I recall, the story ends with only a crippled child left behind," she said. "Seems a little advanced for a seven-year-old."

"Maybe he had help," I said. "It'd either have to be someone from the church or school. Or family. Martha was suspiciously close by on the day Espero went missing, and Gavin's apparently being blackmailed by the sheriff. Meanwhile Archer's still stuck on Frizelle. He's either got serious tunnel vision or one hell of a guilty conscience." I waited. "You're thinking about something. What's wrong?"

"Why did the sheriff think he could blackmail you?"

I said nothing.

"The Office of Professional Responsibility never actually charged you with manufacturing evidence," she said. "We all know you didn't plant that camera, right? So who gives a rat's ass?"

"What if . . ." I took a deep breath. "What if I did, Peg?"

She didn't answer for a long time.

"'Then I guess you got away with it." Her voice was empty.

"Sure," I said. "The herd stays happy."

I could hear snoring in the background.

"Is Punkin already asleep?"

"Not everybody on this planet is an insomniac," she said. "It might be a good idea if we . . . forgot about this part of the conversation."

"I should have told you, partner. I let down the team."

"Yeah. Well. I didn't tell you about Taylor."

"Tyler," I said. "I don't think there's much comparison there."

"Is there somebody for you, Mike? Somebody special?"

"Well, I . . . did discuss Barbie dolls with a teacher today."

"Mike, don't make fun of me."

"There's nobody special," I said. "I didn't mean to kid you about Tyler. It's none of my business."

"I almost wish it was," she said. "When you left . . . I only dated him because I didn't expect it to get serious. Then just in the last few days, things sort of . . ."

"Happened?"

She sighed. "I guess I got tired of pretending there was an easy way back for you and me. That you'd come home . . . and that it would be like none of it ever happened."

"That's interesting."

"What do you mean, 'that's interesting'? You jerk, I'm telling you how I feel."

"No, sweetie. I think you just gave me an insight. Maybe this isn't a cover-up, exactly. Maybe it's . . . denial."

"How so?"

"Like when there's abuse in a family. Everyone's got these . . . strange scars. But if you call attention to it, they all close ranks. 'You never saw that. It didn't happen.' And if that doesn't work—"

"They start getting violent," she said. "Because they're covering up their own guilt?"

"Maybe. Remember what I said yesterday about family secrets? The signature of these crimes points to something very personal. And deeply buried. As long as nobody speaks up . . . it's like it never happened."

"Except that it's happening again," she said. "Which means . . ."

". . . Somebody's trying to break the silence," I said. "I'm glad we had this conversation, Peggy."

"Yeager, you're unbelievable. You call me in the dead of night . . . confess to planting evidence in a major homicide case . . . I tell you I'm with somebody else . . . and you're happy we had this conversation."

"It can't be serious with Tyler," I said. "Has he seen you in your duck pajamas yet?"

"Not yet." We both laughed.

"Be honest, Peggy Jean. You're disappointed in me."

"Part of me always—wondered about that camera," she said. "Jesus. I am disappointed. I mean, I know you were under a lot of pressure . . ."

"It was shameful, what I did. To tell the truth, I was more afraid of losing your respect than anything the OPR might do. But finally I . . . just couldn't live with the secret."

"Mike, never mind my respect. You could have gone to jail."

"Maybe I deserved to," I said. "When I told them, I honestly expected to get crucified. But they decided to cover it up."

"For the honor and reputation of the Bureau," she said. "Same old story."

"Exactly. They'd bury the report, I'd go quietly, and—"

"—It'd be like nothing ever happened," she said. "Strange how these patterns keep repeating themselves."

"Yes," I said. "Strange."

THIRTY-NINE

I worked a while longer on the newspapers, then turned back to the Dupree photo set. The killer's photographs didn't look much like they'd spent the night on a roadside. As a matter of fact, they seemed nearly as pristine as the moment Archer first showed them to me. Still, I checked them . . . studied them . . . held them to the light until I was absolutely certain.

Photograph Number 21 had been changed.

Superficially they were identical: extreme close-up of Dale's neck wound, hands clutching the trachea. There was even a small dog-ear in the upper right corner, same as before. But in the original version, the camera was tightly focused on Dale's Marine Corps ring while the rest of the image blurred away. Now the entire frame was in perfect focus. And the ring was gone.

Who had changed those pictures—and why?

It was past two A.M. and I was wired as hell. My sight was blurred and the base of my skull was on fire, but no way was I going to take Dr. Lund's pills. I was glad of the hurt. I had to stay wired.

The phone rang.

"Mike."

"Who's this, Yoshi?"

"Michael Francis Yeager." The voice was clipped, tuneless. "Of the FBI."

"Yeah?"

"Understand you're looking for assistance."

"I might be. Who is this?"

"Just a couple of questions, Mike. Do you beat off?"

"Do I what?"

"Your dick, sir. Do you masturbate thinking about her little hairless pussy? What gets you off?"

Someone giggled in the background.

"Look, whoever you are, you've just done a very stupid thing."

The phone clicked off. I picked up, dialed the front desk. The manager answered on the seventh ring.

"*Que?*" he said. "Ah, man. You know what time—?"

"Who did you just put through to my room?"

"*Que?*"

"Never mind. I'm coming down."

I slammed the phone down. It rang again.

"Look, I can trace this call—"

"I can trace *you* pictures of her runny little ass," said the robotic voice. "Or her naked spinal column. Dripping pretty pink fluid on the butcher paper."

I steadied my voice. "Maybe this is just a crank call. Or maybe you know something. Either way—"

"Maybe I'll take your pretty blue eyes in exchange," he said. "And fornicate with the empty sockets. You're a very lucky boy, Mikey. You're about to hear the voice of God."

Then he hung up.

I ran downstairs to the lobby. The manager, in T-shirt and jockeys, was staggering to answer his desk phone. I grabbed it away from him. The caller ID briefly flashed UNKNOWN just as I heard the dial tone.

Now the pay phone outside was ringing.

"Stay there," I said to the manager. "Under no circumstances answer that phone."

I ran outside, picked up the pay phone and steeled myself. "Am I speaking to the person who is holding Cassandra Dupree?"

There was no answer. Only a loud hiss, like static. Or . . . a tape recording.

"*Jesus, am I glad to see you.*" It was Dale's voice. "*I'm in a world of hurt.*"

A gospel TV program played in the background. Cloth or canvas brushed the microphone.

"*Oh Christ,*" Dale said. "*Is that . . . omigod, baby! Cassie baby! Oh God, what happened to my little girl?*"

He was whimpering. Something heavy was set down.

"*Cassie, sweetie, it's Daddy, can you talk to Daddy? Can you talk to Daddy—Oh God, she's not breathing—!*"

A sound of scraping metal. Then the moist, sickening thud of steel on flesh. And again. Something wet splashed the microphone, dulling the sound of the blade.

"OH GOD—JESUS GOD PLEASE DON'T—"

The tape recorder clicked off.

"What do you want?" I said.

"Tell him he should have paid attention," said the deadened voice. Then I heard a sing-song response from inside the phone box: *shooda ped attention*. An acrid smell of ozone. Sparks leapt to my hand as I flung the receiver away. I threw the lobby door open.

"Get down!" I shouted to the manager. "Get—!"

The lobby's front window shattered behind me.

FORTY

For long seconds there was only smoke and the feeble whine of a fire alarm. Glass and sheetrock crunched under my knees as I rose from my duck-and-cover position. A few weak flames danced along the smoking shell of the phone booth.

"*Madre santa del Dios.*" Blood dripped from the manager's forehead. "Whatchoo do to my telephone, man?"

Six hours later I arrived in Langhorne to find the town square jammed with cars. People swarmed in and out of the courthouse door while a leather-faced man harangued the crowd through a megaphone.

"*. . . justice for Pharisees and publicans!*" he said. "*But there's no justice for Cassandra Dupree! There's no justice for Mary Dupree's unborn baby! Why are there no protections for the murders of innocent . . .*"

He thrust a tract into my hand: FEAST OF THE INNOCENTS! THOUSANDS DIE IN CULTS EACH YEAR!

"*. . . children?*" he shouted. "*Their blood cries up from the ground, Sheriff Archer! God's judgment will not sleep forever!*"

It was Tuesday, November 4. The people of Dyer County had come to vote.

"You're a lucky man, Mr. Yeager, and no mistake," said Dr. Lund. "But I do wish you'd stop tweaking the nose of the Almighty."

Lund sat pensively on the other side of my desk. Archer was in seclusion at home, so it was just the two of us in my office—and the voices on my speakerphone.

"Whoever set that charge, it wasn't God." I leaned in to the speaker box.

"Sheriff, the other voices you'll be hearing are Special Agents Weaver and Hiraka. Peg runs the Philadelphia child abduction squad and Yoshi works the VICAP databases—the FBI's Violent Crime Apprehension Program. Okay to proceed?"

"Go on." Archer's voice was threadbare, strangely distant.

"It's gonna be a difficult bomb to trace," I said. "You can buy the ingredients at any grocery store. Homemade plastic explosive using paraffin and bleach—plus camp stove gas for accelerator."

Dr. Lund raised an eyebrow. "Bleach?"

"Potassium chlorate," Yoshi said. "There's trace amounts in laundry bleach. Mike, did you recover any part of the detonator?"

"It nearly decapitated the motel clerk," I said. "There's fragments, but they'll take time to reassemble."

"You say you heard a voice repeating something?"

"That's right. The caller said, 'Tell him he should have paid attention.' A moment later, I heard it again. Only this time it was . . . synthesized. Like a computer talking."

"Could be a voice-tone detector," he said. "The subject might have programmed it to recognize a certain spoken phrase and then rigged it to the detonator. Kind of strange that it repeated the words back."

"Maybe he just wanted to make sure the message got through," I said. "Where would he get something like that?"

"These gizmos are everywhere nowadays—cell phones, security devices, executive toys. Check your nearest Radio Shack. He's not gonna risk using the mails."

"He stole that embalming equipment locally," I said. "So he knows where to find what he needs. And the fact that he had to steal could mean he was scrambling for time. Otherwise he wouldn't take the risk." I checked my calendar. "I suggest active planning for the murders began approximately two to three weeks ago—no later than October tenth, the date of the break-in at Freebairn & Son."

"Mike, you do realize," Peggy said, "there could be other bombs waiting around for you to set them off."

"He could have killed me last night if he'd wanted to. Obviously he didn't. Any luck tracing those calls, Yoshi?"

"Hacked cell phone," he said. "Probably threw it away by now. Did you pick anything up from the conversation?"

"He has help. At one point I definitely heard somebody giggling."

"Giggling?" It was the sheriff.

"That's right. High-pitched laughter."

"What about behavioral clues?" asked Peggy.

"Emotionally he seems arrested at the pulling-wings-off-flies stage. He kept parroting my words back . . . a grotesque fascination with body parts. The whole thing almost played out like a prank call."

"Maybe it was a prank," Yoshi said.

"The subject played a tape of Dale's murder," I said. "It confirms that Cassandra was used to control Dupree. At one point—I'm sorry, Sheriff, I have to say this—Dale said, 'She's not breathing.' "

The room was silent for a moment.

"Let's . . . move on," Archer said at last.

"Before he detonated the bomb," Peggy said, "he specifically threatened you."

"Specifically he offered to pluck out my eyes and have sex with the empty sockets."

Yoshi chuckled. "Did he offer to buy you dinner first?"

"Excuse me," said Dr. Lund. "Could you explain just what you mean by 'arrested child'?"

"Peg, you wanna take that?"

"It's a pattern we see in certain adult survivors of abuse," she said. "They can't develop emotionally past the point of trauma. If they grew up with a parent who makes impossible demands . . . cloaks abuse as 'discipline' or 'training' . . . the kid can develop a massive, extremely fragile ego. What we call *toxic narcissism*. This is reinforced if the other parent is absent or extremely passive."

"Thank you. But . . ." The doctor looked anxiously at me. "Obviously there are many abuse survivors. Surely they don't all grow up to kill."

"No, of course not," she said. "There are other factors—brain damage, attachment disorder. Mainly you have to be taught that other people's lives don't matter."

"This guy can torture people to death and wonder what's for lunch," I said. "Maybe he feels guilty afterward . . . but then he does something nice for the victim and the bad feelings go away. His only true emotions are rage—and satisfaction. Like the power rush a kid gets from playing an extremely violent game. It doesn't matter if the victims cry out, because their suffering isn't real. Death is fun."

" 'As flies to wanton boys,' " Dr. Lund muttered.

"Pardon?"

He waved the thought away.

"So why do the children show him without a face?" Yoshi asked.

"It's too consistent for chance," I said. "If he had prolonged contact with the children, then he might have instructed them to draw him that way. Maybe that's how he sees himself. As a faceless man."

Lund raised his eyebrows. "Rafe?"

Archer cleared his throat. "Sounds to me like the little man who wasn't there."

"He's real," I said. "He knows where the bodies are buried in Dyer County. He knows you, Sheriff. And he wants your complete attention."

"Attention."

"Those were his final words. 'Tell him he should have paid attention.'"

Archer was silent a moment. "Mike, is Pete in custody yet?"

"Not yet. You wanna be there when I talk to him?"

"Ain't decided. We done here?"

"I think so. Yoshi?"

"Um, yeah. About that request for information on the church. What was that Bible verse again . . . ?"

Lund looked at me in alarm.

"Lemme get back to you on that, Yosh. Peg—thanks for the support, guys."

"Be careful, Mike." They clicked off.

Lund leaned into the speakerphone. "Rafe, we gonna see you at the funeral today?"

"I dunno, Sig. I'm feelin' poorly. Musta drunk outa the wrong side o' the glass. Mike, those other folks still here?"

"No, they're gone."

"Pick up a second." I lifted the receiver.

"You're gonna be the one to question Frizelle," he said. "That boy won't talk to me. He hates my guts. Even more, I reckon, since what I did to his mama's whorehouse. Use it, understand? Use his hatred for me. Tell him he could have been the one. Say exactly that."

"What does that mean, Sheriff?"

"And don't be fooled by his guile. You back off, give him wiggle room, he'll repay you with a fang in your heel."

"Guilty or not, we've got him cold for interstate flight from a homicide. If he has information, he'll trade." I waited. "Cassandra, Rafe."

"You don't need to remind me about my granddaughter. Now I'm grateful for all this outside help, but this is still Dyer County. No deals. Frizelle's gonna burn for what he did."

"And if he hasn't done anything?" He didn't answer. "I think you should know, I did invite Detective Tippet to this call. It seems he's busy planning an afternoon press conference with Mr. Warburton."

"You were right about Tippet," he said. "Little bastard sold me south."

"I need to ask you something point-blank. Did you replace any of the photographs in the Dupree set before you gave them back to me last night?"

"No. Why?"

"One of the pictures is different. And I don't know why. But it seems like there was important information, and now it's gone." I listened. "Sheriff?"

There was no answer. Archer had hung up.

"Doc, do you think we're dealing with an officer of the law here? Or just a grieving parent?"

"I've never seen him this bad," said Lund. "Never."

"Did he even know what we were saying half the time?"

"He knew." Lund went to the window. "The real question is, why do you persist in telling a man what he refuses to hear?"

"It's my duty to be hardheaded."

"Duty—or punishment?" He peered sideways at me. "Since you came here you've been imprisoned, threatened—and now twice put in danger of your life. Clearly you have friends in Philadelphia who value your life . . . and yet here you are, in a place where no one's life has value. You have little to gain in Dyer County and everything to lose. So what are you really staying for?"

"What happens if I leave?"

He solemnly shook his head. "Nothing that hasn't been happening here for a very long time. The election will end. The reporters will go seeking the next atrocity. Horrors will continue to thrive behind closed doors. Life, such as it is, will go on."

"But not for Cassandra," I said.

He looked straight at me. "And who is Cassandra to you? Merely a way to burnish your laurels? Or atone for past sins?"

"It's my—"

"Your what? Your job?" He raised an eyebrow.

"Yes. My job." I held his gaze. "You know, Agent Weaver asked me a similar question. And I said I wanted to know that I still could. Save a child, I mean. I never used to wonder why. I just did what I did, and I was good at it. Then something happened back east . . . and suddenly I couldn't any more. And if I'm not useful—if I'm not capable . . ."

". . . If you're not someone who saves children, then who are you?" He smiled gently. "Is that it?"

There was no answering that. I paced over to the window. Down in the square, the megaphone man was being herded away by deputies.

"I want that guy's name," I said.

"He's harmless," Lund said. "Loud but harmless."

"What was that you were saying before?" I asked. "About flies and children?"

"It's from Shakespeare's *King Lear*. 'As flies to wanton boys are we to the gods. They kill us for their sport.' For all the wonders of childhood . . . they really don't know what it means to feel another living creature's pain. But what happens to the ones who never learn?"

"They become predators."

"Ah. Then who's more to blame? The monster . . . or the one who makes him?"

I shrugged and closed the blinds. "What exactly does Luke 15:18 mean? Are you pointing the finger at Reverend McIntosh?"

"It means exactly what it says. Four came home from the mountains. But five went in. And now the prodigal has returned."

"Your dead man again?"

"Only to appearances," he said. "*Fronti nulla fides*, Mr. Yeager. First watchword of forensics. Place no faith in appearances."

He opened the door. Deputy Clyde was standing in the hall. There was a fresh bandage on his nose.

"Agent Yeager, sir," he said. "We got Pete Frizelle."

FORTY-ONE

Lund accompanied me as far as the interview room. A fat little man with a briefcase waited impatiently outside.

"Who's the sourpuss?" I asked.

"Attorney." The doctor shook my hand. "Good luck, Mike."

As Lund walked away I introduced myself to the lawyer.

"I don't want to talk to you, Agent Yeager," he said. "I'm here to file a complaint. My client has been held twenty-four hours without benefit of counsel."

"I'm shocked."

"Where's Archer?" came a loud voice down the hall. "Wherezat rascal? Halloo, Sheriff? Ollie-ollie-in-for-free . . . !"

Wild Pete Frizelle.

He wore a bright orange jumpsuit and a deputy on each arm. Handcuffs and leg irons. And grinning like he'd just snuck into a girl's dormitory.

"Don't that ole polecat have any manners?" Pete said. "Shit. I'd come see him if *he* was up for murder." He nodded to the attorney. "You tell my mama it's okay. I got premature decapitation insurance . . . easy, boys! I'm cool!" He said this as the deputies yanked him through the interview room door.

"Mr. Frizelle, I'm Special Agent Michael Yeager." I outflanked the lawyer. "Have you been advised of your legal rights?"

"Yeah, but it seems like my legal *wrongs* is all anybody wants to talk about lately."

Clyde was still standing in the doorway.

"That'll be all, Deputy," I said.

He withdrew uneasily and the door closed.

"Looks like Poppin' Fresh forgot to duck." Pete was pointing at the back of my neck. "That is one bad haircut, friend."

"I'm not your friend, Mr. Frizelle. I'm here to inform you that in addition to first degree homicide, you're now charged with child abduction and endangerment."

The attorney narrowed his eyes. "What's your evidence for these charges?"

"Cassandra was taken from the Dupree home on the night of October thirty-first. Your client was at the scene—"

"I already told you assholes," he said. "All I was doin' was droppin' Mary Frances off."

The attorney waved him down. "I want full discovery. And my own experts to review the evidence."

"Save it for the grand jury," I said. "In light of the physical evidence, your client's record, and his history with the murder victims, there's more than enough to indict—with or without the UFAP violation. My immediate priority is getting Frizelle's cooperation in the safe return of Cassandra Dupree."

Pete's eyes had gone wide. "What did you just say?"

"I said I want you to help me bring Cassie home."

"You said victims." He spoke with growing alarm. "Who else is dead?"

I couldn't tell if he was bluffing or not.

"Your girlfriend, Mr. Frizelle. Mary Frances Dupree."

The blood drained from his face.

"Oh, Jesus, no. Don't you bastards fuck with me any more." He turned to his attorney. "What the fuck is this shit!"

The lawyer looked more scared than his client. "Pete, for Christ's sake, stop it! You're not helping yourself."

Frizelle was thrashing. "Don't you say she's dead, you cocksucker!" The deputies pushed him back down into his chair. Pete's head hung low, his body wracked with sobs.

If he was acting, he was doing a damn good job.

"Aw, Mary." He shut his eyes tight. "Oh, baby. Oh, God. I'm sorry. I'm so fucking sorry."

I leaned in. "What are you sorry about, Frizelle?"

The attorney stood up. "No. Stop right now. This conversation is over."

Frizelle raised his face, tear-stained. "If you're lying to me, you son of a bitch—"

"Do you want to see the autopsy photos?"

Pete looked away. "No. I don't wanna see nothing."

"Agent Yeager," the attorney said. "My client's been through a terrible ordeal. Either you let me speak to him privately, or I will have this whole case thrown out."

"All right," I said. "We'll resume this conversation after Mr. Frizelle has had an opportunity to compose himself."

Deputy Clyde was standing outside the interview room.

"Clyde, is it just my imagination, or are you hovering?"

"I was just wonderin'." He shifted nervously. "Did anybody say . . . if they know how that fire at Deputy Rosario's got started?"

"Somebody tampered with the propane line Sunday night."

"Oh. Okay." He nodded. "I sure was sorry to . . . hear about her."

"You should be. She died in a lot of pain." I watched him turn away. "Clyde?"

He froze in his tracks.

"Tell your partner it's only a matter of time before I nail both your asses to the wall."

He skedaddled. A moment later Frizelle's attorney appeared in the doorway. He didn't look happy.

"Pete wants to talk to you alone," he said.

FORTY-TWO

Wild Pete was cuffed to his metal chair. The fight seemed to have gone out of him. I waved the deputies out of the room and shut the door.

"You okay?" I asked him.

"Oh, yeah," he said. "I'm Julie fuckin' Andrews on the goddamn mountaintop."

"Sorry about before. I figured you had to know about Mary."

He shot me a look: don't bullshit a bullshitter.

"Listen, dude," he said. "You promise me one thing. When you fry me, do it right. I don't want my eyeballs poppin' out or nothin'."

"Why are we going to fry you, Pete? Are you guilty?"

He looked away sullenly.

"Maybe you could petition the governor for a beheading," I said. "I hear you're pretty handy with Japanese swords."

"Mister, I'm a peaceful man. What I like is money. And what money buys. Pussy, weed, and freedom. In that order."

"Sure, but there's easier ways to make money, Pete. Pimping your girl-friend. Dealing drugs. Blackmailing customers at your mom's whorehouse. Nice work with the Nikon, by the way."

"Hell, I like you." An outlaw gleam stole into his green eyes. "You come by Wild Pete's when we reopen, bo, you'll get unlimited credit."

"You're an optimist, Pete, I'll give you that."

"I ain't such an optimist." His smile faded. "What I am is a coward."

"Why's that?"

"I turned my back on Mary to save my own sorry ass," he said. "My life ain't worth a rat turd. Shit, I don't wanna die. But I gotta get right with God. You believe in God?"

I paused, aware that I was being tested. "I believe in setting things right. How did you turn your back on Mary?"

He took a breath. "Couple weeks ago, Mary Frances got it in her head that somethin' bad was gonna happen to Cassie. And we should grab her and go. Which I considered a not-too-well-thought-out plan. But she had her blood up after that hearing—and when Mary's blood was up, the only thing to do was back the hell off. So I figured, give her a few days, she'll calm down."

"You tried to talk her out of it."

"I almost thought I had. Then Friday afternoon, I get this crazy-ass call sayin' she was at the church and they didn't wanna give Cassie up."

"What time was the call?"

"Whatever time the phone company says. Three, three-thirty . . . Anyhow, I was pissed on account I'd just closed on a brand-new Jag—"

"Used," I said. "Thirty-two thousand on the odometer."

"Used, whatever. I get to the church—"

"In the Jag?"

He nodded. "—and find out Cassie's got her dog with her. So now I gotta worry about bein' a fugitive from justice *and* puppy shit on the leather seats. Meanwhile Mary . . . is . . . actin' . . . strange."

"Strange as in drugged?"

"Strange as in I'm worried she's losin' her fuckin' marbles. She's talkin' about . . . well, what happens to kids who, y'know, get abducted. Things a kid Cassie's age should not be hearin' from her mom. I thought I was gonna have to take Mary to the hospital."

"But instead you took her to Dale's house."

"She wanted us to pack a trunk for Cassie. To fit in my two-seat convertible." He rolled his eyes. "By now I am thinkin' she's gotta be back on the meth, and she's wearin' those shades so I won't see she's got pupils big as Pluto. So I yank her sunglasses off and . . . You already know what I'm gonna say, don'tcha?"

"Try me."

"Razor cut." He pointed to his left eye. "She wouldn't tell me who did it."

"You didn't give it to her?"

He eyed me coolly. "I ain't never cut or even hit a woman. Especially not Mary. It ain't right for a man of honor."

I had to laugh. "Honor?"

He straightened his shoulders. "It's why I got into sellin' swords. I always liked them old movies where the samurais followed a code of Bushido—means 'honor,' y'know. Duty. All that jarhead shit Dale believed in. I never was a marine, but I never gave a woman reason to fear me."

"And so you honorably kicked Mary and Cassie out of your nice, clean convertible and drove away," I said. "Where'd you go?"

"Mama's. Fucked the whole night away."

I bet Pete spent the night with his whores. Robbie's words echoed coldly in my head.

"Saturday mornin', Mama wakes me up sayin' that Dale's dead . . . and I got to run."

"Because you might be accused of his murder?"

"Because I might be next." He shook his head. "I ran like a damn rabbit—and in the end, all my Bushido didn't mean dick. Now I'm gonna die anyway."

"Pete, you convince me you didn't kill Dale and Mary. Because a lot of people would just as soon see you fry."

He considered that. "Take my cuffs off."

He wasn't big, but he looked plenty wiry.

"Why?"

"I'm gonna show you my scars."

I unlocked his cuffs. Pete unzipped the orange jumpsuit and stripped himself to the waist. His chest and arms were covered with blue prison tattoos—crosses and sacred hearts and Virgin Marys with double-D breasts.

"What are you, a walking shrine?"

"Just stick a quarter in my ass and light a candle," he said. "Check the flip side."

He turned his back. Blue-black angels' wings covered his shoulders, feathers running down each muscled arm.

"I got this done mostly to cover up," he said. "Can't let folks in prison find your weakness."

I felt an involuntary chill as I realized what he was talking about. A huge gout of flesh and bone had been carved from his right shoulder blade, leaving a deep cavity between the ribs. A very old wound.

"There ain't no bone from hither to yon," he said. "That right arm couldn't swing a broom. And as for usin' a knife, forget it. I cut myself choppin' onions." He pulled the jumpsuit back. "You can put the cuffs back on if you want. I just wanted you to see my wings."

"I'll leave your arms free if you promise not to fly away."

"Much oblige." He stretched. "Know the worst part about that hole in me? It leaves the lung exposed. Whole time I was in San Quentin, I was convinced that was where the shiv was gonna go. Right . . . in . . . that . . . hole."

He grinned—but not quickly enough to suppress a fleeting look of terror.

"Who did this to you, Pete?"

He didn't smile or blink. "Reckon I did it to myself."

"Come on. That's something you expect from a scared child."

He started to speak. Then his eyes went to the ceiling. "I forgot all about them cameras. Archer's watchin' this, ain't he? Hey there, Sheriff. You fuckin' dinosaur." He whistled. "Take off my leg irons, man. I wanna show him somethin' else."

"Nobody's watching, Pete. And Archer's not here. He did ask me to give you a message. He said you could have been the one."

That riled Mr. Frizelle. "Yeah, well, ain't he a big scary man. You send him a message back. Special delivery from Pete's white ass. Don't defecate where you habitate."

"What do you think he meant, Pete?"

"He's got no right playin' God. Bad enough he let others suffer. No-account trash like me and Dale. But he'd force his own flesh and blood to suffer in silence, just to save his own sorry hide. Somebody oughtta hang his dirty laundry out. Somebody should—"

"—put a trocar through his spine?"

"Who you been talkin' to?" he said, petrified. "You swear to God them cameras ain't on?"

"Why are you scared of the cameras, Pete?"

He froze. "You talk to Lund?"

"Lund says his lips are sealed."

"Lund'll vouch for me. He fixed me up when the sheriff . . ." He fell silent.

"When the sheriff what?"

"When he found what was left of us. You can kiss my butt in the county square, but I was there. I've looked into the abyss with my own two eyes. And Lord knows I've seen it stare back."

I didn't answer right away. Either I was being played—and played very well—or he was on the verge of handing me something important. But the stark silence in his eyes told me I wouldn't get another word until I proved I was ready to believe him.

"So the faceless man really does exist," I said finally.

He seemed to look at me with new eyes. "You talked to him, didn't you?" He clucked his tongue. "Man, you are in deep dirt now."

"I talked to somebody," I said. "Who is this guy? What's he look like?"

Pete rubbed his chin. "By now he could look like most anybody."

"All right, Pete. I'm gonna take you at your word. If everything you're saying is on the level, then you're going to start giving me names and addresses. Something real I can use."

"He ain't got no address. And no name either."

"He's got a name, Pete. And right now he's got your flesh and blood. Your daughter."

Pete shrank into his chair.

"He's got Cassandra," I said.

"Gimme some paper."

I pushed a sheet of paper and a pencil at him. Slowly, as if signing his own death warrant, he scratched out two letters:

RD

"What do these initials stand for?"

"Not initials," he said. "Eyes. Starin' outa the shadows."

That was all I got out of him.

FORTY-THREE

Frizelle looked back over his shoulder as we led him to the cell block.

"I answered your questions," he said. "Do I get to ask one of my own?"

"You can ask."

"Mary's baby. Was it a little boy or a little girl?"

I said nothing. Pete dropped his chin.

"Pete, if it's important . . . I'll try to find out."

"I reckon I'll ask Mary Frances when I see her." He smiled timidly. "Hope that pans out for me. You get way better odds in my casino." He turned to the cell block at large. "That's Wild Pete's, boys. Check it out one time."

One of the guards pushed him by his bad shoulder. Pete didn't flinch.

"I thought you were coming back yesterday." The media room deputy scowled as he opened the door to me. "I worked my tail off gettin' that damn Super 8 scanned in."

"Is it ready?"

"As much as it's gonna get. It's only about eight and a half seconds. I got it on continuous loop." He sullenly double-clicked an icon on the PC screen. "I can tell you, though. You're not gonna be happy."

"Why's that?"

"You can hardly see a damn thing."

He wasn't far off. The digitized movie was dark, jerky, a whirl of grains and scratches. At first all I could make out was light reflecting off the curved walls of a narrow tunnel. It bounced left, then right, then left again, seeming to end in some kind of larger space. There was a lens flare as the beam reflected off a polished surface—then the loop jerked back to the beginning. By the third repetition I could see shapes. After the tenth I started to make out details. Blobs of scarlet became red light bulbs. Smudges of gray and brown became chicken bones and candy wrappers.

"Hold it right there," I said. "Go back three frames."

Now I had a sense of the room: fifteen by twenty feet, eight-foot ceiling, cinderblock walls. A wall clock—no, a timer; there was only one hand on it. A metal tub with a garden hose snaking out. Sheets of paper hung from clothesline. And something that looked like a large microscope, or a—

"Photo enlarger," I said. "It's a darkroom."

He squinted anxiously. "It is?"

I nodded. "Play back at two frames per second."

The unseen photographer was holding the movie camera in his left hand, the light source in his right. You couldn't do that crawling on your belly: he had to be walking on his knees, which—given the confined space—could only mean the filmmaker was less than five feet tall. A child.

"Just before he enters the big room, he pulls himself up, like he's trying to get his feet under him." I tapped the screen. "That's when his camera light bounces off a mirror, or picture frame . . ."

"I see it now." Light dawned in the deputy's eyes. "Just before it flares up there's a kinda reflection."

"Close in on it."

He blew the frame up to full screen. Something was indeed being reflected back—a pale, misshapen oval with dark smudges that might have been two eyes and an open mouth. Or a Halloween mask. Or nothing.

"It's not enough to go on," I said finally. "I need at least twice that quality. Send a request to the Vegas field office for digital enhancement. My authority."

He groaned. "So what is this anyway? Some kinda school project?"

I left without answering. Connor Blackwell was sitting in the lobby, looking very pale in a black suit. He held a manila envelope in two trembling hands.

"I was on my way to the funeral." He looked around furtively. "Can we go somewhere private?"

"I presume you mean somewhere that isn't bugged," I said. "Let's try my office."

As we took the elevator up, I noticed that Connor was perspiring a little behind the ears. I thought he might be hungover. He waited until I'd closed my office door before handing me the envelope.

"This is the transcript," he said. "You won't tell anyone I showed it to you?"

"No problem," I said. "Are you okay? You look a little green around the gills."

"Must be the sheriff's bourbon. I really didn't drink that much . . . it's been getting worse as the day goes by." He wiped the back of his neck. "I owe you an apology for the other night. I think I stepped over the line, bringing up your mother's death that way."

I waved him off. "Ancient history."

"I just wanted to help, that's all."

"In a way, you did." I smiled. "If you're feeling up to it, I could use some help right now. A little profiling support."

He seemed surprised. "Well –sure. I mean, I don't have your expertise . . ."

"Don't mistake me for an expert. I was just wondering—can you tell me which areas of the brain correspond to empathy?"

He tapped his forehead. "The prefrontal lobe."

"And if the lobe is damaged?"

"Well, you'd see cognitive defects—impaired social skills or attention span. Lack of spontaneous emotional response. So many higher brain functions concentrate in that area that you could almost say it defines a person's humanity."

"Say you met a guy like this in the street. What would give him away?"

He seemed to ponder carefully. "Most areas would be normal—motor skills, language, spatial recognition. You might expect some mixed dominance. A right-handed person leading with his left foot . . ." He raised an eyebrow. "Why?"

I instantly thought of Espero's church photo. The boy had been holding a stuffed animal in his left hand—and leading to the camera with his right eye. "It's interesting, that's all. Can I trust you to keep something between us?"

He nodded.

"One of our subject's primary features is an absence of empathy. Not simply a cruel streak, but a complete inability to identify with others. You could be on fire and he'd use you to light a cigarette. Have any of your patients ever met that description?"

"Where to begin." Connor exhaled. "There's only one person who completely fits the bill. I don't know his medical history, so I can't speak to any organic defects. And I don't want to take any chances by saying his name inside the building. But he was in the room when you and I first saw each other."

"Good tip," I said. "You've seen evidence of this behavior?"

"I've talked to some of the women he's mistreated. Including . . ." He put a hand to his chin. "Well, one of the victims."

"You mean Mary Frances."

He nodded. "I'm told he was one of her regular clients. Got his kicks beating her up. Not just his fists . . . cigarette burns and razor blades. I never could convince her to come forward. I think at heart she believed she . . . deserved it." He winced. "Her employer seemed only too happy to turn a blind eye."

"You know, I've never been to a place where so many people are under observation. You've got cameras in the cell block, cameras in the neighborhoods . . . cameras watching other cameras. Everybody's looking, and yet nobody sees a thing."

"And where there is no vision, the people perish." He smiled weakly. "You really should read Gavin's book. He talks about this."

"Believe me, I've read plenty. No offense, but—"

The phone rang. The caller ID read FBI PHILADEL.

"I have to take this," I said. "Should we talk more after the funeral?"

He pulled himself to his feet, grimacing. "If I make it that far."

I waved good-bye as I picked up the phone.

"You're still alive," Peggy deadpanned.

"Rumors to the contrary, I'm smarter than my recent behavior might indicate."

"A smart man would have learned not to answer telephones," Peggy said. "I've got a meeting in five. Want to hear what Yoshi got on this church of yours?"

"Shoot."

"The preacher's story is on the level—more or less. Tree of Life started making donations to Cathedral Lake Camp in the early seventies. After the camp closed, money started flowing back the other way."

"Big money?"

"Like a hundred to one. This is where the water comes in. Apparently in Nevada, it's like hog futures. Water rights can be traded on the open market, used to secure loans . . . it's gold. Anyway, most of the water belongs to something Archer and McIntosh organized called the 'Arbor Vitae Improvement District.' "

"Latin for *Tree of Life*."

"That's right. They fund the hospital, a community center . . . as well as a lot of real estate development in the area."

"San Cristobal," I said. "Where the McIntoshes live."

"And Gavin and Martha McIntosh are the sole trustees of the foundation. Your sheriff owns the water—but his daughter and son-in-law are raking in the money like there's no tomorrow. Literally."

"How so?"

"Check your local newspaper for title transfers. The foundation controls the water, but Archer owns the rights. And when he dies, the foundation dissolves. End of gold rush." She waited. "You're welcome."

"Thank you," I said. "I'm just wondering—how the hell did these guys ever get together? I mean, I've seen Gavin and Archer together, and they're not exactly swell buddies."

"Where there's money, there's a matchmaker." She briefly pulled away from the phone. "They're calling for me, Mike. Anything else?"

"What was your read on the conference call?"

She took a breath. "Honestly?"

"That bad, huh?"

"Archer's not capable of running this investigation. He's too close and too distracted. And if he really is blocking the inquiry, then you've got to be prepared to take a more active role."

"In other words, take over," I said. "Is that a suggestion or an order?"

"It's a fact," she said. "Either he steps aside or he's going to get his granddaughter killed." She spoke to someone on her end, then came back to me. "They're calling me in. How did it go with 'Wild Pete'?"

"No help there," I said. "He's one hell of a joker, though. He showed me his tattoos . . . talked about honor and Dale's devotion to the Marine Corps. Then he gave me . . ."

"Sorry. Gave you what?"

"Somebody's initials," I said. "R.D."

FORTY-FOUR

CB: What's that next to you?

CASSANDRA: My puppy.

CB: What's she doing? Is she sleeping? [silence] Cassie, look at me. Can you tell me why Belle's lying down?

CASSANDRA: No.

The interview was dated October the thirteenth. Judging from the number of pages, Connor had spoken with Cassandra for close to forty-five minutes—probably longer once you factored in the pauses. He wasn't kidding when he said Cassie was withdrawn. At times she was damn near inaccessible.

CB: So now your teacher says you get sick every day. Is that right? [silence] When do you start to feel—Cassie, do you feel sick now?

CASSANDRA: I don't know.

CB: What are you looking for? Are you—do you want to keep drawing? Which crayons do you—

CASSANDRA: [inaudible] that one.

CB: Which? This one, or . . . ? Here, it's okay. You don't have to be scared. Go ahead and finish your picture. [silence] Can you tell me who that is?

CASSANDRA: I want that one for the eyes.

CB: Sorry?

CASSANDRA: Can I—may I please have another crayon?

CB: Sure. [silence] Who is that you're drawing?

CASSANDRA: My daddy.

A color copy of Cassie's drawing was attached. Just as Connor described, she had drawn a male figure with Frizelle's brown hair and green eyes. There was a smudge across the face, as if Cassie had started to erase it. The man stood directly over the puppy, crushing it with his feet. Cassie had shown herself at the far edge of the page, arms flat against her body— a posture of helplessness, detachment. Her face had no mouth.

Despite repeated coaxing, Cassie refused to explain the picture, and the interview finally turned to other matters—home life with Dale, her schoolwork, visits from her mother. These things she had no trouble discussing. Then, just as Connor was wrapping up, Cassie made her only unprompted statement:

CASSANDRA: Some of him is still underground.
CB: Some of who, Cassie?
CASSANDRA: He didn't all burn up. Some of him you can see if you go down, down underground.
CB: Who are you talking about? *[silence]* Where underground?

A note had been scrawled on the page in what appeared to be Sheriff Archer's handwriting: "Connor, J. T. will follow up." That had to be Detective Jackson Tippet.

CASSANDRA: You can't just go down there. You have to go back and then up and then you can go down, down, down. Robbie said he can hear him crying down there. And his eyes are . . . what's this color?
CB: Silver.
CASSANDRA: He has those color eyes. They stare at you from the dark.
CB: Robbie took you down this hole?
CASSANDRA: He said not to because I might go down there the wrong way.
CB: What happens if you go down the wrong way?
CASSANDRA: You die.

He has those color eyes. They stare at you from the dark. Pete, I recalled, also talked about eyes staring from the shadows. So now I had a picture of a man with no face. A man with no empathy, who wanted to be God. A man with silver eyes, who hadn't all burned up, who still lived under the ground. A man called the Shadow Catcher, who took away all the parts nobody wanted . . . and turned them into something that ate you up. A man who was dead and yet not dead. And all of this had something to do with the letters R. D.

Peggy had been right about the old newspapers. Looking through my stack of printouts, I found a lot about title transfers—and something more about Cathedral Lake. Every year, the Dyer County *Ledger* published a list of the summer camp's top donors. Archer's name always topped the list, followed by any number of locals—none of whose initials were R. D. But one nameless contributor had advised readers to "See our Special Advertisement on Page 2."

At first I thought it was a glitch—why would anyone ask to be kept anonymous and then refer people to his ad? Then it dawned on me: there were no advertisements on page two. There was, however, the Cute Baby of the Week.

The county clerk told me folks read the paper to know what not to believe. Dr. Lund said to place no faith in appearances. No matter what else was happening in Nevada or the world—war, storm, or locust plagues— the *Ledger* was going to put its Cute Baby of the Week on page two. I'd joked with Yoshi about recycled babies, not thinking it might be literally true. But there they were: the same five or six Cute Babies under different names, week after week. All fake.

But there might still be a few originals around.

Down the hall was Sheriff Archer's gallery of framed newspaper clippings. I took everything from 1978 back to my office. Started cutting away the brown paper backings. There were no Cute Babies of the Week on the backs of those 1978 originals. In their place I found a quarter-page ad.

RUDOLPH DUBLINER PHOTOGRAPHY
Since 1968
Family and School Pictures a Specialty

And then, neatly printed at the bottom of each ad:

Luke 15:18

The logo showed the initials *R* and *D* centered in the lens of an old-fashioned camera—with dots in the loops so that the letters looked like a pair of eyes. That was what Pete Frizelle had called them—not initials, but eyes.

I picked up the phone and dialed.

"Agent Weaver," answered the voice on the other end.

"Yeah, sweetie, it's Mike—"

"—is not here. To leave a message . . ."

I waited for the beep. "Peg, it's Mike. Check on a man named Rudy Dubliner. A photographer in Dyer County from 1968 to 1978. They removed all traces of him when they switched the papers to microfiche. He took school pictures. He had access to children. I don't know what happened to him. But now . . ."

There was a siren outside. The horn of a fire truck.

". . . I know when it happened."

Through my window I saw fire and emergency vehicles leading the hearse. Taking Dale Dupree to rest.

Morningstar Cemetery had no Jesuses at Gethsemane or Cedars of Lebanon. No grass. The headstones were cheap and many were homemade. But it held some of the oldest names in Dyer County. One tall wooden cross from 1869 read:

> *Here Lies the Hunter*
> *Carson Younger*
> *Lost his Nerve*
> *And Died of Hunger*

Nearly lost in its shadow was a plain granite marker:

THEODORE AMBROSE FREEBAIRN

March 13, 1966—November 5, 1978

For this my son was dead, and is alive again

"Theo would be embarrassed by the Scripture," said a man behind me. "But they were the only words that seemed to help."

I turned to face a bantam gentleman in a pressed black suit. He had a hound-sad face and large, sensitive ears—the kind you knew would be cold to the touch.

"Mr. Freebairn," I said. "I'm Mike Yeager. We spoke on the phone—"

"Yes, I remember. That detective never did send a police report. Don't know what I'm gonna do. Insurance won't pay without it."

"I can handle that for you," I said. "As a matter of fact, I'd like to see the damage in person."

"Why the sudden generosity?"

"The stolen articles were used in a recent series of crimes. I think you know which one I'm referring to. It occurs to me that only someone familiar with embalming would know what to take."

"Or how to use them," he mused. "I don't have much of a staff, if that's what you're asking. Just a cosmetics girl—and an assistant who, frankly, is all thumbs. Mainly I'm just one old man plying his trade. Wife died twenty years ago . . . there's 'And Son.' Added those words the day Theo came home to us. Never had the heart to take them down."

"How did he die?"

Cheated rage broke over the mortician's face. "Do you really care? Or is this just morbid curiosity?"

"It matters to me, Mr. Freebairn."

"He was burned in a fire. By a sadist whose name is not worthy to be spoken."

"Rudy Dubliner?"

He said nothing.

"I need someone who's willing to tell me about him," I said. "What he did to Theo and the others. And why the sheriff is so determined to wipe his name from the records."

The mortician laughed bitterly. "Rafe thinks if he didn't hear something, then you didn't say it. He had me fired because I wouldn't toe his line. If I see murder, I write 'murder.' And if I see—"

"Exsanguination?"

He briefly closed his eyes. "Poor Sig. Archer should have left him to his children. One thing I'll say for Doc. He'll keep his word, even if it breaks him."

"He could use some help," I said. "Would you be willing to examine the body of Mary Frances Dupree?"

"Rafe'd never let me within a mile of his daughter," he said. "I'm surprised he let me bury that poor little Mexican boy of his. The man has no Christian morals whatever."

"Then you believe the recent deaths are related to the events of nineteen seventy-eight?"

"A blind man could see that. But it couldn't be Rudy Dubliner this time." He glanced over his shoulder. "The service is starting. I must go to the family."

"Why couldn't it be Dubliner?"

"Rudolph Dubliner is dead," he said, as he walked away. "I watched him die."

"'Man that is born of woman hath but a short time . . . ,'" said the preacher.

Dale's casket was the size of a piano crate, covered with a parade-sized American flag. The pallbearers were big and silent and angry—firefighters and U.S. Marines.

". . . 'He cometh up and is cut down, like a flower. He fleeth as if it were a shadow . . .'"

The six men solemnly faced one another. Lifted the flag, smartly brought the ends together.

". . . 'In the midst of life we are in death.'"

The honor guard tucked the ends of the flag into a triangle, stars outward. Then the tallest marine presented it to an older woman in black. Dale's mother.

"Ma'am," he said with a crisp salute. "Receive the flag of Lance Corporal Dale Dupree and the thanks of a grateful nation."

She cradled the flag like a baby, but didn't weep. She had done this before.

"'I heard a voice from heaven saying unto me, "Write" . . .'"

Gavin McIntosh scattered desert sand over the grave. He looked ashen, exhausted. Then he took the mother's hand and whispered into her ear. Dale's mother closed her eyes, and Gavin nodded to Freebairn. The mortician pulled the switch and the massive coffin ached into the grave. A tape-recorded trumpet played "Taps."

In the end the earth had room enough for Dale Dupree.

FORTY-FIVE

The funeral reception was held at Tree of Life. The mourners, obeying some ancient herd instinct, gathered in a tiny corner of the big room. Some faces were familiar to me. Evelyn Maidstone scooped ginger cookies into her purse while Fire Chief Espy coughed into a ragged kerchief. Whispers flew around like hornets.

"... found under the trailer. What I heard ..."

"Satan worshippers."

"Kiddie porn. All them whores are into ..."

"... vote yet? Tell me how to vote."

"Where's the sheriff, anyhow?"

"... guy from the FBI?"

"Why isn't anybody doing anything about any of this?"

Connor was nowhere in sight, nor had he signed the visitation book. Neither had Sheriff Archer ... or his daughter, Martha. I found Robbie at the buffet table, piling wedge-cut sandwiches onto his plate.

"You got a hollow leg, Rob?"

He barely looked at me. "My legs are spin-dly. I have Fried-reich's A-tax-ia."

"I'm sorry, pal. Bad joke."

"Yeah," he said. "It's a deg-ener-a-tive dis-order. That means it gets worse. Probably I won't be able to talk anymore soon." He lowered his voice. "It sucks shit."

"Well ... I guess it does, doesn't it?" I smiled. "You seem to know a lot of words."

"I like to read," he said. "Plus I can run fast, if I'm on my walker. I'm a super runner."

"I knew that the first time I met you. You zipped off from that parking lot like there was no tomorrow. Mind if I join you?"

"My mom doesn't want me talking to you."

"How about your dad?"

Robbie glanced behind me. "He hasn't seen you yet. Here, you can have a sandwich. I won't eat them all."

"My pleasure." I took one. "I met your teacher. Miss Corvis. She said to tell you they all miss you."

"She's nice," he said. "You should be Miss Corvis's boyfriend. I don't think she has one now. But you better hurry. Tommy Boster says she's a hot piece of—"

"Lemme get back to you on that one, okay?" I looked around. "Where's your mom, anyhow?"

"She's too sick to come," he said. "She has dep-res-sive ep-i-sodes."

"That's not a lot of fun, is it?"

"It makes my dad real sad when she yells at him. He cries and begs her not to, but she does anyway."

"How do you feel when your mom is depressed?"

He touched his chest. "I put my heart in a box. And I hide the box underground."

"Is that where it is right now?"

"Uh-huh. It'll come back up pretty soon, though. Then everybody'll see."

"What will everybody see?"

"It'll get so full, it will blow up," he said. "It'll just blow up."

He took a big bite and swallowed.

"Uncle Dale's funeral was sad," he said. "One time my puppy died? And we put it in a box and we put the box in the ground. He barked and barked and barked and then he stopped. That's how I knew he was dead. I miss him. Did you ever have a puppy die?"

"Sure," I said. "How did your puppy die?"

He shrugged and put another sandwich on his plate.

"So Rob, I've been thinking about what you told me the other day. About the Shadow Catcher."

He said nothing.

"Do you remember telling me he was after Cassie?"

"Some of those things I don't remember."

"What do you remember?"

"I remember you're from Lan-cas-ter County. And it's Ah-mish, not Ay-mish."

"That's pretty good. Why do you like the Amish?"

"They don't hurt anybody," he said. "I'm gonna run away and be like them. Maybe you can visit me."

"You are probably the only person who could get me back to Lancaster County," I said. "If you remember all that, then you've got to remember what you said about Pete. About where he was the night Dale died." No answer. "Was this something you figured out? Or did somebody tell you?"

"That was not a thing I ever said."

"You did say it, Robbie. And you told Cassie about somebody who lives under the ground. Is that the Shadow Catcher?"

Robbie kept piling up food like I wasn't even there.

"Your cousin's life is in danger," I said. "If you know something, you have to tell. Or she could die. Just like Uncle Dale and Aunt Mary. Do you understand? Cassie could die."

Robbie stared defiantly at the carpet, and now I could see under his collar. The back of his neck was freshly bandaged.

"How did you get that, Robbie?"

"I fell downstairs."

"Fell on your neck, Rob? How did you do that?"

"I just did! Shut up!"

I took his face in my hand and turned it toward me.

"Don't do that!" Robbie yelled. "Let go of me, you little fucker!"

The voices in the church fell silent.

"That's what Uncle Dale did just before he shook me." Robbie's voice was cool. "Are you going to shake me now?"

I let go of him. A faint red mark blossomed, just like the one Dale had left on Friday. Robbie never took his eyes from me.

"I'm—sorry," I said.

"Agent Yeager." Gavin stood behind me, flanked by several mourners. "Please leave my boy alone." He strode toward me. "On second thought, I think you should go now."

"I'm not leaving until your son tells me the truth."

"The truth?" His little eyes narrowed. "How dare you use that word to justify hurting—a disabled child?"

A couple of those big firefighters were closing in. I touched the bandage on Robbie's neck.

"Certain patterns repeat," I said. "Do you want what happened to your wife happening to Robbie?"

Gavin opened his mouth but no sound came out.

"Look to your boy, Reverend."

The preacher put his arms around his son. I looked down at Robbie.

"I'm sorry I scared you," I said. "I have no right to do that. Nobody does."

The boy bit his lip. I walked away.

"Lan-caster County!" Robbie cried after me.

"Lancaster County," I said.

FORTY-SIX

Despite its monolithic appearance, Dyer County Consolidated School was a scarily easy place to break into. Behind the recycle bins, right on the shoulder of Highway 313, I found an unguarded break in the fence. As I stepped through, I noticed Dorothy sitting across the schoolyard, watching over a group of third graders.

"Throw it hard, Joey! Jesus, throw it like you got 'em!"

"Go home, crybaby!"

"Hurry up and kill him! *Kill him!*"

The kids were playing dodgeball—some of them aiming for blood. Mostly they were just having fun. Running, laughing, teasing, crying, being rowdy. Being kids.

"Sometimes I think we regress as we get older." Dorothy shifted on her tree stump, making room for me.

I sat down. "How's that?"

"Five-year-olds hug and cry," she said. "Seven-year-olds make up clubs just so they can exclude each other. And by the time they turn eight . . ." She gestured at the yelling third graders. "I see you found the teeny tiny gaping hole in our security system."

"So much for the metal detectors," I said. "Why don't they just fix the fence?"

"They did a couple times, but the kids keep tearing it open. Fact is, the maintenance budget's about dead. We can't even afford toilet paper."

"Right."

"I'm serious! Do you know what it's like having to ask a parent to donate toilet paper? If they put half the money into schools that they spend on prisons . . . no offense."

"None taken," I said. "As it happens, I agree."

"It's just a shame to watch the school fall apart. Now that they've approved vouchers for that new private school, this place is gonna be a ghost town."

"What new private school?"

"Oh—that Arbor Vitae thing."

"That name's been floating around a lot lately."

"Yeah. I mean, they were nice enough to let us rehearse there. I think they're trying to tempt me with all the nice facilities. But kids don't need TV cameras just to put on a show. And I dunno . . . the whole McJesus thing spooks me out."

"See now. I thought you might have been a McJesus person when I met you."

"McJewish." She looked at me. "So is this your idea of a second date, or what?"

"Since when did we have a first date?"

"You showed up, didn't you?" She winked. "Seriously, why are you here?"

"Can you tell me—"

She touched my arm. " 'Scuse me a sec—*Lacey?* I saw that, honey! No aiming at faces!" She turned back. "Sorry. Can I tell you what?"

"Where did Robbie find that play about the Pied Piper?"

She furrowed her brow. "He said it was from his Robert Browning book. Why?"

"There's a line in there about 'should have paid attention.' And just last night I heard somebody else say those exact words."

"Who did?"

"I can't tell you," I said. "But didn't you ever notice how strange Robbie's play is? Psychologically speaking, I mean. It makes several direct references to child abduction."

"You could probably say the same for most of Grimm's fairy tales." She exhaled. "But I know what you mean. He's not the same Robbie I met in September. I thought it might help him to act his feelings out . . . turn it into a game."

"Sure, but—what did you say yesterday? The monster is always real?"

"Yes." She looked at me. "I guess you know what it's like to have monsters that nobody believes in."

I nodded.

"Me, too," she said.

"I think Robbie knows who took Cassandra," I said. "Scratch that. I know he knows. And I may have just blown my best opportunity to get him to talk."

"How'd you do that?"

"I got angry." I exhaled. "He stonewalled—started cursing like a Jersey longshoreman. I got hot under the collar, he clammed up. I may have pushed him too hard."

"You want me to try talking to him?"

I looked at her, surprised. "Have you done forensic interviews before?"

"Me? Sure. Not so much since grad school, but—why?"

"I'm just wondering why they didn't ask you to interview Cassandra."

"They just didn't. Nothing against that guy Connor, but I think they wanted someone . . . compliant?"

"I've got a transcript right here." I took it from my jacket. "I was hoping Connor could answer some questions, but he's apparently out of commission."

"You want me to read it."

"It's not that simple. The document's still under seal of the family court. Legally I can't show it to you. And if you agree to look at it, you could get in trouble."

She raised an eyebrow. "Big-T or little-t trouble?"

"You could lose your teaching certificate. The problem is, I don't have time to get you authorized. I should say, Cassie doesn't have time."

She looked at me, eyes wide.

"Cassie's trying to say something in her interview," I said. "Something Connor wasn't able to get from her . . . and that I frankly don't understand. I can talk to forensic psychologists—what I don't have is someone who knows Cassandra."

"You do now." She tossed her head. "I mean, how much trouble could I get in?"

"Just think about it. I'll call you later."

"No." She took the envelope. "No, there's no time." She turned, distracted by fresh yelps from the dodgeball game. "I gotta intervene, okay? Come back in half an hour, when school lets out." She winked. "You can use the front door this time."

I stood up. "Thanks, Dorothy. I mean it."

"Just make it worth the risk." She smiled. "Or at least worth my while."

"Well—I do have a coupon for free ice cream."

"Hm. Somebody's been a good boy." Before I could stop her she gave me a hug. Fifty children whistled and ooed.

FORTY-SEVEN

A chill came down with the afternoon breeze. I found Dorothy out front in the loading zone, hugging the last of her first graders good-bye.

"Bye, Miss Corvis!" a small Korean girl yelled, trotting off to her father's car.

"Good-bye, Eleanor! Don't forget—sing out, little bird, sing out!"

As she saw me, her eyes filled with concern.

"Did you read the transcript?"

She nodded.

"There's something else I need to show you," I said.

"... *exit polls are to be* trusted," the AM radio bleated at Hardy's drugstore, "*Archer could squeak through this latest challenge. However, we're now told that Buford Warburton and the Dyer County Commission are about to announce a major breakthrough* ..."

We sat at a rear table while two untouched dishes of Rocky Road melted. Dorothy held Cassie's spiral-bound notebook in both hands.

"... *homicide investigation of the sheriff's daughter, a local sex worker, and the ongoing search for his granddaughter* ..."

She closed the book.

"What do you think?" I said.

"I need to breathe a minute," she said quietly.

"It's upsetting, I know. But as you've probably seen, the transcript by itself isn't that revealing."

"Cassie doesn't talk. She draws." Dorothy looked through the pages. "All the way through the interview, she kept reaching for crayons."

"Did Connor share any of this with you?"

She shook her head. "One thing about Cassie, she doesn't invent things. She wouldn't have imagined those images. Someone must have shown something to her. Or described them."

"She might have been drawing from old photographs. Maybe Rudy Dubliner's pictures."

"Who's Rudy Dubliner?"

I was about to answer when Mrs. Hardy, the druggist's wife, walked over.

"Y'all ain't too hungry, are ya? Guess our flavors don't suit ya."

Dorothy brightened. "I'm sorry, Mrs. Hardy. It was lovely. We just . . ."

Mrs. Hardy waved it off. "Honey, I'm teasin'. I wouldn't want you hurtin' that lovely figure. I bet he don't, neither." She winked at me. "Say, I remember Rudy."

I looked up. "You do?"

"Yeah, he used to own a photography studio here in town. Nice enough fella."

"Do you know what happened to him?"

"Well, lessee—I think he got a job in Reno, or was it . . . hey, Spence! Whatever happened to Rudy Dubliner? Did he move?"

"Old Walleyes?" The druggist chuckled. "He's still around. Ain't he?"

Mrs. Hardy waved him off. "He don't know. I think Rudy moved away. Or could be he died. Go ask Dave Freebairn, the undertaker. He knows who's dead around here."

"Why did your husband call him 'Old Walleyes'?"

"Hadda lazy eye. Never knew which one to look in."

"You remember anything else about him?"

"Well, sure, I—" Then she stopped short. "Huh. Thought I did. Long time ago. Well, he's gone now, that's for sure. Maybe he did die." She shuffled back to her Barbara Cartland novel.

"Mrs. Hardy's a sweet lady," Dorothy said.

"Mrs. Hardy has big ears," I said. "Let's take this outside."

"So who was your monster?" Dorothy hugged herself against the cold as we left the drugstore.

"Beg pardon?"

"We've both met our monsters, remember? I was just wondering who yours was."

"I take it you're not referring to the special agent in charge of my field office."

"I mean really. Who was the monster nobody believed in?" She slipped her arm into mine, as easily as if we'd been dating for years. I had to admit it felt nice.

"My father," I said. "Nobody ever believed in him. I think that's what made him such a tyrant. He ran an apple farm . . . preached the gospel . . . raised six kids by himself. And somehow the universe failed to acknowledge him." I laughed. "Those were the worst goddamn apples."

"Why did he have to raise you by himself?"

"My mother . . . died when I was nine years old," I said. "She killed herself."

"Oh, Mike." She pulled me closer. "I'm sorry."

"So am I." We walked in silence till we reached her Vespa, parked beside my Nash.

"I don't mean to sound so offhanded," I said. "It's just that all these years later, I still don't know how I'm supposed to talk about it."

"There's no way you're 'supposed' to talk about these things. You'll know when you're ready."

"I guess there's more important things to worry about right now." I let go of her arm, took her hand in mine. "Anyway, I appreciate your help with the transcript."

"I'm not sure I was that helpful." She shook her head. "You have to be able to see and hear the kids or there's too much you can miss."

"I'll see if I can find the audiotapes."

"Yeah, but it's video you want," she said. "I'd like to stay with you on this. If you want me to."

"I'll let you know what happens. Right now. . . . I think I need to see what's going on at that press conference."

"Do you want me to see if I can track down Robbie?"

"No. I . . . don't want to put you in harm's way."

She laughed. "For asking questions?"

"The deputy who found that notebook was killed for asking questions."

"Oh."

She straddled her bike.

"Can I call you later? Or is that also gonna get me killed?"

"You can call me," I said. "Dorothy, there's something I need to come clean about."

"Uh-oh," she said. "You're married."

"I'm not married."

"You're gay."

"Nothing like that. I don't want to presume anything. But I can't get involved right now. It's not personal. You're . . . great."

She raised an eyebrow.

"Let me start over," I said. "It would be a distraction I can't afford."

"Because of the case."

"I guess so. I mean—yes, obviously. I don't know what I'm trying to say."

"You're saying, 'I like you, Dorothy, so stay the hell away.'" She kick-started her engine. "Don't worry, I'll deal. Just as long as you're not already involved."

"I don't know. I only just found out she's dating again. It's not like things were solid with us anyway . . ."

"Michael?"

"Yeah."

"We don't have to figure everything out right now. We have time."

"Here's hoping," I said. "Robbie thinks I ought to make a play for you. Since you don't have a boyfriend."

"Huh. Who says I don't?"

"You're here, aren't you?"

"Maybe I'm trading up." She kissed me lightly on the cheek and sped away.

FORTY-EIGHT

". . . like to thank you all for makin' time today," Buford Warburton said from behind a nest of microphones. The hearing room at Dyer County Courthouse was packed to the rafters—locals, mainly, but also reporters and TV crews from as far away as Carson City. Mr. Warburton was a walrus of a man, double-chinned and slow-talking, with sagging eyelids and bad hair plugs. Detective Tippet sat gravely beside him in full-dress uniform.

"I have just finished conferrin' with members of the county commission." Buford cleared his throat and the microphones boomed. "They have authorized me to report a major breakthrough in the abduction of—Tip, would you turn that poster so's people can see?"

Tippet flashed a quick look of resentment—he clearly wasn't thrilled to be playing second banana. But he obediently turned an easel to reveal a mounted, poster-sized picture of Cassandra Dupree. Flashbulbs popped all around.

"Cassie Dupree . . . is . . . alive," he intoned. "We have a communication from her kidnapper, which I will now read to you."

A collective hush overtook the galleries. Buford was reading from a sheet of paper, vacuum-sealed in cellophane. I noticed dark spots on the reverse. Dried bloodstains.

" 'I bear no ill will to this little angel,' " Buford recited in a dull monotone. " 'I hold her but in earnest of an unpaid debt. Serve me with justice and she will live to glorify me. Treat me with cowardice and deceit, and you yourselves will answer for her burnt and broken form.' "

"Excuse me." A female reporter spoke above the murmur. "Where and exactly how did you receive this letter?"

Buford was about to speak when Tippet leaned in to whisper. Apparently they hadn't quite decided how to field the question. Finally Buford took his hand off the mike.

"That's confidential," he said.

"Yes, but—how do you know it's genuine?"

This time Tippet got there first. "We've subjected it to rigorous analysis," he said. "The letter was acquired in tandem with what we believe to be the primary weapon used in the murder of Dale Dupree."

I could feel my eyes bulging out as Tippet lifted a plastic evidence bag. Inside was the silver trocar—long and sharp and streaked with blood. He was almost smiling as he dangled it in front of the flashbulbs. An old man beside me covered his eyes.

"This item had been reported stolen by a local establishment," Tippet said in a Sergeant Friday cadence. "With this physical evidence we will conclusively identify the perpetrator. It's only a matter of time."

"How would you describe the perp?"

"Sexual deviant," Buford said with authority. "Satanic ritualist, maybe. Definitely a brain-damaged individual with some facial deformity. We're building a database of names and canvassing the a—"

Another reporter raised his hand. "Officer Tippet—"

"Lieutenant."

"—Was this breakthrough due to the FBI assistance you've received?"

Tippet's eyes narrowed as several cameras wandered my way. I kept my arms folded and my mouth shut.

"I wouldn't say so." Tippet shot me a sour look. "They do what they do. But we have our own resources, and they serve us very well without the need for federal interfer—'scuse me, involvement."

It was an obvious slip, but it did the trick. A dozen pens began writing *interference* onto notepads.

"Are you implying that the FBI has somehow jeopardized Cassandra Dupree's safety?"

"God willing, no." Tippet flattened his brow. "The point is, we are now takin' a down-to-basics, facts-first approach. Seein' as Sheriff Archer is not actively leading this invest—"

"I just wanna say somethin'." Buford swept his hand past Tippet, practically knocking the trocar off the table. "To whoever you are holdin' Cassie. Hide where you will, we are gonna smoke you out. You give yourself up now, turn that little girl in with no harm done, and maybe we can talk. But you harm one hair, and with the Lord God as my witness—"

His voice fell as the door clicked open behind me. Several of the locals were turning around. The cameras followed.

"Oh my God," someone said.

Sheriff Archer was standing in the doorway.

"Least now I know why my station's empty on a Tuesday afternoon." Archer strode into the room, holding a trembling hand to his side. The quaver in his voice wasn't from anger or even fear. It was physical agony, a spectre of age, come at last for Rafe Archer.

"Sheriff," Buford said. "Didn't expect you in person. We know this is your private time of grief."

"I never shot a man in the back, Buford. Don't expect to die that way, either."

Warburton shrank into his folds of fat. "What do you want, Rafe?"

"Coffee, if you can spare it. Ain't slept much."

Buford motioned to an aide. A cup was brought to the sheriff as he turned to face the crowded gallery.

"I know some of you think I don't belong here." His voice was suddenly feeble. "Maybe that's true. But I got things to say. Things you . . . got a right to hear, I reckon."

There were uneasy murmurs. All the camera lights were on him now, leaving Buford and Tippet in the shadows.

"I always thought I was a . . . good man." He took a long swallow of coffee. "I tried, Lord knows. Tried to be a good shepherd to you people. A good father to my little girls. But I've done a great wrong. And—grievous harm to our children."

Some people started to protest. But as he spoke that one word—*children*—it was as if he'd thrown a shroud over the room.

He pointed at me. "There's a man here says I'm facin' death. Reckon we all gotta face that sometime. But I've got to stand naked before God. And be held guilty for others who suffered on my account."

Buford leaned in to his microphone. "Rafe, you don't need to do this."

"I don't want to," he said. "I got to—have to speak. I had bad dreams last night. All the mountains were on fire, and our babies were burnin'. But I . . . couldn't move. My arms were tied to the ground, and . . . my mouth was sewed shut. I couldn't save them all. I just couldn't. God help me—I had to leave him there."

From the corner of my eye I watched Tippet get up and leave, taking the trocar with him. I was about to follow when suddenly the sheriff stumbled. His hand shook, spilling coffee onto the floor.

"I had to make a choice," he said. "Who would live and die. And now finally I see—"

His mouth twitched into a smile—a quivering rictus, inhuman.

"Should have seen—" He gasped for air.

All at once he began to convulse. Coffee shot from his lips in a black jet. I was already rushing to catch him.

"*Omigod he's*—" People in the galleries were screaming.

The sheriff fell backward as if struck, his boots kicking the floor. His back curved in a bow; facial muscles tightened. A rich froth of saliva and coffee tumbled over the sheriff's chin. His cheeks and fingertips were rapidly turning corpse-blue.

I bent down. Took his cold hand in mine.

"So much—pain—," Rafe Archer whispered.

FORTY-NINE

Half an hour later the council chamber was clear and I was on a pay phone with Dr. Lund.

"How is he?"

"They got his stomach pumped and a line in," Lund said. "Frankly, it'll be a miracle if he lasts the night. I understand he was making a speech when this happened."

"He never got to finish," I said. "He must have seen it coming."

"There was nothing you could have done, Mike. He'd ingested the poison at least ten or twelve hours ago."

"Have they made an identification?"

"Phosphorus dissolved in carbon disulphide," he said. "It's used in—"

"I know what it's used for," I said. "My father kept it for putting down sick hogs. He used to mix it with molasses to hide the flavor."

"It attacks the liver and intestines," he said. "Terrible, agonizing way to die."

"Whoever did this really wanted the sheriff to suffer. How did they give it to him?"

"In his bourbon." He sighed. "God knows what's keeping Rafe—hang on, Mike."

As I held the line I suddenly remembered how Connor was holding his stomach in my office.

"Doc," I said, as Lund returned. "Connor Blackwell drank out of that same bottle."

"We'll look for him," he said. "You'd better come on over to the hospital, Mike. The situation . . . it's falling apart."

"Don't remind me. That press conference was a nightmare. Tippet actually showed the murder weapon."

"I'm afraid it's even worse than that."

"How could it possibly be worse?"

"That was Reverend McIntosh," he said. "Robbie's gone missing."

FIFTY

Dr. Lund met me at the nurse's station of the ICU. The funeral director was standing beside him.

We shook hands. "I hope you're not here in your official role, Mr. Freebairn."

"Not yet," he said. "Seems it might be a good idea to put our heads together."

"First things first. What's being done about Robbie?"

Lund held out his hands. "Soon as Rafe took ill—pandemonium. The boy went missing from his own neighborhood."

"Not too long after your little stunt at the funeral," added Freebairn. "Don't think that won't set a few tongues wagging."

"Right now I don't care if they think I'm the Boston Strangler. We need to secure the exits. That's a gated community, right? They'll have security tape of any vehicles entering or—"

"Mike," Lund said. "This isn't your problem any more."

"Like hell. It's why Archer brought me in."

Lund nodded. "And right now Sheriff Archer is incapacitated. That leaves Detective Tippet in charge of the Dupree homicide and all other related cases. You can take it for granted that he's rescinded Archer's request for FBI assistance."

"Let him try."

Freebairn waved me to a sofa. "Mr. Yeager, I'm not an educated person like you or Sig here. Forgive me for plain speaking. What's happening here is beyond you. There are dark powers at work in Dyer County."

"More bullshit about ghosts."

"No, Mr. Yeager. This is very much about the living. Mr. Warburton has friends at the county commission. Right now he's preparing to launch an inquest into your conduct with Robin McIntosh. Apparently he feels you have some prior pattern of negligence."

Lund nodded soberly. "It's true, Mike. Something about a recent case in Philadelphia. . . ."

I looked from one old man to the other. "Maybe if Robbie's parents had been keeping an eye on their son—"

Lund placed a hand on my shoulder. I followed his gaze. Gavin and Martha McIntosh were staring at me from the elevator well.

The preacher still wore his funeral suit. Martha was a broken willow beside him, moving in a zombielike shuffle. Her face was smeared thick with makeup, as if she had forgotten how to apply it. The effect was like looking at a badly painted doll. Her bare legs were covered with fresh shaving nicks. Martha's thick auburn hair was dirty and matted, tied back with a rubber band.

Gavin leaned in to his wife. "Martha, baby, why don't you go in and see your daddy."

Her voice was like cracked plaster. "Don't leave me alone in there."

He touched her hand and spoke in soothing tones. A nurse led Mrs. McIntosh away. Gavin walked over and I stood up to face him. Sheer exhaustion had drawn his cheerful features out like clay.

"I owe you an apology," he said. "You told me to take care of my boy. I should have listened."

I had to admit that wasn't what I was expecting. "What exactly happened, Reverend?"

The preacher shook his head. "It all went so quickly. Robbie got sandwiches on the carpet, and Martha started shouting. They fight a lot. He went out in the yard. I thought I'd give him a moment to cool down. . . . The sheriff told me not to let them play on the grass. And I thought he was being . . . irrational."

"I know a million things are running through your mind," I said. "Try to remember the details. Were any of the sheriff's deputies on duty?"

"There was supposed to be one—you know, the skinny boy with acne. But he didn't show up." He shook his head. "After Robbie vanished, I drove around the neighborhood. The guard was on his lunch break. Everybody was gone."

"Did they check the security tapes?"

"Nothing. They said if any car came through, the cameras would have recorded it. Can that be true?"

"There could have been a malfunction, or . . . was the barrier up or down?"

He rubbed his temple. "Down. I found Robbie's walker on the highway. At first I thought . . . he's just fallen down. Then I saw it was all bent and twisted. Like it had been thrown from a moving vehicle."

"Make sure when you talk to the sheriff's dep—"

He seized me hard on the wrist.

"Please let me help you," he said. "I want to help you look for my son."

"Gavin, I don't know how to put this, but . . . I may no longer be assigned to your case."

"I don't understand." He blinked. "You said you were here to protect us. Was that a lie?"

"Reverend," I said. "Did you never think this could happen to your own children?"

He stared blankly. I looked past him. Martha was standing in the hallway, a feral light in her eyes.

"Mr. Yeager." She curled a finger at me. "Come here."

"Martha, don't," Gavin said. "I'm handling this."

"Shut up." She sounded remarkably like her father. "You can't even handle yourself. You, Mike Yeager. Front and center."

A raw smell hung around her—heavy perfume and unwashed underarms. "What do you want, Mrs. M—"

She spat in my face. "That's what," she said with a triumphant gleam. "We were fine until you came here."

"I didn't make this happen, Mrs. McIntosh."

"You watched it happen." Her voice was strangely calm. "Don't you know when a family is dying? It's when they start hiding things. Like so many rotten Easter eggs in the back yard. Shh. Mustn't talk about that . . . strange smell rising from the ground. Then one day . . . the eggs begin to hatch." She tapped my chest. "Peck, peck, peck. All the baby chickens come home to roost."

"Martha." The minister took her hand. "Darling, please."

"Gavin doesn't understand." She leaned forward, as if confiding a choice bit of gossip. "But just today I woke up and realized . . . I've lived my whole life in a funhouse. You keep looking for someone to lead you out . . . and it's just your own cocksucking reflection. And just when you think you're free and clear . . . big joke. There never was an exit. And you never had a chance in hell."

Gavin was on her. "Darling, for God's sake. You're talking very loud."

"Not a fucking chance!" She writhed in his arms. "My sister is dead! My father is dying—and you don't care about anything but my *talking?* My *volume?* Can you hear me *now,* Gavin? How loud am I *now!*"

"If you don't quiet down," he said in a low voice, "somebody's going to give you a shot. Is that what you want? Think about the baby, Martha. The baby."

Her mouth bent crookedly at me. "What happened to your face, Mr. Yeager? Is that some of me on you?"

This time she didn't struggle as Gavin took her away.

"He was so *small,*" she said to him. "What did they do to make Daddy so—small?"

"It's all right, Martha. He'll be at peace. We just have to keep praying. We'll go home . . . and we'll pray."

He led her to the elevator well. As the sliding doors closed, desperate unhappiness broke across Martha's face.

"There's no me anymore," she said.

Lund handed me a tissue. Mrs. McIntosh's spittle smelled of alcohol.

"Let's go see the sheriff," I said.

FIFTY-ONE

The glass-walled ICU was roughly the size of the execution chamber at Leavenworth—even had a small observation room, where a bored nurse worked cryptograms. EKG machines and saline regulators stood guard around the sheriff. Tubes grew from his arms like vines. Martha said her father looked small. Without his hat or leather jacket, Rafe Archer looked tiny indeed. His eyes fluttered behind half-closed lids. His chest rose and fell raggedly, as if he were buying each breath with a piece of his soul.

"Somebody said he talked to you before he passed out," Freebairn said. "What did he say?"

" 'So much pain.' "

"The poison," Lund said. "Must have been eating him alive."

"Something more than that." Freebairn looked at me. "Silence kills, Mr. Yeager. It killed my boy."

"Tell me about him."

With delicate and reverent slowness, the undertaker handed me a photograph from his suit pocket. An old matte color print from the late 1970s, showing three preteen boys holding brand-new 35mm Nikons. I recognized Dale and Pete. Between them was a plump boy—frizzy hair, pasty skin. There was something fragile, almost frenzied, in his bright blue eyes.

"My wife and I never could have children," said Freebairn. "So we decided the Lord had intended us to adopt. We brought Theodore home from a woman who'd . . . well, she'd treated him badly. But he was a bright boy, smart as a whip. Wanted so much to come home with us. We thought maybe we could . . . save him."

"Who took the picture? Dubliner?"

Freebairn nodded. "Turn it over."

I did as he asked. "What's this written on the back? Something in Japanese?"

"Lakota Sioux," answered Lund. " *'Nagi Wa Oyuspa.'* An Indian word for *photographer.* It literally means, 'He captures the spirit.' A more familiar translation would be—"

" 'Shadow Catcher,' " I said.

"That was what he made the children call him," Davis said. "Rafe never knew I kept this picture. I want you to have it now."

"Thank you." I turned to Dr. Lund. "Okay, Doc. Time for answers."

Lund put a hand to his face. "I gave my word."

"Sig," Freebairn said. "Like the man said: we all have to stand before God."

"I've lived too long in shame," Lund said. "There are only three living witnesses to the events I'm about to relate, Mike. They're all in this room."

"I'm listening."

"Rudy Dubliner came here in nineteen sixty-eight. Said he was from Montana, but he never kept his story straight . . . not that anyone was listening. Right off, Rafe put him on his Pay-No-Mind list. You tended to forget about Dubliner when he wasn't around. You'd pass him in the grocery store, and five minutes later ask your wife who you'd just said hello to."

"What did he look like?"

He shrugged. "Everybody. Nobody. He had congenital amblyopia—lazy eye. Strong as a bull, though. Toted those big cameras around like a bunch of daisies. Picnics, christenings, softball games . . . folks got so used to seeing Rudy, he just blended in."

"The point being," I said, "he liked to be wherever children were."

"He got to know those kids better than their own parents," Lund said. "Birthdays. Favorite bands. Crushes. People just figured it was Rudy trying to drum up photography work."

"And always watching," Freebairn said. "Always studying our babies."

"When did he start hunting?"

"Not for years," Lund said. "My guess is he wanted people to get used to him. Especially his victims. And he needed time to . . . prepare."

"He built himself a special place," Freebairn explained. "Dug it out . . . Rafe said he covered up so well you could walk right over it. And a bloodhound wouldn't smell what was . . . down there."

"By the winter of 1977 he was ready," said Lund. "All that remained was to choose his victims. He was very careful about that, too. Took his time getting to know the kids. Children who were . . . well . . ."

"Kids who were at odds with their parents," said Freebairn. "Like my Theo with me. Kids who had weaknesses or fears he could use. Play hero to. Tell 'em they was right for hatin' their folks."

"We just never saw Rudy that way," said Lund. "But to those young ones he became everything. Poet, friend, advisor, teacher . . ."

". . . God," I said. "The center of their universe."

"Exactly. He made them feel special. Beautiful. Understood."

"Theo was the first," Freebairn said. "Always a bit feisty . . . but a good heart. Then he just changed. And now he was smartin' off, yellin' . . . terrible things he did. One day I found these—picture books in his room."

"What kinds of pictures?"

"Pervert pictures," he said. "He'd scratched the faces out . . . wrote cuss words in 'em. Soon after that he was gone. Left this awful note sayin' he'd run away. We didn't know what to do but pray, hoping Jesus would keep sending him our love. But then Dale went. And Pete."

"And finally he came for Martha and Mary Frances." I looked at Archer. "And you couldn't close your eyes any more . . . could you, Sheriff?"

"Oh, Rafe was an avenging angel in those days," said the doctor. "Strong and sleepless. He lit up that whole county with searchlights. But even the brightest lamp can't shine everywhere. Two weeks after Mary and Martha went, he started to break down. We didn't know at the time—but he'd begun to receive pictures of the children. Showing precisely what had been done to them. And every one that came took a little piece out of Rafe. Looking into his eyes was like staring down the black barrel of his Colt revolver. Nothing alive in 'em."

"Is that how Dubliner gave himself away? By sending pictures?"

Lund shook his head. "Not exactly. You must remember, Rudy knew how to blend in. But his ego wouldn't let him hide. He had to prove how brilliant he was. How powerful. And so he broke his own cover."

"He joined the search party," I said.

"Just so," Freebairn said. "I remember thinking, 'That man is a true Christian.' Every day, there he was. Making coffee, markin' trails. And all the while leadin' us a merry chase. Laughing at our sentimental weakness in his black heart."

"Right away Rafe starts to wonder," Lund said. "How is it the kidnapper manages to stay ahead of him? Sheriff figures it has to be somebody inside the search. So one night he looks to one side . . . and it's just a bunch of grab-ass deputies who think they're looking for runaways. Then he turns to his other side . . . and he sees parents too scared to think about anything. And then he looks ahead of him . . . and he sees Rudy Dubliner. Old Pay-No-Mind Rudy, always on your elbow like a trusty hunting dog. Good old Rudy, with his cameras."

"What did the sheriff do?"

"Nothing right away," Freebairn said. "Last thing he wanted was a trial, with all the reporters and lawyers sayin' the sheriff couldn't protect his own kids. But he also knew . . . no way in hell could he let Rudy get away. And if Dubliner got a whiff that Archer was onto him, he might just kill his hostages. So overnight Archer became Rudy's best buddy—even deputized him. Rudy lapped it up like a cat eatin' cream. Then one evening, Rafe calls me and says, 'I want you to drive tonight. Bring thus-and-such in the back of your wagon. And come alone.' Doesn't say what he wants it for. But from the list he gave me I know it's gonna be bad."

"Same with me," said Lund. "He told me to bring my kit—extra bandages and sutures—and prepare for the worst."

"That Halloween night there was no moon," said Freebairn. "Cold and dark as the heart of hell. Archer made some excuse to send his deputies off. 'Cause what he wanted to do, he aimed to keep quiet. The four of us drive far out into the central valley. I'm behind the wheel, and Sig here is next to me. And Sheriff's in the back with Rudy."

"The whole time, Rafe is talking," Lund said. "Reminiscing about his little girls. How sweet they were as babies. What they'd wanted to be for Halloween. In all the years I'd known Rafe, I'd never heard him open his heart so much. Never saw him . . . so vulnerable."

"Meanwhile our friend Mr. Dubliner is as quiet as you please," Freebairn said. "Then Sheriff points off into the desert and says, 'Davis, park over there. Some kids left a campfire burnin'. Sure enough there's a fire. And a blanket on the ground . . . and a ten-gallon can of gas. Usually when you see something like that you kick it out, so it won't cause a brushfire. But Archer just reaches down and says, 'Well, look here. I think we've got our man.' And he opens this envelope . . . and there's photographs inside."

"He gave them to me first," Lund said. "The moment I saw what had been done to these little ones . . . it was like a knife in my heart. Even in Korea I'd never seen such things—and never, never with children. I wept . . . I couldn't breathe. Then he says, 'Give 'em to Davis. His turn.'"

"... And I take them," said the mortician. "And I swore right there I would tear the living heart from the man who harmed my Theodore."

"That's when I realized what Rafe was doing," the doctor said.

"He was watching," I said. "To see what was in your eyes."

Freebairn nodded. "Then Archer said, 'Now show 'em to Rudy.' And Rudy took 'em as cool as a postman stampin' a letter. He looked ... and looked ... and he kept on looking. Longest of any of us, he stared at those pictures of our children."

"How did he react?"

"He remarked on the quality of the pictures. Said, 'This is one fella who knows his craft.' It was then I understood what Rafe had brought me out there to do. And I was glad."

Lund rubbed his eyes. "Rafe pulls the blanket aside, and there's four stakes set in the ground. On each stake is a chain ... and a hook, like you hang meat on. Sheriff's quiet. Never seen a man so cool. He put his hand on that Colt revolver and says, 'Rudy, I think you better lie down.' And Rudy just laughs! He says, 'Sheriff, you can only kill me once.' Rafe doesn't bat an eyelash. 'Mr. Dubliner,' he says, 'I can kill you so bad it'll feel like it happened a thousand times. Now I've appealed to your compassion. And I'm appealing right now to your common sense. But if that don't work either, there's something else that will.'"

"Pain," I said. "Pain is justice."

Freebairn nodded. "That's just how the sheriff said it. 'We're going to take turns,' he said. 'I'll ask the questions. And if I don't like your answers, Mr. Freebairn here will take something from you. What he takes—and how he takes it—is absolutely up to him. And then I'll ask again. And if you still won't cooperate, then Sig's going to do something even worse.'"

"What was that?"

"It was my job to keep him alive," said Dr. Lund.

We listened to the grinding hum of the respirator. Archer's chest rose and fell in its slow ride toward death. "How long did it take?"

"All night," Lund said. "By the time it was over, there was very little of Rudy Dubliner left. But give the devil his due—he was still alive."

"And he still hadn't told us where he'd taken our children," said Freebairn. "By then it was maybe an hour before dawn. You can tell Sheriff is gettin' not just angry, but stone mean. Even I'm afraid of what I'll have to do next. Then Rudy starts makin' this funny dry sound in his throat, like *eh-eh-eh*. The son of a bitch is laughing at us!"

Lund nodded. "And he says, 'Sheriff, I'll make a deal with you.'"

"He told us, 'I have a witness,'" Freebairn said. "'He's with the children right now. Awaiting my return. If I'm not back by sunrise, the children are dead. But if you agree to my terms, then he'll set 'em free.'"

"Now we didn't know if he was just crazy with pain, and right then we didn't particularly care," said Lund. "I thought he was bluffing. But Archer says, 'What do you want?' And Dubliner juts his chin at Rafe like he's the man in charge, and says—"

"'You have to kill me,'" Freebairn said.

"Rafe nodded," Lund said. "And Dubliner—devil knows how he's breathing by now—says, 'Come closer, and I'll whisper it in your ear.' I honestly didn't think he would do it. But Rafe kneels down, and puts his ear to Rudy's lips. And Rudy whispers something only the sheriff can hear. And then . . ." Lund trembled. "He plants a bloody kiss right on Rafe's neck."

"Rafe stands up like a snake bit him," said Freebairn. "And Dubliner says, 'Well, Sheriff? Do we have a deal?' Rafe don't say a blessed word. Just draws that Buntline Special, slow and careful . . . and puts a .45-caliber bullet through Rudy Dubliner's left eye."

"Archer told me that Colt would do terrible things to a man."

"It does worse to the man that fires it," Lund said. "Rafe left us to deal with the body and drove away. An hour later he came back, covered with soot and ashes . . . and he had the children with him. They were unconscious . . . in terrible shape . . . but they were alive."

"Not all of the children." Freebairn's eyes were red. "He looked at me and said, 'I'm sorry, Davis. Your son . . . burned to death.'"

Freebairn covered his face with his hand.

"So he never told you where the hiding place was?"

Lund shook his head. "You can probably guess. That was the night of the Cathedral Lake fire."

"And the witness?" I said. "Where was he?"

The men looked at each other. "There was no such person," Lund said. "Or so we decided. I thought it was all over but the grieving. But then—"

"Archer came to me the very next morning," said Freebairn. "Tells me to write out Theo's death certificate. And put down he had a hiking accident, or whatever wouldn't get people too curious. And I said, 'Rafe, this is my son you're talking about. What you're asking for is plain wrong.' He just stares at me. 'And what do you call what you did last night?' I said I had no trouble with what we did to Rudy, and I'd just as soon never hear his name again. But I wouldn't dishonor my son's memory with a lie. Got my walking papers that very day."

"That was when Rafe came to me," said Lund. "I told him pretty much what Davis did. But then he said, 'Sig, I need you to do this. Because if word gets out what happened, then these children will carry the shame their whole lives. No one will understand they were forced. We have to bury all this so deep that it can never rise again.' And finally . . . I agreed to help him."

"And that was the beginning of the lie," I said.

"Yes," said Lund. "And that was the life and death of Mr. Rudy Dubliner, who called himself the Shadow Catcher. Rafe didn't even bother making up a story about him. He figured . . . correctly . . . that people would barely remember Old Walleyes a year or two down the road. Except for those few of us who had looked into Rudy's soul . . . and we were bound by the pact of silence."

"But somebody broke the pact," I said. "And the Shadow Catcher has returned."

There came a soft tapping at the glass. The nurse, pointing at her watch.

Lund stretched. "Gentlemen, we have outstayed our welcome."

I stood up as he opened the door. "Doctor, I'd like a moment with the sheriff alone. Something I need to say to him."

"He won't hear you," Lund said.

"I'll hear me."

Lund nodded as he and Freebairn left, closing the door behind them.

I stood over the bed, took Archer's rough knotted hand in my own. His fingers curled around mine, like a baby's. Even in the space of a few minutes the old man had withered. Yet some part of him still forced that heart to beat. Something more than hatred. More than the poison in his body.

"It's more than pain, Sheriff. It has to be more than pain."

FIFTY-TWO

Lund was waiting outside under a copper-colored dusk.

"Davis went on home," he said. "This was very hard on him. Theo was his whole life."

"And you?"

"I'll manage. Whatever happens, I think my days of turning a blind eye are done."

"Too bad the sheriff never made that decision," I said. "How do you suppose a man as suspicious as Archer could be fooled by someone like Rudy Dubliner?"

"I suspect that like most men who consider themselves hard to fool, Archer had a massive blind spot. In his case it was a bad habit of confusing submission with loyalty."

"Incidentally, whatever happened to Dubliner's photographs? Any chance they could have survived?"

Lund thought a moment. "If they did—which I doubt—then the only person who could have preserved them would have been the sheriff himself."

"And, of course, the witness."

"If there ever was any such person."

"I think he's real. And so do you." I held up the photo of Theodore Freebairn. "Theo's gripping the camera in his left hand . . . but focusing his right eye on the camera. Just like Espero. Mixed dominance."

"You'd have made a fine physician." Lund studied the photograph carefully. "I remember when Davis first brought Theo to me . . . angry, distractible, highly destructive. There'd been trouble at the funeral home. Davis wouldn't say exactly what. But I gathered the boy had . . . done things in the embalming room."

"With a trocar?"

"Yes." Lund shuddered. "I diagnosed him as hyperactive and prescribed Ritalin. Of course, Ritalin's a stimulant . . . when his condition worsened, I realized it wasn't ADHD at all. I took a head X-ray and found the contusion. It was very old . . . almost certainly predated the boy's adoption."

"Did you ask him how it happened?"

"I did. He started screaming. 'Don't send me away. I want to stay here. Please don't make me leave.' I'd never seen a child so terrified."

"You didn't happen to keep those X-rays, did you?"

"Yes—but it doesn't matter. Theodore Freebairn is dead."

"You saw him die? Or is that just something Archer told you?"

"Of course I wasn't there, but—Davis buried him, for God's sake."

"Did you ever look inside the coffin?"

He said nothing.

"Doctor, just suppose for a moment. If Theo had lived, impossible as it seems—wouldn't he make a likely suspect?"

"Yes, but . . ." He thought for a long time. "He would have needed to transform himself radically. Enough to fool his own father. People do change over the years. Even so . . ." Lund looked at me, bewildered. "At this point, Mike—and I say this with complete honesty—you know as much as I do."

"Let's hope it's enough."

His eyes widened. "Then you are staying."

"Let's say I'm about to find out how much pain I can take." I smiled. "I have to ask Tippet for my job back."

He looked at me earnestly. "Thank you, Mike."

As the doctor walked away, I noticed that he seemed to stand a little taller.

FIFTY-THREE

As far as anyone at the sheriff's station knew, Tippet had gone straight from the courthouse to the lockup. Then, at 5:58 P.M., he checked out a cruiser from the garage and left. The evidence room deputy hinted that Tippet might have stopped by to check the trocar back into custody—or he might not have—but to find out either way, I'd have to get direct authorization from Tippet, or the sheriff . . . or the acting sheriff in Archer's absence.

"And who would that be?" I asked.

He held up both hands. "You tell me and we'll both know."

I left him and headed for the lockup.

Pete Frizelle stumbled into the interview room, sporting a fresh bruise on his cheek. He hadn't lost his swagger, though. He sat down at that table like he was about to make me an offer for it.

"What the hell happened to you?" I asked.

"Slipped in the hot tub," he said. "Keep up the shitty service, I'm gonna file a complaint with management."

"Sorry to say I don't have much pull with the new administration."

"You think maybe Buford's havin' second thoughts about the job?" He grinned. "Life span of the average sheriff's been droppin' pretty steady last few hours."

"How do you feel about what happened to Archer?"

"Man got his comeuppance. How'm I s'posed to feel? Sorry? I'm sorry I might be joinin' him."

"He did save your life, once upon a time."

"Yeah. Well. Remind me to send him a card next St. Asshole's Day.

Didn't do my worthless butt no favors." He shivered. "Where the hell is Buford, anyhow? Fucker was supposed to get me outa here. That Jaguar's got shitty transmission, too."

"I don't think anybody's coming to get you this time, Pete. Right now it's just you and me. Worthless or not, you're my only link to the man who killed your girlfriend." I slid the photograph of the three boys to him. "Tell me about Theodore Freebairn."

Pete stared at it like a cat watching a mean dog. "Just some kid me and Dale hung out with."

"But not just any kid, right? And not just anybody taking the picture. R. D.—Rudy Dubliner? You remember what you told me this morning?"

"Hell I can't remember my own name. Tippet musta knocked half my brains out." He looked away.

"Right. Well, thanks for cooperating." I took the photo and stood up.

"Where you goin'?"

"I'm not wasting any more time on you. Hope you kept up the premiums on your decapitation insurance."

"Mr. Yeager, wait."

In two meetings he'd called me *dude, bo, Poppin' Fresh.* Now for the first time he was addressing me by name.

"If I tell you things . . . important things . . . just don't walk out, okay?" He laughed weakly. "Maybe a man could get a bite to eat? Strictly of the nonpoisoned variety? Ain't swallowed much lately 'cept my own broke teeth."

I sat down again. "If you tell me the truth, Frizelle, I'll bring you a turkey sub with extra mayo and a bag of Funyuns. On the other hand, maybe I'll pour it down a tube in your nose. I'm not much on witnesses who threaten hunger strikes."

"That what I am now? A witness?"

"Were you?"

He thought a moment before answering. "You ever hear of somethin' called the Witness Protection Program?"

"I've had some dealings with it."

"They give you a new life, right? New name, new Social Security . . . one thing they can't give, and that's a new you. They can't put back what some other sumbitch took away. I look at that picture of me . . . I don't know that boy Pete. All I remember's bein' with Rudy. That crazy eye of his. Any part of me worth keepin', he took."

"I notice you kept that Nikon he gave you."

"So in other words what?"

"He couldn't take everything," I said. "And your daughter is still alive."

"Gimme that back." He took it from me. "This picture got took at the Secret Camera Club . . . also known as Chez Rudy. Hadda been before the girls came into the picture."

"And Theo?"

"Theo." He drew the word out. "Mr. D.'s favorite little pet. Smart as a whip . . . but a total spazz. I don't mean to speak ill of the dead. But he could suck the life right out of a room."

"Why'd you hang out with him, then?"

"You kinda felt sorry for the little fucker—at first. He was so eager for people to like him. I knew how that was, my mom bein' in the whorehouse business. And Dale . . . well, Dale was everybody's friend. So we let Theo pal around—till he started to creep us out."

"How so?"

"He thought death was funny." Pete shook his head. "One time he snuck us into his dad's funeral home . . . round back where they worked on the bodies. Man, I'd never seen a corpse before—bet your ass I was scared! There was this fat old lady dead on the table. Theo picks up her hands and starts wavin' 'em around, singin' *meow, meow, meow, meow*—like that cat food commercial. Dale said she deserved respect and he'd kick Theo's ass for him if he didn't quit. He sure had it in for Dale after that."

"But you stayed friends."

Pete raised his hands. "He had all these pictures o'naked women! Said he knew a guy who took nudie shots of Vegas strippers, and if we came by we could have some. Well, of course that guy turned out to be good ole Rudy. We got the pictures . . . plus all the weed we could inhale . . . then one day when we was all good and juiced and stoned, Rudy says, 'How's about we liven up the party?'" His face darkened. "After that . . . things got weird."

"Did you try to tell anyone what happened? Your mother?"

"I was afraid people would think I was a homo." Frizelle stared away. "Anyhow, Rudy used Theo as a kind of middleman. So's nobody could connect him to us. Only Theodore was useless when it came to girls. That's where I came in handy."

"Another go-between," I said. "Did you think at the time you were doing a bad thing, bringing Mary and Martha into the Camera Club?"

"No, 'cause by then I was halfway turned into a little Rudy myself." He shook his head. "Sounds crazy now. But Mr. D. made us all feel like we had permission to do anything—as long as it was what he wanted us to do. Always acted like he was tryin' to teach us. I guess to God he did."

"But you're not like that now."

"No, but I ain't exactly a role model neither." He rubbed his cheek. "Only one of us ever came out with his head held high, and that's Dale. And he's the one Rudy messed with worst of all."

"How do you think Dale managed to survive?"

"No question about it. It was his daddy's ring."

"His ring."

Pete nodded. "The whole time we was down in the dungeon, Dale talked about his dad who died in Vietnam. He said they could take anything from him, but as long as he had that ring, he knew we was gonna come out okay. 'Cause he was gonna be a U.S. marine one day like his daddy. And marines are not allowed to die without permission."

"That's why he always wore it."

"Yeah." He looked down, red-eyed. "Shit, I always thought I'd feel better after I talked."

"Someday, maybe. What about Theo? What did he want to be when he grew up?"

"Why're you askin' so much about a dead kid?"

"Is he dead?"

"I hope to God." Pete thought. "Every time you turned around, Theo wanted to be somethin' else. Mind, it always hadda be huge, like brain surgeon or multibillionare movie director. But one thing he always came back to, and that was bein' a government spy."

"Really."

He nodded. "And he was a regular little spook, I tell ya. He could do voices—imitate people, y'know. Had all these books tellin' you how to make homemade bombs—mail-order catalogs for guns and electronics and ninja shit. Oh, and weapons. Theo loved his weapons. He was the one who got me interested in samurai swords."

"Did he ever own any swords?"

"Oh, yeah. I'll never forget the time he put one to my neck and said he was gonna cut my head off."

I forced myself not to react. "What did you do?"

He laughed harshly. "Turned around and knocked that thing outa his hand. Sometimes I think he really woulda done it. But he was a regular coward when you took his toys away."

"So if he'd lived, you think he might have tried to go into law enforcement?"

Pete shrugged. "My mama always says you can become anything. God knows Theo tried. But one thing he couldn't become, and that was a plain old regular human being. He could be smart or friendly or mean or you-name-it . . . but he had dead eyes, like a corpse. And there weren't anything he could do about that. We used to say Theo was a nobody because he couldn't make anything else of himself. Maybe that's why he loved Mr. D. so much. Rudy gave him somebody to be."

"Well, I think that's worth a sandwich, Pete."

He grinned. "And Funyuns?"

"For Funyuns you have to work a little harder," I said. "What did Detective Tippet want you to talk about?"

Pete laughed. "It's what he didn't want me to talk about."

"And what was that?"

"Everything I just got done tellin' you." He gave me an appraising nod. "Say if that ain't worth a bag o'chips."

FIFTY-FOUR

"Ye—? Wh—you want?" The voice on Tippet's cell phone was peppered with silence. Since I was speaking from my office, I had to assume the breakup was on his end.

"It's time we started sharing information," I said. "Screw the politics. I'm willing to give you what I have if you'll do the same."

"What makes you th—need anything from you?" He was coming through clearer now. Sounded like he might be out of doors. "Makin' this case just fine, Yeager, and good riddance."

"Quit showboating, Tippet. If you had the case, you wouldn't have high-tailed it out of that press conference. Something Archer said must have got you running scared."

There was a long silence, and for a moment I thought I'd lost the connection. Then an eighteen-wheeler's horn sounded on his end, a sharp Doppler shift roaring by.

"What do you have?" he said finally.

"You tell me where you found that eight-millimeter film, and I'll tell you what it means."

"Go on."

"You can take the credit for whatever happens," I said. "We nail this guy, bring the kids home, it's all yours. All I want is a look at the physical evidence. That includes whatever you took when you jumped me Sunday night."

"Yeager, you are one paranoid bastard," he said. "Thought you said you had somethin' to share."

"I know all about you and the sheriff's daughter," I said. "You can burn those negatives, but there's always going to be a few more you couldn't find. And even the Frizelles aren't going to cover for you if Cassie's life is on the line. So make your choice. Be a hero . . . or watch your career go up in cinders."

I could hear him breathing hard. Then the signal died.

At first I cursed myself for letting him hang up, all the more when he didn't pick up again. But as I thought about that eighteen-wheeler's horn, I realized there weren't too many places he could be. The tractor-trailer had been moving too fast for anything but Highway 313. All I had to do was keep driving south. And the closer I got to Caritas, the more certain I became of where he'd gone.

The moon over Morningstar Cemetery was hidden behind storm clouds. From a distance I saw the blue lights of Tippet's police cruiser, parked near the gate. He wasn't in the car. I approached cautiously, sweeping my flashlight in a broad circle. Not for the first time since coming to Dyer County, I found myself wishing I was armed.

The driver's side door was slightly ajar. The interior was warm and the police radio was on. I checked the dashboard computer. Apparently he'd only just begun the process of pulling up a vehicle ID but hadn't input any data. Something—or someone—had persuaded him to break procedure and get out of his cruiser before identifying the potential threat.

A clatter of wild *yips* startled me—coyotes, down from the mountains. I picked up the radio microphone.

"Dispatch," said a voice, heavy with static.

I gave him my name and location. "Lieutenant Tippet is not in or near his cruiser. We may have a man down."

"Understood, sir. Please stay with the vehicle and await backup."

I was about to do just that when my flashlight caught something near the gate. The olive-drab sleeve of Tippet's uniform jacket.

"Tippet?" No answer. It was only the empty jacket, hung neatly over an old wooden cross like a scarecrow. I swept the graveyard with my flashlight, then pushed the gate open and walked through. Tippet's Durango boots were lined up at the foot of the cross. His gun belt dangled beside the jacket. I took out his .38, still fully loaded. As I cocked it, something moved behind me, running lightly.

I wheeled around, gun in hand. A pair of yellow eyes gleamed at me, then cautiously stepped into the light. A coyote. Something was in its mouth that might have been a sock. It stared, frozen still—then trotted away, as if I was of no account. It dove behind a backhoe, reappeared beside a large pile of freshly turned earth. And leapt nimbly across the open grave of Theodore Freebairn.

As I approached the grave I heard a sound over the high wind. A faint knocking. I leaned over the open pit. There at the bottom, cradled in a concrete vault, was a white coffin. There were scratches near the hasp, as if someone had recently broken it open.

"Good Christ," I said.

The brass handles of the coffin jumped.

Jesus fuck.

"Hello?" I said. "Can you—"

This time I definitely heard a pounding inside the casket.

Don't do this, Mike, I told myself. For chrissakes, get out. But someone could be in there. Alive and in pain.

"Okay, I can hear you. Just hang on."

The thumping grew louder. Frantic.

"I'm not going to leave you here. I promise you'll be okay." I was beginning to feel silly without knowing why.

I heard moaning inside. Whimpering. Before I knew what I was doing, I'd jumped down into the grave and landed hard on the coffin. The top half of the lid shook violently. I pocketed the .38 and fumbled for the casket's broken lock.

"Okay, okay," I said, conscious of my own breathing. "Let's get you out of th—"

As I raised the lid a large, naked man pushed himself up from the coffin and collided against me. His fleshy palm, slick with blood, struck me in the eye. I fell backward and he landed on top of me. A weird moaning rose from his throat—not quite human, strangely muffled. My flashlight shone into the face of Jackson Tippet.

His eyes and mouth had been sewn shut.

"MMMMNNHHH! MMMGGHHNNHH!" He pawed at me like a drowning man trying to push the lifeguard under. Blood and fluid trickled from the closely spaced stitches in his mouth—which curved up at either end, giving him a rag doll's mindless grin. The eyes were thick upward slits, a caricature of sleepy contentment. His nostrils frothed and spat as he tried desperately to breathe. And as the scream forced its way through, stitches tore at the flesh around his lips.

"Calm down!" I shouted. "Just calm down! You're gonna be—" *All right?* I thought. *Sweet Christ.* His knee drove into my chest and he pushed himself over me. He slammed into the side of the vault like a side of beef—then fell back into the silk-lined casket. Now I could see why his boots had been removed. He wouldn't need them any more.

Tippet's feet had been cleanly severed at the ankles.

FIFTY-FIVE

I drove hell-bent to the station, drawing stares all the way up to my office—my shirt was still covered with grave dirt and Tippet's blood. The phone was ringing as I opened the door.

"Yeah?"

"Mike, it's Peggy. I've been trying to get you all—what the hell's going on?"

"Everything. Robbie went missing, and—did you get my message? The name I left on your voice mail."

"Rudy Dubliner, yeah. Look, this thing of yours is starting to make serious waves. I've got calls from the OPR, the Vegas field office, and the deputy director—all wanting to know what the hell happened to your sheriff on live television today. And why the Bureau's name is getting dragged in. What's wrong?"

"Thirty minutes ago a blind, naked man jumped out of a coffin at me."

She took a breath. "Did he tell you why?"

"That would be a real trick, considering they also sewed his mouth shut. It's Tippet."

"My God."

"He's not dead, but—he's not talking, that's for sure. Look, I'm gonna call you later."

"Mike, w—"

"I gotta get on top of this, Peg. I'm a little messed up right now."

I hung up the phone, still shaking from adrenaline rush. I took several long breaths, then called Dr. Lund.

———

The doctor was waiting as I came out of the washroom.

"Any word on Tippet?" I pulled on a borrowed sweatshirt from the gym.

"Alive at last report. What time did you say you spoke to him?"

"I talked to somebody on his cell phone around eight o'clock. But it was only twenty minutes later when I found him."

"It wouldn't have been enough time to . . . do what was done to him. You must have spoken to someone else."

"Pete did say Theo was good at imitating voices," I said. "Does Davis know what happened to his son's grave?"

"No. But I don't think he deserves to hear about it on the radio."

"Let's bring him into protective custody," I said. "I take it Buford's ready for us."

He nodded. "And the judge."

Both men were waiting in Archer's office. The judge sat idly sipping the sheriff's whiskey. I had to force myself to picture him in his judicial robes, and not as I saw him in those Sweet Charity photos. Buford paced the floor like he wanted to sit in the sheriff's chair, but couldn't quite get up the nerve.

"Gentlemen," I said. "Thanks for coming out on what has to be a busy night for you both."

"Sure as hell is," Warburton grumbled. "I'm assumin' you do know this case is no longer in your jurisdiction."

"I'm afraid it is whether you like it or not. The subject made an attempt on my life. Threatening harm to an FBI agent is a federal offense."

"Bull hockey."

The judge peered over his highball glass. "Let's hear the man out, Buford."

"Tippet was almost certainly attacked to shut him up," I said. "Which makes you a target as well, Buford. I suggest you open your mouth while you still can."

His mouth was already open as I said this, and it took him a moment longer to speak. "You don't call me Buford, hear? As of the close of polls today, I'm the duly elected sheriff of this county."

I looked at the judge. "Is he?"

"Well—maybe," the judge said. "As you may know, the ballot was in two parts. Part one was on the question of the sheriff's recall. In the event the recall succeeded, he would vacate office as soon as the votes were certifled. Part two would have chosen his successor. We're still counting ballots, but it appears Buford has won a clear majority among the candidates."

Buford raised his hands. "That's all I'm sayin'."

"Even so," the judge continued. "Amazing as it may seem, part one of the ballot doesn't look like it's going to pass. Rafe Archer may not live the night, but he seems to have survived the recall."

Warburton blinked.

"So who's in charge now?" I asked.

"The county bylaws are quite plain. In the event of the sheriff's death or sudden incapacitation, the role of acting sheriff automatically goes to—" He gestured at Lund.

"The district coroner." Lund sighed. "I was afraid of that."

"Now that we've cleared that up," I said. "Let me ask you politely . . . Buford. Where did Tippet find those items you showed at the press conference today?"

He reddened. "I don't know anything. Tip did all the legwork. I just—"

"—made big speeches, I know. That's the problem. If you'd bothered to learn anything about the subject, you'd know he's got a pretty sizable ego. I don't think he liked being called a brain-damaged Satanist."

Buford gulped. "Tip found that needle at Dale's house. And the letter. I ain't sure exactly where. He called me first thing Saturday . . . I said it was a good opportunity and we oughtta take advantage."

He spoke without the slightest hint of shame.

"Tip said we couldn't outright hide what he found," he continued, "or that would be suppression of evidence. But I figured we could take a chance buryin' 'em at the bottom of the inventory, where Archer wouldn't be so quick to notice. So instead of *trocar* he wrote *metal object* . . ."

The judge winced.

"Where's the letter?" I asked.

"I don't have it. Or the murder weapon. Swear on my mother's grave, Tippet took 'em when he left."

I looked at the judge. "Your Honor, I'll leave you to deal with Mr. Warburton and the election commission. Dr. Lund and I have some urgent matters to attend to."

"Surely." The judge rose as Buford skulked away.

"Tell me," I said. "You wouldn't be the same judge who presided over Cassandra's custody hearing, would you?"

"I would," he said with an affable air. "Why?"

"I was just curious why you accepted a transcript of her interview when most family courts require video."

He throttled back his smile. "We had video. I viewed the tape in chambers."

"Where's the tape now?"

"Somewhere safe, I'm sure." He shrugged. "Have we by chance met . . . ? You seemed to recognize me as you came in."

"I've seen pictures of you," I said. "Fourth of July."

"Oh." The judge blushed. "My."

He beat a hasty exit.

I turned to Lund. "Well, Mr. Acting Sheriff, shall we see what's in the evidence locker?"

Several file boxes were brought to us in a downstairs conference room.

"Tippet's been a busy fellow," I said, as we sorted through the inventory. "Here's his report on my fight with Dale . . . the B&E at Freebairn and Son . . ."

"What exactly happened at the cemetery, Mike?"

"Damnedest thing I ever saw. Someone had dug out the grave with the groundskeeper's backhoe."

Lund winced. "For God's sake, why?"

"I think it was to prove the coffin was empty," I said. "Our boy wants people to know he's alive. Probably he put Tippet in the casket as a joke—leaving the flashers on to make sure somebody found it right away."

"Tippet didn't even put up a fight?"

"There's a fresh pair of tire treads in front of his cruiser. As near as I can figure, he drove by, saw somebody leaving, and pulled them over. Then he approached the other vehicle—and got one of these in the eye." I held up the bagged trocar.

"I can't imagine anyone getting him to drop his guard like that."

"We'll have to see whose car it was. I don't think Tippet was there by chance. He ran out of the press conference right after Archer said, 'I had to leave him there.' "

"You really think Rafe was talking about Theo."

"Yes, and I think Tippet was beginning to figure that out. Maybe because of something in this letter."

I held it up—a single sheet from a PC printer, spotted with dried blood. "Buford only read the first part," I said. "Here's the rest."

Treat me with cowardice and deceit, and you yourself will answer for her burnt and broken form.

Do not think you can kill me again. You are old now and I am immortal. You are hollow and I am full of light and fire. Your seed will fail and mine will soon find a new vessel. Remember, remember.

Say nothing of this or she will bleed.

"Thinks well of himself, doesn't he?" Lund said, when I finished reading.

"Does it sound anything like Rudy Dubliner?"

"Like a voice out of the grave," he said.

"You know, when Buford read the note, he said 'yourselves'—but here it clearly says 'yourself' in the singular. This must have been intended for Archer's eyes. Only thanks to Tippet, he never saw it." I turned it over. "That's all there is. What do you think 'remember, remember' refers to?"

"It's part of an English children's rhyme for Guy Fawkes Day. 'Remember, remember the fifth of November—gunpowder, treason, and plot.'"

"November fifth is the date of death on Theo's tombstone."

Lund nodded. "And the anniversary of the Cathedral Lake fire."

The evidence room deputy put his head in the door.

"Here's that list of Tip's interview reports," he said.

"Deputy," I said, "I brought in a latex sample yesterday. Any chance of getting an analysis?"

"Talk to the lab." He gave a what-can-you-do wave.

"Latex sample?" Lund asked, as the door shut.

"Something I found up at the camp. It had a partial palmprint. The evidence technician brought it to the lab; the lab claims it came back here. Somewhere in between it disappeared." I started looking through the interview reports. "Let's see who Tippet's been talking to. Davis Freebairn . . . Evelyn Maidstone . . . hm."

"What?"

"Lake Mead Hospital Burn Unit," I said. "Here's another one. A call to the director of the Northern Nevada Medical Center for Plastic and Reconstructive Surgery."

"Did he write down what they talked about?"

"Just says, 'background interview.'" Then I noticed the date. "Wow."

"Seems Tippet had more on the ball than I'd guessed."

"More than any of us would have guessed. Take a look." I turned the file around.

"The date's wrong."

"No, it's not," I said. "He's been following up on this facial reconstruction stuff since the middle of October. Two whole weeks before Cassie's abduction. Now what was happening in mid-October that might have sent him down this path?"

"Espero's disappearance," Lund said.

I nodded. "And Cassie's custody hearing. They both took place on October the thirteenth."

FIFTY-SIX

"What could Tippet have found?" Lund said, as we walked down the hall. "You'd have to believe that he started investigating before there was anything to investigate."

"Not really. During Cassandra's interview, she told Connor something about a hiding place—'Some of him you can see if you go down, down underground.' Archer wrote a note on the transcript advising Connor that Tippet would follow up. I don't know exactly where Tippet looked or what he found—but he must have discovered something that got him interested in burn centers and facial reconstruction."

"Probably the camp," Lund said. "I'm almost certain that's where Rudy held the children."

"I was up there yesterday. I didn't see anything like what you've described."

He shrugged. "Rafe did say it was well hidden."

"Archer was up there three times this weekend. If he'd found anything important, he'd have concentrated the search there, instead of spreading it over half the county."

"Not necessarily. Remember, secrecy has always been Rafe's paramount concern."

"I'm starting to get an idea why. Just before he collapsed, the sheriff said, 'I had to make a choice.' He couldn't take all the children. Maybe he left Rudy's witness behind in that fire."

Lund frowned. "Tomorrow is the fifth, Mike. What do you think will happen?"

"He's already told us. 'Say nothing of this or she will bleed.' And now—for good or ill—the case has gone public."

"Doc." The evidence room deputy leaned into the hallway. "Call for ya."

"I'll be right there," Lund said. "What now, Mike?"

"I'm going down to the media room."

He looked at me, surprised.

"Archer and Gavin asked Connor to interview Cassandra. When the judge said he saw video, I realized—if you were Rafe Archer, and your granddaughter was involved in a custody battle, where would you insist on holding the interview?"

"Right here." His eyes lit up.

"Go take your call. I'm going to find that tape."

The media room kept its surveillance tapes neatly ordered—by date and location—in six rows of metal racks.

"'I'm getting' that film of yours worked on, like you wanted." The technician looked back at me. "Your Vegas people said it's gonna cost a bundle to get it done by tomorrow."

"Tell them to send me a bill." I compared the tapes against the inventory book. "Who's authorized to check these tapes out?"

"Nobody." He looked at me with quiet pride.

"What if it's for the sheriff?"

"If the sheriff wants something, we make him a copy." He pointed to a VCR. "But nothing ever leaves. His orders."

Dr. Lund joined me a few minutes later. "Any luck?"

"I'd need a week to find everything. But take a look at this." I showed him a page in the inventory. "Connor Blackwell was assigned to Conference Room Three from eight till nine A.M. on October thirteenth. Mind you, nothing ever leaves here, but—" I pointed to an empty space on the shelf "—that particular tape appears to be AWOL."

"The judge said he watched a videotape in chambers."

"Right. Let's hope that copy still exists." I exhaled. "I hope you have better news than mine."

"I'm afraid not. That was the hospital."

"Archer?"

"Tippet," he said. "Died fifteen minutes ago. Apparently he pulled his own sutures out."

"I wasn't his biggest fan, but . . . he deserved better." I thought for a moment. "You know, there weren't any marks on his forearm."

"Why would there be?"

"Two guys jumped me Sunday night," I said. "I hit one of them in the face—next day Clyde's got a broken nose. I wrapped a bicycle chain around the other guy's right arm. At the very least it would have left a red mark . . . but Tippet didn't have one."

"For what it's worth," Lund said, "I just spoke to the technician who was supposed to review your latex sample. He never got a chance to analyze it . . . but after some prompting, he finally remembered who had it last."

"Not Tippet."

Lund shook his head. "His partner, Deputy Clyde. It seems no one's seen hide nor hair of him since the funeral." His eyes narrowed. "What about that bothers you, Mike?"

"He's the deputy who was assigned to guard Robbie," I said.

One look at Clyde's personnel file told the entire story. In a small department, one deputy could wear a lot of hats . . . and Clyde seemed to have worn them all. Patrol division. Evidence technician. Administration. Impound. Courthouse security. Like he told me outside Archer's office, he did get moved around.

"All last week, Clyde worked graveyard shift in the media room," I said. "People were so used to seeing him that they stopped noticing."

"You really think he could have taken that videotape without getting caught?"

"You and I just walked out of there. Did we get searched?" I kept looking through the file. "I should have arrested the little slimeball when I caught him snooping around. To hell with that—I should have flattened him."

"Well, at least we've still got the transcript."

"No, we don't," I said. "Shit."

"Who does?"

"Somebody I may have just put in a lot of trouble."

I put the file down and started walking.

"Mike, where are you going?"

Half a dozen deputies sat around the break room, drinking coffee and talking in low voices. They all fell silent as I rapped on the doorway.

"Anybody here know where to find Clyde?" I asked.

One of them tentatively raised his hand. "I know where he does his drinkin'."

FIFTY-SEVEN

I stopped to make one call on my way out the door.

"Dorothy, it's Mike."

"Michael! My God, have you been watching the news?"

"That's why I'm calling. Things are . . . getting ugly. I don't think you should be alone tonight."

"Oh, so? You gonna put me up in one of your cells? Or is this a bona fide proposition?"

"I don't want to take any chances," I said. "Give me your address, I'll send a squad car."

"Michael, I live all the way out on the edge of creation. And with the rains coming . . . anyway, I don't want to ride in the back of some police car."

"All right, I'll come get you. It may take awhile. I have to stop somewhere first."

"Just for clarification," she said. "Are you offering to protect me . . . or asking to see me?"

"A little of both, I guess."

"Well, I don't need protecting."

"I want to see you," I said. "I need to."

She paused. "Let me come to you, okay? It'll be faster."

"I really don't think that's a good idea."

"Then I guess you're just gonna have to swallow your male ego and trust me," she said. "I promise not to stop for strangers."

She was off the phone before I could protest. Dr. Lund was waiting in the lobby, a raincoat over his arm.

"We're getting the search parties reorganized," he said. "More people have volunteered since the news broke on Robbie." He handed me the raincoat. "You're sure of what you're doing?"

"I'll stand a better chance of taking him off guard this way." I saw what was in his other hand. "What's that for?"

"You may need this," he said. "And I think Rafe would want you to have it."

He handed me the Buntline Special.

Thirty miles north of the crossroads, the Amargosa Roadhouse was said to be the only place in Dyer County where you could get a beer, an ounce of crystal meth, and a mouthful of broken teeth—all without leaving your bar stool. My hiding place was an old pumphouse. It didn't offer much protection from the wind, but it had a good line of sight on the exits.

It was spitting rain as the Amargosa's customers started rolling out. *"God damn it's cold!"* cried one drunk biker after another. Finally the last of the Harleys and Dodge Rams disappeared into the night . . . leaving only a white Chevy Silverado with broken headlamps.

Five minutes later the batwing doors opened again. Clyde poked his head out cautiously—then unzipped his fly and urinated right off the front porch. He swayed a little as he shook himself off, eyes closed in relief. It would be such a beauty shot, I realized. I could take him down by the thigh, the shoulder, anything I wanted. But I needed him in condition to talk.

Clyde zipped himself up and ambled off. I walked quietly behind him, heel-toe, maintaining stride with the Colt upright. The noise of the rain covered my footsteps perfectly. Clyde tried to find his key and wound up dropping his whole ring into the mud. As he bent down, I spun the revolver around in my hand and struck it against the base of his skull. His feet shot straight out, throwing his face against the truck door. He fell limp to the mud like a crash test dummy.

"Deputy Clyde," I said, "you are under arrest."

Pete's old Silverado didn't handle too badly, I thought as I drove the winding road back to the crossroads. Occasionally the tires slipped on the slick asphalt. I kept her under sixty and watched for curves.

"So you were the one who took Frizelle's truck from the impound," I said. "And Tippet wasn't with you Sunday night, was he?"

Clyde hadn't said much since regaining consciousness. Handcuffed to the sissy bar and trussed up with duct tape, he mostly looked out the window and whimpered.

"Why do you keep checking the side-view mirror, Clyde?"

"I'm so dead," he slurred. "So fuckin' dead."

"Not that I'm complaining, but maybe it wasn't too smart of you to stop for a drink on your way out of town."

"S'posed to meet somebody," he said. "Hadda hand somethin' over."

"You mean this?" I held up the half-inch videocassette. "What were you going to do, sell it to the media?"

"My head hurts." He winced. "You gotta know somethin'. That whole beatin'-you-up thing was not my idea. Nor killin' Ada. I got roped into it, and right now I just want out."

"Who roped you into it?"

He looked at me, quivering.

"Clyde, the minute your fellow deputies find out you helped burn Ada Rosario, your life's not going to be worth a Confederate nickel. Maybe if you cooperate, we can talk about this at the station. But if I think you're trying to dodge me . . ."

He watched me downshift into second. "What are you doin'?"

"I don't like to drive angry." I pulled over to the shoulder. "You try and shit me, Clyde, and I'll take care of you right here, where there aren't any surveillance cameras. Now who were you working for?"

"It wasn't what I wanted." I could smell the alcohol sweating out of him. "All it was supposed to be was framin' Pete. It wasn't to hurt no kids. Swear to fuckin' God."

"You're not convincing me, Clyde."

"We gotta keep movin'." He gulped. "I'll tell ya anything you want, honest injun, but not here. There's somebody followin'. If he sees me talkin' to you—"

I pulled my fist back. He flinched.

"Christ on a pony, man—look in the rearview!"

I didn't want to take my eyes off Clyde, but something told me he wasn't kidding. I glanced quickly at the mirror. About half a mile back, barely visible through the heavy rain, was a pair of yellow high-beams. A truck, maybe, or four-wheel vehicle. I had seen it before without taking much notice. Now it was on the side of the road. Waiting.

"Who is it?"

"Just drive. Oh God, please drive."

"Close your eyes," I said. "Do it."

I waited till he shut his eyes, then slid the tape under the dashboard. As soon as we started moving again, the headlights began to follow, matching our speed.

"I was at a dead end," he said. "Couldn't get nowhere workin' for that old buzzard Archer. Then he came to me, and said him and some other folks were gonna work it so there was a recall. And when that happened, I'd finally get to move up."

"Who did? Tippet?"

"No, god damn it. The preacher. Brother Gavin."

I looked at him. "You're telling me Gavin McIntosh was behind the recall."

He nodded.

"And kidnapping his own son, too, I guess?"

"Oh man, he's gainin' on us!"

I checked the rearview. The other vehicle was five hundred yards away and closing.

"Hang on." I shifted into overdrive, feeling the tires spin as we crested the hill.

"Here's where the real fuckin' begins," he said.

"Clyde, do me a favor and shut up till I get back on the highway." I pushed it up to eighty. There was no way I was going to outrun this bastard. And it was ten miles back to the crossroads.

"Oh shit watch out—!"

I put on the brakes a second too late. Rocks had fallen across the road. I swerved and we hydroplaned over the narrow shoulder. The truck skidded more than a hundred yards down the hillside. I felt the tires give as we bottomed out. For long seconds there was only darkness and heavy rain.

I looked around. The four-wheel vehicle was nowhere in sight. "Where did it—"

Clyde had pushed the passenger door open and was trying to get out. He slipped in the wet sand and fell, still handcuffed to the overhead bar.

"Clyde, get your ass back in the truck!"

I grabbed him and he screamed, yanking the chromium bar loose. He landed on his feet, hopped a few yards with his legs taped together, and fell. The rain was coming down in sheets now, lit by occasional flashes of lightning.

I circled in front of him. Clyde was crawling.

"Yeager, you gotta let me go, let me go. He's gonna kill me."

I held the Colt to his upturned face. "Look, I will personally ventilate you if you move one more inch. Who's driving that other vehicle?"

He pulled himself up, kneeling.

"He got inside me," Clyde whimpered. "I was in trouble, I was weak, and he got inside. I said I'd help, but I wouldn't hurt no kids. But then the little girl talked, y'see? And that's when Tip found somethin'."

"What? Found what?"

"Pictures," he said. "I told him to leave 'em alone, but he wouldn't listen—and now Christ, look at him—"

"Clyde, did Archer ever explain the philosophy of the Buntline to you?"

He shut his eyes tight.

"So you know I'm not screwing with you." I pulled the hammer back. "Who has the children?"

"*Don't make me say it!*" His eyes broke wide open. "Please, Yeager! You'll never see me again, I swear—"

I felt my finger tighten on the trigger.

"Last chance," I said.

"*Omigod Yeager he's here—!*"

I turned. And faced a wall of darkness.

FIFTY-EIGHT

The dark man was tall, snarling. I turned just in time to see a diagonal streak of silver slicing down.

"*Oh Jesus!*" Clyde yelled. "*Oh man!*"

The Colt fired wild. I fell hard against the side of the truck. There was no pain in my right hand, and for a few seconds I thought he might have cut it off. My attacker raised the sword high. I rolled away and it cut through my jacket like gauze, striking sparks off the truck body. That gave me a bead on him. I dealt a side thrust kick straight into his solar plexus. He landed with a dull sound.

The gun was lying barrel-down in the mud. I retrieved it and backed away. The dark man was getting up. His eyes were points of silver in the dark.

I brought the Colt up in both hands. Lightning flashed. Suddenly he wasn't there. A second later my hand jumped as he kicked the gun away.

Where the fuck is he? Where the f

My head struck the ground.

Clyde was screaming.

My next coherent thought was that I'd better get inside, because it was really coming down like a drunken sailor. Water fell in black sheets, striking my bare neck and shoulders.

"Clyde?" I said. "Where the hell—"

Clyde was gone. Duct tape lay in ribbons. There was a shallow trench in the mud, stained with blood, as if an animal had dragged him away. I rose to my feet, staggered to the white pickup and pushed the driver-side door open.

Where the hell is that tape? I remembered shoving it under the seat—no, the dashboard. If I was lucky, it was still there. He might not have had time to look. Or he might be waiting for me to show him where I'd hidden it.

The gun! I threw on the headlamps. *It's gotta be here,* I thought as I stumbled around the truck. *I can't be caught out here unarmed.*

A single headlamp shone in the distance, fifty yards away. It skidded into the turn, then bounced over the highway shoulder. A dark, hooded figure rode down on me.

"Michael?" A high voice on the wind.

I shielded my eyes against the light. "Dorothy . . . ?"

"Oh God," she said, running from the Vespa. "Michael. What did they do to you?"

FIFTY-NINE

There were periods of blackness as I rode behind her on the bike, and once or twice I had to stop myself from falling. We were climbing narrow switchback roads. Finally we made it above the treeline, where dry scrub and bare rock gave way to aspens and pines: I could smell Ponderosas through the rain. At the end of the road was a small wooden cabin. Wind chimes were blowing. A warm light shone from within.

"Okay, we're here." Dorothy pulled a tarp over the motorbike. "Come on, you'll be all right."

The shower was barely a trickle—but it was warm, and afterward I felt cleaner than I had in days. It wasn't until I saw myself in the bathroom mirror that I realized what a beating I'd taken.

"A face only a mother could love," I muttered to my reflection. "On payday."

Thunder rolled. The lights dimmed, then struggled back.

"Hey, Aquaman!" Dorothy said from the other side. "Heads up!"

The door cracked open and her tiny hand thrust a plaid nightshirt at me.

"Where are my clothes?"

"Drying," she said. "You gonna wear this, or am I gonna have to come in there?"

I grumbled and slipped it on. Dorothy's lonely cabin, high in the north hills, was decorated with throw rugs and Kokopelli figurines. Her living room smelled of incense and last night's wine.

"I look like Grampa Walton in this thing." I closed the bathroom door behind me.

"You look a lot better now than you did when I found you." Dorothy wore a blue terry-cloth robe and thick hiking socks. She took me into her arms and pressed against me. "Mm. You smell like my shampoo. It's—oh, you're shaking." She brushed my hair lightly with her fingertips. "How are you feeling?"

"I've been better," I said. "How did you find me?"

"That's the road I always take to the highway. I didn't know it was you at first. I just saw a truck at the bottom of the hill. If you hadn't turned your lights on, I probably would have gone right past."

"Didn't you promise not to stop for strangers?"

"It's lucky for you I did. You weren't making a lot of sense at first. And it's a long way to the hospital."

"What was I saying?"

"You told me somebody was watching us and we had to keep moving. But we couldn't leave without the tape."

"The tape," I said. "Do you have it?"

She nodded. "It was under the dashboard, like you said." She took it from her raincoat by the door. "PROPERTY OF DYER COUNTY SHERIFF'S DE- PARTMENT. Is this what I think it is?"

"I hope so." I looked around. "We need to get it back to the station. Where's the phone?"

She pointed. "Right by the door. But—"

I picked it up. No dial tone. "Shit."

"The phones are always the first to go," she said.

"How are the roads?"

"I wouldn't want to try them till the rain stops. Not on my little Italian bike." She joined me at the window. "Michael, I really think you need to rest. You look like you're still in shock."

I looked outside. The wind had picked up speed, buffeting the trees. Wa- ter and mud slid down the wet road into the valley. And beyond that only darkness.

"Let's take a look at the tape," I said.

We watched on Dorothy's secondhand VCR. The first few minutes were only static, and for a second I thought I'd been hoodwinked. Then the screen cut to an overhead view of an interview room. The colors were washed out and the audio was mostly hiss. But I immediately recognized Cassandra Dupree. She sat with her arms folded, a tiny figure in pink and purple, alone in a white room. Once or twice she glanced upward with mild interest.

"She's so tiny," Dorothy said.

"Do you see what she's doing?"

Dorothy nodded. "She's looking at the camera. Probably just nervous about being taped."

"I've been in those rooms. The camera's not easy to spot unless you know to look for it. That or she's got really sharp eyes."

"She sees a lot."

A moment later the door opened and Connor Blackwell entered. He set down a plastic tray full of paper and crayons.

"You doing okay in here?" he said. *"Want something to drink?"* Cassie said something in reply, but even with the volume up I could barely hear.

"Do you still have the transcript?" I asked.

She nodded and left the room. On-screen, Connor was sitting down with what looked like a printed list of questions. Every time Cassie answered one, he checked it off. There seemed to be few checkmarks on that page.

Dorothy came back with the transcript. "Did I miss anything?"

"It's like he's following a script," I said. "He keeps asking the same questions, but she's not cooperating."

"Well, no wonder." Dorothy thumbed through the transcript. "I mean, they're okay questions. Nothing misleading or coercive. But you can tell he's nervous. And she's picking up on that."

"What would you have done differently?"

"I wouldn't interview her in jail. She might think she's being punished."

"It is unusual."

"Not that unusual," she said. "I remember this girl I worked with once. The father had raped her . . . the whole family turned against her. But she stuck to her story. Then they put her into that interrogation room, and she just broke down. Eight years old and everyone treated her like a criminal."

"Everyone but you, of course."

She shook her head sadly. "They never heard a word I said." She turned back to the transcript. "I gotta think that's why Connor's so anxious. He knows the sheriff's breathing down his neck. And all he can do is follow his script."

"Connor admitted himself it wasn't a good interview."

After a few minutes we reached the section where Cassie began to describe her nightmare.

"What else happened to you in your bad dream?" Connor asked. *"Can you tell me about it?"*

"It didn't happen to me. It happened to Belle." As she said this, Cassie reached for the tray of paper and crayons.

There was a deadly seriousness to the way she chose each crayon. She drew herself first, then stared at the page for a long time before putting Belle at the bottom—leaving an empty space at the center.

Connor turned his head to look. *"Are you sure you're done drawing yourself?"*

She nodded.

"Well, where's your mouth?" he asked with a gentle laugh.

"I don't got one in my sleep. Only when I wake up." Then she went back to work on Belle.

"What do you think that means, 'only when I wake up'?"

"Not sure." Dorothy furrowed her brow. "It could mean that whatever she's not supposed to talk about only happens at night."

"Who gave you that puppy?" Connor asked.

"My daddy," Cassie answered simply.

I paused the tape. "I never noticed that before," I said. "Her father didn't give her the puppy. Her grandfather did."

"Are you sure?"

"The sheriff told me it was a birthday present."

"A lot of my kids call me 'Mommy' by accident," she said. "Sometimes they get a little mixed up. All men are daddies and all women are mommies."

"How smart a kid would you say Cassie is?"

"Very."

"She's not mixed up." I tapped the screen. "She's looking straight at the camera. Cassie knows where she is. She knows her grandfather's watching." I reached for the remote. "Let's skip ahead. She called the man who killed her puppy 'my daddy,' too, but—"

The screen went black as the lights flickered. Thunder. A moment later we were in the dark.

"Great."

"Give it a second," she said. The lights popped back up, then faded and died. "Okay, I think we're out for the duration."

"So what do we do?"

She looked at me solemnly. "Revert to cannibalism," she said. "Or maybe just eat brownies. And storm or no storm, I'm going to have some wine."

SIXTY

I lit as many candles as I could find. A moment later Dorothy was back from the kitchen with a platter and a bottle of red. As she sat her robe fell slightly open, revealing the curve of her breast. She adjusted it unconsciously.

"Okay," she said. "If this doesn't help, I don't know what will."

I picked up a brownie. "Betty Crocker or Alice B. Toklas?"

"Only one way to find out." She took the brownie from my hand and popped it into my mouth. "You want something to go with that?"

I chewed. "Nothing that would slow me down."

"Maybe that's not such a bad thing." She poured herself a glass. "You always seem to be charging into things."

"It's one way to avoid indecision."

"Now that's strange." She rested a hand on her cheek. "Why would you be afraid to doubt yourself?"

"Working kidnapping is like trying to solve an arson case while there's still people trapped in the fire," I said. "Your best chance of finding a child alive is always in the first forty-eight hours. After that the kidnappers get desperate, the trail goes cold . . . children are fragile. There's no room for hesitation. You're running on nerves and adrenaline."

"What do you run on after the adrenaline wears off?"

"Sometimes you don't. No wonder so many agents burn out."

She drank. "I just wonder why you're still alive."

"I've been asking myself that question for days," I said. "This guy's had at least three chances to kill me. First on Sunday night, then with a bomb in the pay phone. And now tonight. He doesn't want me dead—so what *does* he want?"

"He wants you to feel the way he does," she said. "He wants you to be afraid."

"You've got a profile on this guy, do you?"

"I know about cruel people," she said. "They think they're the victims. It's like what Dale said about the baby crying. There's always a child inside."

"He can't kill unless the victim is vulnerable to him," I said. "They have to be weak and afraid."

"All right. So you're him. What would you be doing right now?"

"Trying like hell to find out what scares Mike Yeager."

"And what do you think that is?"

I bit into another brownie. "I fear nothing."

"Really," she said. "Then what are you running away from?"

"Who's running away?"

She brushed crumbs off my face. "Nobody comes to the desert unless they're trying to leave something else behind."

"Even you?"

"Yeah, but I like it here," she said. "Wait till you see it at sunrise."

Dorothy smiled. Until that moment I hadn't realized how close she was.

"I wouldn't call Philadelphia home," I said finally. "Or even the FBI. In a way, I've always lived on the run."

"You had a place you grew up, didn't you? I know you had sisters who played with corn husks."

"Sure. And two hours reading the Bible every day, and all those goddamn apple trees. And my bastard of a father, whose only real pleasure was seeing which of his children would be the first to crack. Do you know, we got to be so scared of him that if one of us got hit, the rest would just stand there and pretend it wasn't happening?" I took a hard breath. "Sometimes he made us watch."

"And your mother?"

"I barely knew her," I said. "She was just this . . . ghost in a nightgown. It was my job to watch over her—make sure she didn't, you know . . ."

"Hurt herself." Dorothy nodded. "Was she depressed?"

"We were never allowed to give it a name." I began to see her in my mind. Long, dark hair, matted and twisted around her neck like a noose. Fingernails that had to be cut every night so she wouldn't use them to claw herself. And those eyes. Those aching blue eyes of hers, forever searching.

"When I was nine years old I had a nightmare about her," I said. "One of those dreams where you think you're still awake. She was right in front of me . . . and she was sinking into the floor."

"Into the floor?"

"Yeah, like quicksand. And she was screaming. 'Somebody help me. Please help me.' Only . . . I couldn't move. I just had to watch her disappear."

Dorothy brushed my hair. "What a terrible dream."

"It wasn't really a dream." I reached for the wine. "My kid brother shook me awake and I could still hear her downstairs, shouting for somebody to help. My dad was talking back to her—his voice was too low to make out. But whatever he was saying . . . seemed to take her apart."

All at once the room seemed enormous and Dorothy a mile away. But the sound of my mother's voice was as close and steady as my own heartbeat.

"What did you do?" Dorothy asked.

"I didn't, Dorothy. I pretended to be asleep, and finally my brother went back to bed. Like I said. We were that scared."

"You were nine years old," she said. "You couldn't have stopped him."

"I didn't even try," I said. "The next morning we found her in the basement. She'd taken a lot of care to make sure the gas didn't escape . . . sealed all the vents. My first thought was that she looked . . . pretty good. Her skin was bright pink. Of course it was just the carbon monoxide flushing her capillaries. I didn't believe the old man when he told me she was dead. So I had to put my head on her chest to be sure. And he said—'Don't you dare cry. This was your doing.'"

"Oh, Michael."

"He was right. It was the first crime scene I ever worked. And it was from the wrong side."

"Michael, he was wrong. And so are you. You can't go through life—punishing yourself."

I smiled at her. "Oh, I think I can. You asked what keeps me going when the adrenaline runs out. Sometimes it's the smell of that basement I think about—sometimes it's my father's voice. But most of the time . . . it's the dream I have of my mother, sinking into the floor. It doesn't feel great, but it usually works."

"That's not what keeps you going," she said. "It can't be."

"What else is there?"

"Come here," she said.

And then I was in her arms.

Her lips were full and soft, touched with red wine and her sweet breath on my neck. Light at first, tentative kisses as she murmured against my skin. *Love, my love.* Words I could barely understand. She held me for the longest time. I was taking her into my arms. She was letting me press against her, letting her robe fall open.

". . . rid of this," she was saying.

"What's that?"

"The nightshirt," she said. "I think it's served its purpose."

"I don't know if you're gonna . . . like what you . . . oh . . ."

She had lowered herself to the hem and was finding her way up, softly burrowing as her dark hair fell against my thighs. I was naked in her arms. The robe dropped from her shoulders and was gone. I reached to snuff the candle and she took my hand.

"No," she said. "I want to see you."

Now she was above me, round young breasts heavy on my chest. "All these scars . . . ," she said. "What did they . . ." She touched her lips to the bruised rib.

I reached for the curve of her hip against mine. She drew her mouth across me—to my neck, my face, kissing each cut and scar as her hands traveled my body, chest to thigh. She smiled and arched over me, giving me room. Dorothy's hand sought between my legs. Brought me hard against her smooth warm belly. Rubbing me against her.

"You're trembling," she said.

"It's been awhile," I said. "Dorothy, I don't think I can do this."

She raised an eyebrow. "You seem pretty capable to me."

"I want to," I said. "Do I ever. But . . ."

I pulled away.

"Are you feeling guilty?" she said after a long silence. "Is it . . . your old girlfriend? Or what we just talked about?"

"No." I put a hand to my forehead. "I don't know, Dorothy, it feels wrong. We're up here fooling around, and people are down there looking for the children. And the children are waiting . . . and I'm not with them. It would be pretty rotten of me to make love to you, knowing that."

"And if I can make love to you—what would that make me?"

"That's not what I meant. But the fact is, this isn't your responsibility. You have no idea what I have to deal with."

She reflected a moment. "Someday, maybe, I'll tell you my own story. It might change your mind."

She put her hand on my shoulder. I took it in my own. Kissed it softly.

"I'd better go," I said.

"Michael, you can't. It's not safe."

I stood up. "Where are my clothes?"

She frowned, pointing to the bedroom. "On the rack."

I went in and found my jeans on a drying rack beside the heater. As I pulled them on I noticed she'd followed me in.

"Honey—" I turned. She was already putting on a sweater. "Dorothy, what are you doing?"

"I understand, Michael. I really do. I think you're crazy to want to be on the road tonight, especially in your condition. But you don't want to leave the kids in the lurch. Neither do I. So we're both going back to town."

"Baby, it's not safe."

"Really? Whose butt needed saving tonight?"

"Mine." I took a breath. "Look, I shouldn't have shown you the transcript, and I really shouldn't have let you watch the tape. It was pure selfishness on my part."

"You needed my help."

"Yes. But people have died because they came close to identifying the killer. And if you got hurt because I let my guard down . . . I couldn't forgive myself."

She looked at me with aching compassion. "You don't even know why you're hurting. It's not me you're trying to protect. And it's not him you're trying to punish. It's just you, Michael. It was only ever just you."

"What does that even mean?"

"Think about it." She walked past me to the closet. "History does not repeat itself. You think if you care too much about me, then I'll hurt you. Or I'll die. Well, I'm about to prove that everything you've ever learned is wrong."

She opened the mirrored closet door . . .

"Dorothy, stop!"

. . . and the darkness fell on her.

SIXTY-ONE

He filled the closet. A tall man in black, with a pair of silver eyes shining through slits in his hood. He held her pale flesh in two clawed hands. Dorothy was screaming.

"Oh God Michael help me God it hurts—!"

I threw myself on him. His muscles were hard, impossibly strong. Fingers like metal forceps. The gloves tipped with blades, tearing at her white skin. Lines of blood breaking across her belly.

"—cutting me oh please MICHAEL—"

I slammed my first hard against the side of his head and he snarled. An inhuman noise, rabid. Even as he held Dorothy with his left hand, his right slashed at me, flinging me against the bedroom wall.

"Letmegoletmegoletmego—"

Dorothy was struggling. She grasped the jamb of the closet door, her fingers sliding down. He was falling with her, down into the floor.

I leapt forward. "Dorothy, hang on!"

"Oh God he's cutting me—"

He was taking her from me. I grabbed her hand, slick with wet earth and her own blood.

"Cuttingme . . ." Her keening voice rose to a scream. Her hand slipped from mine: gone.

There was a wide black hole in the bottom of the closet. I could still hear her screaming beneath the floor.

I leapt after them.

At first there was only darkness and mud. Then a flapping noise, a dim gray opening in the foundations. As I crawled through, an eight-cylinder engine roared into life. Muddy tires spun hard as two red taillights plummeted out of sight.

I was screaming. No words. A sound that seemed to writhe out of the base of my spine. I was repeating her name, again and again.

Get on top of it, fight it! Control yourself. I pushed myself to my feet. *The motorbike.* I ran to the Vespa, pulled away the plastic sheet, then pushed the bike to the crest of the hill. The vehicle was too far away to make out. All I could see were the brake lights, fading into darkness.

I mounted the bike and began to roll downhill. The other vehicle was half a mile away, beginning its slow turn into the canyon. Now the Vespa was picking up speed. I pushed the clutch in and let it ride down. The wheels didn't so much spin as slide, handlebars bucking and twisting. A cold wind on my face. Blue-black canyon walls rushing past.

I'll only get one shot at this. I popped the clutch and the bike recoiled hard. But the Vespa's engine kicked into life, just as the red lights disappeared around the curve.

I tried to remember the way we came up—the road switched left, then right, then left again. If I went over the edge, I'd go straight into the ravine. The Vespa overbalanced, skidding almost sideways. I leaned right to compensate and just barely recovered. The taillights were back in view, half a mile ahead. It bucked as it hit a bump in the road, then upshifted and roared away.

I was losing her.

He swerved hard to the right. I was just close enough to see into the side-view mirror. The driver was pulling away at the black hood covering his face.

Any second now I'll see his face. That was my last clear thought before being thrown from the bike.

SIXTY-TWO

The wind had begun to die by the time I reached the canyon floor. Night came to charcoal, then ash. Blades of red cirrus clouds cut the sky open as dawn came to Dyer County, Nevada, on the morning of Wednesday, November 5. Dorothy was right. The desert was beautiful at sunrise.

I followed the road wearing only my dirty trousers, glued on like a second skin. My face was dark with mud. My ears were filled with mud. I saw Dorothy falling, slipping away from me. Sunrise reached like bloody claws over the black Sangre de Los Niños. A funeral procession of telephone poles. And Highway 313.

"Hey, buddy."

Someone was calling to me.

"Over here." A young guy with fat sideburns sat behind the wheel of an old Dodge Ram.

"Kinda lost." He grinned. "You know where a man could find some pussy 'round here?"

Half an hour later I stood in front of the Lucky Strike Motel. The storm had blown more letters from the sign, so that it now read:

BLE   E
D   MOV E
KID   S   FR

Bleed. Move. Kid Suffer.

I pulled myself up the concrete steps to my room. There was an unfamiliar blue windbreaker thrown over the TV set. The curve of a woman's back on the bed.

"Dorothy . . . ?" My throat rasped.

"I fell asleep," she said, stretching. "I dreamed . . . Jesus, Yeager. What have you been rolling in?"

She turned on the bed lamp.

Peggy Jean Weaver.

SIXTY-THREE

"So what looks good here?"

Peggy was scanning the breakfast menu at the Silver Star Café. The restaurant was crowded—but no one was talking, apart from sparse thank-yous and please-pass-the-ketchups. The last few days had taken a heavy toll on Dyer County.

". . . you asked for," Peggy was saying.

I looked up. "Sorry?"

"I've got that background on Rudy Dubliner you asked for." She set down the menu. "Seriously, Yeager. When did you last sleep?"

"I think I may have . . ."

"Now what can I get for ya?" Meghan, the waitress from Friday, smiled nervously at me. She wore long sleeves and a fresh black eye.

"Scrambled eggs and orange juice," Peggy said. "Mike?"

I'd nearly forgotten how together—how complete—Peggy Weaver always seemed. Her black travel blazer had fallen open, showing the leather pancake holster strapped tight against her ribcage. The 9mm Glock she preferred to the standard-issue .38, with its spare 16-round clip.

"Mike." Peggy waved her hand in front of my face. "Don't go into the light, sweetie. Stay here with us."

The waitress was gone.

"I ordered for you," she said. "What were you saying?"

"We're just sitting here," I said. "Why are we just sitting here? He's got her, Peg. We've got to move."

She looked at me with concern. "We talked about this, Mike. We're going to look for her. But right now you've got to eat. You're not any good to anyone this way."

I took a breath. "I guess I'm kinda messed up right now."

"That's why I'm here." She handed me a paper napkin.

"What's this for?" I said. "Am I bleeding?"

"You're crying," she said. "It's all right."

"So here's our boy." Peggy spread the file across the formica table. "Rudolph Ignatius Dubliner. Born nineteen thirty-nine in Missoula, Montana. Father was a traveling rep for a school yearbook company—probably that's how the boy learned photography. They lived on the road until Rudy Sr. died in nineteen fifty-five."

I studied the picture of the two. Young Rudy had a lazy eye and a strangely toothy grin. The father's attitude seemed paternal at first—until I noticed how high his hand was resting on the boy's thigh.

"How'd he die?"

"Supposedly a hunting accident. If so, it's the first recorded case of someone getting accidentally shot in the mouth with a rifle. He'd just beat the rap on child molestation in Orme, Tennessee. Apparently the fathers decided to make their own justice."

"To protect the children from shame," I said.

"Same old story. The son made the initial contacts, then Daddy swooped in for the kill. Rudy was still a minor then. He went straight to the police and told them his father was an abuser. When that didn't work, he tried to kill himself."

"Then what?"

"They sent him to a Catholic hospital for observation—made a friend of the chaplain. Father Whatshisname got him transferred to an Iowa farm for boys, where Rudy worked in the slaughter pens. Two years later, they kicked him out for raping a twelve-year-old boy. This time they tried him as an adult—only the complaint didn't stick because—"

"—he'd used another kid as a go-between."

She nodded. "After that he bounced around the Midwest, mostly working in construction. In nineteen sixty-six Dubliner was busted as part of a cottage-industry pedophile ring. Served eighteen months on a ten-year bounce."

"And then?"

"Then he got his second chance," she said. "Right here in Dyer County. Sex offenders didn't have to register then, so he was able to leave his past behind."

"He got forgiven," I said. "To guys like him, forgiveness always equals permission."

She closed the file. "Is this helping at all?"

"It might, if I could keep my head straight." I rubbed my temples. "I can't help but think . . . if I hadn't gone to Dorothy's house last night, he would have left her alone. I killed her, Peg."

She leaned back. "How did you do that?"

"By letting him know she mattered to me," I said. "By letting him know. . . . I wouldn't forgive myself."

She watched me carefully. "Mike, are you gonna be able to get on top of this?"

"I'm trying," I said. "God help me, but if I came face-to-face with the fucker right this minute, I think I'd take him apart."

Peggy glanced around uncomfortably. "Let's move."

As she went up to pay the breakfast tab, I heard familiar music from the next room. I leaned in to see two preteen boys crowding that video game Robbie had been playing on Friday.

"Behind you," the first one said. "Bust his ass!"

"Shit, I'm surrounded!"

For the first time I could see what was on the video screen: DEMON FIGHTER II. A blond warrior, armed with a flashing sword, slashed his way through a subterranean maze. Computer-generated hellbeasts attacked from all sides, spitting blood and slime as the hero hacked away.

"Jump! JUMP! Aw, dude—you choked."

"Chill." The second boy tapped his friend on the shoulder. They both turned to face me.

"What are you boys up to?"

They backed away casually. "Just playin'."

"How's it work?"

"You're fightin' your way into hell." As he said this, demons crowded in and tore the warrior limb from limb. "The farther down you go, the more demons there are."

GAME OVER flashed across the screen, and now the list of high scores was rolling up.

The boy laughed. "You're dead now."

SIXTY-FOUR

We drove to the crossroads in Peggy's white rental Honda. Snow had fallen with the rain, dusting the peaks of the Sangre de los Niños.

"Guess who's Dyer County's Demon Fighter II champion?"

"I wouldn't presume to know," she said.

"Robin Archer McIntosh. The kid who wanted to go live with the Amish. You wouldn't believe how bloody this game is. I'm talking intestines."

She looked over. "Who's the second best player?"

"There isn't one. R. A. M. owns all top ten slots." I paused. "The student outshines the master."

"Meaning what?"

"I'm starting to appreciate the subject's interest in Robbie," I said. "Frizelle told me Dubliner took the role of a teacher—passing on the lessons his own father taught him. How to hunt in remote areas where law enforcement is limited. How to use other children as go-betweens. And Theo was always his best pupil."

"You think the unsub wants his own go-between?"

"Or an heir. In his note to Archer, he said, 'Your seed will fail and mine will soon find a new vessel.' "

"Why would the subject want a handicapped child for his successor?"

"Robbie's legs are handicapped," I said. "His mind isn't. It's Robbie's imagination that makes him a target."

"Or makes him dangerous," Peggy said.

We approached the Unocal station, where two police cruisers waited.

"Peggy, where's my blind spot?"

"Hm?"

"Dr. Lund said Archer had a blind spot for people like Rudy Dubliner . . . the pay-no-mind guys. Where's mine?"

"You're asking me as a former supervisor or former girlfriend?"

"Whichever."

"You have the overachiever's natural tendency to distrust anything that comes too easily," she said. "If I wanted to make absolutely sure you found something . . . I'd put it in a place that was hard to reach."

"And if you wanted to make sure I missed something?"

"I'd glue it to your forehead." She pointed to the road ahead. "Isn't that your coroner?"

I nodded. "So wait. Was that the ex-supervisor or the ex-girlfriend?"

She smiled and unlocked the rear passenger door for Lund. "Doctor, I'm Special Agent Weaver. We spoke on the phone this morning . . . ?"

"Of course, Miss Weaver. How do you do?" Lund climbed into the backseat. "Mike?"

"I'm hanging in there." I reached back to shake his hand. "How's the sheriff?"

"No better and no worse. Breathing's stabilized . . . still on dialysis. He might live to see another sunrise."

"Let's hope we all do."

We drove back toward the Amargosa. Finally we came to the white Chevy, now buried in silt to the wheel wells.

"There's been some minor progress," Lund said. "We tracked down that missing latex sample you found at the camp. No identification on the print. But the material appears to be heavy-grade concealer makeup."

"Right," I said. "Peg, didn't you work a juvenile case involving facial reconstruction?"

She nodded. "In Harrisburg, yeah. That was horrible. Three years of treatment. Thank God it was all middermal."

"How's she doing?"

"Well, they can never give you back your old face. But the skin grafts healed well . . . she's regained a lot of muscle movement. And, you know, she does use a latex concealer to hide the scars."

I turned back to Lund. "How are the autopsy reports coming in?"

"I've got Davis Freebairn temporarily assigned as coroner. He's supposed to call in at ten o'clock." Lund checked his watch. "Which is less than a minute from now. You two go on ahead."

We got out. "Were you able to get a look at your attacker?" Peggy carefully sidestepped down the loose gravel.

"I almost wish I could forget. He was about six feet tall—strong as hell. I remember he had silver eyes."

Peggy raised an eyebrow. "You mean gray, right?"

"Silver. Just like Cassie described in her interview."

We had reached the canyon floor. "There's tracks in the sand," Peggy said. "Down and back again."

"They must have come here after the rain," I said. "Some kind of off-road vehicle."

"Brand-new tires." Peggy knelt down. "I'll say Pirellis . . . top of the line. We should get Highway Patrol working on this."

"No need," I said. "It's a black Nissan four-by-four. Belonging to Gavin McIntosh."

"Are you—"

She looked back over her shoulder. Dr. Lund was clumsily making his way toward us, a look of mortal terror in his eyes.

I took him by the arm, steadying him. "What's the matter?"

"Are you absolutely certain Mary Frances was seen at the church on Friday afternoon? And at the Dupree house?"

"Unless all the witnesses are lying. Why?"

"Davis has completed his autopsy of Mary Frances. And he's quite certain that she died at least five days before you found her under the trailer on Monday."

"How is that possible?" Peggy asked.

"She has a twin sister," I said.

SIXTY-FIVE

Lund stayed behind while Peggy and I drove the road to San Cristobal.

" 'There's no me anymore,' " I said.

"Hm?"

"All those crazy things Martha said are finally beginning to make sense. She told me that when her sister got a spanking, she was the one who cried. And when I asked her how it felt to be separated from Mary Frances, Martha said it was like being amputated."

"Sounds like she's emotionally fused to her sister." Peggy looked at me. "You really think she could pull off the masquerade?"

"With the right hair color and makeup, maybe. I doubt she would have fooled Cassie. But I'm starting to figure out why she wore those dark glasses around Frizelle."

"And you're sure about that four-by-four."

"Martha McIntosh was driving it near the Rosario ranch on the day Espero went missing—no explanation what she was doing up there." I exhaled. "The woman is crazy . . . but I can't see what motive she'd have for participating in her sister's murder."

"It's like you said. All families have secrets."

"Yeah. I did." I looked at her. "Peggy . . ."

"Yeah?"

"It . . . means a lot, your being here," I said. "Between the Bureau politics and—well, everything else—it couldn't have been easy."

She paused, as if wrestling with her answer. "Let's not worry about that right now." Then she looked into her rearview mirror.

"What is it?" I asked.

"Ambulance," she said. "Coming in fast."

She pulled over. The EMT wagon barreled down, lights flashing—then swept away south.

"Peg, lemme borrow your cell phone, okay?"

She handed it to me. I spoke briefly to dispatch, then passed the phone back.

"The ambulance is going to San Cristobal," I said. "Shots have been fired at the McIntosh home."

As we passed the guardhouse, I saw that someone—probably the EMTs or the sheriff's deputies—had driven right through the barrier, knocking the gate to splinters. The ambulance and two cruisers were parked across from the McIntosh house. Two deputies were on the door. Neighbors watched from the safety of their window curtains. The black Nissan was parked askew in the driveway.

"Mike." Peggy pointed to fresh mud on the brand-new Pirelli tires. I nodded.

"What's the situation?" I asked a young deputy crouched behind the mailbox.

"Wish the hell I could tell you, sir. There was a nine-one-one call—lotta screamin', neighbor said. Then a shot fired. Preacher said he'd shoot anybody who tried to come in."

"We have to defuse this," I said. "Under no circumstances attempt to enter the house."

Peggy and I crept up to the door.

"Mike, is this preacher violent? Unstable?"

"No. Martha might be a different story, though." I tried the doorknob. "How do you wanna go in?"

"Ring the doorbell, for starters."

She pushed the button. Heavy chimes sounded. Then a sound of shuffling feet.

"Who's there?" Gavin said from the other side.

"Reverend, it's Mike Yeager. Can we come in and talk to you?"

He hesitated. "Why?"

"We just want to make sure you and your family are okay."

"Do you have a gun?"

"No, Reverend. I'm not armed. The paramedics aren't armed either. They want to help you and your wife and daughter."

"We're fine," he said. "Thank you for your concern. But we're very tired now and we just want to rest."

"Reverend McIntosh?" No answer. "Gavin?" I looked to Peggy. "You're the negotiator."

"Ask about his little girl. By name."

"Reverend, could you do us a favor? Could you take a look at Hannah and tell us if she's okay?"

There was a long silence.

"If I open the door," he said, "will you promise not to attack me?"

"I will not attack you. May I bring the paramedics?"

Another pause. "Whatever you think, I guess, is fine."

I waved the EMTs forward. Peggy took me by the arm.

"He didn't mention his little girl," she said.

There was a sound of turning deadbolts and falling chains. The door cracked open. Reverend McIntosh stood wearing a T-shirt and pajama bottoms. His arms and the front of his shirt were drenched in blood. A small pink kernel of bone dangled from his forelock.

In his right hand was the Buntline Special.

"Reverend," I said. "Where did you get that gun?"

"Martha . . . brought it home this morning," he said in a lifeless voice. "She . . . found it last night. I was going to surrender it to . . . proper authorities. But she said it belonged to her father, and . . ."

He held it like a baby for christening. There was blood on the walnut grip. And one chamber empty.

"You had no right to keep it." He looked at me. "That's what she said. I tried to take it away from her . . ."

"Gavin, give me the gun."

He pulled it to his chest.

"I'm not going to hurt you," I said. "And I don't want you to hurt yourself."

He nodded. Timidly placed the revolver in my hand.

"Mike." Peggy pointed into the living room.

I remembered how clean the room was the first time I visited. Two small children and not a mark anywhere. Now Martha lay spread-eagled on the carpet, her housedress pushed to her waist. Her left eye was a well of blood. The fireplace was spattered with bone and tissue.

"I tried to take it away . . . ," Gavin said. "I begged her . . . not to hurt our baby."

"Reverend," Peggy said softly. "Where is Hannah now?"

"Upstairs," he said, weeping.

Twenty minutes later Dr. Lund met me in the stairwell.

"The child's stable enough to be moved," Lund said. "The paramedics got to her just in time."

"The preacher?"

"I've given him a mild tranquilizer," he said. "He can answer questions, but please be careful. He's in shock."

"Doctor, Martha's baby . . ."

He shook his head wearily.

"She was so determined to protect that child," I said. "Does it seem likely that a woman trying to kill herself with a twelve-inch revolver would put the muzzle to her eye? Especially if someone was trying to take the gun away?"

"It seems—awkward. But that doesn't mean it didn't happen."

"Didn't Sheriff Archer shoot Rudy Dubliner in the left eye?"

He didn't answer. Peggy was coming downstairs, followed by the EMTs carrying Hannah. The child's fingertips were a bluish white, oxygen-starved. A mask covered her mouth and nose. Her thin chest barely moved.

"You're doing fine," Peggy whispered to her. "We're taking you to the hospital. And you're gonna be feeling better soon. Okay, sweetie?"

Hannah's eyes darted anxiously around her. As she came close I could see the thin red mark on her neck.

"Now close your eyes," Peggy said. "I don't want you hurting your eyes out in the bright sun."

As Hannah obediently shut her eyes, Peggy stood between the stretcher and the archway, blocking Martha from view.

"Mike . . ." Lund's eyes followed them out.

"It's okay, Doc. You go on to the hospital. We'll take it from here."

I entered the living room. For some reason I found it impossible to take my eyes off those shaving cuts on Martha's legs. They reminded me a lot of the ones I'd seen on her sister's body at the morgue. Then I knelt down to eye level. Blood had obscured the left half of Martha's face . . . but as I touched her left cheek, the flesh-colored concealer makeup came away easily. Underneath it was a partly healed razor cut.

I opened the drawer where I'd found the summer camp picture: gone.

"Did Hannah tell you what happened?" I asked Peggy.

"Mother tried to put a plastic bag over her head. Said her mother claimed she was . . . protecting her."

"From what?"

"She just said—the bad man, the bad man." Peggy tilted her head back. "Mike, she was blue. Why the Christ wouldn't he let the EMTs in?"

"Let's ask him," I said.

"You go in first," she said. "I need a minute."

I gave her arm a quick squeeze. Then I went into the downstairs bedroom.

Robbie's room was barracks-clean, dark except for a fluorescent desk lamp. Gavin lay semifetal on a narrow bed, clutching a pillow to his chest. His son's photos were taped to the wall. Mostly still lifes—doorknobs and blades of grass, a child's first halting experiments. He seemed to like using macro lenses. Another picture showed Robbie and Cassie holding identical beagle puppies. They were smiling, but there was something like quiet terror in their eyes.

In the drawer was a traveler's map of Dyer County, marked with tiny red dots. The desk held a single row of books. *The Annotated Alice. Ozma of Oz. Stories of Robert Browning.* All stories of magic and escape, of absolute good and evil.

I opened the Browning book to the tale of the Pied Piper. FUCKING BULLSHIT was written across the page in childish red letters.

"He's a beautiful boy," the reverend said. "Don't you think?"

I looked back. Gavin sat on the edge of the bed, rubbing his cheek.

"Reverend." I flipped through the book. "Have you ever taken a close look at your son's library?"

Gavin blinked. "They are a bit advanced for his age. But then, we were home schooling him at four. His teacher assured us—"

I held the book open. "How old was he when he started doing this?"

The preacher's eyes grew wide.

There was not a single page in the book that hadn't been defaced. Obscenities in childish handwriting. Dark lines like needles sticking out of the children in the illustrations. Fire. Blood.

Every single face had been rubbed out with an eraser.

"Where did . . . what were you doing . . . ?"

Peggy came in.

"It was right there on the shelf." I opened another book, then another. "Here. And here. That's your son."

Peggy's eyes darted across the pages. "Mike, what's going on?"

"The McIntoshes have an unusual take on home schooling," I said. "Who taught him to do this, Gavin?"

"It can't be." He stared at me, ashen. "Robbie doesn't do this any more. He . . . stopped."

"Excuse me," I said. "Did you just say 'he stopped'?"

"Mike," Peggy said.

I bore down. "He *stopped?* What else did Robbie stop doing?"

"My son is a good boy, Mr. Yeager. A kind and Christian child. He isn't capable of—he would never—" Gavin began to whimper. "I am not a bad father."

"Mike." An edge was growing in Peggy's voice. "Let's take this outside and give the reverend a chance to—"

"I know what you're up to," Gavin said. "You think I'll confess to murdering my wife. Why don't you just accuse me of all those other people, too?"

"Was it worth it?"

"What?"

"All those water rights are yours now, Gavin. Think that'll comfort you in the dark hours?"

He was turning red now. Peggy stared at the floor.

"My wife is dead, Mr. Yeager. I will not have you assault her memory—or my reputation—with these gutter accusations."

"*Her* memory? *Your* reputation? What about your son, Gavin? Or is he just one more dead child you're trying to sweep under the rug?"

He cooled. "You would know more about that than I do."

Peggy caught me by the shoulder. "That's enough."

"Peg—"

She didn't budge. "Go handle the scene, Mike. I'll talk to the reverend."

"He's all yours," I said.

SIXTY-SIX

I stayed long enough to watch them carry Martha McIntosh out. Then I went upstairs.

Hannah's bedroom was a study in pink chiffon and My Little Ponies. At the foot of the bed lay a plastic bag and a length of fishing wire, tagged for evidence. And a bright red teddy bear with its back ripped out.

My bear got broken, Hannah told me. *She used to could talk. Then Robbie broke her.*

Fifteen minutes later Peggy found me on the front steps.

"Yeager, what the hell was that about?"

"You saw Robbie's photographs," I said. "I just now realized how much they look like one of the Dupree photos. Number 21. Same bad focus, same tight close-up."

"What are you talking about?"

"Robbie said he took pictures, and I didn't listen. If Robbie made that photograph . . . then he was on the scene. And Gavin knew. If you don't arrest him, I will."

"Nobody's arresting anybody right now." She sat beside me. "What are you doing with that teddy bear?"

"Oh, this." I held it up. "Apparently this is Sing-to-Me-Strawbeary. You talk to her, and she sings back to you. A very expensive toy. Only somebody's removed the speech synthesizer."

"So now you're telling me a seven-year-old boy helped put a bomb in a phone booth."

"I don't know," I said. "But Robbie's behaving a lot like Theo did after Rudy Dubliner got his hooks in. The pictures, the obscenities . . . We've gulla reel this in fast. Get the preacher under the hot lights, find out who else has been with the kids—"

"Mike." She sat down. "Please just stop."

"What's the matter?"

"I should have told you before." She took a long breath. "They're going to make me pull the case."

"What?"

"The deputy director sent me here to make an assessment," she said, "and then oversee the transition to local jurisdiction."

"The Bureau doesn't want to touch this case because it's looking like dead kids at the end of the day." I stared at her. "Why you?"

"I asked them to send me. I thought it would be easier. And I kept hoping you'd show me—something."

"Something that would indicate the case was good for the Bureau's image. And that I hadn't lost my marbles."

"That's not what I meant. But you know as well as I do that you're too wrapped up here to be effective."

"Look, I got hot under the collar with Gavin. But if you'd been through what I have—"

"That's exactly what I'm talking about. You've been through too much. And if that isn't enough, I'm talking about Dorothy Corvis."

"What about her?"

"How much does she matter to you?"

I hesitated before answering. "I liked her, Peggy. A lot. I felt . . . I wanted to open up to her."

"Did you sleep with her?"

I raised an eyebrow. "Who wants to know?"

"Take this from an old friend and colleague. You can't work this part of the investigation. Not if she got under your skin the way she seems to have."

"I didn't sleep with her," I said. "I wanted to."

She didn't flinch. "Why didn't you?"

"All I know is that I didn't." I looked at her. "You think I can't be objective?"

"I believe your exact words were, 'If I came face-to-face with the fucker, I think I'd take him apart.' And that you couldn't forgive yourself for letting him know how much she mattered to you."

"Are you . . ." I stopped, suddenly dizzy. "Are you sure you're being objective yourself? That you're not just—"

"Jealous?" She shook her head. "For Christ's sake, Yeager."

If she'd been angry I could have handled it. Instead she was looking at me with deep and honest concern, and finally I had to look away.

"Let me finish this," I said. "You can take over, bring in anybody you want. But don't take the bat out of my hand. I am so unbelievably close."

"You're too close. If you don't fall back, you're going to be the one who burns when this case blows up."

"And if I do fall back?"

"The last thing the director wants is another PR fiasco," she said. "You make this an easy transition—with any luck, you'll take early retirement in three years."

"Giving two children up for dead," I said. "What do you think about that deal?"

"I think it stinks . . . and I think it's the best you're going to do, Mike. I'm sorry."

I paused. "How long do I have to think it over?"

"I wouldn't let the sun set on it."

"We don't have much longer than that anyway. Today is November fifth." I stood up. "I'm gonna check out the front gate. Will you do one thing for me?"

"What is it?"

"Have someone run a background check on Dorothy Corvis."

SIXTY-SEVEN

The tiny guardhouse was unmanned. I watched as an old lady in a green Eldorado pulled up to the entrance, punched in her access code, and drove through without even noticing the damn thing was broken. Just as the splintered nub of the barrier raised, the security camera's recording light flickered on.

"Afternoon." The guard whistled as he approached the gate. "Jumpin' Jiminy. When did that happen?"

"About an hour ago," I said. "Don't tell me you've been on break all this time."

He wrinkled his nose. "It was not on break, sir. I was tendin' the sprinklers. We've got a foolproof security system here, and—"

"—And the cameras record everyone entering and leaving," I said. "But only when somebody triggers the gate."

"I guess they wanted to save on tape." He unlocked the guardhouse.

"Sensible," I said. "So who knows your schedule around here?"

"Only my supervisor. And the people who live here, of course."

As I slipped past the barrier, I noticed two grooved indentations in the grass: wheel tracks.

"Son of a gun," I whispered.

If Robbie really had been abducted from his own front yard, the kidnappers wouldn't have needed the walker. But if he'd been traveling on his own, there would have been just enough space between the gate and the fence for him to slip through undetected . . . assuming that someone was waiting for him on the other side.

I turned back to the gatekeeper. "You didn't see any strange vehicles yesterday? Maybe parked just down the road?"

"Nope. And before you ask, I already told the other cops—I did not see Robbie near the gate but one time since he got dropped off Friday afternoon, and that was to go to the funeral. And his dad was with him then."

I nearly did a double take. "His dad dropped him off at the gate on Friday?"

He rolled his eyes. "No. His dad took him to the funeral. That other fella dropped him off on Friday."

"What other fellow?"

"I don't know his name. He's here all the time. Nice enough gentleman." He locked himself into the gatehouse. "Works for the preacher, I believe."

It was only a few minutes past four o'clock when a deputy and I arrived at the Arbor Vitae Community Center—but the place was dark and shuttered, as if in preparation for a siege. The parking lot was empty. A note taped to the door read: ALL ACTIVITIES CANCELLED UNTIL FURTHER NOTICE.

"Locked." The deputy tried the door a few times. "What do we do? Go back to the preacher's house?"

I looked through the door glass. "Somebody's still inside. I see a shadow moving back and forth." I rapped on the door, then again. No answer. "Let's go around back."

The rolling steel door of the loading dock was up. As we entered I noticed cardboard hills and mouse costumes hanging from hooks. We were on the auditorium stage—dark except for a safety light. I turned a switch and nothing happened. All of the big spotlights had been removed.

"This place sure is empty now," said the deputy.

"Looks like they got the cameras, too," I said. "Somebody's hauling ass out of town."

We left the auditorium and came to a hallway intersection. I indicated that he should go left and continued on to the administrative wing. As I approached the office I heard grinding machinery—a paper shredder, from the sound.

"Hello?" Silence again. A shadow moved across the door. I instinctively pressed myself against the wall. A moment later a teenage girl in yellow pigtails emerged from the office, carrying a stack of papers and singing to herself.

"Miss—" She didn't look my way. Then I noticed she was wearing earphones. I tapped her on the shoulder and she squealed.

"Holy fucking *shit!*" The papers flew from her hands, scattering in all directions. She whirled around at me, scared and extremely pissed off. "You get the hell out, mister, you hear me? I know karate and I am not fucking kidding."

"Just calm down." I called to the deputy. "I'm the law, okay? FBI."

"Huh?"

"Take out the earphones, miss."

She finally got the message and turned her MP3 player off. By then the deputy had arrived.

"Hey, Leta."

"Hey." She looked down at her feet. "I'm not doin' anything wrong bein' here, y'know. I got a key."

"I take it you didn't load out all that TV equipment by yourself," I said.

"I don't know a thing about that. I just got a call to come in and do some work, is all."

"Meaning these papers you're shredding?"

"Yeah, but—hey! You can't touch those. Not unless you got a warrant."

A triumphant smile stole across her face as I hesitated.

I straightened my shoulders. "Your name's Leta?"

She nodded cautiously.

"Leta Brauning? From the church after-school program?"

"Um, yessir."

"You're the one who was on duty when Cassandra Dupree was taken away on Friday afternoon."

Now it was her turn to blush.

"I ain't never said I saw a white Chevrolet. No way." Leta sat across from me in the director's office while the deputy watched the door. "I said I saw Pete come in the door and that was all. But he kept askin', 'Are you sure you didn't see that pickup? It woulda been parked right in front of the window. Are you sure?' And I wasn't sure, really. So finally I said there was a truck."

"Who was asking you this?"

She paused before answering. "Brother Gavin."

"Did he prompt you in any other way before you talked to Detective Tippet?"

She shifted uncomfortably. "Well, he never exactly said I should lie. He just kept askin' questions till I figured out what I was supposed to say. Like he sorta hinted it wouldn't be a good idea to let anybody know he was still at the church when Miz Dupree came by."

"He was?"

"Oh yeah! I know that for a fact 'cause I went to get him to come talk to her. But she didn't wanna see him—and he sure as hell didn't wanna see her. Just sat in his office, talkin' on his cell phone."

"On his cell phone."

She nodded emphatically. "I thought that was kinda weird, 'cause he had a regular phone right on his desk."

"What was he saying?"

"Well, he was askin' if it seemed all right to let Miz Dupree take Cassie— and would whoever it was mind pickin' up Robbie from the Silver Star, 'cause his wife wasn't answering her phone." She cringed. "I ain't in trouble for all this, am I?"

"You mean, for giving false statements in a homicide investigation?" I offered her a patented FBI glower. "Why don't you and the deputy bring me those papers you were so busy shredding."

Leta gulped. "Yessir."

"I'll hold onto your keys in the meantime."

She nervously handed me the ring and disappeared. I let myself into the room next door. Connor Blackwell's office.

I'd only glanced over his library on Sunday, but now I gave each one a careful look. *Your New You. Making Friends For a Lifetime. Overcoming Social Anxiety Disorder.* And one called *The Reality of Demons.* A white audiocassette was sitting on the desk—the same one he'd been listening to in his car stereo. It was titled *A Master and Companion.* I popped it into the boombox.

"The greatest punishment of all is neglect." The voice was even more familiar now that I realized how much it sounded like Connor's. The pitch was slightly lower, but it was the same soothing cadence—confident, intelligent, warm. *"You must be prepared to withhold attention in order to maintain control and respect. Never allow an animal to think of you as an equal. Remember, you are the master. You are the human. You are the alpha."*

"What the hell . . . ?" I ejected the tape and read the subtitle: *Effective Discipline For Your Dog.* This was the guy who changed Connor's life? Apparently so. Because even though his audiobooks were written by at least twenty different authors, every single one had been read by the same actor. I put one in titled *Blue Colorado Skies.*

"That summer at Vallecito Reservoir was my last happy memory for a long time." There was that calm, compassionate voice again. *"I caught a cutthroat trout. Four pounds. Dad made me throw it back. He said—"*

" 'Nothing has to die to prove a man's worth,' " I muttered to myself, noting how precisely Connor had copied the actor's gentle sadness. Now that I looked more closely at that alleged picture of young Connor and his parents, I could see how imperfectly grained it was—like something scanned out of a book.

IT'S NEVER TOO LATE TO HAVE A HAPPY CHILDHOOD. I tapped the mouse and the screensaver vanished. An e-mail program came up. One of the recent messages was titled RE: MFY PATIENT FILES TRANSFER. I immediately recognized the name of my own psychiatrist in Philadelphia—the one whose phone number was on my bottle of antianxiety medication.

> Please see attached files on Michael F. Yeager, pursuant to receipt of patient confidentiality release signed by Mr. Yeager and verbally confirmed in his conversation on 11/01.

Apparently at some point while I was warming a cell in the Dyer County lockup, I had found time to call my psychiatrist and fax over a release form. I opened the attachment. Everything was there—my nightmares over the Madrigal case, my insomnia—even things I'd forgotten, like wanting to join the ministry. Everything but the one thing I'd never talked about. My mother's suicide.

"He's not supposed to be in there." Leta was approaching with the deputy. "I could get fired."

She was holding a stack of pages. "Let me see those," I said.

"They're patient interviews," she protested. "They're supposed to be confidential. You can't look at them. I'll get in trouble."

They were patient interviews, all right.

SIXTY-EIGHT

Half an hour later, I was standing in a conference room at the sheriff's station. Five others were arranged around the table—Peggy, Lund, Freebairn, and the sergeants in charge of Warrants and Patrol divisions.

"Tree of Life has a novel recruitment plan," I said. "The church refers its members to the counseling service—and vice versa. The transcripts include interviews with Dale Dupree, Mary Frances Dupree, Martha McIntosh, Ada Rosario—and our friend, Deputy Clyde."

"We can't use them to make arrests," the warrants deputy said. "Not if they're patient records."

"Correction," Peggy said. "The notes can be used in court if they reveal Connor declined to report evidence of child abuse."

"And do they?"

"We'll see," I said. "I did find it interesting that it was Gavin who called in Leta to shut the center down and shred the transcripts. He did that precisely five minutes after shots were heard at his house."

"After?" Lund shook his head in disbelief.

"After. With his wife lying dead on the floor and his daughter barely breathing upstairs." I picked up the remote control. "I asked Leta how she made the transcripts and she explained that Connor usually gave her audiotapes. Only for this one particular interview he gave her video. After some prodding, she finally showed me the safe where Tree of Life kept their copy—I should say, original."

I held up the high-res videocassette.

"Hell and damnation," Lund said.

I turned out the lights and started the tape. The quality of the VHS original was amazing—crisp colors, high-quality audio. You could practically see the sweat beading up on Connor's forehead. And Cassie's purple spiral-bound notebook, only just visible on her lap.

"What are you looking for?" Connor said. "Are you trying to—do you want to keep drawing? Which crayons do you—"

Cassie pointed directly at the crayon box. "I want that one."

The colors on Dorothy's VCR had been too washed out to see properly. But in the original, it was absolutely clear that the crayon Cassie was reaching for was tan, not brown. The exact color of Connor's hair.

"Which? This one, or . . . ?"

Connor pulled the tan crayon away and rolled a brown one toward her. She didn't pick it up.

"Here, it's okay." He spoke as cheerfully as ever. "You don't have to be scared. Go ahead and finish your picture."

She reached for the tan crayon. Once again he slid it back and pushed the brown one toward her.

"Can you tell me who that is?" he said, even though she still hadn't drawn anything.

"I want that one for the eyes." She stared defiantly for several seconds. Then he casually began to wave a red crayon back and forth across the bottom of the page.

"What's he doing?" asked Freebairn.

"He's drawing blood on Cassie's dog," I said.

"Sorry?" Connor said in a pleasant voice.

Cassie was close to crying now. "Can I—may I please have another crayon?"

"Sure." He pushed the brown crayon toward her. This time she picked it up.

"Now who is that you're drawing?" He tapped the blank space at the center of the page. His body language was subtle but adamant: it was not a question but a command.

"My daddy." Defeated, she began to draw. She was beginning to sob.

I stopped the tape. Of all the faces in the room, it was Davis Freebairn's that seemed most horror-struck.

"Connor Blackwell used his patients to gain information about their children," I said. "Over the course of ten years in therapy, Martha McIntosh had fallen almost completely under his domination. He could make her do anything—from lending him the keys to her four-by-four to posing as her own sister and serving as accessory to homicide."

"How did he do it?" Peggy asked.

"He'd known how to dominate her since childhood," I said. "It was partly a trade. He'd leave Hannah and her unborn baby alone if she gave him full access to Robbie. This was one of Connor's favorite domination techniques. He made threats against the children's pets to control Cassie and Robbie. And it almost always worked—except for this one interview in which Cassandra Dupree seized the opportunity to send a message directly to her grandfather. Look what she does at the conclusion of the interview."

I fast-forwarded to the end. On-screen, the door to the interview room had opened, and Deputy Ada Rosario entered. I felt a slight chill seeing her alive.

"The audio's a little harder to hear because of all the shuffling," I said. "Ada's telling him that the judge wants all the materials logged in right away. Connor protests a little, but Ada wins. And for the split second his attention is distracted—"

I froze the tape, pointed at Cassie's hand on the screen.

"Cassandra puts her spiral-bound notebook into the stack of materials headed for the courthouse. Ada picks them up and goes. And Connor never saw a thing."

"Good girl," Lund said.

"Where is . . . this person now?" Freebairn was very pale.

"No one's seen hide nor hair of him," said the patrol deputy. "Apartment's empty. It's like he never existed."

"I'm starting to think he never did," I said. "Peggy?"

"Good work, Mike." She nodded quietly, a boss's approbation. "We've managed to get helicopters through the Marines at Ft. Sherman, as well as mountain rescue from the National Park Service. We're going to concentrate our search on the Sangre de los Niños mountains, starting in exactly—" She checked her watch. "Fifteen minutes."

I looked at Lund. "Are we done?"

The doctor nodded. "Davis, are you okay?"

"I don't know." Freebairn seemed barely to breathe.

They filed out of the room, leaving me and Peggy alone.

"Here's something else to give to the search team." I handed her the map of Dyer County from Robbie's room. "Nearly all of the red marks are centered around the mountain roads. Plus a few more close to Cathedral Lake."

"You think the boy knows what's supposed to happen tonight?"

"Robbie's central to his plans," I said. "Theo was Rudy's witness. And now Robbie is the witness. It's almost exactly the same as what happened in 1978."

"The same but different," Peggy said.

I nodded. "The student has learned from his master's mistakes. Dubliner's father got sloppy; Rudy himself had a death wish. Somehow I don't think Connor is looking to go out in a hail of gunfire. He's already beaten death once before. My guess is that he's determined to achieve something even Dubliner never could. To prove himself the better man."

"You're sure it's Connor."

"All I need is confirmation. We've got the digital enhancement on that 8mm film. . . . With any luck we'll soon have something to put through age progression software. We'll have the bastard's face." I paused. "I did okay, huh?"

"You did good." She said it gently this time. "We found a lot of shipping invoices in the reverend's study. Including one for photo developer. Ilford Perceptol."

"Is Gavin McIntosh in custody?"

"On his way," she said. "He wants to talk to you only, though. I think he's going to confess to the murders."

"I figured he'd try that next. All right, I'll talk to him. It'll make me late for the search party."

"Just follow the big white glow," she said. "I hope you're right about that camp, Mike. We're going to have more warm bodies up there than the Army had on D-Day. Not to mention all the media waiting for scraps. Whatever happens tonight, it's going to be very public."

"It's a long shot. But I think it's one we have to take."

"Agreed." She started to turn away, then stopped.

"What is it?" I asked.

"You wanted to know about Dorothy."

She handed me a file from the San Francisco field office.

"Dorothy Corvis isn't her real name," Peggy said. "She legally changed it from Rebecca Ann Morgenstern. Her father was a behavioral scientist at Berkeley."

"I saw her degrees on the wall," I said. "Child Psychology, Education . . ."

"The degrees are real. She earned them under the new name. Here's why she changed it."

She picked out the faxed newspaper obituary. Dr. Morgenstern had Dorothy's luxuriant black hair and keen eyes. Only her smile was missing.

"When she was eight years old, her mother brought her in for stomach cramps. The doctor found genital and rectal bleeding. She accused her father, but the family closed ranks. Inquest went nowhere—Papa had too many friends."

"And the police interrogated her in jail," I said. "Treated her like a criminal."

"She told you this?"

"She said it was a girl she was working with," I said. "What happened after the inquest?"

"They hanged Dorothy by her ankles from the basement rafters," she said. "She finally got herself loose . . . kept pounding on doors until someone opened up. Her father opened his veins in the tub . . . Rebecca went into foster care. Somehow through it all, she managed to survive."

"How did she survive?"

"It's not an answer, Mike. It's just information." She took the file back. "Why did you need to know? Do you suspect she's involved?"

"No. But she's vulnerable. And I need to know what he's going to try to take from her."

"What he's going to take from her?"

"Robbie told me the Shadow Catcher takes the dark parts of you away. The parts nobody wants. And uses them to destroy you. Your fears. Your shadow."

She nodded, understanding. "Does he have yours?"

"I'm afraid he does." I looked at my watch. "I'd better go talk to the preacher."

"Mike . . ."

She kissed me on the cheek: the kiss of an old and very dear friend.

"It's only your shadow," she said.

After Peggy left I called the desk deputy with instructions to notify me as soon as Gavin McIntosh arrived. Then I sat down for another look at the digital transfer of that 8mm movie.

I was interrupted a few minutes later by a knock at the door. Davis Freebairn.

"You don't look surprised to see me," he said.

"I could see your face during the meeting."

"Why do you . . ." He reddened. "Why did you say that this Connor Blackwell . . . knew Martha from childhood? Who do you think he is?"

"We both know who he is," I said. "We both know he didn't die in that fire."

"My Theo . . . is dead." He closed his eyes, halting back tears. "The man you showed me is someone I've never met."

"But not entirely unfamiliar, I take it." I picked up the remote. "Do you see what it is I'm watching now?"

He nodded without looking.

"Do you recognize the face on the screen?"

It took a moment. But at last Freebairn opened his eyes.

The image was clear now—clear enough, at least, to show that the face in the reflection was not a mask. The boy was half-bald, his left ear missing. His nose had nearly melted away. The lower lip hung and drooled, the skin around it burned and puckered like old bacon. Theodore Freebairn's eyes stared into the camera. Dead eyes, just like Pete said. He seemed to be trying to smile.

"He's my son." Davis wept. "God forgive me."

SIXTY-NINE

The sergeant in charge of Patrol division gave me a message from Peggy; one of the advance search parties had found something in the foothills and she was going ahead to investigate.

"Did she say what they found?"

"Phone cut off," said the sergeant. "It's those mountains. I'm just headed out myself. The reverend's upstairs for you. Here's all the invoices we found in his office."

"These are all from contractors," I said. "Bulk tanks and generators."

"Yessir. Supposed to be for that new hospital wing. Only guess what? Nobody at the hospital's ever seen 'em. I been tellin' people for years that guy's crooked."

I stopped myself from suggesting that we were trying to break the reverend for homicide and kidnapping, not graft. But then I remembered the missing TV cameras. And what Robbie had said about keeping his heart underground.

"Just how big are these gas tanks?" I asked.

"Pretty damn big," he said.

The voices on the police radio were thick with confusion:

"... Calling FBI escort. Say 20, escort."

"... We have lost contact with the advance party."

"Dispatch, we have a civilian caller reporting an explosion two miles north of Madre de Dios Pass ..."

"Two officers down. Subject has fled the scene."

"There is fire in the Sangre de los Niños foothills."

Peggy did not answer her cell phone.

Gavin McIntosh was sitting in my office, arms folded.

"There's nothing you can do to stop it," he said. "It's in God's hands now."

"What's he planning to do with all that equipment? Some kind of private Armageddon? Is he going to film himself killing the children?"

"He won't kill them," Gavin said. "You will."

"For God's sake, Reverend—"

"Don't you blaspheme in my presence, sir."

"We don't have time for this!" I yelled.

Gavin crossed his arms tightly.

"He couldn't have meant to kill Martha," he said. "God had forgiven him. I can't have helped . . . create a monster. We were going to make this desert green again. . . ."

I sat down, bringing myself eye to eye with him.

"Reverend," I said. "Who was Connor Blackwell before you took him in?"

He looked at me a long time before answering.

"He was a soul in pain, Agent Yeager. That's all he was. A soul in pain."

"Exactly what kind of pain?"

"He was burned," Gavin said. "Came into a Las Vegas emergency room—and they turned him away like a dog in the streets. What could any decent person do and still call himself a Christian?" He held up his hands. "Tree of Life paid for everything. With time, and prayer . . . with God's love . . . we gave that boy a new face. A beautiful, kind, courageous face." He released a deep breath of resignation. "We called him our Prodigal Son."

"You have reached the mobile phone of Special Agent Weaver. To leave a voice message . . ."

Peggy's phone never went out of range. Never. Either she was under fire . . . or it had been taken from her. I didn't want to consider the latter possibility. But if she'd seen the explosion, she would have called at the first opportunity.

"Hello?"

I was so used to the recording that I nearly hung up. The signal was heavy with static.

"Peggy?"

"Sorry," said the voice on the far end. "Agent Weaver can't come to the phone. Would you like to leave a message?"

"Connor," I said. "Or do I call you Theo?"

"Up to you." He yawned. "Tell me, Mikey. How does it feel to have two more bitches on your conscience?"

I said nothing.

"Did she let you come in her mouth?" he said. "Was it all warm and gooey? Like a butterscotch parfait? Don't think those seeds will have time to sprout, do you?"

"I know what Rudy did to you." I paused. "But you don't have to kill them."

"Don't I?" His voice deepened, a parody of his concerned-therapist voice. "You seem a little upset, Mike. Is there something you'd like to get off your chest?"

The line died.

Half a dozen impulses darted through my mind. Before I knew what I was doing, I'd grabbed my jacket from the door hook, ready to run headlong into the night. Archer's Colt revolver was still in the side pocket, right where I put it when I took it from Gavin. Still spotted with Martha's blood. Still loaded. Why had Connor left it behind? He must have realized I'd take it.

Then the answer came:because he knew I'd take it.

Connor had planned on everything, even our assault on the mountains. Just like Rudy, he'd prepared for years. The only thing he couldn't plan on was my arrival—and even that he'd adapted to remarkably well. Even I had become part of Connor Blackwell's plan.

I punched to a fresh line, dialed.

"FBI," came the answer.

"Yoshi, it's Mike. I need the precise GPS coordinates for Agent Weaver's cell phone. Stat."

"We can't do that, Mike. Not without at least two levels of app—"

"Her life is in danger," I said. "Make it happen."

He took a breath. "Okay, boss. Hang on."

While he hunted the information, I placed calls to the search party. Then I rang down to the lockup and told them to get Pete Frizelle ready.

SEVENTY

"What the hell's this?" Pete looked up as I emptied the envelope on the table.

"Your wallet," I said. "Car keys, condoms. It's all there."

"You're givin' me this? What for?"

"Let's say I'm about to find out what you're made of," I said. "Right now I've got people covering all the access routes to the Sangre de Los Niños. But if we go up there guns blazing, he's going to kill Cassandra. As well as some other people who don't deserve to die. I need to know a way up that won't be watched."

Pete suddenly went pale. "What makes you think I can do that?"

"Because you've been there before," I said. "A long time ago."

He nodded. "Lost Lake."

". . . *bringing you live coverage* of *the standoff in Dyer County, Nevada, where at least a hundred armed deputies under the direction of federal agents stand ready . . .*"

I turned the radio off.

"I bet everybody's watchin' this," Pete said. "I bet the whole goddamn county's glued to their TVs."

I didn't answer. We were taking a fire trail this time—narrower, steeper, but clearly less traveled. Fresh motorcycle treads led the way.

"Tell me what we're headed into, Pete."

"You go in through the main lodge," he said. "Behind the fireplace, there's a kind of stairway down to the basement, where they used to keep fuel oil. It's not a big room—got a cement floor. I can't tell you much more, 'cause I was blindfolded. I remember they used to hoist us up and down in a leather harness."

"What's down there?"

"There's the room where he cleaned us up every night, after he was done." He shuddered. "It's all white. And tunnels, too. Rooms with . . . hooks in the ceiling. And . . ."

His voice faltered. Pete was close to hyperventilating.

"What do you remember about the night of the fire?"

"It was the only time I ever saw Theo scared," he said. "Every night, Rudy left him with orders to kill us if he didn't come back by morning. And for the first time it looked like Theo was gonna have to go through with it. Martha was beggin' him not to—said she'd let him do anything if only he wouldn't murder us. But Theo was too scared for that."

"How'd the fire get started?"

"Well, there was always them gas tanks, and Theo wavin' matches around like he was the god of fire. Finally Dale just looked at me and said, 'Either way we're gonna die, Pete. We may as well die fightin'.' So he got us both untied. And we was gonna get the girls loose. That made Theo panic, so he lit the fuse. Place went up like a Christmas tree fire."

"Then what?"

"Then Archer showed up," he said. "I remember he had blood on his uniform. And Theo's beggin' and cryin' that he was a victim like us. Mary said, 'Daddy, don't believe him. You don't know what he made us do.' Archer draws his pistol, aims it—but then he just says, 'Help me, Theo. Help me get them to a safe place.' "

"What did Theo do?"

"Ran away," he said. "Right into the fire. Meanwhile Dale's head's still busted open, and my arm is no good. And the girls are—bloody as newborn babes. But Archer got us all out." Pete scratched his head. "We're all screamin' at him to drive, 'cause the fire's everywhere. But he says, 'We can't leave him. He's just a child.' Finally, though . . . he drove on."

"You didn't see what happened to Theo?"

"Heard him scream," he said. "Thought that was the most beautiful sound in the universe."

"I see the fire." I navigated a tight turn. "That's Peggy's car a hundred yards to the right. You see that other trail leading up?"

"Where—"

Then the front end of the car jerked upward, nearly flipping over. Shattered glass from the windshield sprayed us both. As the vehicle settled I could feel the front tires caught on something.

"What the hell—?" I got out and looked at the busted grille. Black smoke billowed from under the hood. The explosion had gone off a fraction of a second early; otherwise it would have ignited the gas tank.

"Tripwire explosive under the car," I said. "We've gotta move."

That was when I noticed Pete was wheezing. He touched his chest, looked at the slick blood on his palm. And laughed. A shard of metal had imbedded itself in his sternum.

"Right—in—that—hole," he said. "This is—funny."

"We'll laugh about it later." I dragged him to a safe distance, leaned him against a scrub pine. "Keep breathing, Pete. I'm gonna bring Cassie to you."

"Agent Y—Mike . . ."

"Yeah, Pete."

"Don't let him—fuck with your head."

"I'll try not to."

I drew the Colt and climbed along the ridgeline. By then I could hear the shots.

SEVENTY-ONE

The underbrush was burning as I reached the other fire trail—where the blackened shell of a sheriff's department off-road vehicle lay on its side, still warm from the blast. Two men lay dead on the ground. The deputy's sidearms were missing. A voice crackled on the hand radio.

". . . Say 20, Unit Four. Do you copy? Please come—"

I picked up the radio. "Base, this is Special Agent Yeager. Unit Four is down."

I could already hear the sound of approaching helicopters.

"Sir, we have hostage rescue and assault teams on approach—"

"Negative—10-22. You will adhere to my previous instructions. No attempt will be made to approach the perimeter without my coded authorization. Get those helicopters back."

"Sir." It took a few seconds, but finally the sound of the propellers faded away. If Connor was listening—and he had to be—then he knew he wasn't going to get his bloody standoff. Not unless he could wring the code out of me.

. The fire roads ended there, and motorcycle treads snaked up a narrow horse trail. Peggy's footprints were fresh in the red dirt. And now I heard another high, flat snap of gunfire. Peggy's Glock. She wouldn't fire if a child was in the crossfire. And she rarely wasted a round.

"*Robbie, stay down!*" she shouted.

I followed her voice through a stand of dead aspens. She was kneeling behind a boulder, aiming at the stone fireplace of the main lodge. As I stalked over a rise of land, Peggy pivoted the Glock at me. She had a fresh bruise on her forehead and a red stain on her collar.

"It's me." I crept to her. "What's the condition of the kids?"

"I haven't seen Cassandra. He's using Robbie to draw fire." She pointed at the main lodge. "These buildings must be interconnected—bastard keeps popping up like a mole."

"There's tunnels," I said. "Armed?"

"Everything those deputies had—shotgun, thirty-eights. Plus something close-quarters to control the kids. One of those big blades. Meanwhile I'm down to twelve rounds. I hope you brought your six-shooter."

I nodded. "Is he talking?"

"Not since he grabbed my cell phone," she said. "I think he's been trying to call somebody."

"Probably Gavin," I said. "He's disintegrating."

"Any chance of the cavalry riding in?"

I took a breath. "I've given orders for them to hold back."

"What? Mike, are you insane?"

"He's got every approach to this mountain booby-trapped—just like the bomb that killed those two deputies. He wants his Armageddon, Peg. On live TV, with the eyes of the world glued to him."

"Why?"

"So we'll all finally pay attention." I looked closely at the lodge for signs of movement. "What was Robbie's condition when you saw him?"

"Scared."

"Okay, I'm going in. Save those twelve rounds for a clean shot."

"Forget it. I'm coming with you."

"One of us has to be ready to call in the strike." I handed her the walkie-talkie. "The code to the command post is *First Corinthians, 13:12*. I love you."

"Mike."

I high-crawled from one burned-out cabin to the next, keeping the Colt on hair-trigger. Even if I was lucky enough to spot him first, I'd have less than a second to aim. And Robbie, at least, was with him.

SIGN UP HERE FOR ACTIVITIES. The sign had been pushed aside, revealing an open trap door beside the stone fireplace. And a short wooden ladder leading down.

I listened, hearing only a light breeze and my own rapid breathing.

Then I leapt into the opening.

The ground was hard cement, just as Pete said. I backed against the corner, shone my flashlight around. No fuel cans, no other exits. The room was completely empty. But I could hear muffled voices. A man and a crying child. At first I couldn't tell where they were coming from. Then I looked back at the ladder.

You can't just go down there, Cassie had said in her interview. *You have to go back and then up and then you can go down, down, down.* Halfway up to the trapdoor was a break in the ladder. Behind it was a spring catch, neatly concealed in the supporting iron rods. I pressed it and the top half of the ladder swung out, revealing an opening in the wall.

Then I could hear Robbie's voice, echoing in the darkness.

"Please don't make me," he said. "Don't make me be mean to her anymore."

Something about the simplicity in his voice chilled my blood. I pushed myself through. The hidden door opened into a narrow cement tunnel, forcing me to crawl. I was about six feet in when I came to a dead end. What had Cassie said about the tunnels? If you go down the wrong way, you die.

I could hear the voices more clearly, as if they were only a few feet away. Connor was speaking to Robbie in a tone that was utterly unfamiliar. It wasn't his therapist voice, and it wasn't the robotic cadence of my midnight caller. It was the high, petulant rasp of a child.

"Blah, blah—you're such a fucking milk-baby," he was saying. "Just shut up a minute, you little faggot, and let me th—what was that?"

I stopped moving. Silence.

He chuffed. "It's a little late to find out you don't have any balls, Robbie."

There was a scrape of metal drawing back. A moment later the bottom of the tunnel dropped, and I was falling into darkness.

SEVENTY-TWO

It seemed to take forever to hit bottom. I landed badly on my ankle, losing my flashlight. The gun went off, throwing a split second of light into the tall chamber. The floor was soft, mossy. The air was rank with the smell of ketones, of garbage. Of death.

Someone above me was applauding.

"It's one thing to watch somebody else sink into the ground, isn't it?" Connor's voice was about twenty feet above me, flat and strangely calm. "It's something else entirely to go down into that darkness yourself."

He was standing in a doorway, a dark silhouette against a gray rectangle. Mirror eyes glowed dimly.

I pulled myself to my feet, trying not to betray a limp. "Why don't you come down here and find out?"

He yawned. "I've been down there. I didn't like it much. Say hi to your mommy for me."

He disappeared; there was a loud click. Harsh yellow floodlights came on, blinding against the white tile walls. A row of bare metal pipes were set in the ceiling, fitted with shower heads. They began to knock, spraying cold rust-brown water down. The water turned lukewarm, then hot. Then scalding. I pulled my leather jacket over my head.

I looked around the porcelain floor. Thick slime and bath toys began to slide down to the metal drain. The Colt had lodged against a rubber duck. Boiling water peppered my cheek as I scanned the ledge above me. There was a chain in the ceiling, and a leather harness hanging down from it, maybe six feet above my head. I took a leap, then slipped back and fell against the floor. I thought I heard Connor laughing.

I took another running jump and this time my fingers caught the bottom of the harness—barely. Then, inch by agonizing inch, I pulled myself up level to the exit and swung in. The water instantly shut off.

"That was just for fun." Connor's voice was amplified now, echoing against concrete. "You smelled like you could use a bath."

I was in another tunnel now. I crawled along—left, then right, then left again—holding the revolver in my blistered palms.

"Ooh, Mikey don' wanna pway?" His voice dropped several octaves. "Mike, I'm your father and I order you to suck my cock." The last word was lost in a bray of laughter.

The space in front of me was dark. But from the zigzag of the tunnel, I was fairly certain where I was now: Theo's darkroom.

"Here's the part you don't get." His voice seemed to vibrate inside my head. "You—don't—understand—these—kids. I understand. I've spent my whole life studying them. I don't *have* to feel sorry for them because I am *above* feeling sorry for them. And I am *not* brain-damaged, asshole."

Keep talking, I thought. *Tell me how far I am from the walls.* My feet crunched candy wrappers and Coke cans.

"I want you to know I heard everything," Connor said. "I saw what you let that cunt do to you. I know why you couldn't fuck her, even if you don't. Every secret in your heart belongs to me." He laughed. "*I know you.* I've seen how you operate. And I know you just can't help yourself from what you're about to do."

My fingers touched cold cement. Now all I had to do was keep moving till I found the way out.

"But don't worry, Mike. I won't let you die like a dumb animal."

Gray-white rectangles flickered over my head. TV monitors.

"See now. There's everybody . . ."

The screens showed the distant flashing lights of police cars, the satellite dishes of news vans. All ranged at the bottom of the canyons, waiting.

"And there's you . . ."

Now it changed, and I saw myself standing with my hand against the wall, a blur of green light and shadows. Night vision. I could just make out the edge of a doorjamb five feet to my left.

"And there's you again . . . and her. Naughty, naughty."

The monitors now showed two naked forms moving against each other through a window. I recognized Dorothy's dark hair, the swell of her breast.

". . . And here's her again."

A woman's pale, nude body hung upside down, fingers brushing the floor. Dark streaks of blood trickled down like paint. As the rope slowly unwound, her face turned to me.

"Oh, by the way—did I mention this is all going out *live?*"

"Dorothy," I said. "Oh, baby."

"Don't you dare cry," he said, the mock-father again. "This was your doing."

"That's enough. Oh Jesus, enough." I threw myself against the door beside me. It shuddered open, and now I was in a low wooden room, smelling strongly of gasoline.

Connor Blackwell, head to toe in black, stood before me. Half his makeup had streaked off, showing blotched corpse-white skin. Mirrored contact lenses. Without his false hair or beard, he seemed less a man than an ancient child. He held Robbie under his arm like a broken toy. The other hand gripped a two-foot embalming trocar.

"So now you see," he said. "And now you know. You won't be able to stop me without killing her, too." He grinned. "But you can watch."

"Robbie," I said.

But Robbie looked away from me. Connor smiled and ran. I followed him down to the end of a wide tunnel. The drainage pipe that emptied into the lake.

"Peggy, hold your fire!" I shouted. *"He's got Robbie as a shield!"*

A motorcycle kick-started into life and thundered away. I started to follow . . . then someone coughed in the room behind me.

"Hello," a thin voice said, as I turned.

"Hello, Cassandra," I said. The child sat with her back against an ancient boiler, hands behind her. "Are you okay? Can you walk?"

"I can't get up." She watched me with piercing green eyes.

I bent down. "Want me to pick you up?"

"I can't get up. I *can't.*" And then I saw.

She was tied to the wall with a length of piano wire, looped around her wrists and disappearing over a spring pulley. I could just barely see the end of the shoelace—the homemade fuse, leading to a length of metallic ribbon. With Cassie's slightest breath the wire moved, threatening to scrape the fuse against a wad of dried white paper. Friction explosives.

He won't kill them, Gavin told me. *You will.* I would have grabbed her without thinking.

"Okay, sweetie. Don't move." I cast about, looking for anything with a cutting edge. "Peggy!" I called back down the tunnel. "Clear!"

"I watched him tie it up," Cassie said simply.

"Cassie, do you remember what color the fuse was? Was it black or white?"

"Black." She didn't hesitate. "Mister?"

"What is it?"

"He's taking Robbie to kill her."

"Kill who?"

"Miss Corvis," said Cassandra. "He's going to make Robbie kill her."

Several agonizing seconds later, Peggy appeared in the tunnel.

"Mike," she said. "They're gone."

"Peg, we've got a short fuse here. Black powder. As best I can tell, it's rigged to go whether we cut the wire or try to pull her out."

"All right. So we wait."

"Can't wait," I said. "The primer's iodized ammonia. Touch explosive. The slightest bump sets it off."

"He said I'd be blown to shit," Cassie said.

"That's not gonna happen, baby. Can you remember how long the black string was? Was it a foot long, or—"

"I don't know that," she said.

I held my hands twelve inches apart. "Was it this far apart?"

"It was half that."

"Forty seconds an inch," I said. "That's less than four minutes on a black match fuse." I looked to Peggy. "Your call."

She handed me her pocket knife. "Cut her free."

"All right, Cassie. Agent Weaver's gonna keep tension on the wire. You're gonna breathe in deep so I get a little slack. And I'm gonna cut the wire and get you out. Then we're all three of us gonna run like heck. One-two-three. Understand?"

Cassie nodded solemnly. Peggy braced herself against the wire.

"Ready," I said. "One . . . two . . . thr—"

"Mike, the fuse!"

I looked up. Crystals were popping and sparking from the wadded paper. I cut through the wire, pulled Cassie into my arms. We ran to the end of the tunnel, into the night air. Then I put Cassie into Peggy's arms.

"There's defilade behind those big rocks at the top of the banks," I said. "Get her as far away as you can."

"Mike, where the hell are you going?"

"After him," I said. "Once you get her to safety, look for the generators. Shut them all down. Every one."

"The what?"

"Cut the power," I said. "Kill his cameras."

She started to answer. Then she looked over my shoulder. "He's halfway across now."

I ran down the banks, following the tracks of the motorcycle. Listening to the engine fade away. Tall arc lights shone down over a vast ocean of white.

Lost Lake.

SEVENTY-THREE

He had made it as far as the sailboat—a tiny black spot on the white lake bed. I leapt after him, scrabbling down loose soil.

Then I felt the explosion.

It wasn't a single noise, but a string of loud reports—trash cans falling down stairs. And then the big charge, a rush of hot air hurling me. I wiped out against the bottom in a spray of sand. Flames clawed the air. As I looked ahead I saw the explosion had rocked Connor as well. His motorcycle treads wove, then skidded. They crashed fifty yards away, a smear of black against white. And a thin ribbon of steel.

"That's close enough," the frozen voice commanded. Connor had raised himself from the fallen motorcycle and was holding Robbie to his chest. The sharpened trocar point lay against the boy's earlobe.

I aimed the pistol.

"You can't kill me," he said. "And if you try—" He nudged the blade against Robbie, drawing a point of red.

"If you kill him," I said, "there'll be no one left to become you when you die."

"I will never die." Connor laughed. "Go on, shoot. Everyone will see there's no justice in you. Only the same shit that lives inside everybody. They'll all see."

"You mean, because of the cameras?"

He smiled.

"They're not going to see a thing, Connor. Not what you want them to, anyway. The cameras aren't working anymore."

He started to speak. But then the floodlights abruptly shut off—first one bank, then the other. Now there was only moonlight and the stars above.

"Sorry I had to take your toys away," I said.

He drew the trocar back, poised to strike.

Robbie was watching me.

"Robbie, get down!" I shouted.

Connor swung the trocar down. I pulled the trigger and blood exploded from his hand. The metal tube clattered to the ground as Connor Blackwell sank to his knees, clutching the stump of flesh at his wrist. Stared at me with his wounded mirror eyes.

Then he leapt.

It was nothing like fighting a human being. We were locked together, rolling on the sand. He clawed with his good hand like a rabid animal. His teeth closed hard around my thumb, snapping his head back and forth. The pain was a needle of white through my arm. I placed my left hand against his throat and pressed. Then I rolled on top of him, choking. Still he held on.

"Nobody's watching you anymore." My heart was pounding, lead in my chest. "Nobody—sees."

All at once he was like a puppet with his strings cut. He fell to the sand, whimpering.

"It wasn't my fault," he said. "He forced me. He . . . made me do it."

"It was never him, Connor. It was always you."

I sat back, cradling my wounded hand.

"Mister Yeager . . . ?"

I felt the needle point against the back of my neck.

"You shouldn't hurt people," he said.

I turned to face him. He was on his knees, staring at me with Connor's lifeless eyes. The trocar was close enough to kill if he chose to put it through my eye.

"Robbie . . ."

He didn't move.

"You asked me the other day," I said. "If somebody was hurting a kid, would I shoot him until he died?"

"I remember," he said.

I put my hands up. "Don't you think it's time to stop hurting yourself?"

Robbie looked to Connor. Then back to me. And lowered the point of the blade.

SEVENTY-FOUR

Peggy was the first to emerge from the helicopter.

I handed Robbie to her. "Frizelle?"

"He'll make it," she said. "Nice shooting, Agent Yeager."

"I only took his weapon," I said. "His real power was in those cameras."

Connor now lay semifetal, blood oozing into the sand.

"He's in shock," I said. "I wonder if you'd mind reading him his Mirandas."

"Where are you going?"

"Across the lake," I said.

There was only one building left standing. An old stable, plain and laid with straw. A rope thrown over the ceiling beam, a metal hook dangling down. A video camera on a tripod, its red recording eye dark. And nobody hanging from that hook. Empty coils of rope and an empty blindfold. Bloody footprints leading from the door.

Once again, she'd found a way to survive.

SEVENTY-FIVE

On Friday afternoon I found Peggy Weaver with the children in a private ward of the hospital. Cassie and Robbie were drawing directly on the wall with crayons.

"What's that you're drawing?" Peggy held Cassie from behind.

"That's when you cut the wire," Cassie said. "And we almost died."

Robbie had drawn a large, surreal image of Dale's severed head. Next to it a large, hooded camera. A pair of silver eyes shining in blackness. And a lone man with a gun.

"And what are you doing over here?" Peggy asked.

"Over here we're safe." Then Cassie looked at me. "Hi."

Robbie smiled up at me.

"That's you." He pointed. "You're stopping Connor from killing me."

"How does it feel when you make these drawings?"

He pulled back from the wall, squinting as he examined his work. His legs, freshly clad in plaster casts, stretched out from the wheelchair.

"It's hard to get close," he said. "My casts make me turn sideways."

"Did you have another dream about him last night?"

"I guess." He looked at me. "I guess that's a thing I'll always have."

". . . And that right there is my cat," Cassandra said. "Inky runs away when you try and pick her up . . ."

"She's a chatterbox," Robbie said.

"What's in this part of the drawing?" I pointed to a row of crosses.

"It's where my mom and dad are buried," she said. "Did you go to their funeral?"

"I went to your dad's funeral, sure."

"I'm gonna have their funeral when I get out," she said. "And for Aunt Martha, too."

"I think that would be a good idea," I said. "Kids, do you mind if I borrow Agent Peggy for a moment?"

"Are you going away?"

I smiled. "Just for a minute. You keep drawing."

"And then are you going away forever?"

"Not forever," I said. "But for a little while. I have to talk to some people and make a report."

"And then what?" Robbie asked.

"Then you just whistle. And I'll be there."

"For real?" Cassie asked.

"Yes. For real."

I drew Peggy into the hallway.

"Crayons on the walls?" I asked. "You're gonna be real popular with the hospital staff."

"It was a desperation move. I couldn't get them to play with the sandbox toys."

"And?"

"It's still not real to them. Next week I'm coming back with that therapist from Alexandria . . . that's when the real work starts." She looked at me. "You took a big risk, putting yourself at his mercy that way."

"I knew Robbie didn't really want to kill anyone," I said. "Photograph Number Twenty-one was the key. It was the only picture that showed the victim as a human being—able to suffer. Wearing his father's ring. I had to make sure Robbie knew I could see him with the same empathy."

"I heard you did some digging in Gavin's backyard today."

"We found Robbie's puppy," I said. "Connor buried it alive."

"He told Robbie that's what would happen to Cassie if he tried to tell," she said. "I think you need to be the one to let Robbie know that's not true."

"I'll try," I said. "I just got the film back from the lab."

"And?"

"Some of them are old . . . self-portraits Theo made after the fire, like the ones Tippet probably found during his own search. I also discovered some that were much more recent . . . Espero, and Dale, and Mary. Connor documented everything as a kind of how-to manual. So that Robbie would know how to follow in his footsteps."

"But you didn't kill Connor," she said. "And now Robbie's got a chance to learn something different."

"Let's hope it's enough," I said. "Oh, and we found Clyde too. What was left of him. I'd show you the pictures, but I'm assuming you haven't eaten yet."

"You assume right," she said. "You wanna grab an early dinner? I've gotta get up at six A.M. for my flight to Philly."

"Who's picking you up on the other end?"

She smiled. "I left my car at the airport."

"Let's make it a late dinner." I hesitated. "Peggy, I don't know if I'm coming back to Philadelphia. Even if the Bureau wanted me back . . . I'm still a long way from knowing what to do about my career. And about us."

Peggy looked closely at me, loving and honest.

"What to do about us?" she asked. "Or what to do about her?"

I said nothing. I had no answer.

Dr. Lund met me in the hallway.

"Frizelle sends his regards," he said. "He said he's looking forward to spending some time with Cassandra. And getting that turkey sandwich you promised him."

"You really think he's ready to raise a child?"

He shrugged. "We learn by doing."

"Speaking of which, are you going to take my advice and hold onto that sheriff's badge?"

"For now." Lund made a diffident wave. "I think it's time we had a little new blood around here, don't you? Besides, I'm going to have my hands full as temporary guardian to those two children."

"Given your options, I'd say you're making the right choice."

We shook hands and parted. I went on alone to the ICU wing. Sheriff Archer lay flat on his bed—bloodless, withered. Eyes open. Waiting.

"The children are safe," I said.

He stared at the ceiling, silent and still. Then, very slowly, he turned his head to me.

"Safe . . . ?" he asked in a voice like ground glass.

I nodded. Then I took off the gun belt with the Colt revolver. Laid it across the foot of his bed. "If you want my opinion, the philosophy of the

Buntline needs revising. You don't always have to shoot to kill."

"And justice . . . more than pain?"

I started to answer. Then I realized he was beyond hearing me—or anyone—ever again.

SEVENTY-SIX

Sunset in Dyer County.

I walked out into the hospital parking lot and awaited the inevitable. For two days Peggy had dropped hints about bringing me back—if that's what I still wanted. I'd promised to listen. Dinner would be nice.

I took a deep breath of clean Nevada air. For the first time in days, I had no calls to answer, nowhere to go. I was myself again—not Special Agent Yeager, but just plain me. Covered with scars and full of memories that would be slow to fade.

"What are you looking so down about?" said a woman's voice behind me.

I turned.

Dorothy.

She stood on a pair of crutches, fresh bandages around each ankle.

She smiled weakly. "You expected maybe a ghost?"

I took her into my arms. Felt her lips against me, warm and soft. Breathed the perfume from her hair. The herbal shampoo that made her smell like a garden. My hand in the small of her back. And the feel of her.

"Where were you . . . ?"

She eyed me quizzically. "With the kids," she said. "And your FBI friend. She's . . . very nice. They told me you were just there, and you went outside. And . . . here you are."

"I came for you," I said.

"I know," she said. "And now you've found me." She lowered her face. "So you wrecked my bike, I hear. So . . . okay. Your place next time, maybe."

I laughed, brushing tears. "I'm not sure if I know where my place is."

"Want to go find it?" She waited.

"Dorothy. I . . ." I looked for words and found none.

"Come on," she said. "Let's sit down."

We sat on a bench by the hospital doors.

"I should have been more honest with you." She cast her eyes down. "I've had trouble with people in your line of work. You didn't seem like the cops I'd met before. You seemed kind, and decent. And gentle. And you are."

"A lot of us are. More than you might think."

"I hope so." She paused. "Anyway, I thought it would be good to help you. And when it ended, there might be a chance of you leaving it all behind."

Then she looked at me. "But you're not going to, are you?"

I released a slow breath. "It's my world, Dorothy. It's the only one I know."

She put her hand on mine.

"Call me when you're ready for a new one," she said.

Then she kissed me softly, and a moment later the nurse came to help her back inside. I nearly followed her. But finally I just sat on the bench. I hadn't realized until then just how exhausted I was. And how alone. And how alive.

And it was my world after all.

I looked up at the Sangre de los Niños—still scarred from the flames, but ancient and strong, made of red stone and legends of sacrifice. They would outlast everything that had ever happened there. I would live and die . . . Robbie and Cassie would watch their own children grow old . . . Dyer County itself would fade into dust. But still those mountains would remain, beyond the reach of human understanding. And keeping their secrets well.

I never realized just how beautiful they were.